Dragon Soup for the Soul

ALSO BY EMILY MARTHA SORENSEN

Dragon Eggs

Dragon's Egg

Dragon's Hope

Dragon's First Christmas

Dragon's Fire

Dragon's Song

Dragon's First Valentine

The End in the Beginning

The Keeper and the Rulership

The Fires of the Rulership

The Magic or the Rulership

Fairy Senses

Fairy Eyeglasses

Fairy Compass

Fairy Earmuffs

Fairy Barometer

Fairy Pox

Fairy Slippers

Fairy Lunchbox

Fairy Icepack

Fairy Stopwatch

Fairy Toothbrush

Fairy Perfume

Fairy Crown

THE NUMBERS JUST KEEP GETTING BIGGER
Twenty-Four Potential Children of Prophecy

TRILOGY OF A TEENAGE WEREVULTURE
Trials of a Teenage Werevulture
Trifles of a Teenage Werevulture

THE VIRGO CURSE
Not Quite a Curse
Not Quite a Blessing
Not Quote Changed

WICKED WITCHES OF RESTVA
Black Magic Academy
White Magic Academy

THE ZODIAC CURSE
Aquarius
Gemini
Cancer
Sagittarius

SHORT FICTION COLLECTIONS
Worlds of Wonder
Magic and Mischief
Tales of Tie-ins

Dragon Soup for the Soul

EMILY MARTHA SORENSEN

HEMELEIN PUBLICATIONS

Dragon Soup for the Soul

Legacy of the Corridor, volume 2.

A Hemelein Publications Original. Copyright © 2021 by Emily Martha Sorensen. All rights reserved. Except for brief excerpts in the case of reviews, this book may not be reproduced in any form without prior written permission of the publisher. All stories and essays published by permission of the authors.

Additional copyright and first appearance information for individual stories is found at the end of the book.

The works in this book are fiction. Any names, characters, people, places, entities, or events in these stories are products of the author's imagination, and any resemblance to actual people, places, entities, or events is entirely coincidental.

Cover artist: Meredith Dillman, meredithdillman.com.
Cover art and "Mossy Fairy" used in the "About the Cover Artist" section both copyright © 2021 by Meredith Dillman. Used by permission of the artist.
Cover and interior layout and design: Joe Monson

Managing Editor: Joe Monson
Publisher: Heather B. Monson
Published by Hemelein Publications, LLC.
http://hemelein.com/

First Edition
First Hemelein printing, December 2021
10 9 8 7 6 5 4 3 2 1

ISBN:
978-1-64278-016-1 (trade paperback)
978-1-64278-017-8 (ebook)

Library of Congress Control Number: 2021947105

❀ Created with Vellum

To Ben:
The best husband ever.

TABLE OF CONTENTS

Legacy of the Corridor	xi
On Dragons and Curses	xiii
Joe Monson	
Introduction	xv
The Dragon and the Santa	1
The Apple of Discord	7
Advanced Precognition	13
The Spinning Talent	19
On a Long Camping Trip	36
On the Way Through the Woods	38
Ogre in Boots	44
Entrance Interview	51
Knock Three Times	52
The Mark on Her Right Hand	55
Third Princess	59
His Unicorn	69
Dragon's Egg	74
Dragon's Dawn	119
Dragon's Hope	123
Dragon's Yowl	170
One Midsummer's Night	171
The Rise of Starlight	173
To Prevent Similar Views	197
Not Quite a Curse	212
Not Quite a Blessing	255
Not Quite Changed	299
About the Author	343
About the Cover Artist	344
Also from Hemelein Publications	349

LEGACY OF THE CORRIDOR

Way back in 1994, M. Shayne Bell put together *Washed by a Wave of Wind*, an anthology of short works by authors from "The Corridor", an area that covers Utah, most of Idaho, parts of Wyoming and Nevada, and stretches into Arizona and parts of northern Mexico. Sometimes, the area around Cardston, Alberta, Canada, is included, too. For those unfamiliar with this area, it was settled by Mormon pioneers, members of the Church of Jesus Christ of Latter-day Saints.

Shayne's anthology highlighted science fiction and fantasy works by authors from the area, as The Corridor contained an unusually high number of successful authors—for the population in the area—both genre and non-genre, both members and non-members of the predominant religion. That legacy continues today with an impressive list of authors such as Jennifer Adams, D. J. Butler, Orson Scott Card, Michaelbrent Collings, Ally Condie, Larry Correia, Kristyn Crow, James Dashner, Brian Lee Durfee, Sarah M. Eden, Richard Paul Evans, David Farland, Jessica Day George, Shannon Hale, Mettie Ivie Harrison, Tracy and Laura Hickman, Charlie N. Holmberg, Christopher Husberg, Matthew J. Kirby, Brian McClellan, Stephenie Meyer, L. E. Modesitt, Jr., Brandon Mull, Jennifer

A. Nielsen, James A. Owen, Brandon Sanderson, J. Scott Savage, Jess Smart Smiley, Eric James Stone, Howard Tayler, Brad R. Torgersen, Dan Wells, Robison Wells, David J. West, Carol Lynch Williams, and Dan Willis.

That's a big list of names, and it only barely scratches the surface.

Hemelein Publications created this publication series to highlight authors from The Corridor, both well-known and lesser-known. We think Shayne did a wonderful job drawing attention to these amazing writers back then, and we want to continue what he started.

You can learn more about the series at:

http://hemelein.com/go/legacy-of-the-corridor/

Joe Monson
Managing Editor
Hemelein Publications

ON DRAGONS AND CURSES

JOE MONSON

I first met Emily about a decade ago at *Life the Universe, & Everything,* the local academic science fiction and fantasy symposium in Provo, Utah. She has been busy since then, building up a prolific list of shorter and longer works. If she continues at this rate, we'll need to to produce a few more of these collections of her writings.

When I came up with the idea for the *Legacy of the Corridor* publication series, she was one of the first authors I added to my list. Her stories are usually humorous, and they have a good flow. I tend to enjoy her stories, wherever I find them.

I'd previously read about one-third of the stories included here, so it was fun to read a bunch of new (to me) stories. There are several standalone stories, three poems, and several sets of stories set in the same universes. I think my favorite of these universes is the *Dragon Eggs* series. Maybe I have a penchant for nostalgic period pieces, maybe I like dragons, and maybe I just like these characters. I hope you enjoy them (and all the rest of the stories) when you read them.

Now, regarding the cover. I've never met Meredith Dillman in person (maybe we'll meet at a convention one of these years), but I've worked with her for well over a decade through the art shows

I've directed and volunteered at. She's one of my favorite artists, and I have dozens of her works. She reminds me a lot of artists like Pauline Baynes, Arthur Rackham, Barbara Freeman, Edmund Dulac, Ida Outhwaite, and Anne Anderson, all from the late 1800s and early 1900s. I immediately thought of her when I read the *Dragon Eggs* stories here. The dragon on the cover isn't based on these stories, but it makes for a great cover image. Meredith's style complements Emily's stories very well.

The variety of stories contained herein is a good mix, and can best be enjoyed by bundling up with your favorite warm beverage and blanket in a soft, comfy chair. Take your time to savor the stories as you read them. I hope they make you smile.

Joe Monson
Managing Editor
Hemelein Publications

INTRODUCTION

"Okay, what is this book about, and what do you write?" you may be thinking.

Well, I'll tell you.

I write stories that are funny, touching, oddball, and deep. Sometimes one of those things. Sometimes all of those things. And it may depend on your perspective which ones are which.

I think humor is a great way to deal with complicated subjects. It's also a great way to goof off and be silly and relax.

I like stories about love. Sometimes family love. Sometimes friendship love. Sometimes romantic love. Sometimes self love. The important thing to remember is that I don't write stories about hate. I write stories about relationships that uplift and strengthen.

I prefer a positive perspective to a negative one. If you like characters who angst and whine about how miserably the universe treats them, go elsewhere. If you like characters who face very challenging situations with courage and determination and rational thought, look here.

I am a very religious person who puts God first and foremost in everything. I try not to be preachy, and I think I succeed, but I *always* think through what message a story is sending. Even my silliest, most whimsical stories often have multiple levels, because I try to make sure everything is consistent with truth.

I hope you'll find these stories playful, heartwarming, and thought-provoking.

That's what I write.

Emily Martha Sorensen
December 2021

THE DRAGON AND THE SANTA

*I*rri's stomach growled as he flew. He hadn't eaten in three days, and he was extremely hungry. The elders had *warned* him against flying too close to the worldgate, but had he listened? Of course not, because he was the great Irri.

Irritably, Irri scanned the sky for birds. He'd seen precious few since he'd come here to this wasteland, and they had all escaped him. What kind of planet was this, all snow and ice? How could any reptilian person live in such a place?

A jingle made his ears prick up. In a distant cloudbank was the slightest red glow, dancing through it. He dove, roaring fire in his wake.

He seized his prey, a big woolly horned thing, and prepared to gulp it down.

"RELINQUISH RUDOLPH!" a voice roared.

Irri paused, looking down at the prey in his talons. It bucked and reared, showing the whites of its eyes. Defiantly, he moved it back to his jaws.

A blast of energy blew him back. With a shriek of terror, the woolly thing wriggled free. Eight more woolly things writhed from the cloud, and all nine stampeded away.

The cloud was silent for a moment. Then it said, "Blast."

Irri growled in frustration.

A round, red-and-white head popped through the cloudbank. From the lack of fear in its eyes, Irri surmised that this was not a prey species.

"Thank you very much!" the creature snapped. "Do you have any idea how long it takes to breed a reindeer with a glowing nose? Not to mention one that can fly! And they'll have scattered miles away! How am I supposed to deliver my presents *now?*"

"Need food," Irri growled. "Or I'll eat you."

"Dragons," the newcomer muttered. "Wait there."

The head disappeared for a moment. There was a rustling sound. Then a huge chunk of raw meat dropped from the cloud.

Irri shrieked in triumph. He seized it in his talons, tore his teeth into it, and gulped strip after strip of flesh. As the meat sizzled in his stomach, he began to feel a trifle better.

"You really shouldn't be in this world at all," the creature said, poking its head back up through the fog. "The last time I saw dragons was—oh—back when they still called me Odin."

"Came through by accident," Irri snarled, snarfing through his meat. "Flew too close to a gate. Turns out it was open. Closed behind me again."

"Ahh." The creature rubbed his eyes with two fat fists. "Of course. I could have told the humans that concentrating their world's magic on top of a pole, right around a solstice, was asking for trouble. But does anyone ever listen to me? Noooo. All they let me do these days is give their children presents. It almost makes me wish I was still Odin, even without the depth perception."

Irri bolted his last scrap of meat. He reared backwards, flapping his wings, and snuffed loudly for more. Sensing nothing, he narrowed his eyes in the direction of the escaped prey.

"Oh, no you don't!" the creature said from behind him. "You scared away my reindeer—*you're* going to pull my sleigh."

Sudden weight fell onto Irri's wings. He hissed and bucked in fury. But the creature behind him paid him no heed. More and more restraints fell around him, across his nose and face, until even his flame-centers were extinguished.

"Horrible creature," Irri gasped. "Release me!"

"No, I don't think so." There was a jingling behind him, and a string of little bells was heaved over his back. Irri bucked and shivered as the freezing metal itched him. The red-and-white creature paid this no heed. "I have few enough believers these days. I refuse to let you jeopardize the few I have left. Besides, there's nothing you can do about it. My magic's at its peak today."

Irri tried to spit fire, but nothing came. He writhed in fury.

"My current name is Sinterklaas, by the way," the round creature said, tying the last tether of its sleigh in place. "Or Weihnachtsmann. Or Santa Claus, if you insist."

"Hate you," Irri hissed.

"I'll send you home when we're finished. Unless you'd rather wait until the gate opens in another year?"

"*Hate* you!"

"If you must, but we've no time to waste on that silliness. Now ... which one is closer from here, Greenland or Norway?"

IRRI'S OPINION of the Santa did not improve as they continued on their journey.

The creature kept an enormous list that it flipped through incessantly. "Joseph ... Emma ... Johnny," it would murmur, making notes with either a thick feather or a black stick it called a pen. "I wish they'd let me upgrade to a smartphone, but not enough folks envision me that way."

"Why do you let them determine your life?" Irri growled. "It is stupid."

"Magic works best with the rules people believe in. I like magic. So I use the role they give me."

"It is stupid!"

"I've been worse," the Santa murmured, squinting at its long list. "Naughty ... nice ... I wish they'd give me a third option. Most children are both, and many things in between. Ah well, I never leave coal anyway."

Irri licked his teeth. Coal sounded tasty.

"There!" the Santa shouted, pointing at a cluster of lights. "Hold still while I freeze time so we can get down there safely."

THE CREATURE also had an irrational prejudice against hunting.

"No cats," the Santa told him firmly, as they hovered right over a rooftop with some tasty-looking fuzzballs on it. "No dogs, either. And if I catch you eating a horse, I will trap you until the next solstice comes, so help me."

Irri sulked as the round creature squeezed down a too-small chimney.

And then there was the food that the Santa *did* bring him.

"My reindeer are supposed to eat these," the creature said, dumping a pile of plants by Irri's mouth while they stopped to rest. "That means they're yours tonight."

Irri stared at the orange roots incredulously. "Do I look like a prey species?"

"Try eating like an omnivore for one night. It won't kill you."

Irri picked up the offending roots in his talons and flung them away.

The most annoying thing, however, was the way the creature kept *humming*. Sometimes it even added words, and the words were always inane.

"Up on the housetop reindeer pause ... out jumps good old Santa Claus ..."

"Do you *mind*?" Irri roared. "I'm trying to concentrate on flying!"

"Good for you. I'm trying to enjoy my one day out. I enjoy singing."

"You are tone-deaf," Irri growled.

"No, I'm not. Dragons just compose differently."

"You sound like half-dead rodents," Irri snarled.

"If you say so. But it's my sleigh. And there's nothing you can do to stop me. On the first day of Christmas, my true love gave to me ..."

Irri wondered if the Santa was *officially* on a list of non-prey species.

"THAT'S IT," the Santa said finally, pulling off Irri's restraints after a night that felt like it had lasted for weeks. "We've finished the last house. We're back at the pole. Ready to go home now?"

"Past ready," Irri growled. "Never want to see you again."

The Santa laughed. It sounded like a drum bouncing on a rock. "You know, you're the first six-limbed steed I've had since Sleipnir. It's been fun, hasn't it?"

"No," Irri retorted.

"You actually might stay," the Santa said shrewdly, unstrapping the harness. "Dragons are getting more popular every year. I'm sure you could cash in on quite a bit of magic."

"Not interested," Irri growled.

"In fact, given the hoards humans believe dragons have, you could even do what I can't, and accumulate a lot of money." The Santa brightened. "Money that could fund Hollywood movies to shift public opinion about me ..."

"Not listening!"

The creature put its arm around Irri's snoot. "We should talk about this further."

"You should *open the gate!*"

"One year. I'm sure you could stand that."

"I'm sure I could find a way to eat you."

The Santa paused. "Ah. Perhaps I shouldn't teach you magic to rival mine."

Irri showed off his teeth.

The Santa sighed and waved its hand. The portal opened.

Irri flapped his wings, rose in the air, and darted through it.

"Tell your friends the offer's open!" the Santa called as the portal sealed again. "Any dragon who wants to come next year could cut a great deal!"

Irri snorted fire in derision. He backwinged up into the red sky. As if he would send any of his friends into such a fate.

His *enemies*, however ... now, that might be worth considering.

AUTHOR NOTE:
Santa Claus really is Odin. Seriously. Go look it up.

I enjoy Santa Claus as a character in a mythology. I find it unwise to tell children he literally exists, because that is a) lying, and b) telling children to believe in a pagan deity. My parents decided to stop doing Santa Claus after my sister decided to start praying to him.

But as a character in a fantasy story ... sure! Great!

And dragons, of course, make everything awesome.

THE APPLE OF DISCORD

I picked up the golden apple. It felt cool to the touch, even in the hot morning sun.

I knew it, I thought. *I knew it was magical.*

"Is this what you saw?" I asked Cassandra.

She shivered and backed away.

I gripped the apple. This was why I was here. This was why I had gone straight to see Cassandra. I knew she could find it for me.

"Let's destroy it," I said.

"*No!*" Cassandra yelped, seizing my arm. "You can't! The Fates—!"

I stared at her, astonished. "You dreamed your entire nation was going to die if your brother finds this. And you're worried about the *Fates?*"

"I've angered a god before," Cassandra muttered. "It doesn't pay."

"You had every right to refuse Apollo," I began heatedly.

"Men hold women as slaves," she snapped. "Gods hold mortals as slaves. Fates hold everybody as slaves. It is the way of things."

She pried the apple from my hands and plonked it back on the grass. "And as you are *my* family's slave," she added sharply, "you will do as I say."

I decided that I did not like Cassandra.

I WAS NOT, in fact, King Priam's slave. I was not even a mortal. I had been a guest at Peleus's wedding, which my sister had planned. And I'd watched the apple create jealousy and rage within every goddess present.

I made myself invisible and waited until Cassandra had forgotten me. Then I returned to my mortal guise and snuck back to the orchard. The apple lay there, glinting in the morning sun.

Paris picks it up and chooses a goddess, I thought, staring pensively. *Cassandra says that will start a huge war among the mortals. But would that be preferable to a war across Olympus?*

I wasn't sure I could destroy the apple. Destruction was not my specialty. Therefore, *someone* had to keep the apple—and that someone shouldn't be me.

But I wasn't so sure the whims of Olympus should be allowed to cause millions of mortals' deaths—again.

Slowly, I picked up the apple. I stared at it.

Kallisti, it said. *For the fairest.*

I had been the only woman not affected. Even both my sisters had fought for it. The brawl had pushed the apple out over Olympus, down into the world of mortals. And I had known something must be done to stop Eris's gift causing further chaos.

A brilliant light exploded from the sky. Dazzling, the queen of the gods stood before me.

"The apple," she said, her voice echoing. "Give it to me."

I felt my eyes widen. The queen of the gods. Hera. I had spent my life avoiding her, afraid of what she might do to me.

Another light grew, this one up from the ground. It billowed into a rose and exploded into Aphrodite. She stood, radiantly, wearing absolutely nothing.

Hades, I thought numbly.

"*I* deserve the apple," Aphrodite sneered. "You must see I'm the fairest of Olympus."

"I am your queen!" Hera snarled.

Aphrodite smirked. "And men actually take an interest in me."

A third light stabbed the air and snapped into Athena. Clad in battle armor, she was wielding a spear.

Oh, HADES, I thought.

"Nothing is fairer than wisdom," Athena announced. "The apple belongs to me."

I felt myself sweating. All three goddesses had gone mad for the apple at the wedding. And a worse three, I could not have chosen. They were all infamous for their capriciousness and jealousy.

No wonder Cassandra predicted war would come of this. I felt sick. But I still had one hope: my mortal disguise was even better than Athena's.

"How could I choose?" I asked piteously. "You are all lovely beyond comprehension. I could never discern which is the fairest!"

Of course I was lying. It was clearly Aphrodite.

Aphrodite tossed her hair. Hera just stared at me stonily.

"I know!" Aphrodite cried. "Choose me, and you'll get the love of any man you wish!"

I tried not to show how revolted that idea made me. I knew what Aphrodite's idea of love meant. Cassandra had experienced that already.

Hera caught on quickly. "Give the apple to me," she commanded. "I'll give you power. Power over others, as well as your own destiny."

If I *had* been mortal and a slave, I would have gone for that instantly.

"Wisdom is greater than power," Athena said coldly. "Without wisdom, power and love will fade."

That gave me pause as well. But the real question was not whose gifts I wanted: it was whose anger would most likely be fatal to me.

Unfortunately, the answer seemed likely to be "all three."

"Will she who benefits protect me from the others' wrath?" I wheedled, making a show of cringing.

All three goddesses frowned. Athena looked suspicious, but

nodded. Aphrodite sniffed and waved her hand. Hera folded her arms and glared.

"You'll find me very grateful," Aphrodite purred, holding out her hand.

"Nothing could protect you from *my* wrath," Hera growled.

"I defend those I like," Athena said coolly.

"All right." I swallowed. Here it was, then. "I give the apple to Aphrodite."

Aphrodite squealed and snatched the apple from my hands. "I knew it!"

Athena's eyes flashed. "The goddess of war is not the wisest person to offend."

"Nor the Queen of Olympus!"

"My reward, please!" I cried.

"Oh —" Aphrodite looked up from the apple. "Of course. Certainly. Who shall I enchant?"

"Zeus," I said.

"*Zeus?*" Hera roared. "My *husband?*"

"To fall in love with Hera," I added.

There was a stunned silence.

"You want ... Zeus ..." Athena began slowly.

"To fall in love with *Hera?*" Aphrodite squeaked. "That's disgusting! I never enchant married people to fall for each other!"

"Please," I said, my palms sweating. "Please, Aphrodite. Half the problems on Olympus spring from Zeus's unfaithfulness. You could end it easily."

"Lose my greatest bargaining chip?" Aphrodite asked incredulously. "How would I make deals with mortals who want to have affairs with him?"

"Not to mention the power that would give Hera," Athena muttered.

"APHRODITE!" Hera roared. "You made an agreement! NOW FOLLOW THROUGH!"

"Fine," Aphrodite snarled. "I'll do it." She jabbed a finger in my direction. "But *you* get no protection from me."

Light exploded like sharp spikes, and she vanished.

I stood alone before Hera and Athena.

I swallowed, rubbing my sweaty palms on my tunic. *Please let them not recognize me. Please let them not recognize me ...*

"You know," Athena said shrewdly, "one might say you benefited more than Aphrodite, Hera."

Hera's eyes went hard. She stared at me like she was tempted to blast me into ashes. "That mortal still chose *Aphrodite,*" she spat.

"Then I'll punish her," Athena said coolly. "I've received no benefit. And you know what I can do to mortals who offend me."

A slow smile spread across Hera's face. "Like Arachne ... very well. I'll leave this mortal to be your plaything."

With a roar of thunder, she vanished.

Now I stood alone before Athena. Athena, who had turned a mortal into the first spider just for beating her in a weaving competition. Despite knowing the uselessness, my legs tensed to flee.

Athena surveyed me. Her face betrayed nothing.

"Which one?" she asked casually.

I gulped. "I—I don't know what you —"

"It never ceases to amaze me how imperceptive others can be," she murmured. "No mortal would make such a request. No mortal cares so much about wars on Olympus."

"They should. Wars on Olympus tend to affect all."

Her eyes narrowed. "And now you make me certain you are not what you seem. Who are you?"

"Aglaia," I admitted, raising my head. "Of the Graces."

"The goddess of *beauty?*" she asked incredulously.

"That's why the apple did not affect me," I said.

"Clever." She frowned at me. "I respect cleverness." Her frown deepened. "I suppose I'll spare you, as well."

She sliced the air with her spear, and stepped through the portal it created.

I closed my eyes, breathing raggedly. *I survived. Oh, thank Zeus, I survived.*

"Sister!" Thalia cried, dropping down beside me. "What did you think you were doing?"

"Fixing your mess," I retorted without opening my eyes. "Whose bright idea was it to invite every deity but Eris to a celebration?"

"Thetis just wanted the perfect wedding! You know what a dreadful guest she is."

Euphrosyne giggled, dropping down beside her. "Well, I think you did a good thing. Now we can go back to the festivities!"

I laughed. I hoped they were right.

But, after all, it isn't every day the Fates bow to Graces.

AUTHOR NOTE:
I have a bone to pick with Greek mythology.

Actually, I have about a million bones to pick with Greek mythology, most of them revolving around how misogynistic it is. One of the most annoying things is the cause of the Trojan War. Paris, selfish jerk, drives me crazy.

So I decided to find an in-universe way to fix it.

ADVANCED PRECOGNITION

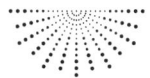

"All right, class, get out your assignments. Yes, Miss Baker?"

Startled, Sarah raised her hand.

"*Yes*, Miss Baker?" the professor repeated, sounding impatient.

"Um," Sarah said nervously, "I thought this was our first day. What —?"

The professor let out a long, dramatic sigh. His eyes rolled heavenwards. "Every class I get a slacker. Of course I haven't announced the assignment yet; the *point* of this class is to remember things I haven't asked yet. As per our course aims?"

Sarah gulped, sliding down in her seat. "I—I don't think you've —"

"I hand them out on the last day of class." The professor gave her an irked glare. "Honestly, how —"

The whole class tittered.

"— did you even *pass* Beginning Precognition?" he finished.

Face burning, Sarah slid further down in her seat. She hadn't passed Beginning Precognition; she hadn't even taken it. She was here on a dare from her roommate, who had claimed that students on the Reason track couldn't possibly handle classes in the Mysticism building. Now she was beginning to wonder if her roommate had been right, and she'd been an idiot.

"No," the student next to her said.

Sarah stared at him, befuddled. What was he talking about?

"Miss Baker!" the professor barked. "Why aren't you taking notes?"

Sarah fumbled in her satchel for a notebook and pencil, and found her pencil had snapped in half. She turned to her neighbor. "Could I borrow —?"

"I already said no."

"Here." Someone held a pencil over her shoulder. "I brought this for you."

Sarah took it, relieved.

The professor put his feet up on the desk, pulled out a thick tome, and started to read. Sarah stared at him, stared the blank paper in front of her, and looked around at everyone else. What were they all writing? How could they be taking notes when the teacher said nothing?

With less than five minutes of class-time left to go, the professor leapt up from his seat and talked at such a break-neck pace that Sarah barely managed to record five sentences. At last, humiliated, Sarah dropped the notebook into her satchel and buried her head in her hands.

I'm never, never, never going to pass this class.

"Don't worry about it!" the student behind behind her said cheerfully. "You've saved me enough times when I've forgotten things!"

Sarah turned around, startled. "Oh—uh—thank you for letting me borrow your ... uh ... pencil."

"Nice to meet you, Sarah! I'm Tanja. We're friends next week."

Sarah blinked. "Huh?"

"I have next period free, too!" Tanja looked delighted. "We spend it trying to figure out which paradox you have a mental block against. We figure out it's Salinski."

"*Huh?*" Sarah stared at her.

"Uh ..." Tanja looked worried. "Did I forget to let you introduce yourself again?"

"Do you have trouble remembering the past?" Sarah asked weakly.

"Yeah," Tanja giggled. "I have an awful memory. The last time I tried taking a class in the Reason building ... brrrrr." She shivered. "Can you believe the Logic professor claims looking at the answers on a test ahead of time is *cheating?*"

"You two might want to study together," the professor said from the front of the room, packing up his deck. "It's the only way either of you are going to pass."

"Do you think that's a threat or a future-seeing?" Sarah whispered, alarmed.

"Both," Tanja grinned. "'Foretelling your own actions and thereby making them happen.' That's Salinski!"

TANJA WAS A VERY, very confusing person to study with. If you could decipher her madcap insights and put them into some semblance of order, it was impressive how much knowledge she had. Unfortunately, she rarely remembered even half of what she knew.

"I hate this class," Tanja wailed, throwing her midterm in the trash. Both of them had failed it. Sarah was starting to get very, very worried about the final exam. "All the other classes I can just coast on through. Mind-reading? Easy. Clairvoyance? Please. I passed Supernatural Studies without even studying. But here, it's like the professor is trying to—to—to—*challenge* me!"

Sarah looked at her own test gloomily. She had only answered three questions correctly, and she wasn't even sure if that had been foreseeing or just guesswork. So far, she had only had two future visions she was sure were real, and both had involved Tanja complaining.

"And just *tell* Raine you're sorry," Tanja said, looking peeved. "It's getting ridiculous."

Sarah stopped. "What are you talking about?"

"The feud. It's so utterly stupid."

"Who's Raine?"

"It's not fair!" Tanja wailed. "If I'd lived two hundred years ago, people would have thought me brilliant! But now that we know paradoxes, seers can't sound mad anymore! We're supposed to make *sense!*"

"You could take medication," Sarah suggested. "I've heard time-drift potions can do wonders for —"

"And take a chance of losing all my precognition?" Tanja asked incredulously.

Sarah sighed. "Maybe we're doing this all wrong. You don't need help seeing the future; you need help remembering what you've seen. Have you tried using mnemonics?"

"Men-what?"

"People who can't see the future use them to study." Sarah looked at her test grimly. "People like me."

"I dunno." Tanja looked unenthusiastic. "If you mean memory tricks, those don't work on me."

"All right." Sarah held up a notebook. "Let's try something else instead. You have trouble keeping memory in your brain. So why not keep it on paper instead?"

Tanja stared at her. "On paper?" she repeated.

"Yes." Sarah tossed the notebook at her. Tanja fumbled to catch it a second early, and it fell to the ground. "Try writing whenever you remember something. Write in blue ink if you think it's the past, red if you think it's the future. I'll space it chronologically after the final exam. Then you can look at it during the final and see the whole class in logical order."

Tanja looked surprised. "That might actually work." She flipped the notebook open, grabbed a blue pen, and stopped. "It's blank!" she cried in horror. "All my hard work —"

"You haven't written anything in it yet."

"Oh. I could have *sworn* ..." Tanja shook her head, dropped the blue pen in her pocket, and grabbed a red one instead. She plonked to the ground and started writing.

Sarah sat beside her and pulled out her home-made flash cards.

She flipped the first one over and squeezed her fist in frustration. Eight times a day, she had reviewed these. She recognized the writing, the dents, the worn edges. But the terms had disappeared from her mind again. She *hated* those paradoxes.

"You're going about it all wrong, too," Tanja mumbled, not looking up from her notebook.

Startled, Sarah looked over at her.

"Studying. This isn't a class where you can learn things logically. You've got to use your intuition."

"What intuition?" Sarah muttered, glaring at the flash cards in her hands. "I don't *have* any intuition."

"Sure you do." Tanja snatched the flash cards and threw them over her shoulder. "Tell me about Jinkan."

Sarah squeezed her eyes shut, rubbing her fists into them. "Jinkan Paradox. Jinkan. Jinkaaaaaaaaan ..."

"Stop trying so hard. Paradoxes only work if you're *not* trying to remember them. What did you eat for breakfast this morning?"

"Huh?" Sarah gaped.

"Or tomorrow. Or yesterday. What did you eat?"

"E-eggs," Sarah stammered. "And toa— *Remembering the future at all when it is not predetermined!*"

"See?" Tanja said smugly. "Now tell me about Harighan."

"I don't —"

"For crying out loud," Tanja said in exasperation. "Just tell Raine to quit it and stop being stupid."

"*'Changing what you remember from the future so that it does not occur'?*"

"*See?* Now try Dinskan."

Sarah tried to let her mind wander. She stared at the walkway, the trees ...

"'Confusing the future with the past'?" she asked slowly.

"No, that's Dinskan."

"You just asked me about Dinskan!"

"Really?" Tanja squinted at her.

"*You're* Dinskan."

Tanja grinned. "Kinagar."

"'Forgetting things you've prevented'—hey, this works!"

"Just try not to overuse it," Tanja cautioned. "Wringalin Paradox says the better you remember paradoxes, the more difficult it can become to think logically."

Sarah stared at her in horror.

"But I'm the living proof that's not true!" Tanja said happily.

IN THE END, Tanja passed their final exam with flying colors. Even Sarah, with the vaguest, fuzziest beginnings of future memory forming, scraped by. For some reason, that made the boy sitting beside her fly into a rage.

"She can't pass when I didn't!" he screamed. "It's not fair! She sat beside me to distract me! She *knows* I hate her! Of *course* I couldn't concentrate!"

Sarah turned and stared at him. "Who —?"

"You're such a jerk! I hate you!" He threw his test at her and stormed out of the room.

Sarah stared after him, jaw dropping as a fuzzy future memory tickled the back of her mind. "*Who ...?*"

Tanja yawned. "Raine."

Sarah clutched her forehead. "There's someone just as crazy as you."

"Crazy, but with a passing grade!" Tanja crowed, waving her final test.

AUTHOR NOTE:
I was in class at BYU one day, thinking, "Wouldn't it be annoying if the teacher expected us to turn in our final exam on the first day of class? What kind of class would do that?"

The result was this story.

THE SPINNING TALENT

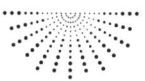

"Aria, you idiot!" Della shouted as her roommate walked in through the door, humming dreamily to herself. "What did you think you were doing down there?"

"I'm in love," Aria told her, falling happily onto her bed and staring up at the ceiling. "He promised he'd come back tomorrow, Delly! And I gave him Papa's old ring to remember me by——"

"That's what I meant," Della moaned, putting her head in her hands. "The headmistress will kill me when she finds out I let you give that away. It was enchanted to protect you from your birth-curse!"

"But who better to protect me than my true love?" Aria asked earnestly. "Besides, I don't believe I *have* a birth-curse. Papa's overprotective, that's all."

"This is supposed to be a school for the intelligent," Della groaned. "How did you even get in?"

"Daddy's rich," Aria shrugged, staring dreamily at the ceiling. "And I know I'm not as smart as you are, but nobody is, so there. Besides, he's my true love, and everyone knows true love conquers all!"

"Exactly *how* long have you known your 'true love'?" Della asked nastily.

"I've seen him from a distance before," Aria sighed happily. "But we've never spoken till now. Oh, Delly, wait till I tell you all about him! He's so handsome and brave and smart and witty, and he danced with me all night, and—"

"At the ball you went to *after* curfew," Della muttered.

"That's the one," Aria murmured. "And, oh, so *handsome!* I never realized from a distance just how *handsome* he is! Just wait till I tell you how we met—"

"I'm not interested in hearing how you met," Della snarled. "I don't even care who he is. Just make sure you get that ring back tomorrow, you hear?"

"Oh, Delly, you're so obsessed." Aria pouted. "His true love will protect me better than any old enchantment could. Just look at history."

"You're flunking history."

"Oh, don't bother me with lessons while I'm basking in true love's light!" Aria cried, flinging her arms out. "What do I need with school when I have *him?*"

Della groaned loudly, pinching out the candle by her bed. "Will you please promise to get your ring back from him the next time he drops by?"

"Oh, Delly!" Aria giggled uncontrollably. "You miss the point completely!"

To Della's fury, Aria spent the next three weeks sneaking out past curfew, chattering about her "true love" to every other girl who would listen, and evading every conversation about her ring. Her true love was apparently the second prince of the royal family, at least according to her horde of admiring classmates.

"Oh, he's so gorgeous," Lesias whispered, peeking just over the top of Della's dorm window to watch them. "Everyone says Havol's going to inherit the throne, but Tendar's the cutest. Aria's so lucky, I could just *die!*"

"Don't die," Della said sourly, "and get out of my room. Both of you."

"Oh, but I haven't had my turn yet!" Stellar cried, leaping up from Aria's bed. "Lessie, let me see! Please! Just one peek!"

"I don't suppose she's asked for her ring back yet?" Della muttered.

"OH, GOSH!" Lesias cried. "Stellar, look! They're *kissing!*"

That did it. Della slammed her textbook shut and stormed downstairs to the library. How could she expect to keep her scholarship if nobody would let her study?

TWO WEEKS LATER, the headmistress called an all-school assembly about a truly horrifying prospect.

"King Jerold has announced a wish to find a new goldspinner," she informed the chattering crowd. "To facilitate this, we'll be holding tests for the spinning talent all day. Once you've been tested, you may have the rest of the day off, though normal classes will resume tomorrow."

Excited buzzing broke out among the crowds of girls.

"The spinning talent!" one of Aria's friends cried rapturously. "Imagine if I had it! Goldspinners don't have to worry about *anything*—they're in highest demand of *anyone!*"

"If I had the spinning talent, I wouldn't have to worry about marrying rich," another girl giggled, clapping her hands. "I could choose whatever cute husband I wanted, and make us *both* wealthy."

"I'd like to spin straw into gold," Stellar said dreamily. "Then Aria wouldn't be the only girl here with a chance at winning a prince."

Della listened in cold horror as the headmistress announced where the testing would take place and the order they'd be tested in. She didn't want to take a goldspinning test, didn't want to take the risk that she might pass it. Her grandfather had had that talent, and he'd been worked to an early grave as a result.

Besides, who wanted suitors who only liked you for your gold?

"It's fairly easy," the history mistress told Della, threading several long, thin straws through her wheel. "You spin this, chant the words, and see if anything happens. Are you enjoying that book about King Jerold's great-grandfather, by the way?"

"Oh ... yes," Della said nervously. "Interesting man. He *really* used to be a beast before some princess kissed him?"

"Most historians suspect lycanthropy," the history mistress said. "Which means it may not have actually vanished. But it doesn't really matter as long as true love won, now does it?"

"Sure," Della muttered, her stomach tied in knots. She glanced across the room, where Aria was struggling to thread straws through the spokes of her wheel. The protocol mistress, looking exasperated, pulled the straws away from her and demonstrated how to use the wheel properly.

"Well, go on!" the history mistress smiled, patting Della on the shoulder. "Let's get this over with!"

Hands shaking, Della adjusted the spindle and twitched the straws into place. She'd used spinning wheels before, back home, but never for this—never to attempt this.

She squeezed her eyes shut and took hold of the wheel.

If I say the words wrong, there's no way it'll work.

"Straw into glunnnmmmb," she muttered. "Stlllmmmmm into gllllrrrd. Stlaaaa into ..."

"*ARIA!*"

Della's eyes flew open. She jumped to her feet, knocking her wheel over.

Aria lay slumped across her own spinning wheel, its spindle clutched upside down in her hand. She didn't appear to be breathing.

Della ran to her fallen roommate.

"Aria!" she cried. "Aria! Wake up! Wake up, wake up, wake up, and *breathe*, you idiot!"

Aria gasped, and kept breathing. But her face remained still.

"I—I—I don't know what happened!" the geography mistress was babbling, near tears. "She just seized it, and it pricked her finger, and—and look what happened!"

A crowd of girls leapt up from their spinning wheels, clustering around Aria and murmuring excitedly.

"Out of the way!" a loud voice barked, pushing through them. Through a haze of tears, Della recognized the face of their headmistress.

"What happened here?" the headmistress demanded. "Was she starving herself? Does she need her corset loosened?"

A babble of excited theories sprang up from the crowd of girls around Aria.

"SHUSH!" the headmistress shouted, cutting them off. "Della, you're her roommate—do you know what caused this?"

"N-n-no," Della stammered, her whole body shaking. "I mean, she ate like a horse—she doesn't lace her corsets too tight—headmistress, I think it might have been her birth-curse!"

Gasps rang across the whole room.

"Didn't she have a ring to protect herself from that?" the headmistress demanded, her voice dangerous. "I recall her father saying she had to keep it on at all times."

"There's no ring on her fingers!" a girl called from the crowd.

Della gulped back a sob. "She—she gave it to a—a suitor, a few weeks ago."

"And you didn't inform me *immediately?*" the headmistress roared. "That neglect may have cost your roommate her life!"

Della burst into tears.

"*You!*" the headmistress shouted, pointing at the history mistress. "Find out who that boy was, and get it back!"

"I know who the boy was!" Lesias squeaked. "It's Tendar, our second prince! He's Aria's true love!"

"Prince?" The headmistress's voice sounded hoarse. "Prince of *our* kingdom? The king never answers inquiries. We'd never get through in time ..."

Della shook all over.

My fault, she thought numbly. *This is my fault. If I had just told the headmistress, instead of worrying I'd get her into trouble ...*

"We should send a message to the court anyway," the protocol mistress said shakily. "I'll figure out a way to make them listen to us. Surely nobody would argue when a girl's life is at stake."

"King Jerold is a stubborn man," the headmistress said hollowly. "And greedy. If he said he wants a new goldspinner, he's not going to listen till one arrives. He might not even listen after."

Della squeezed her eyes shut, stood on trembling legs, and forced herself to look up at the headmistress.

If this is my fault, she thought numbly, *then I have to be the one to solve it.*

"I might be able to speak with him," she croaked.

"You have the *spinning talent*?" Headmistress Riena demanded, her sharp eyes pinning Della.

"Not for sure!" Della shook her head, shaking. "I don't know for sure! But— my grandfather had it. Mom's kept that a secret since ... since I was teensy ..."

"How could you keep something like this from us?" the magic mistress squealed. "Why, even the *possibility* of such a rare gift —"

"*Hush,*" the headmistress said, flicking a glare over at her. "Clearly Della didn't cherish the idea like you do."

"Yeah," Della said miserably. "Why can't the king just find an alchemist if he wants more gold?"

"Alchemy's notoriously unreliable," the history mistress murmured. "No one's made a philosopher's stone in centuries."

"Besides, goldspinning has more mystique!" the magic mistress squeaked.

"Perhaps for a king," Della said bitterly. "Headmistress ... how long do you think Aria's got before she dies from that spell?"

"Well ..." The headmistress looked reluctant. "She's essentially in a coma, and she's very skinny. I don't think she'd digest anything but water. Perhaps ... a week?"

"A *week?*" Della cried. "It's a three-day journey just to get to the castle from here!"

"All the more reason to run the test quickly!" the magic mistress cried, eyes gleaming. "There's no time to waste!"

"There's no call to rush her!" the headmistress barked. "We'll wait until she's ready."

Della took a deep breath, closed her eyes, and steeled her shoulders. "No. It's all right. If Aria's time is limited, the sooner we test me, the better. If I have the talent, I may have a chance to save her. If I don't ... well, better to know quickly."

The magic mistress ran to fetch a spinning wheel. The headmistress picked up a pile of papers and shuffled through them, not seeming to want to look Della in the eye.

"A goldspinner ..." she murmured. "I never dreamed we might have one in our midst."

IT WORKED. Of course it worked. Three spins of the wheel, concentration, and a few magic words were all it took. Looking at the string of wire and the magic mistress's ecstasy, Della felt a wave of misery and relief.

I have a chance to save my roommate, she thought, closing her eyes. *But at what cost to me?*

"GOLDSPINNER, GOLDSPINNER!" The fat king clapped his hands, his belly jiggling. "How fast are you? What high quality? Show me!"

Della fought to keep from glaring at him. "Fetch me a spinning wheel, sire, and I will do as you say."

The king waved his arms wildly at a pair of servants on the other end of the room. "Spinning wheel!" he hollered. "And lots of straw!"

Della scanned the room as thoroughly as she dared, but Prince Tendar was nowhere in sight. One snooty courtier stood in the corner, his arm around the waist of a sour-faced lady, but they looked like the crown prince and his newly-betrothed.

Where was Tendar? She had to find him as soon as possible. She had to get that ring back.

"So!" the king crowed, as four servants lugged in an enormous spinning wheel and six bales of hay, "prove your worth! Turn these all into gold!"

Della gaped at him. "*All?*"

"That's right!" The king rubbed his piggish hands together gleefully. "*All* of them!"

But that could take weeks! Della thought desperately. *Goldspinning works one straw, one thread, at a time—how can he expect me to do it all at once?*

Della's mind flew furiously, trying to think of an answer that wouldn't enrage the king.

"Have you ever seen a goldspinner in action, sire?" she burst out.

"Well." The king's brow wrinkled. "Not precisely."

"Well, that's because a ... a goldspinner ... needs privacy, sir." Della gulped. Would he buy it? Just one minute alone would let her sneak away and speak to Tendar ... "We can't produce on demand without—um—while people are staring at us, and —"

"LOCK HER IN A DUNGEON!" the king howled. "If she can't produce gold from these by morning, kill her!"

"*What?*" Della gasped.

"Then you can *prove* you have the gift," the king leered. "See you in the morning!"

Della screamed and tried to run, but three of the king's servants grabbed her.

"And fill the dungeon with straw!" the king shouted. "I want to see all of it turned gold by morning!"

DELLA SPUN two long gold wires and then gave up in despair. Over an hour had passed, and the tiny threads looked worthless next to those giant mounds of straw. Besides, her fingers were sore and blistering.

Yesterday I was free, she thought, flinging a huge pile of straw at her spinning wheel. *I chose to come here to save my roommate. Now all that's going to happen is that we'll both die for nothing.*

"The universe is unfair!" Della shouted.

A shadow bubbled in front of her, and a hideous man slurped out of it.

"Agreed," he said.

"Who—what—?" Della gasped.

"A friend." The ugly man smirked. "Do you need help?"

"I don't—I can't—it's impossible!" Della gulped back tears that sprang to her eyes. "Even if you goldspin too, there's no way all this straw could turn by sunlight!"

"Sure there is." The man's face turned crafty. "Quite easily."

"How?" Della demanded, yanking a straw off her blouse and flinging it to the ground. "Even with a dozen goldspinners, this work would take weeks!"

The small man coughed. "Well, I am not, in fact, a goldspinner. But I *am* an alchemist. And I happen to have a philosopher's stone with me."

Della froze. "A philosopher's stone?" she whispered. "Aren't those nearly impossible to make?"

"Yes, nearly." The man smirked. "But I happen to be brilliant. Masterful. The greatest alchemist in hundreds of years—"

"Get to the point," Della muttered.

The man coughed. "Well. It so happens there's something you could do for me."

"I'm not marrying you," Della said flatly.

The man looked insulted. "Nothing like *that*. I just need a favor."

"I'm promising nothing about my first-born child!"

"Just a small favor!" the man shouted. "A teensy thing! You'll barely notice it!"

"What?" Della demanded.

"I ... er ..." The man coughed and looked away. "I'd rather not say ... just yet."

"Then I'm not agreeing."

"Thankless, aren't you?" The ugly man eyed her. "Do you want your life saved or not?"

Della hesitated.

"Fine," the man said. "I'll just go back."

"All right!" Della shouted. "Help me!"

The man smirked. He reached into a shadow and pulled out a tiny gold ball. He tossed it in the air and caught it again.

"You get the straw," he told her. "I'll turn it. And let's hurry. We don't have much time left."

THE KING'S fat jowls turned crimson at the sight of all the gold in the room. He wept with happiness as he flung himself into a huge pile of it.

His wife surveyed Della with a highly suspicious eye.

"None of that looks spun," she said, her mouth a thin line. "It's still shaped like straw."

"W-well, that can happen sometimes," Della stammered, her palms wet with fear as she held them behind her. "It—depends on the goldspinner, you see. Your majesties, may I ... may I please see Prince Tendar? It's really urgent. You see —"

"Oh, certainly!" the king cried jubilantly, tossing handfuls of gold-straw in the air. "Whatever you wish!"

"*No.*" The queen shot him an angry glance. "I don't like this. There's something wrong. Besides, if she can turn one room of straw into gold, why can't she do another?"

The king froze, seeming stunned by that idea.

"N-no!" Della stammered. "I was—I've—I can only do so much at once! The magic's exhausted for now!"

The queen smiled thinly. "Well, you'd better hope it finds its way back soon, hadn't you? Guards, lock her up again. Let her sleep and eat. Then kill her if she isn't finished making more gold in the morning."

DELLA STARED at the mounting piles of straw with mounting despair.

"Won't you let me out, please?" she pleaded to one of the strong-armed servants, lugging in hay. "Even for one minute? I'll pay you all the gold you want. No one would notice ——"

"Nah." The servant shrugged. "Gold's going to be worthless if the king spends any of this. And he's bound to. Doesn't know the first thing about how economy works."

"I'll find some other way to pay you, then!" Della said desperately.

"Can't pay me if I'm dead," the servant smirked. "Face it, gold-spinner—you're stuck here."

"But Prince Tendar!" Della cried as he left. "At least bring him here! I just need to talk to him for a minute!"

The servant burst out laughing.

"You and half the kingdom, missy!" he called, waving. "But you're not nearly luscious enough for his taste!"

DELLA SLUMPED IN THE CORNER, staring at the endless straw that towered to the ceiling.

"Need help again?"

Della gasped, spinning around. "You!"

The little man pulled his arm from the shadow with a slight *slurp*. "For another favor, I could save you again."

"No way." Della smacked a handful of straw, which went flying. "If I change all this tonight, I'll just get stuck with more tomorrow. If I do it long enough, gold will become worthless, and the king will blame me. I'm dead either way."

The man considered, looking at her. "That's pretty accurate," he admitted.

Della closed her eyes and breathed in slowly. "I—I don't suppose you can take people with you when you're shadow-walking?"

"Welllll," the little man said slowly. "Maybe ..."

"Yes or no."

"I've never tried it," the man muttered.

"Then let's try it." Della opened her eyes. "Take me out of here. Or at least to Prince Tendar. I need to speak with him."

"Prince Tendar?" The man looked stunned. "Why him?"

"None of your business!" Della shot back.

"Then I won't help you!"

"Then I won't live to do *your* favor!"

The man seemed struck by this.

"I mean, you do have a reason to keep me alive, don't you?" Della asked.

"Fine." The man looked surly. "I'll take you to Prince Tendar, then out of here. But after that, you have to do my favor."

"Only if you say what it is," Della said peevishly.

"It's a *small* favor," the man muttered, looking angry. "*Reasonable.*"

"Then tell me what it is!"

"Not till you've agreed!"

"That defeats the *purpose!*"

The man spun on his heel and folded his arms.

"*Huh!*" Della flopped onto the spinning wheel and sat there, waiting for him to change his mind.

Minutes passed. Silence.

Minutes more passed. Stony silence.

Every minute delayed is another minute lost of Aria's life, Della thought unwillingly.

"All right," she muttered. "You win. Once we leave, I'll do your favor."

"Promise?" the man asked eagerly.

"If I have to," Della muttered.

The man grinned and grabbed her arm. Della gasped as her body liquefied. It felt like her whole self had turned into nausea.

They zipped up the wall outside the castle, around to a window, then right through it.

There, in a curtained bed, lay a beautiful prince. Asleep, he looked like an angel.

He's gorgeous, Della admitted, weak at the knees. *But he likes Aria*, she reminded herself quickly. *And really, that doesn't say much for his taste.*

"Here to give him a kiss?" the ugly man asked, smirking.

"Shut up," Della muttered. She walked over to the prince and put her hand on his mouth.

The prince's eyes flew open. "WHF——!"

He relaxed, catching sight of Della's face. She pulled her hand back slowly.

"Hel-lo, beautiful." The prince held out his arms. "Are you here for me?"

Outraged, Della smacked him.

"*Ow!*" the prince cried, clutching his jaw. "What was *that* for?"

"Aria's ring," Della hissed, checking over her shoulder for guards. One might arrive any minute. "Give it to me."

"What are you talking about?" The prince scrambled back, looking alarmed. "I don't have any ring!"

"*Aria's ring!*" Della hissed in a strangled shout. "Your *true love's* ring! She needs it to protect her from her birth-curse! Give it back!"

"I don't have a true love!" Prince Tendar scrambled back further, looking scared. "I've never had a true love! I don't want any ring!"

Della leaned forward. "Give—it—back," she hissed.

"GUARDS!" Tendar shouted, scrambling out of bed. "GUARDS! There are assassins in here! GUARDS!"

The door flew open. The ugly man lunged for Della, and they slurped into the shadows again.

Over walls. Through the doors. Faster, faster, away from the castle, through the forest, into wilds Della had never heard of before. Then, at last, they bubbled upwards again.

Della grasped a tree branch, dizzy. "That—has got to be—the most unpleasant way to travel," she gasped.

"But the fastest." The ugly man sat down. "If only at nighttime. You, ah ... back there ..."

"I—I failed." Della turned away, gripping the branch. "I totally failed. What's *wrong* with him? How could he pretend to have forgotten? *She's* spent the last few weeks obsessing!"

"Ah ..." The ugly man sounded very awkward. "That ... well, see, things ..."

"I can't believe he's such a creep!" Della exploded. "He said she was his one-and-only! What a liar! What a *creep!*"

"He's ... ah ... well ..." The man's voice fumbled. "You know ... about that favor you said you'd do ..."

"I've got to get that ring back," Della moaned. "I've *got* to get it back. But where's he *hiding* that thing?"

A lint-covered ring appeared under her nose. Della stared at it.

She turned around slowly.

"*You?*" she asked in a strangled voice. "*You*—*you* —"

"It was love at first sight!" the man cried piteously. "I'd never seen a maiden so enchanting!"

"SHE COULD DIE BECAUSE OF YOU!" Della shouted.

The man's eyes widened. "Die?"

"She's been in a coma for five days because she was missing that ring! She has a birth-curse! That was enchanted to protect her!"

"Here! Here!" The man dropped the ring in her hands. "Take it! Save her! She never said anything!"

Della snatched it. "How did you—*why* did you —"

"Just a whim." The small man looked away, his voice red. "I'm good at magic. Sometimes I want to look handsome. Desired. Popular. So I use illusion. Then I met Aria."

"And the favor?" Della snarled.

The man pawed the ground with his foot. "I just ... wanted somebody ... to tell her the truth. Slowly. So she'd accept me. You're her friend. Her roommate. I thought, if anybody ..."

Della closed her eyes, sighing. "Aria's shallow. All the clever lead-ins, all the careful explaining, won't make her accept you. Her 'true love' was the prince you pretended to be."

"But if you just explain —" the man said desperately. "The real me —"

"She'd see nothing in the real you."

The man stumbled back. "But I'm *brilliant!*" he snarled. "I'm a *genius!* I *invented* shadow-walking! I created a philosopher's stone! I could give her *anything* —"

"EXCEPT POPULARITY!" Della shouted. "Brilliant magician you may be, but you're a *dunce* socially!"

The man's shoulders slumped. He turned away.

Della closed her eyes.

Harsh tongue, she thought. *Harsh words. Mother would whip me.*

"I'm sorry," she said quietly. "But it's the truth."

"I'll take you back," the man said dully, without turning around. "You save her. It's the least I can do, if she's dying."

ARIA'S EYES OPENED SLOWLY, looking into Della's face and yawning widely.

"Hello, Delly," she chirped. "I feel *marrrrrrvelously* well-rested today!"

"I'm glad to hear it," Della muttered. "You almost died."

"Oh, don't be so *dramatic!*" Aria giggled, slapping her arm. "Delly, you think everything's life-or-death, *seriously!*"

"Ask anyone," Della snarled. "You've been asleep five and a half days. Your birth-curse nearly killed you. I had to get that ring back from your 'true love' in order to save you."

Aria stared at her blankly. She lifted her hand to her face and peered at the ring.

"Then where's Tendar?" she asked tremulously. "Why'd you wake me? He should have done it. He should have kissed me. Tendy?"

"Right here," a voice said dully.

Aria peered around her roommate's shoulder and screamed.

"MONSTER!" she shrieked. "MONSTER! DELLY!"

Della slapped her.

Aria gasped, clutching her cheek.

"He's the one you fell in love with," Della snarled. "He made himself look like Tendar so you'd fall for him, too. But he has plenty of other qualities. He's a genius —"

"Stop it!" Aria sobbed. "Stop lying! I don't want some stupid genius! I want Tendy!"

Della stood up, slowly, struggling with her fury.

"I wrecked my life for you," she said coldly. "The king will kill me if he ever finds me. I'll live in hiding for the rest of my life. And I did it for you. The least you can do is listen to him."

Aria hesitated and peeked over Della's shoulder again. She yelped, dove under her covers, and shook her head.

"Nooooo!" she cried. "No, no! He's too ugly!"

Della's face turned hot with fury.

"It's all right." The man's voice sounded wooden. "Everyone hates me. Everyone rejects me. Why should she be any different?"

"Because she claimed she loved you," Della snapped.

"Doesn't matter." The man's eyes looked dead. "It was based on lies anyway."

Something in his voice scared Della. *He might do something drastic now*, she realized.

"I don't care what you look like," she blurted out. "I mean, yes, you're hardly pretty. But I'm an outlaw too, you realize. That makes us equals."

Slowly, the man looked up at her.

"You're brilliant," Della said, swallowing. *Oh, how ugly he looks. But that doesn't matter. Or at least it shouldn't. I can't let it matter. I can't.* "All I ever wanted was an education. If we stayed together ... would you teach me?"

The man stared at her. Fear and hope and anger flitted across his face.

"You feel sorry for me," he accused her.

Della looked down. She couldn't deny it.

"But I also feel sorry for *me*," she insisted. "I'm dead if the king finds me, and you're the only person who'd be able to keep me safe. As for you ... well ... I can't offer love, but I can offer companionship. Better than loneliness."

There was silence a long moment.

"You mean we could be friends."

"Yes," Della said quietly. "We could be friends."

Slowly, the man held out his hand.

"All right," he muttered. "Friends."

They slurped into the shadows. There was silence.

"Does this mean I need a new roommate, Delly?" Aria cried from under the sheet.

AUTHOR NOTE:
I've always thought there was good crossover potential between "Sleeping Beauty" and "Rumpelstiltskin," given that both fairy tales involve a spinning wheel.

Naturally, my take on this had to be humorous.

ON A LONG CAMPING TRIP

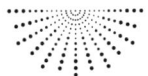

On a long camping trip that our dad made us take,
We went out snipe hunting (that was a mistake).
Because, quite on purpose (in pranks he's a whiz),
My big brother lost me, the jerk that he is.
In twilight I screamed and I screamed to be found,
But I just heard him laughing (he oughta be drowned).
I took off alone and hid in a dark cave,
Resolving to forget that creep and be brave.

But a horrid black shadow, more oily than air,
Then burbled behind me (it just wasn't fair!).
I let out a shriek ('cause the thing had no shape)
And a horrible tree root tripped up my escape.
Another more ghastly shade, double the size,
Appeared right before me (I feared my demise).
It shrieked in shrill laughter and snatched at my wrist.
I howled and fell backwards (the tiny one hissed).
I grabbed a dead branch that was knobbled and jointed,
Which went through the monster (it looked disappointed).
I pulled back, surprised, and I realized at last

That the thing couldn't hurt me (I coulda just asked).
I looked back behind me, and saw that the small one
Was scared, not of me, but the hideous tall one.
And that's when I knew, like a big neon sign,
That the smaller one had a big brother like mine.

My parents believed, when my big brother claimed,
That I'd just run away (shoulda known I'd be blamed).
But it's not a big deal, because my brand new buddy
Came back home with me (it's a really quick study).
So now, under his bed where the shadows are dim,
My big brother has a surprise waiting for him.

AUTHOR NOTE:
I enjoy rhymed and metered poetry. I cannot for the life of me figure out what the appeal of free verse is supposed to be. When I want to tell a story without meter and rhyme, I write prose.

This may be an unpopular opinion. Or maybe you're going, "Yes, thank you!"

> *Well, whatever you think,*
> *This poem forges a link*
> *Between giggle and blink.*
> *(I hope it doesn't stink.)*

ON THE WAY THROUGH THE WOODS

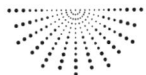

"I say your charm thing is broken," Topaz yawned, dragging a brush through her unruly curls. "We've been walking for hours and haven't seen anything."

"The Forest Beyond is huge," Mildred said testily. This princess she'd run into was starting to drive her crazy. "Besides, I thought you weren't in a hurry."

"Oh, sure, sure." Topaz waved her hand lazily. "*You're* the one on an errand for your High Witch. I'm just off to teach my dad a lesson about frogs as suitors. Gingerbread?"

Mildred eyed the chunk of windowsill the princess had stolen from a house earlier. They had barely escaped from an angry, dessert-loving witch, and she wasn't eager to relive the experience. "No, thanks."

"Well, then," Topaz licked the last bit of sugar off her fingers, "want to make a detour? I see bushes off that way. They might have berries."

Mildred's stomach growled. "That might be okay ..."

"Great!" Topaz hopped up and brushed the crumbs off her elaborate gown. She tugged her stockings straight, shook wrinkles out of her skirts, and marched towards the bushes. Mildred eyed the thick, dark trees in every direction and carefully brushed dirt off her black cloak.

"Hey, these aren't brambles!" Topaz called from ahead of her. "Come look at this!"

Mildred ducked under a branch and hurried over. Growing from the brambles were what appeared to be ... "Flowers?"

"Not just flowers. *Roses.*" Topaz wrenched one off its stem and poked it behind her ear. "In the middle of a forest. Who would think?"

Mildred stared at the row of thornbushes, mind working with misgiving. They seemed much too tidy to have grown naturally —

A roar sounded ahead of them.

Mildred yelped, startled.

A figure in shredded clothing thundered through the brambles, shoving them aside in his wake. He looked like some monstrous cross between a human and dragon, with huge leathery wings and a fanged tail. His eyes glowed red with fury.

"YOU STOLE ONE OF MY ROSES!" the monster roared. "People who steal my roses must pay! People who —"

The monster stopped abruptly.

"*You stole one of my roses!*" he shrieked in an entirely different tone.

"You said that already," Topaz said helpfully.

"But you *actually* stole one of my roses!"

Topaz's eyes narrowed. "What, were you just going to accuse us either —"

"YOU WILL FOLLOW ME!" the monster roared, grabbing Topaz's arms with a clawed hand. "YOU WILL FOLLOW ME *NOW!*"

Without even seeming to notice Mildred, he wrenched Topaz's arm and dragged her off. In a moment, they had disappeared behind a thick clump of trees.

Mildred stood frozen, petrified. She was a witch. She was supposed to be powerful and terrifying. But she'd barely started school, and Menacing Spells was her worst subject. No matter what her teachers said, she didn't want to hurt anybody.

"You'll stay here till you've learned some MANNERS!" the monster roared.

"Really? That might take ages."

"*FEAR ME!*"

"No, thanks. Dad's got a much worse temper."

Mildred closed her eyes, breathed, and quelled the fear in her heart. She couldn't leave the princess alone with a monster, even if the princess seemed unworried. Slowly, she forced her quavering legs to move forward.

Past the brambles, beyond the thick clump of trees, she reached an enormous stone tower. Two massive rock doors were shoved open, and the monster stood in front of the opening, glowering. Inside sat Topaz on a spiral staircase, fluffing her curls and making kissy faces at the mirror she kept in her satchel.

"H-hello," Mildred said hesitantly. "Are you—are you a human under a spell?"

"Who wants to know?" the chimera growled.

Mildred swallowed. "W-well ... you have an accent from Guraton. I wondered ..."

"Oh!" Topaz's eyes brightened. She tossed the mirror back in her satchel. "Are you from the royal family? Your face looks sorta like the old king's!"

The chimera glared at her. "That's none of your business."

"I heard a rumor one or two escaped the revolution," Topaz pondered. "You must've been cursed by the witch who helped it."

"*None of your business!*"

"A beast-curse," Mildred said, awed. "It must be. They're really tricky. In Traditions, we learned that the first was cast in the year —"

Topaz rolled her eyes. "Irrelevant, Mildred. How do we break it?"

Startled, Mildred shook herself. "Well ... a kiss from a princess should work."

Topaz turned around and scrutinized the monster. "Yeah, not happening. Any other ideas?"

Mildred chewed on her lower lip. "One curse can supplant another—but it needs to be as powerful, and I'm not at that level yet—"

"Not a good idea to mess with curses. I've heard they can cause damage you don't predict."

"My Menacing Spells teacher said that doesn't matter."

"Your Menacing Spells teacher is a jerk."

Mildred fell silent. She didn't disagree.

"What part of 'none of your business' did you two not understand?" the monster rumbled.

"Wait a minute!" Topaz cried. "You know that spell someone used on my great-grandmother?"

Mildred scoured her memory. "You mean the standard rose-curse?"

"Exactly! Makes coma patients healthy, but puts anyone else in a coma. Don't you think this tower looks *awfully* like one of those?"

Mildred looked up. The enormous tower was covered in brambles, despite the fact that there were no cracks in the smooth stone to encourage this. The top window was covered in shutters with thorny vines growing into them. It had clearly not been opened in a decade.

"Is someone up there?" she asked softly.

The chimera snorted and folded his arms, turning away.

"Please," Mildred whispered. "We just want to help."

The wings flapped sharply and settled back onto his back.

"My sister," he said finally.

"Okay." Topaz hopped up. "I know what worked on my great-grandmother. Just a minute."

She skipped up the stairs. There was silence for a moment. Then an unearthly shriek.

"You *SLAPPED* me!" a woman's voice howled.

The monster gasped. He raced up the spiral staircase, tail crashing against the walls and smashing holes in his haste.

Topaz bounced down the stairs, looking pleased with herself.

"What did you do?" Mildred demanded. "What worked?"

"Same thing that worked on my great-grandmother." Topaz

pulled an empty bottle from her satchel and shook it. "Revoltingly strong perfume. I keep one around in case I need to throw it at somebody."

Mildred stared at her. "The slap wasn't part of it?"

"That was for letting herself get cursed. I hate victims who play for sympathy."

"Rosa!" the monster howled from far above them.

"Beirran!" a woman's voice sobbed.

"And now his sister can kiss him," Topaz said with satisfaction. "Which is good, because I'm sure not gonna."

Mildred smiled. She set the directional charm again and pointed it towards their destination. "Should we give them their space?"

"Sure." Topaz hauled a rock candy cobblestone out of her satchel. "Want some?"

Mildred shuddered. "No, thanks."

They headed back into the woods. Mildred took one last look back at the stone tower as the view was covered by trees. She felt happier than she could ever remember being.

Witches aren't supposed to do good deeds, she thought, humming, *but the High Witch doesn't have to know about this, does she?*

"Besides," Topaz said casually, "I already stole the satin bedsheets."

AUTHOR NOTE:

This started out life as a chapter in my first published book, Black Magic Academy. *I axed it because it was unnecessary to the plot, but it was fun enough that I decided to adapt it into a standaloneable short story instead.*

When I was in junior high school, I was sick to death of damsel-in-distress princesses and tomboy princesses. I wanted a character who was super girly while also being feisty. So I created Topaz, the kleptomaniac princess who is a royal pain in the neck.

There need to be more tough girl characters who are feminine. Not just tomboys. Girly girls. Those were the role models I wanted when I was a kid, and they're still hard to find.

OGRE IN BOOTS

*H*orinwa was just sitting down to his usual breakfast of snake egg omelets and hemlock syrup when he heard a loud, insistent whamming on the front door. Annoyed, he got up to go see who it was.

On the way, he cheerfully entertained the notion that it might be a Normal stupid enough to believe that pestering a wicked witch was a good way to get a curse put on somebody they didn't like for free. He had gotten a few visitors like that over the years. He always found them to be amusing test subjects.

On the other hand, it might be someone else after his daughter.

If I have to put down another assassin from those sore losers who pass for teachers at Black Magic Academy, he thought darkly, *I'm going to lodge an official complaint.*

So his daughter had been the pride of the school. So she'd managed to keep a horrifying secret hidden from them for well over a year. So she'd outwitted them all and escaped. They really had to learn to have a sense of humor about such things.

He fingered a charm in his pocket, one he kept ready all the time just in case, and flung open the door, ready to face whatever was waiting for him.

There was no one.

"Ahem!" a voice called from below.

He looked down. A tom cat with long, thick whiskers stood on his front porch, lashing his tail. Oddly, the tom cat was standing on his hind legs. Even more oddly, the cat was standing awkwardly inside a pair of oversized boots.

"My name," the cat said grandly, "is Puss."

"No, it's not," Horinwa said.

The cat looked nonplussed. "Excuse me?"

"That's a name used for female cats. You're clearly male."

"W-well, take that up with the human family who adopted me!" the cat sputtered.

"Mm-hmm," Horinwa murmured. He was already bored with this conversation. "I don't lift curses on enchanted princes. If you keep on pestering me, I'll cast a new curse on you, though." He turned to shut the door.

"I'm not a prince!" the cat yelled.

"A helpless bystander, then." Horinwa kept on shutting the door.

"I'm an ogre!"

Horinwa paused. He glanced idly down at the cat through the sliver of openness that remained between them. "Oh?"

The cat stood tall and preened his whiskers proudly. "A human, indeed! I'm a magnificent ogre. Greater and mightier than any such puny beings!"

"Uh huh. You realize you're a cat now, which means you're smaller than me."

The cat's whiskers wilted. "Well ... yes, but that's temporary."

"Is it, now?"

"It is. Because you're going to break the curse on me."

Horinwa laughed out loud and shut the door.

He headed back to the kitchen to finish his omelet. He would have to heat it up again now, and Rulisa wasn't home to make it simple, more's the pity. He missed having a fire witch around the house.

It wasn't that Horinwa didn't know how to perform temperature spells. Of course he did. As a former teacher of Kraken Institute, it would have been ridiculous for him to not know the basics of any field. But that branch of magic tended to come easier to fire witches than any other element, and Horinwa was a water witch.

Of course, the fire witch he missed the most of all wasn't his daughter. It was his deceased wife, Welsa. Horinwa sighed moodily, sitting back at the table and poking at his cold omelet.

An irritating caterwaul howled from outside.

Horinwa plugged his ears and muttered a soundproofing spell, but it only muffled the noise a little. Wind witches were better at spells than water witches, just as water witches were better at brews. If he had a torrent of water, he could soundproof the cat ...

He got up from the table and fetched a bucket of dirty dishwater from the kitchen that he hadn't yet bothered to dump outside. Then he headed for the front door.

The tom stopped mid-cauterwaul. "Now, as I was saying—"

Horinwa dumped the contents of the bucket over the cat. The sodden feline shrieked in horror. With a smile, Horinwa snapped his fingers and sent the cat reeling backwards across the fields at a rapid pace. Back, back, back, back ...

He chuckled and slammed the door. The booted tom cat would be miles away by the time he stopped. No doubt he would take the hint and go off to pester some other witch who was both closer and a little more amiable.

But the tom cat was back in the morning.

"Now, as I was saying—" the irritating feline began as Horinwa stepped outside his back door to fetch a bucketful of water from the well.

He ignored the chatter, plunged his bucket into the well, and marched back to dump the water onto the cat. When he did, it showered around the tom, leaving a bubble of dryness around him.

Horinwa paused. "You've seen another witch."

"I have, yes."

"From the looks of things, a wind witch."

"Indeed."

"Then *why*," Horinwa asked with exasperation, "didn't you just ask *that* witch to help you?"

The cat preened his whiskers, looking aloof. "I have my reasons. Now, I want you to turn me back into an ogre now."

"I can't imagine why you think your desires will affect me."

"I have mounds of treasure back home," the cat said. "I could pay you."

Horinwa paused. As a member of witch aristocracy, he had no particular need for money. Village witches used it, but when a member of witch aristocracy wanted something from a Normal, they tended to simply take it. Still, he couldn't deny that coins tended to smooth over negotiations with particularly well-armed Normals who didn't take kindly to their natural place in the pecking order.

"All right," he said cautiously. "But why would you want *me*, in particular?"

"I have my reasons," the cat said mysteriously.

"So explain them."

"I'm willing to negotiate the payment, but the reasons are my own. And I have an additional condition: you must come to my home to change me back."

Horinwa paused. That sounded obviously suspicious, and he wasn't fond of walking into traps. On the other hand, he'd always survived before, and some of his best brew materials had come from innocently wandering into a trap that he pretended he couldn't see and harvesting rare materials he couldn't have accessed otherwise while there.

Welsa had once yelled at him for walking into an obvious trap by her death-enemy just because it had allowed him to amble through the gardens of her family's manor for several minutes unmolested before the trap sprang.

Oh, true, he still had the scar on his leg from where the cerberus had bitten him. On the other hand, he'd also gotten some clippings from the enhanced poison ivy that grew along the walls, and those had enabled him to invent a superior itching brew.

Horinwa sighed. He missed his wife a great deal, and his teenage daughter, who spoke to everyone with condescension, was little comfort. Rulisa's haughty scorn simply wasn't as fun to provoke as his wife's rage.

He weighed the risks of following the cat. The chances of finding interesting brew materials in an ogre's home weren't terribly high. On top of that, his wife wasn't here to shout at him for his incaution, which stripped most of the entertainment from the prospect.

Still, the house was awfully quiet with his daughter away at school. He was bored.

"All right," Horinwa said affably. "Let's negotiate on the price."

They negotiated for a long time, arguing until both sides were satisfied that they had successfully cheated the other.

"About food," the cat went on, "I intend to forage for myself. If you want to have a food allowance for the days spent traveling—"

"Days?" Horinwa asked, puzzled. "Why would I spend days? I'm going to fly."

The cat looked alarmed. Its eyes grew large, and it stumbled back and nearly toppled out of its too-large boots. "Fly?"

Horinwa laughed out loud. "Yes, fly, you silly tom named Puss. Don't tell me you've never flown before?"

"I'm an *ogre!*" the cat hissed.

"No excuse," Horinwa said blithely. "There's nothing to it. Just try not to fall, because then you'd turn into a dead little splat."

"We're going to walk!" the cat screamed in panic.

Horinwa laughed. "No, no, we're taking the broom."

The cat seemed deeply unhappy when they departed about an hour later, Horinwa's pockets full of empty vials for new samples and full ones of useful brews.

Horinwa could, perhaps, have been more wary, but he was having too much fun to waste energy on worrying. And thus it was that the trap he had halfway expected managed to catch him completely off guard anyway.

As they arrived at the ogre's hut, Horinwa's feet touched the ground, the broomstick clattering beside him.

A hand made of earth exploded up beside him and clenched him tight in its fist.

Horinwa gasped for breath, finding it difficult to inflate his lungs. This artificial hand-shaped rock was much more powerful than he would have expected. *Blast it. He's hired an earth witch to create protective wards against me.*

"Like it?" the cat taunted, leaping from the bag that was still attached to the end of Horinwa's broomstick. The broomstick that was now, unfortunately, several feet out of reach. "I hired a witch to trap you. Your daughter's the one who cursed me into this form, and I owe her payback! She's too far away for me to get revenge on her now, but you're conveniently nearby. And I'm sure killing you will distress her terribly!"

Horinwa struggled against the earth-hand's tightening grip, his blood boiling. A brigand seeking his money or life was an enterprising businessman who he could respect. A fellow witch wanting to make a name for herself by killing someone as powerful as Horinwa was being perfectly rational. An angry customer trying to repay him for tricking them into buying useless garbage was just part of the game.

But going after his daughter? That was beyond the pale.

Nobody went after his daughter and lived.

A gush of water exploded upwards, shooting torrential arcs in every direction. The arcs danced in dazzling jets and plunged down into the earth again, a constant loop of water rushing from the underground river beneath him.

The hand of earth attempting to squeeze Horinwa to death struggled desperately to keep its shape, but it melted into a soggy mass in no time. In seconds, Horinwa was merely covered with mud and sore and bruised.

He lashed his hand out and a hiss of water responded, twisting and twirling around his arm, undulating like a deadly viper as it flew through the air around him.

"P-please," the cat stammered, taking several steps backwards. He stumbled out of his boots, leaving them soddenly strewn in the mud. "I made a mistake. I-it wasn't Rulisa I wanted to hurt. It was somebody else. It was her death-enemy! Yes! It was her death-enemy I was after! That's right, I remember now, ha ha ha ha!"

"Don't worry, I don't believe in revenge," Horinwa told the cat comfortingly.

The cat-turned-ogre began to relax.

He shot the water-viper at the cat and sliced off its head.

"But I *do* believe in killing threats to my daughter," Horinwa added amiably, ambling over to inspect the corpse for potentially useful brew ingredients.

It was a shame about there being no payment. There was a con he wanted to try with jeweled eggs that would hatch into frogs and snakes, and paying an earth witch to turn dirt into gemstones could be expensive. He would rather pay with much-less-valuable coins than from his personal stash of rare brew ingredients.

Still, he'd protected his daughter from an enemy. That was always worth doing. It was a shame she had so many of them. In witch society, the more enemies you had, the more respected you were, so he ought to be proud, but she never seemed to kill any of them herself, so he kept having to do it for her.

Horinwa picked up his broomstick and sprayed the mud off of it. *Well, a good day's work for a wicked witch. If only my wife were here to laugh over it with me!*

Author Note:
Rulisa is the rival in Black Magic Academy, *and the protagonist of* White Magic Academy. *Her father is a highly entertaining not-very-nice person. Think "totally shameless con artist". So I thought I'd write a standaloneable short story from his point of view.*

Has anyone else ever noticed the oddity of a male cat being named Puss?

ENTRANCE INTERVIEW

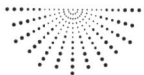

"So, why do you want to attend the Sukanil School of Magical Studies?" High Witch Dal asked, smiling.

"I don't," Rulisa said flatly.

"You don't?"

"No, but it's not like I have much choice. I got expelled from my first school, and I broke the second one I wanted to apply to."

"You broke ... the school?"

"Yes, but don't worry, it was on purpose. I'm not incompetent enough to do it by accident."

"And ... what happened at the first school?"

"I guess you could say I broke that, too."

There was a long, long pause.

"We'll get back to you."

AUTHOR NOTE:
Rulisa is not the best student to have in your school.

KNOCK THREE TIMES

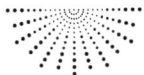

Ellie cleaned the house because she absolutely had to.
Her stepsisters were slobs, and her stepmother was quite
   bad, too.
"Your standards are just way too high," her stepmother
   protested.
"You cleaned the grate an hour ago!" her stepsisters attested.
But Ellie couldn't help it, be it crumb or dust or hairs—
She simply had to keep perfection up and downstairs.
"It could be worse," stepmother sighed; "her father spoke
   rhymes.
At least she only cleans a lot, and knocks three times."

A messenger came to the house with fancy invitation
For them to all attend a three-day royal celebration.
But on the first night all of them were heading out the door,
The younger sister tripped and splashed ink all across the
   floor.
"Don't clean it up!" the older cried. "We shouldn't delay!"
"Then go without me!" Ellie shouted. "I have to stay!"
Her sisters waited half an hour, but she'd found new grimes.

KNOCK THREE TIMES

So they left as Ellie fiercely scrubbed and knocked three times.

At last, her task completed, Ellie sat back and cried.
She'd wanted to go to the ball, and now had no ride.
The front door then burst open; her godmother barged in.
"Your whole family is worried, Ellie! Where to begin?!
It's a good thing I have magic, girl. I'll make you a coach.
Fetch me pumpkin, mice, and lizards now," she said with reproach.
Soon the pumpkin was a grand coach with the faintest of slimes.
Ellie vigorously cleaned the seats and knocked three times.

When she found the royal ballroom, all her tensions relaxed.
She had never seen a floor quite so exquisitely waxed.
She squealed about it to the prince, and he was bemused.
"Is it really that exciting?" he asked. "Yes!" she enthused.
He found this so entertaining that they danced for hours long,
And before either had realized it, the night was half-gone.
At her curfew, she was dragged away with the midnight chimes,
With her mind so full of him ... she didn't knock three times.

On the next night, the prince watched the door like a hungry hawk,
But she had to stay home because she'd forgotten to knock.
So her sisters dropped her shoe into the lost and found claims.
(A subtle hint because the prince was awful with names.)
The prince found it, and cried out that he wanted to date
The girl who'd worn this tiny slipper! (It was size eight.)
Five hundred ladies claimed it theirs and other such crimes,
But none of them were her, and none knocked three times.

He went from house to house to find the girl of his dreams

(Not noticing her address had been sewn in the seams).
At last he found the right one, where her family was housed.
"It's past time; it's been weeks now," her two stepsisters
   groused.
"She's hiding in her bedroom now. She's locked herself in!
She thinks you made her commit some unpardonable sin."
He stared; then they explained it all in whispers and mimes.
So he went to Ellie's door, and then he knocked three times.

There was silence for a moment, and then Ellie emerged.
Hopefully, the prince asked, "Has the problem been purged?"
Shakily, she nodded. So he grabbed both her hands.
"In that case, do you think that we could make dinner plans?"
The stepsisters squealed loudly and clapped hands in delight.
Ellie's face was crimson and now glowing quite bright.
"I guess it's not so bad if you distract me sometimes ..."
The prince grinned, and together, they both knocked three
   times.

AUTHOR NOTE:
Why does Cinderella *clean the house when she's so unappreciated? Well, maybe because she has obsessive-compulsive disorder and can't handle it when things aren't perfect.*

What if her stepfamily isn't the problem?

What if her mental illness is her real enemy?

THE MARK ON HER RIGHT HAND

Cara flopped down by the window seat of the train, sighing. It had been a long day at work. She couldn't wait to get home to Nora.

Other commuters got on the train after her. One of them was a handsome young man who was heading towards her, his eyes on her unmarked left hand.

Cara shifted her position so that her right hand was evident.

The young man noticed the mark, seemed to lose interest, and sat elsewhere instead.

Cara breathed a sigh of relief. It was always uncomfortable when a guy tried to flirt with her. It was always a relief when they caught the hint from her right hand.

A mark on the left hand was a sign one was married. A mark on the right was a sign that one had a teff, a celibate romantic life partner. Usually that was a same-sex relationship, because sex outside of marriage was forbidden, while romantic love wasn't, and life partnership wasn't.

Cara's teff was Nora, a woman she'd been in love with for nearly a decade. They'd become teffs eight years ago, the best day of her life.

The train slowed to a halt at the next stop, and more people got on. A middle-aged man sat down by Cara, stowing his bag under the seat in front of him.

Cara was startled to see he had a mark on both of his hands.

That was rare. It was allowed—you could have as many spouses and teffs as you wanted, as long as you kept every promise you made—but most people only wanted one. Most of the time when you saw someone with two marks, both were on the left hand, and it was because they'd been widowed and remarried later.

It was odd to see both hands marked. Usually when someone decided marriage was possible for them, they preferred marriage.

"Can I ask ..." Cara asked, pointing at his hands. She hoped it wasn't rude, but she wanted to know. "... how that happened?"

The man looked over at her. She saw him glance down, taking note of her right hand. He nodded.

"Ellen came first." He held up his left hand. "We had a pretty typical courtship. We've been married for twenty-four years, and we have seven kids. She's the love of my life."

"Still living?" Cara asked.

The man grinned. "I sure hope so. She was this morning."

Cara looked at his right hand.

The man's gaze followed hers. Gently, he touched the mark on it. "That's Tad. He's been my best friend since I was eight years old. A few years ago, I asked him, 'Why don't you ever date?' and he said, 'Because I'm not into girls.' I'd already figured that out, so I said, 'Why don't you date guys? You could look for a teff.' He looked at me for a long time and finally said, 'The guy I'm in love with is married.'"

The middle-aged man stopped abruptly, looking choked up.

Cara searched in her purse for a handkerchief.

The man waved it away, shaking his head. After a moment, he continued. "So I talked to Ellen, and she said, 'If you want Tad to be your teff, I'm okay with it.' I asked Tad if he wanted to be. He bawled. He said yes. That's how it happened."

"Are you in love with him?" Cara asked quietly.

"No. Doesn't matter."

"Do you kiss him?"

"Of course. He's my teff."

"Do you enjoy it?"

The man smiled. "Not as much as kissing Ellen, but I don't do it for me. I do it for Tad. He loves being kissed, and I love making him happy."

Cara was quiet. That wouldn't have been enough for her. She'd always thought the whole point of having a teff was that it was mutually romantic. But not everyone was the same.

The train stopped at her station, so Cara got up to leave. The middle-aged man got up to make it easier for her to get out.

Cara thought about that conversation all the way home. She thought about everything she had, and was grateful for.

When she got to the apartment, she unlocked the door and found Nora in the kitchen, already having started on dinner.

Cara pulled her away from the cutting board and kissed her.

"What was that for?" Nora said with a laugh.

"For being in love with me."

"Thanks for making it so easy." Nora stroked her cheek.

Cara watched her go back to cutting the vegetables.

"Hey, Nora?" she asked, screwing up her courage. "Have you ever thought you might want to get married?"

It was something she couldn't offer the woman she loved.

"Well, yeah." Nora turned to look at her. "That was what I originally wanted, after all: a husband and kids. You know that. But anytime I tried dating a guy, I felt cold and empty. Whenever I'm with you, I feel warm and full. I'm open to the idea of marriage someday, but I'm not looking for it. If I ever did decide to, you know I'd keep my promise to you."

"I know." Cara wrapped her arms around her waist and put her head on her shoulder.

Nora ran her fingers along her arm. "How about you? Have *you* thought about it?"

Cara shook her head. "I've never had the slightest interest in guys. I knew when I was a kid that I wanted a teff, not a husband. You're exactly what I've always wanted."

Nora laughed. "You're not at all what I expected, but I'm happier with you than I ever was before I met you. Thank you."

"You're welcome."

"I love you."

"You, too."

Cara reached out and placed her right hand on top of Nora's. The marks of their love seemed to shine in the light.

AUTHOR NOTE:

God draws the line where God draws the line. It is not the business of humans to draw the line for other people before that.

There is room in Zion for a system like this.

THIRD PRINCESS

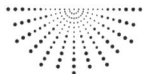

"Send in my eldest daughter," the Queen ordered. "Penelope."

The butler cleared his throat. "Ah ... your majesty, your eldest daughter's name is Prunella."

"Whichever." The Queen waved an imperious hand. "The eldest."

"As you wish." The butler bowed and hurried off.

The Queen knew the youngest of three was always successful in her quest or adventure or engagement, so she'd devoted all her time to Arabella. Thankfully, Prunella and Penelope weren't too much of a bother, but she'd be glad when they got themselves out of the way. After all, Arabella couldn't succeed in anything until the older two had failed.

Prunella stumbled into the room, tripping over an uneven hem on her gown.

The Queen sniffed, pretending she didn't notice her eldest daughter's disheveled hair. She'd been in that no-good library again, no doubt, and probably even had a half-finished book hidden behind her back right now.

The Queen summoned an insincere smile. "Dearest Prunella, how very good to see you."

Prunella tried to smooth her hair down, and sighed. Why had

Mother called her? She'd been in the middle of an excellent book, one of her favorites.

And why was Mother looking at her like that? Oh, no —*surely* she hadn't made some kind of plan —

The Queen made an imperious wave at the butler, who made himself scarce. "Now that we're alone ..." she purred. "I suppose you've heard of the prince of Arvakhia?"

Prunella blinked, uncertain of what to say. Everyone knew about Alfonse, the crown prince of Arvakhia. Probably even Arabella knew who he was. People said he was cagey and impossible to reach. Or did she mean the younger brother, Spenser?

"Crown prince or the one who disappeared off on a quest?" she hedged.

"Crown." The Queen's smile was icy. "I'm sending you to Arvakhia."

Prunella stared at her mother in disbelief. "What for?"

The Queen's eyes flashed in annoyance. "To *attempt* to win his hand in marriage, you fool."

"M-me? But Mother—"

"No buts." The Queen waved her hand. "Our kingdom needs an alliance with Arvakhia. I'm counting on you to succeed."

Prunella left, more than a little bewildered. Mother had never done more than barely acknowledge her existence before. Why Arvakhia? Why so suddenly?

"Her royal highness — the Princess of Sveilian!"

Prunella's eyes widened as she entered the Arvakhian throne room. It was barely decorated, tastefully minimalist, so much more appropriate than their castle back home. It seemed to say, "Dear peasants: we are not wasting your tax money on fripperies."

She curtseyed awkwardly to the king and queen, then fastened her eyes on the doors that were open a crack behind the throne room. She saw *books!*

Before the introductions were even over, to the scandalous cry of a butler, she ran to the doors and peered right through them. Before her was the most awesome sight she had ever beheld in her life. Bookcase after bookcase, filled to capacity, spilling out all over the floor and across several tables.

She ran straight to the nearest and pulled out a handful. It was only then somebody cleared his throat.

"Oh!" Prunella leapt back, dropping the books. She realized, suddenly, in horrid embarrassment, that she had probably just shamed her family. "Oh—er—sorry ..."

"It's quite all right," the young man smiled, picking them up for her. "Are you the eldest princess of Sveilian? The one I'm supposed to meet?"

"Oh—" Prunella felt her face flushing. Of course she should have thought before running off. Of course. But Mother had never really bothered to drill the etiquette of courtly behavior into her. "I think I may have just done something terribly rude—"

"It's quite all right." The young man smiled brilliantly. "I'm not offended, and my parents are used to me doing exactly the same thing. So why should anybody else be?"

THE QUEEN STARED at the message in dismay.

The butler coughed. "Is ... something wrong, my queen?"

"*Wrong?*" The Queen exploded. "*Wrong? Wrong?* I'll tell you what's wrong! There's been a terrible mistake made, that's what's wrong!"

The butler hesitated, but there was no backing out. "Your majesty?"

"This!" the Queen sputtered. "*This!*" She waved the message in the air.

The butler cleared his throat. "Ah ... a great shame, your majesty."

Her eyes narrowed. "Have you been reading my messages again?"

The butler coughed and tried to look innocent.

The Queen's face flushed. "I want live messengers from now on, do you hear? No more of these notes that anybody can read!"

The butler sighed. "Yes, your majesty."

The Queen flung the note on the floor. "How could she, the little sneak? Stealing Arabella's rightful husband ..."

The butler cleared his throat, curiosity getting the best of him. "Your majesty?"

"The first daughter, Penelope, you fool! She's gone and gotten engaged to the prince of Arvakhia!"

Try as he might, the butler couldn't see a problem with that. "But your majesty, weren't you *seeking* for an ... alliance ...?"

"He was meant to be *Arabella's!*" the Queen shrieked, towering above him. "Arabella's husband, not the eldest daughter's! The eldest *never* wins the man!" She sat again, breathing heavily and glaring. "Send in Prunella. Now."

The butler cleared his throat. "Your majesty, Prunella is—uh—in Arvakhia."

"Penelope, then! Whichever is the second!"

PENELOPE SCOWLED as she entered the throne room. She didn't appreciate being interrupted when she was at the archery range. Especially when she was on a winning streak!

She shoved open the doors and strode in, heavy boots clomping across the painted marble.

"Yes, Mother?" she barked, folding her arms.

The Queen looked her up and down and shuddered. "You smell like cattle."

"I was shooting arrows with the stableboys." *And winning,* Penelope added sourly.

The Queen sighed. "Of course, of course ... but right now, I have a task for you."

Penelope eyed her mother suspiciously. The last time she'd said something like that, it had been to demand her daughter grow out her hair longer than a quarter inch. Mother had wept and howled when she'd refused to be obliging.

"You're going to Arvakhia!" the Queen cried, clasping her hands. "Isn't that magnificent?"

"Are we invading?" Penelope asked hopefully.

"No!" the Queen scowled.

Penelope sighed.

"We are trying to prepare a *proper* alliance to Arvakhia," the Queen said icily. "Do you understand my meaning?"

"Do you think I'm going to marry on your say-so?" Penelope asked incredulously.

"No!" the Queen roared. "I'm sure no prince in his right mind would even glance at you!"

Penelope rubbed her hands over her peach fuzz and smirked.

"I'm sending you," the Queen said in a brittle voice, "to arrange *Arabella's* marriage, not your own."

"Oh!" The light dawned. Penelope chewed her thumbnail for a minute. "Does that mean she'd be living somewhere far away?"

"Her husband-to-be is their prince! She will, of course, remain in Arvakhia!"

Penelope grinned. "Then I'm in."

"PENELOPE!" Prunella ran to meet her on the road, tripping all over her lace petticoats. "The carriage arrived here without you!"

"Did it?" Penelope spat on the ground and jumped off her horse. It whinnied. "Drat. I bet the driver I could beat him."

"Are you all right?" Prunella gasped for breath and clutched her sides. "We were so worried!"

"Yeah, just wounded pride." Penelope groaned and rolled her shoulder. "Do you know where the prince is I'm supposed to meet?"

"Oh! Prunella's face glowed as she clasped her hands to her chest. "He's the most beautiful, wonderful man you will ever meet! He has the heart of a dreamer and the soul of a poet, and he—"

"Er—yeah—" Penelope was taken aback. "Er ... are you in love with him or something?"

"Yes!" Prunella squealed and hugged herself. "We're engaged!"

Penelope stared at her, aghast. "But ... Mother sent me here to arrange him marrying Arabella."

"Oh, no." Prunella shook her head earnestly, eyes wide. "He's going to marry me."

"Hhhmm." Penelope chewed her thumbnail in confusion. "Is there some other prince here?"

"Penelope," Prunella sighed, "don't you ever listen to your studies? The second prince, Spenser, got captured by giants two years ago. The family has given up hope he's still alive."

Penelope's eyes lit up. "That's it! Of course! I'm supposed to rescue him!"

"Uh ..." Prunella stared at her with wide eyes. "He's probably dead ..."

"No problem," Penelope said confidently. "If he is, I'll bring his bones back, get some closure to the family. Well, what are we waiting for? Come on! I've got to equip for a journey!"

"*Married?*" the Queen shrieked. "To *WHOM?!*"

The messenger looked back at the butler helplessly. He shrugged and gestured for the young man to continue. Looking miserable, the messenger did. "The—ah—the prince, your majesty."

"The *prince?!* First he think he's going to marry Prunella, and then—!"

"Oh, no, no!" the messenger hastened to reassure her, relieved to understand the cause of her worry. "This is the second prince, your majesty. Apparently he was captured by giants, and Miss Penelope mounted an expedition to save him, and the two fought back-to-back to slay all of the ... ah ..."

He trailed off as the Queen's face darkened with further fury.

"You're telling me," she said with barely restrained rage, "that she *found the other prince* and *eloped with him?*"

The messenger whimpered and looked back for the butler, who was now discreetly hiding.

"Get out!" the Queen screamed. "Get out of my sight!"

The messenger scrambled from the room as quickly as his skinny legs could take him.

"Butler!"

A very unhappy butler returned to the room.

"Bring Arabella in here. Now!"

THE QUEEN MANAGED to calm herself as her youngest daughter flounced in.

Arabella was everything a proper princess should be—beautiful, dainty, and with perfect manners and grooming. The Queen had given her everything she could possibly desire since the day she was born, and Arabella had blossomed under that care.

"Dearest daughter, come here."

Arabella pouted. "I was in the middle of having my nails done. And my hair isn't *half* finished."

"Now, now," the Queen soothed, "I have something more important than that to divert you."

Arabella's pout deepened. "Last time you said that, it was just some boring diplomacy."

The Queen smiled indulgently. Her youngest daughter was too delicate for matters of state; she should have known that. "Of course, pet. Now, listen to this: I've found the perfect husband for you, though your incompetent sisters haven't quite managed to secure him yet. So I'm going to send you to Arvakhia to catch him yourself."

Arabella pondered for a minute. "Is he rich?"

"*Very*," the Queen assured her.

The princess's face lit up. "All right," she said eagerly.

The Queen beamed. "What a lovely, dutiful daughter you are. Don't you even care who he is?"

"Doesn't matter, as long as he's rich."

The Queen gave her a warm, loving smile. That was dear

Arabella—always willing to make sacrifices for the good of her kingdom.

PRUNELLA'S EYES widened as she read the message delivered with breakfast. "Arabella's *here?*"

Spenser choked on his steak. Penelope thumped him hard on the back.

"Your youngest sister? The one I've heard about?" Alfonse said in horror.

"Let's hide in the library," Prunella said desperately. "Arabella would never go near it."

"Good idea!" Alfonse scrambled out of his chair, and clasped her hand. They hurried down the hallway.

Spenser stopped choking and nodded jerkily at Penelope. "Thanks, thanks. Hey, look, what's up with this girl?"

She pondered. "You know those weak, whimpering damsels you were locked up with?"

Spenser made a face. "Urghhh. Wouldn't lift a finger to help themselves. Kept telling me I had to choose one of 'em to marry once we escaped. That's why I kept plugging all the escape routes."

"Yeah. She's worse. No brains, no guts, and no wits."

"Uckhh!" Spenser shoved his chair back. "I'd rather muck out the stables!"

"Me too," Penelope grinned. "The smell would keep her away from us."

"Well, then," he said, and whacked her on the back. "Let's go do it, shall we?"

ARABELLA SNIFFED in disapproval as she took in the throne room's furnishings. The styles were old and shabby, nearly sixteen years out of date, and she saw no jewelry on either the king or queen. This was clearly no rich country, as she had been led to believe; this was a land of poverty.

This king and queen also had no proper manners or courtesy. Why, they had tried to fob her off with only a ten-minute introduction ceremony! It wasn't until she reminded them of the four-hour-long version due to her rank that they consented reluctantly, and even then, she caught them trying to read books secreted in the folds of their sleeves!

Arabella was most displeased.

Fortunately, the butler was more pleasing.

"I must say, your majesty," he burbled proudly, as he led her to a guest suite, "it's a delight to host someone who understands the importance of full ceremonies with all the trappings. In fact, your taste for ostentation exceeds even my own. Your taste in fabrics is truly exquisite, and it does my heart good to see proper jewelry worn, and not just paste."

"This castle is abominable!" Arabella complained. "They have nothing! They must be in the most abject of poverty!"

"Ah, no," the butler lamented, twisting the diamond-and-ruby bracelet and tapping at the matching belt at his waist. "They simply have an appalling lack of taste. They are wealthy enough to pay me generously, as you can see."

"The height of fashion!" Arabella gasped, choked up.

"It is yours, my dear," the butler sniffed, handing the bracelet over. "I share your joy in the discovery that somebody here has taste."

"It can't be." The Queen's face was ashen as she read the news. "It simply—can't—be."

The messenger gulped, looking for the butler, who had removed himself from the throne room.

"Your majesty?" he ventured timidly.

"Arabella—" she gasped—"the butler—marrying a *butler*—"

The Queen slumped into a dead faint.

Seeing his chance, the messenger fled from the room.

The butler poked his head in and scooped up the note out of curiosity. He frowned as he read it, as perplexed as the Queen. Arabella was going to marry a butler, was she ...

What self-respecting butler would agree to the arrangement?

AUTHOR NOTE:

I wrote this short story a long time ago, in high school. If I were to rewrite it now, I would put way more emphasis on the romances. But I do like the way it is now, with a bare bones minimalism that focuses on the humor of it.

HIS UNICORN

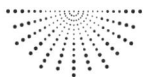

A light shone through the window. Brendan rolled over and rubbed his eyes. He looked blearily at the curtains. It wasn't the dim glow of sunlight; it was more like the piercing radiance of a unicorn, impossible to miss or ignore. But he hadn't seen his unicorn since ...

Since ...

Wait, where was Billie?

Brendan leapt out of bed and ran to the window. Looking out, he saw his wife standing next to the glowing white creature with a long spiral horn.

His breath caught in his throat in shock. It *was* a unicorn!

Was it *his* unicorn?

He didn't even stop to put on shoes or grab a coat. He ran to the door in pajamas and bare feet, flinging it open and slamming it behind him.

He hadn't seen his unicorn in a month. He'd thought she'd abandoned him.

Was she back?

At the slam of the door, Billie spun around, her eyes wide.

The unicorn stiffened and jolted a step back.

"Please don't go!" Brendan exclaimed. He had meant to run over, but instead he slowed his pace, walking slowly and carefully. "Please don't go."

The snow was thick, and his feet were bare. He shivered as he reached where he wife stood. He took Billie's hand.

Nobody spoke or moved.

Brendan tried not to show his bitter sadness.

This wasn't his unicorn. This one was male. He had the same shining whiteness and luminous horn, but he was taller, more muscular, and had hard, wary eyes.

So she really was gone. His unicorn had abandoned him. He'd lost her forever when he'd married Billie.

It was worth it for Billie. Everything was worth it for Billie. But oh, if only he'd known. If only he'd known.

Perhaps he would have moved more slowly. He'd married Billie only two days after meeting her. He'd needed her the moment he'd seen her, and she'd felt the same way.

If he'd known he'd lose his unicorn, perhaps he could have at least said goodbye.

Brendan drew in a breath, fighting back the urge to cry.

"You can see unicorns?" he asked, trying to keep his voice level.

Billie nodded.

"I thought I was the only one."

"You're not." Her voice was quiet.

He knew so little about her. She'd mentioned having a sister once, and that was it.

He hadn't pried. He'd assumed her family was a touchy subject. Now he wondered if it went deeper than that. He wondered if she'd always felt disconnected from the world around her, just like he did, because she could see things that nobody else could.

He eyed the male unicorn, grief and jealousy filling him. *Are you her unicorn? Did she love you as much as I loved mine?*

"Why's he here?" Brendan spat.

"His mate needs help giving birth. Her baby's upside down. I have human hands, so I can turn him around."

Brendan could barely get out the words. The words that had

haunted him for the past month. "But you're not a virgin. Unicorns won't go near anyone who isn't."

"That's a myth."

"Oh." He supposed that was obvious, given present company. But that just made it worse.

The unicorn swished his tail and waved his head in agitation.

"I have to go now." Billie looked anxious.

"Can I come?"

Billie hesitated. She looked at the unicorn, who pawed the ground with his cloven hoof and tossed his head.

"Okay," she said quietly. Her hand shook a little as she pressed her hand to the unicorn's flank, then pressed Brendan's hand on top of hers. "Don't let go, or you'll be lost somewhere along the way. It would be hard to find you again."

He wrapped his other arm around her waist. "I'll never let go of you."

She let out a shuddering breath.

The world began to blur around them, as if they were moving with incredible speed, though he felt no sense of motion. A new place popped around them in sudden clarity.

They were in a clearing in a forest of trees, trees of numerous species he'd never seen before. Were they in a different part of the world, or ... somewhere else?

There was a snuffling noise, and he looked down. Lying on the ground was a female unicorn, snuffling in great distress.

Not his unicorn.

Billie fell to her knees and put her hand on the unicorn's flank. "I'm here," she said. "Let's get your baby out safely."

Brendan stood out of the way and watched Billie work. He'd seen birth many times, having grown up on a farm.

Sweat beaded on her forehead as she turned the baby, beginning to drip in her eyes. Brendan came over and wiped her face with his sleeve. Billie nodded at him in thanks.

The feet of the foal emerged, with the soles pointing downwards. He breathed a sigh of relief; that was normal for equines.

When the baby had wholly emerged, he looked at the forehead.

There was a small nub covered in fur. How long would it take for the horn to grow out? As long as antlers for deer?

The foal wobbled on unsteady legs, went in search of a teat, found one, and settled down to suck on it while the placenta was delivered safely.

The female unicorn ate the placenta while the male nuzzled her, resting his head on her neck.

Billie let out a sob of relief and moved back, sitting by Brendan. "She's safe. She's okay."

Brendan took a deep breath. He had a feeling he knew what he'd missed now. What he should have seen from the beginning.

"She's your sister," he said into the silence, "isn't she?"

"Yes." Billie's voice was very quiet.

"You're a unicorn. You're *my* unicorn. The one I've known since childhood."

"Yes."

Brendan let out an explosive breath. "Why didn't you *tell* me?"

He couldn't keep the accusation, the hurt, out of his voice. He'd thought all this time she'd abandoned him.

"Because you were human. I thought you wanted a human."

"Of course not! I wanted *you!*" He grabbed her shoulders.

"Oh." Her voice was barely audible. "Really?"

"Yes! And I would have preferred for us to both be unicorns!"

"Oh." Her voice shook. "W-we ... we can."

Hope exploded in his heart. "Yeah?!"

"Yeah." She swallowed. "But ... the path to changing species is very difficult. Very painful. I only made it through because I wanted to be with you so badly."

He stroked her forehead, where her horn ought to be. He wanted it back. He wanted *her* back. "Would you rather we be unicorns, too?"

She nodded. She was shaking.

"Then let's do it."

Joy lit up her face. "Really?"

"Really."

"But it's painful."

"It's worth it."

She hugged him with her neck wrapped around the back of his.

Of course she was Billie. How had he missed that? Why else had he been so desperate to marry her the minute he'd seen her? He'd loved her for nearly two decades.

She was his unicorn. Truly his.

And soon, he would be hers.

AUTHOR NOTE:

The more years I've been married, the more I yearn for stories about happily married couples.

Why are all the romances about getting together?

Where are all the romances about staying together?

I need those stories. I think we all do. Stories are how we learn. When there are no stories about how to move from Point B to Point C in a relationship, how are we supposed to know how to do that? Much less Point C to Point D, and Point D to Point E.

I find a lot of series that include long-running couples put less and less focus on relationship development as the series progresses, making it only a background detail. There need to be more stories about marriage continuing to grow and deepen. That's how we learn how to improve our own.

This is a story about a pair of newlyweds, but ... it could very easily have happened ten years later.

Sometimes important turning points happen after the wedding.

DRAGON'S EGG

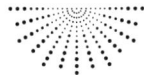

Chapter 1
Eggs

Rose twisted her finger through her long, piled-up hair, crumpled her hat in her hand, and stepped into the dragon wing of the Museum of Natural History, her favorite place in the whole city.

She hoped the trilobites and dragon claws would help her get up the nerve to talk to Papa. He hadn't exactly been receptive when she'd mentioned fossils before.

"Hello, Miss Palmer," Mr. Teedle greeted her. He was the curator of the dragon collection, and he knew her well. "Back again?"

"Yes." Rose hesitated. "I'm going to tell my father today."

"You don't need his permission!" Mr. Teedle said encouragingly. "It's not the nineteenth century anymore. It's 1920. Women have been paleontologists for over a hundred years!"

"I wish he understood that," Rose said, shaking her head. "I *do* need his permission to study geology. He pays my tuition and housing."

"I suppose he thinks you should simply get married?" Mr. Teedle asked with exasperation.

"No ..." Rose hesitated. "It's my mother who'd like to see that. It's just that he thinks a woman's work is in the classroom."

Mr. Teedle shook his head and sighed heavily. Then he brightened. "Come see what we just brought in! It's astonishing!"

Rose followed him further into the room, her fears evaporating in the familiar place. A dragon's skull hung on the wall, enormous horns protruding from its head and nose. The right horn was broken, with fractures running all down it. She passed a glass case against the wall that was filled with rocks imprinted by dragon claws.

They were coming up on her favorite exhibit: two stones scorched by dragon fire, a rare treasure. There were only a few dozen around the world, and it was thought that they might represent some kind of writing system, given that the patterns seemed highly precise, yet irregular. It was hoped that these stones, or those like them, would be the key to uncovering what dragon fire had been used for, which might in turn be a clue to whether there were dragon species that had been intelligent.

It was the unanswered questions that Rose found the most fascinating. She itched to find the answers to them. She craved the thrill of discovery, and longed for the long hours of careful puzzle-solving. She envied even the assistants who did nothing but brush dirt off fossils, day after day. To be that close to newly-discovered fossils, to touch them daily, would be a dream.

And dragon fire was one of the most puzzling questions in paleontology. Nearly as puzzling as the question of whether any dragon species had been intelligent. Rose dreamed of being the one to find the answers to them.

"Here we are!" Mr. Teedle said proudly. "What do you think?"

Rose shook herself out of her reverie.

The glass case in the center of the room no longer held her favorite exhibit.

"Dragon eggs?" Rose asked, trying to hide her dismay. "What happened to the dragon fire stones?"

"On loan to The Academy of Natural Sciences," Mr. Teedle said.

"These are our newest acquisition. They were uncovered in a hidden cave near the bone beds in Vernal. Aren't they something?"

Rose stared at the twelve eggs in the case. Whole dragon eggs were rare, though eggshell fragments were common. Twelve real ones found in one place would have been quite exciting. But these were clearly *not* real dragon eggs: they were dusky orange with brown spots. Real dragon eggs would be fossilized.

"An artist's recreation. How nice," she said politely.

"They're not an artist's recreation," Mr. Teedle said excitedly. "They're not calcified at all. We're not sure what the shells are made of, as we haven't been able to shave a piece off of any of them to test. They were found by the bones of adult *Deinonychus antirrhopus* dragons, and they match the shape of fossilized eggs we have found of the species. Aren't they *something?*"

Rose's eyes widened. She stared at the eggs, riveted. "Are you quite certain they aren't fakes?"

"We haven't been able to prove that they originated in the Mesozoic Era, so no, we can't be certain. But the material they're made from doesn't seem to be one anyone is capable of fabricating."

"How do we know they're dragon eggs?" Rose blurted out. "How do we know they're not just ... just some undiscovered reptile that lives in that part of the world?"

"Excellent question," Mr. Teedle said. "That's a hypothesis that several people have put forth. But the prevailing theory currently is that these are *Deinonychus antirrhopus* eggs, somehow preserved by a mechanism we don't understand."

"They should be decayed by now," Rose breathed. "They should be impossible."

"Well, I certainly hope they're possible, or else the museum has spent a lot of money on fakes," Mr. Teedle chuckled.

"How could the Dragon National Monument bear to part with these?" she blurted out. "Were they mad?"

"They found hundreds, all in one place," Mr. Teedle said. "The Smithsonian has bought six. The Field Museum of National History has bought eight. The Dragon National Monument has a clutch of sixty currently on display."

"Perhaps the species is still alive," Rose murmured. "Is that possible?"

"Who knows what's possible?" Mr. Teedle asked with a smile, spreading his hands. "It's an exciting time to be in paleontology."

Rose nodded emphatically.

Another patron wandered into the room from the hallway. He wore a well-worn suit with a short jacket, and carrying a black fedora in his hand. His hair was oiled and slicked back, but still looked mussed, and he had no mustache, which made his face look bare. "Excuse me, is this the Hall of Ornithischian Dragons?" he asked.

"Check the signs," Mr. Teedle called back. "This is the Hall of Saurischian Dragons."

"Thank you," the man said, turning to walk out of the room.

A vision slammed into Rose's mind.

She was a tiny infant, crawling across the vast, dry landscape under a beating sun. She shivered, her whole lizardly body wriggling from head to tail. She stumbled forward, her tiny claws grasping for purchase, her tail sagging and sticky.

She wriggled around and turned back, and found herself looking back at a broken eggshell, slathered with a trail of goop after her. She smacked the dry ground with her claw and looked up, terrified.

There, high above her, were the comforting presence of her parents. She knew their minds, and their faces from what they had shown her. She opened her mouth and let out a small, shrill cry, and her mother reached out a claw and gently removed a sliver of shell that was trapping her tail.

Stumbling forward again, she at last collapsed in a heap, and her father carefully reached down to pluck her up. In the sizzling warmth of his palm, she let out a soft sigh and dozed off to sleep.

Rose gasped and returned to being human, standing in the Hall of Saurischian Dragons, right outside the case full of dragon eggs.

"Did you ... did you ...?" she stumbled.

"Yes," Mr. Teedle said, his eyes huge and his forehead sweaty. He ran his hand down the slick surface of his greying hair, over and over again.

"I saw it, too," the stranger said. He walked toward them and the case. "In the hot sun, slithering forward ..."

"... but I felt cold," Rose finished for him.

"My tail felt sagging and sticky ..." Mr. Teedle whispered.

"... until my mother pulled the eggshell off me," the stranger finished.

They all stared at each other.

"It wasn't *my* memory," the stranger said. "I've never hatched from an egg."

For some reason, that struck Rose as funny. She started giggling.

The stranger's eyes fell on the display right beside them. "Those eggs," he said. "Is one of those eggs alive?"

Rose fell silent. Her heart hammered. The blood rushed to her ears.

"Of course not," Mr. Teedle said. He hesitated. "At least ... we don't *think* ..."

They all stared at the display case. The twelve matching eggs did nothing.

Chapter 2
Evaluation

"One of those eggs is alive," the stranger said. "I'm sure of it."

"How can you be sure?" Rose asked skeptically.

"Those things *look* alive. The skeletons don't." The stranger waved his hand around to indicate the rest of the room. "Besides, the vision was about hatching. Where else could it have come from?"

"That's not particularly sound reasoning," Mr. Teedle said. "But it's a valid hypothesis. These are the newest addition to the room, and nothing else like that has ever happened before."

"This implies that there might be living *Deinonychus antirrhopus* in Vernal," Rose breathed. "Imagine what we could learn from a fertile egg."

"There can't be dragons still alive," the stranger objected. "People would have found evidence of it by now."

"What do you think this is?" Mr. Teedle asked.

"I think it's an egg that's survived for millions of years. Hibernating or something."

"How could an egg survive for millions of years?" Rose asked skeptically.

"How could a dragon breathe out fire without self-injury?" Mr. Teedle shrugged. "How could a dragon even produce it? There are still many unanswered questions about them. Almost anything is possible."

"But this means we will be able to find out the answers," Rose breathed. "With a *live dragon* ..."

"Assuming the assumption is correct, I can hardly wait to study it," Mr. Teedle said gleefully. "We'll have to set up a laboratory on the facilities ..."

"Hang on," the stranger objected. "If this is a live animal, it doesn't belong in a museum. It belongs in a zoo."

"I imagine there could be a collaborative project," Rose said, waving her hand carelessly. "Every scientist worth their salt will want to study it."

"Imagine what this will do for the museum," Mr. Teedle said, his eyes shining. "Imagine the prestige. Imagine the number of visitors. Imagine how many fresh expeditions this will finance."

"Imagine that this is a living creature that should have some say in where it's going to live!" the stranger shouted.

"The eggs are the property of the museum," Rose said. "I'm sure a great deal of care will be made to make proper arrangements."

"Actually, the young man has a point," Mr. Teedle said solemnly. "We don't know how intelligent *Deinonychus* dragons were, but there's a great deal of evidence that they may have been as intelligent as apes. Perhaps even as intelligent as humans."

Rose felt a thrill down her spine. There'd be an answer to that question, at long last. Someone would be able to assess the behavior of a living specimen and evaluate it. Would she have a chance of being involved in the project? Even as an observer?

"Intelligent as humans?" The stranger stared at both of them, slack-jawed. "Then this isn't an animal we're talking about at all. This is a child. A baby!"

Mr. Teedle looked troubled.

Rose wasn't sure if she should keep arguing her point, but the concern was valid, and it was worrying.

"You're right," she said. "We have to proceed on the assumption that it might be. It's silly, but harmless, to treat an animal like a person. It's potentially very harmful to treat a person like an animal."

"But it would not be very practical to proceed that way," Mr. Teedle said, rubbing his oiled hair. "The egg is, as you mentioned, the property of the museum. It might be as intelligent as humans, but it won't have the legal rights."

"If it's a person, then it needs to *get* legal rights," Rose said. "The sooner, the better."

The stranger smiled at her. "What's your name, Miss ...?"

"Rose Palmer," Rose said. "I'm a student at Hunter College."

"Henry Wainscott. I'm a student at City College."

The men-only college with the gorgeous Gothic architecture? Rose thought. She envied him. The academic standards of his school were probably far more rigorous than her women-only college.

"Pleased to meet you, Mr. Wainscott," she said formally, holding out her hand.

He shook it.

"So we have a plan, then," Rose said briskly. "Assuming that the egg is alive, and assuming that it was the source of the vision we saw, we shall assume it is intelligent unless proven otherwise. We should probably speak with the director of the museum and see what protections can be applied right away."

She said that with a hint of hope, because she had wanted to meet the director for a long time. She knew nothing about him save what Mr. Teedle had mentioned: that he was a busy man who rarely ventured out into the museum during the hours it was open. It would be an honor to become acquainted with him.

"No, it won't do," Mr. Teedle broke in, interrupting her thoughts.

"It's all very well to say that, but the egg is the property of the museum, and we paid a great deal of money to acquire it."

"You paid for *twelve* eggs, didn't you?" Henry demanded, jabbing his finger at the exhibit. "Look! You'll still have eleven!"

"And lose the most valuable artifact this museum has ever acquired? I'm sorry, but the director would not stand for that. Neither would I, I'm afraid."

"It's not an artifact, it's a baby dragon!" Henry shouted. "Stop thinking about what's good for the museum, and think about what's good for the *child!*"

He was saying *child* now, Rose noted. As if it were an absolute certainty.

"There's a simple way to resolve this dispute," Rose said firmly, taking a step forward as if to curtail the altercation by inserting herself between them. "We ask the egg if it is intelligent, and if there is anything it wants. Perhaps it can communicate more clearly than it has already."

"And if it doesn't?" Henry demanded.

"And if it does?" Mr. Teedle asked.

"Then we evaluate it from what it says. Perhaps the egg is intelligent. Perhaps it isn't. Perhaps the egg is content to stay in the museum, or actually wishes to be here. That's a possibility that neither of you seems to have considered."

The two men exchanged uneasy looks.

"It can't do any harm to try," Mr. Teedle said.

Henry walked over to the display case and knocked on the glass.

"Mr. Wainscott!" Mr. Teedle said sharply.

"Helloooooo," Henry said loudly, paying the curator no heed. "Hello in there! Are you the one who sent us the vision? Are you one of the dragon eggs? We want to know what you want. Can you understand me?"

A wave of memory and emotion bowled Rose over.

Why hadn't they answered before? He had given them his mother's memory of hatching. Wasn't it clear? He would give them one of his ancestors' memories. His father had given it to him.

It bubbled to the surface. It felt muted, like the original experience had been muffled by the interpretation of many minds.

She was very cramped and uncomfortable. Her legs felt powerful, but her neck was weak. Her mother and father had instructed her to strengthen her neck so that she could use the egg tooth to chip her way out, but she had been lazy.

Suddenly, there was emptiness where the father had been. She thrashed and kicked and screamed out, but only the mother's mind answered. She sunk into a deep despair. Cold filled her heart, her mind, her limbs. She fell asleep.

After a long time, a new presence in her mind dawned. It was a new father, chosen by the mother to replace the one they had lost. Uncertainty gave way to relief, and she awakened fully. She worked to strengthen her neck and burst out of the egg at last.

Rose drew a breath, but there was no time to think. Now there was a raw memory again, unfiltered from being passed through other minds.

His parents had vanished. His parents had vanished! In terror and despair, he retreated to the special sleep his parents had shown him how to do in case they vanished.

At some point, other minds came. Not his parents. He didn't want them. He refused to wake up. They went away.

There was movement. There were more minds. Sometimes many, mostly two minds at once. Every so often, he would wake up. But he never liked them, so he always went back to sleep.

There were no minds at all for a very long time. The emptiness was so complete, consciousness faded entirely. All sense of time was lost.

His mother's mind was there.

He jerked awake, disoriented, but it wasn't her mind. It was good, though. Similar. Where was his father's mind? He couldn't hatch without them both. He wouldn't! Maybe he would go back to sleep.

There it was! His father's mind! He exulted, waiting for the minds to greet him, but they didn't. The father's mind was going away. No!

Didn't they know he was here? He'd give them the memory of his mother's hatching so they would understand.

They didn't answer. They didn't answer. They didn't answer. Why didn't they answer?

They had to stay. They had to raise him. Didn't they know the rules?

The memory ended, and Rose drew in a breath, gasping. Her heart was filled with terror, and her arms were shaking.

Chapter 3
Experience

Henry stood there, frozen, shell-shocked.

"I have to go," he blurted out. He started to back out of the room.

"Wait," Mr. Teedle said. "Why—?"

"I have to go, too." Rose scrambled away from the case, terror lancing through her mind like jagged rips of lightning. "I'll be back—be back—thanks, Mr. Teedle."

She turned and fled after Henry, racing down the stairs from the fourth floor. She nearly bumped into another patron ascending in her haste.

"Wait!" Mr. Teedle shouted after her. "What did you see?"

Rose leapt down the last few stairs and raced for the exit. In blind terror, she ducked under the arm of someone opening the door to the museum and raced down the street. Tears stung at her eyes. So desperate—terrified—so lonely—

Central Park was across the street. Rose slowed while cars drove past, her heart hammering. Those weren't her memories. Those weren't her feelings. Those weren't her loneliness, her desperation.

But it was her terror.

Her arms were shaking, she realized numbly. She must look dreadful right now. What must people be thinking?

Maybe she should have stopped to tell Mr. Teedle what the dragon had said. Maybe she should have explained.

But she couldn't face going back. Not in the face of such desperate need. She waited for a gap in traffic, and then crossed the street into Central Park, her mind numb as she took in the late summer's afternoon.

Two women passed her pushing prams. They chattered to each another as a small child trailed after one of them. It was impossible to tell what gender the small child was, as the child was wearing a sailor suit with an overlong blouse, and she couldn't tell if there were shorts or skirt underneath. Most likely a boy, as the sailor suit was pink. But you never knew.

A woman sat on the grass nearby, watching two small boys wrestle with a huge dog. A third boy ran over, waving a shredded scrap of cloth, and the dog lunged for it, snapping excitedly. The boys screamed with laughter.

Rose glanced out over the Lake, where a couple drifted by on a boat. The woman wore a ruffled blue dress and held a flower-shaped paper parasol over her head, the black feather at the top of her hat tickling it. The man was wearing a green belted suit and a hat with a ribbon around it. At first Rose thought they were alone, and then she noticed the man was clutching a small baby in the crook of his arm.

There are so many parents around, Rose thought, swallowing. She'd never noticed it before, but children were everywhere. She walked slowly down the path, feeling a breeze whip the skirt around her ankles. *All out here with their children.*

Would a dragon child even be allowed in Central Park? No one knew when they first started to breathe fire. Perhaps a dragon child would be dangerous.

No, no, no. She couldn't even fathom having a human child yet. She wanted to study dragons, not raise one.

She started to pass by a man sitting under a tree, twisting his hat in his hands, and did a double-take as she recognized his clothing.

"Mr. Wainscott," she said. "What are you doing here?"

He looked up. "Miss Palmer," he said. His voice was strained. "Did you get the same message I did?"

"He wants ..." Rose's voice faltered. She swallowed, gathered her skirt, and sat down in the shade beside him. "He wants me to be his parent."

She couldn't bring herself to say the word *mother*. Somehow, that seemed much more personal. More alien. More not-what-she'd-intended-for-her-life-path-at-all. Sure, there were some women who had children at eighteen, but she had never wanted to be one of them. She wasn't ready for that kind of commitment. How could the dragon ask such a thing?

"He wants me to be his father," Henry said.

"I can't do it," Rose blurted out. "It's an outrageous demand."

"Children aren't known for being undemanding," Henry said. "Just ask my brother. He has six-year-old twins."

"I can't do it," Rose said. "I won't do it!"

Henry was silent as he picked at the grass.

"At least we know for sure that he's intelligent," he said. "He thinks we're the equivalent of his parents."

"We don't know for sure that's what it means," Rose said, but her heart wasn't in it.

It might not be objectively sound, but the dragon had felt intelligent. Frighteningly intelligent. She didn't know of any human baby who could think so clearly. Though perhaps that was simply because she had never had the opportunity to compare: human babies lacked the ability to communicate telepathically.

"I had a professor last semester who brought up the question," Henry said. "He said they couldn't have been because there was no evidence of any written language."

"That was Edward Cope's argument," Rose snorted. "As if there haven't been human societies with no written languages! I much prefer Mary Anning's hypothesis. She said that dragons might have used scorched stones as a method of recording information, since the structure of their throats and jaws suggests that they had multiple glands for controlling the temperature of their fire and the chemicals that produced it. In the same way that some animals used scent to communicate, dragons may have been so sensitive to temperature differentials that they could use them as a form of language—"

She stopped, seeing Henry watch her with a smile on his face.

"What?" she asked.

"You're very smart, aren't you?" he asked.

"I'm very interested in the subject," Rose said, a little embarrassed.

Henry grinned. "I guess we know the answer to whether they had a written language now, too."

"We do?" Rose asked quizzically.

"Sure. This means that dragons didn't need a written language to record information permanently. They just passed down memories directly."

"No, no, no." Rose waved her hand. "That would be no more than a sophisticated oral tradition, which means it would still be colored by interpretation every generation. That doesn't mean there was no written language. We'll have to see if the dragon has any memories from ancestors that would be relevant to other questions about dragon society, or whether all that was communicated to him were memories of hatching. It would be amazing to interview him—"

"Miss Palmer," Henry interrupted. "You're very smart, but you're being very dense."

"What?" Rose faltered.

Henry sighed heavily. "This is a baby, remember? His primary concerns will be food, drink, and loving parents. He's not going to be receptive to being interviewed, especially by someone who apparently plans to reject his request."

Oh. Rose swallowed. She'd almost forgotten that, in the heat of her excitement.

"What should I do, then?" she asked in a small voice. "I don't—I don't want to be a parent right now. You can't ask that of me. That's too much to ask."

"I'm not asking it," Henry said. "He did."

"I still can't do it," Rose said. "I just—I just can't."

"Don't justify yourself to me," Henry said. "He's the one you owe an answer to."

Rose wrapped her arms around her knees. A breeze picked up and tried to snatch her hat off, but she grabbed it in time. She began to twist it around in her hands, as Henry had been doing earlier.

"If this had only happened a few years later," she said, "I might have been in a better position to say yes."

"Children aren't known for their spectacular timing, either," Henry said dryly. "Ask my sister-in-law how many times she got woken up at three am to change horrendous diapers of two screaming babies."

"Are you going to accept?" Rose asked, looking up at him.

Henry pondered for a moment. He ran his fingers through the grass. "Yes," he said at last. "I think I am."

"How?" Rose asked in amazement. "How can you be prepared to do that?"

"I like children," Henry said. "I've always wanted to have them. This isn't quite the way I had anticipated it happening, and it's not ideal, but ... he chose me. He rejected hundreds of dragon parents, but he chose me. That's quite appealing."

Rose squeezed her hat tightly. Her thumbnails dug into the brim. To her that didn't seem appealing at all. It seemed terrifying. What would it be like to fail, under all that pressure? What would it cost to succeed?

Chapter 4
Essence

"The dragon must be waiting for an answer," Henry said, standing up. "He's likely frantic by now. I would be, if I were in his position. I'd better go."

Rose watched him walk off, his stride sure and purposeful, and it seemed incomprehensible to her. How could he be so sure of his choice after barely half an hour? Was he the sort who made decisions quickly?

She wasn't. She didn't enjoy adapting to new situations. And this one was too overwhelming for words.

You owe the dragon an answer, Rose told herself, trying to breathe slowly and think rationally. *Think about it. What are you going to say?*

Rose picked at the brim of her hat while she thought.

There were all kinds of good reasons why she couldn't do what he was asking. If she listed them one by one, maybe he would understand.

First: she was too young to be a mother. Not in an absolute sense, certainly, because there were many married women with small children her age. But she didn't feel mature enough or wise enough now. Maybe she never would. Parenthood had always been an abstract, something to consider in the future, not a priority to anticipate this year.

Second: she had her future to consider. It would be hard enough to be taken seriously right now, given her gender. If she had a child in tow, it would make her even less attractive a prospect for hiring.

A small voice in her head said, *Although maybe you could use him as a way to get hired, given his species ...*

No. Rose shook her head. She couldn't think in those terms. She hated it when people saw her as a woman first, and a scientist second. To accept him because of his species would be atrocious hypocrisy, not to mention an atrocious reason to become a parent.

Third, then: she was too biased. It would be hard for her to resist the fascination of his species to see the person within. She'd have to work hard at it. It would be better for him to have somebody who wasn't interested in dragons.

Fourth: she had no experience with babies. None of her acquaintances or friends had children, and her cousins were all younger than her. She had two younger sisters, but they were both close enough to her in age that she could barely remember what they had been like as small children.

Fifth: she had no *interest* in babies.

That might be a logical fallacy, her rational mind prodded. *Didn't you just declare it would be better for him to have somebody who wasn't interested in dragons? By the same logic, someone who had no interest in babies would be better suited to raise them.*

Rose waved the thought off irritably. That was different. The dragon would have people treating him as nothing but a member of his species for his entire life. He needed somebody who would scarcely notice it.

Sixth. Sixth ...

There had to be a sixth reason. There had to be a whole host of them.

Ah, yes. Sixth: he had to see that it would be far better to have parents who were married to each other than two strangers who had never met in their lives.

If she didn't accept, Henry and the dragon could pick out some other woman at their own pace. Any woman would do. Any woman would be better at it than her.

Seventh, Rose thought firmly, *there are five million people in this city. It doesn't have to be me. No matter how much like your birth mother I seem to you.*

Although that raised a question.

Why *did* she remind him of his birth mother?

Eighth, Rose thought hesitantly ...

It was no good. Now that she was wondering, she couldn't concentrate on anything else. A familiar feeling of insatiable curiosity crawled up her spine and settled fixedly in her mind.

She had to know the answer to that. She had to.

Surely there couldn't have been *that* much in common between them. There were so many objections, so many reasons she didn't want a child right now. Not to mention that his mother had lived millions of years ago, in another civilization. The dragon had been sure his mother loved him, and Rose didn't know how to love a child.

Restlessly, Rose stood up. The only person who could answer that question was the dragon. She marched down the path back towards the museum, determined to find out. She entered the museum and walked up the stairs.

When she reached the top of the stairs, she walked around the bend to the Hall of Saurischian Dragons, where she spied Henry standing by the display case, speaking in soothing tones, while Mr. Teedle hovered nervously behind him.

"Miss Palmer!" Mr. Teedle said with some relief, running over to her. He ran his hand through his hair and wiped his sweaty brow.

"Mr. Wainscott refuses to explain to me what's going on, and the dragon has been throwing a fit. I think I have a decent idea what a *Deinonychus antirrhopus* dragon roar must have sounded like, because the egg has been projecting memories of it across the room since you left. I had to clear the hall because the patrons were complaining! He only stopped when Mr. Wainscott came back! What happened?"

"I'll explain to you later," Rose said. "I need to go talk to the dragon egg n—"

"William, don't lick the wall, that's disgusting!" a chubby woman shouted from the hallway to three children who were wandering around her. "George, stop making that noise. Leslie—"

"Excuse me! I'm sorry!" Mr. Teedle said, hurrying over. "I'm sorry, ma'am, but this room is closed. Would you please make your way over to the Hall of Ornithischian Dragons instead?"

"What? But we were just there," the woman protested. "George wants to see the *Tyrannosaurus rex*."

"I want to be one when I grow up," a fat-cheeked boy informed him, flapping his arms. "I want to fly like they did."

"*Tyrannosaurus* dragons didn't fly; the wings were vestigial," Mr. Teedle said. "If you'd like to see a flying dragon, we have a lovely *Stegosaurus stenops* on display in the Hall of Ornithischian Dragons—"

"I wanna see the T-rex! I wanna see the T-rex!" the boy shouted, hopping up and down in rage.

"We came all the way here because he had to see his favorite dragon," the boy's mother said huffily. "There's no sign saying this hall is closed. Why can't we just—"

While the two were arguing, Rose slipped away to the display case with the *Deinonychus antirrhopus* eggs. Henry was still talking to them in quiet tones.

"No, I can't speak for her," he was saying. "Yes, it would be nice to all be a family together. No, you'll have to ask her that question, not me."

"I'm here now," Rose said.

A feeling of joy burst up from the display case. The dragon sent her a flash of bubbly, happy memory of Henry's mind returning, and then a similar memory of his father returning from hunting—had that been a *Tenontosaurus?*

Rose shook her head. No. The dragon's memories of his father, or the tantalizing glimpse of a *Tenontosaurus tilletti* from the shard of his father's memory that had been included, were not important right now.

"You told us I reminded you of your mother," Rose said. "Why?"

A feeling of confusion bubbled up from the display case.

Rose tucked a strand of hair behind her ear, and tried a different approach. "Can you show me what your mother was like?"

A mix of eagerness and sadness, and then—

She was picking up several rock specimens carefully in her claws and sorting them according to classification. Some of them would be suitable for public display in the vast rock collection cave later.

And then—

She was irritated that a feathered pest had interrupted her work. She wasn't hungry, so she swiped it away with her tail. Her father, who had flown by despite all her wishes, informed her that she should have kept the thing for later. She wished he'd mind his own business and leave her alone.

And then—

The seasons had changed. She hated change. It always made her grumpy. She flicked the egg with her tail to get him to stop asking the same question for the billionth time, and wondered if the child had gotten the same maddeningly inquisitive nature that had made her parents so incessantly weary with her.

Her husband rolled the egg over with his claw and sleepily explained the answer to the question for the billionth time.

And then—

The egg was crying silently, forcefully. It was the first time his father had left to hunt since the child had gotten old enough to wake up. He had been a surprise, this baby, much earlier than she had wanted, but she'd get used to him. Perhaps she shouldn't let him know she thought him a pest sometimes. Quiet, quiet now, little one ...

The flashes of memory ended.

Rose burst out into hysterical giggles. The dragon child was right: the two of them had been extremely alike.

Chapter 5
Element

"So ... did he answer your question?" Henry asked. His hands twisted a little, like he was nervous. Perhaps he was.

"He did," Rose giggled. Why couldn't she stop laughing? "Perhaps you ought to ask why you remind him of his father."

Henry shook his head. "No, thanks. I'd rather not live in the shadow of somebody I can never replace."

For some reason, that struck Rose as hilarious, and she let out a long spurt of laughter.

"What's so funny?" Henry asked. "What did he show you?"

"Oh, he just—it's just—I—I don't know!" Rose started to cry. It came out in choking sobs.

Henry stared at her in real alarm now. "Miss Palmer!"

"It's no problem! I'm fine! I just—I—I—I—" Rose burst into sobs again.

Henry drew back in horror.

You're hysterical, the part of Rose's mind that was still rational informed her. *Calm down. Stop being so emotional. Think rationally.*

Rose drew in a deep breath and managed to clamp down on her feelings. Her arms shook, but when she spoke, her voice sounded passably steady.

"His mother and I were very alike," she said. "Including having the same doubts and worries. She was out of her element, too. But she loved him."

Hysteria threatened to bubble up again, so she clamped down on her feelings tightly.

Rational, she told herself sternly. *What would be the rational thing to do?*

Most of her objections had been effectively rebutted. All the ones that were left seemed selfish and whiny.

Logically, if his mother had loved him ... then she could, too.

"All right," Rose said, her voice cracking a little. "All right. I'll do it. You win, demanding brat."

Henry stared at her in astonishment. "First you outright plan on rejecting him ... and then *that's* how you accept?"

"It's good enough for him," Rose said. The faintest hint of terror leaked through her mental shield, so she clamped down on it hard, clenching her fists as she did so. "His original mother would have said the same thing."

"Your hands are shaking," Henry said. "Are you sure you're all right?"

I never said I was, Rose thought. She breathed in deeply, and then breathed out again. The shaking in her hands quelled.

"I'll need time to get used to it," she said. "I will be."

The dragon's mind bounced with excitement. He was going to hatch and be with his new mother and father, who were just like his old ones. They would teach him how to run and fly and play, and they would all soar off together —

"Hold on," Rose said. "We're human. We can't fly. You're going to need to understand that."

— and it would be so much fun! Hatching was a while away, but he would grow nice and strong so that he could burst out and they'd all breathe fire together —

"We're *human*," Henry said. "We don't breathe fire."

— and his father would teach him how to hunt those tasty meat creatures he brought home, crunch crunch —

"I don't think he understands," Henry said with exasperation.

"How can he?" Rose said. "He's never seen a human before. He's never seen anything before, except through another dragon's memories."

— and he could hardly wait to stretch out his tail, and they would teach him to swipe things with it!

"He's in for a world of disappointment, isn't he?" Henry sighed.

"Maybe not," Rose said. She felt a tentative brush of anticipation.

"For a curious child, a world unlike anything in his ancestors' memories might be wonderful and fascinating."

Crunch crunch! The dragon sent them memories of the noise his father made while eating. Crunch crunch!

Henry shuddered.

"You realize he's a carnivorous dragon," Rose said with amusement. "We're going to be hearing a lot of that. For that matter, we're going to need to figure out what he can eat."

Henry rubbed the side of his face. "That's going to be really expensive, isn't it?"

Rose felt a little perverse satisfaction that he hadn't thought everything through before he'd agreed. "Unless he can eat primarily rats and pigeons."

Crunch crunch!

"Stop that!" Henry shouted. "That's enough of that noise, thank you!"

His new father didn't like the noise. That was strange, because his old father had made that noise. He'd share a new noise his old father had made.

"What is that sound?!" Henry yelped, putting his hands over his ears, as if that would help. "It sounds like nails on a chalkboard!"

Rose barely kept her face straight. She was glad she wasn't the only one who was out of their element. "I think it's his father sharpening his claws on a rock."

Henry squished his fingers against the glass of the display case. "That is NOT AN IMPROVEMENT," he said. "NO MORE NOISES."

"Excuse me," a very cold voice said from behind them. "Please don't touch the glass."

Rose spun around to see Mr. Teedle standing by a man she didn't know who emanated an air of condescending authority. His suit was very well-tailored, and he held an elegant, matching derby hat in one hand, and an ornamental cane in the other.

"Oh," Henry said, taking his hand away from the glass and turning around. "I'm sorry, sir. I'm afraid we haven't had the pleasure of being introduced?"

"My name is Director Campbell," the man said coldly. "I am in charge of this museum. Teedle wanted to acquaint me with the dragon eggs. He claims that one of them is alive. What is this tomfoolery?"

"It's not tomfoolery," Henry said hastily. "He *is* alive. We were just talking with him when you came in."

"Talking with a dragon egg," the director said in a flat voice. "How charming. And I suppose next, you will have a conversation with the *Tyrannosaurus* skeleton?"

"That wouldn't do much good, seeing as a skeleton's not alive," Henry said with evident annoyance.

"Neither are fossilized eggs," the director said in a clipped voice. He paused, flicking his gaze over to the display case. "Forgive me. Un-fossilized eggs, but ones that are still at least one hundred million years old."

"Director." Mr. Teedle cleared his throat. "One of those eggs does seem to be alive. I have experienced it. That's why I brought you here. It seems to have some kind of telepathy. It showed visions of its ancestors' memories to us, and then it made a mental version of a roaring noise. All of the patrons in this hall heard it, which is why I had to clear it out. I'm sure the egg can share some memories with you, too, director. They're quite fascinating."

Rose recognized a cue.

"Dragon?" she asked, turning around. "Would you please share a memory with everyone in this room?"

He was sullen. His new father didn't like his noises. He was going to take a nap.

"No, don't *sleep!*" Henry cried.

Nothing.

Rose swallowed. She had always wanted to meet the director of the museum. Looking like a fool was not the way she'd hoped to do it.

CHAPTER 6

ENTRANCE

"WHAT KIND of joke are you trying to pull?" the director demanded. "Teedle, if this is something you are in on, I'm not amused."

You don't look like you have much of a sense of humor about anything, Rose thought. But she said nothing. She couldn't blame the man for being offended. The story sounded crazy, and it was unreasonable to expect him to believe such an outlandish claim without evidence.

"I'm sorry to have wasted your time," she said, bowing her head. "The dragon will, perhaps, offer communication to you another time. My apologies for this inconvenience."

"Actually, we need to talk to you about something," Henry said.

Rose's head shot up. *What are you doing?*

"What would that be?" the director asked frostily.

"The egg," Henry said. "It can't stay here. This isn't an appropriate environment for a living being."

Rose stared at him in horror. *Are you out of your wits?*

The director stared at him with absolute incredulity. "And I suppose you'd like to take it off our hands and move it to a more appropriate location?"

"Exactly," Henry said, looking pleased. "Miss Palmer and I will take care of it jointly."

"I suppose that's you," the director said sharply, looking at Rose. "What do you have to say?"

Rose was silent, gripping her hands into fists.

"Sir," she said at last, keeping her voice level, "we believe this dragon has petitioned us to be his caretakers. We humbly ask for your permission to be present at all important events relating to his care and hatching."

She purposefully did not use the word *parents*, though the dragon's meaning had been clear. That word would only cause the man to think she was a sentimental female who thought of nothing but marrying and babies.

The director gave her a narrow-eyed, measured look.

"If the dragon does not hatch, of course, I ask for no more than what any patron of the museum would: to visit the egg regularly, not to touch it or to interfere with the exhibits in any way. When the dragon does hatch, I ask to be present, to be a part of the studying, and in anything further, for the dragon's preferences to be weighed."

The director's eyebrows softened. He looked suspicious, but not nearly as angry as before.

"To suggest that a creature could hatch after millions of years is ludicrous," he said. "There's simply no good reason it could happen."

"Yes," Rose agreed. "But if it should, imagine what can be learned about the species."

The director looked thoughtful.

Rose's heart pounded.

"Your point is well-made," he said. "Very well. I see no reason why you cannot visit regularly, just so long as you pay the entry fee and don't disrupt the other patrons' visits. And if the creature does hatch, not that I believe such a thing will happen, I will consider your request to be present at the event."

Rose fought to keep the joy from showing up on her face. *I did it!* she exulted. *We'll have all the access we need!*

"That's not enough, sir," Henry said bluntly.

Rose stared at him in horror. *What are you doing?*

"That dragon—velociraptor or whatever it is—is far more than just a species. This is an individual, with very definite wants and needs."

"*Deinonychus antirrhopus,*" Rose murmured, humiliated. "*Velociraptor mongoliensis* were tiny."

"Whatever," Henry said, waving his hand, as if that had no bearing. "The dragon's telepathic, and plainly intelligent. Leaving him in the museum, away from his parents and surrounded by nothing but corpses, would be cruelty."

"Well, unluckily for it, all other *Deinonychus antirrhopus* dragons are dead," the director said sharply.

"Yes, but *we* are his new parents," Henry said sharply. "That's my son in that display case, and I demand to take him home with me."

The director stood very stiffly and said nothing.

"Mr. Wainscott!" Rose hissed. "May I please talk to you?"

Henry ignored her. And, incredibly, he actually managed to make things worse.

"I don't know which one is our egg," he said, "so we should probably pick them all up, shake them around, see if that wakes him up—"

"Disregard all that!" Rose said, breaking in desperately. "We've no intention of disturbing any of your very valuable and well-cared-for exhibits. Mr. Wainscott, we should *go*."

"I'm not going anywhere until I have my son," Henry said stubbornly. "How do you think he's going to feel when he wakes up and he finds we're not here? Not to mention that the museum will be closed tomorrow. We can't leave him alone for a day and a half. That's unpardonable!"

"You know what is unpardonable?" the director said with cool composure. "This blatant effrontery and abominable rudeness."

"Let's go," Rose said, pulling on Henry's sleeve.

He shook her off angrily. "You think that was rude?" he demanded. "I can be rude. Let me tell you what I think of someone who thinks it's all right to keep a child from his parents."

Then he began to let loose a string of insults that would have made a sailor blush. In desperation, Rose slapped her hand over his mouth.

The director looked at Mr. Teedle in amazement. "Is he out of his senses?"

"Apparently so," Mr. Teedle said, looking weary. "Mr. Wainscott, there is no way you are taking any exhibit out of this museum, living or not. I will make sure to explain to the dragon egg the situation before we close for the day."

"I'll tell him myself," Henry said, ripping Rose's hand off his mouth, "because if he's not leaving, neither am I."

"Oh, aren't you?" the director asked.

THE DOORS SLAMMED SHUT behind them with a whoosh of finality. Inside, a burly security guard eyed them through the glass, his arms folded menacingly.

"You got me kicked out, too!" Rose snarled. "Why did you do that? *Why?* Do you have any idea how stupid you were? Learn to compromise!"

"But I was right!" Henry protested.

Rose shoved her hat on her head and glared at him. *How could any woman with a personality like mine have married an idiot like this?*

"Don't worry," Henry said, eyeing the grandeur of the pillars on either side of them. "There must be a way to get back into the building. Maybe I could break one of those windows, or ..."

"Mr. Wainscott," Rose said with extreme exasperation, "I believe you have caused enough disasters for today. Please try not to get yourself arrested by destroying or intruding on private property. Rest assured that if you intend to try, I would be the first to report you to the authorities."

"It wouldn't work, anyway," Henry murmured, putting his hat back on. "I'm sure they have security guards at night."

"If that's your primary concern, I remain apprehensive," Rose said icily. "Mr. Wainscott, negotiations would have been possible in a few days, after it had become evident the child was alive and requesting our presence. Now, you have poisoned the director's goodwill. I am not pleased."

Henry's shoulders drooped.

Without a word, Rose turned on her heel and walked away.

Chapter 7
Excuse

It wasn't just that he had gotten her thrown out of the museum, Rose reflected as she walked down the street, swinging her arms fiercely as her heels clicked against the sidewalk. If she were truly honest with herself, she would admit that she was glad for the excuse to leave the dragon there for as long as possible.

Normally a person has time to acquaint themselves with the idea that they are going to raise a child, Rose thought. *Surely it is not unreasonable for me to be glad it wasn't reasonable to bring him home today.*

Not to mention the exhausting question of whether she or Henry would have been the one to bring the egg home. That was a question she would rather leave for another day, too. She had roommates, and she didn't know how she would explain the situation to them when she didn't even know how to sort through it herself.

Rose turned a corner out of habit, and then realized she should have turned the other direction, towards her family's house instead of her apartment. She turned around and nearly bumped into Henry.

"Mr. Wainscott!" she cried, startled. "Were you following me?"

"No! Well, yes. I figured I should apologize to you. And maybe we should talk about what we're going to do."

"Very well," Rose said, folding her arms. "Apologize."

"You're not going to make this easy on me, are you?"

Rose stared at him frostily.

Henry sighed. "All right. I'm sorry. I might have gotten overexcited. I told you I love children, right?"

"I believe you mentioned it."

"I *hate* it when children cry. He was in a panicked frenzy by the time I got back. The thought of leaving him alone for a day and a half, without being able to comfort him ..."

"He's currently in an egg," Rose said flatly. "There will be plenty of time to coddle him and allow him to be clingy. Have a little patience."

"I'm trying to apologize!" Henry cried.

"Then apologize, don't make excuses."

"I'm sorry," Henry said huffily. "I'm sorry that we got kicked out of the museum. I'm sorry the director got mad. Happy?"

"You've just said you're sorry about the consequences of your actions. You've said nothing about your actions. That still doesn't constitute an apology."

Henry glowered at her.

Rose walked around him and continued towards her family's house.

"All right, I'm sorry!" Henry said, running after her. "I'm sorry I got hotheaded and didn't leave well enough alone!"

"Thank you," Rose said, stopping to glance back at him. "That's an apology." She resumed walking.

Henry trotted after her. "So ... why are you still walking away?"

"I'm not walking away," Rose said. "I'm late. If you want to talk, we'll have to talk on the way."

"Late to what?" Henry asked.

"Dinner with my family. My mother insists on it every week."

"Oh." Henry walked on silently for awhile. "Should I meet your family?" he asked hesitantly. "Given the circumstances ..."

"I suppose you could," Rose said, increasing the pace. It occurred to her that the later she was, the fouler a mood her father would be in. She still had to talk to him about changing her classes next semester. "Don't mention the egg."

"Why not mention the egg?" Henry asked, hurrying to keep up with her.

"Because the story would sound mad, and it would only complicate the conversation we need to have tonight. It would be best if my father isn't in a bad mood. He'd be apt to refuse."

"Oh, right," Henry said. "Of course."

It wasn't long before they reached her family's house. Rose rang the doorbell, hoping her father was in a patient mood.

Her mother opened the door. She wore an old-fashioned shawl bedecked with flowers, and a lovely blue dinner gown that looked like it had seen better days. Rose's mother's taste in clothing was quite nice, but the budget her parsimonious husband gave her was quite slim. She spent most of her effort in making sure her three daughters were properly dressed, in the hopes that they would all land suitable husbands quickly.

"Rose!" her mother cried, throwing out her arms and embracing her. "We wondered where you were. Your papa's quite annoyed that you're late."

"I'm sorry," Rose said. "I was ... delayed."

"Hello," Henry said from behind her, reaching out his hand.

"Would you be Rose's mother? My name is Henry Wainscott. I'm Rose's fiancé."

What? Rose spun around and gaped at him. *What in the world is he saying?!*

"Oh," Rose's mother gasped. "I—I never even heard that Rose had a beau—George! George, you'll never believe who Rose brought with her! You'll never believe what they said!"

She ran into the house, leaving the door wide open.

"Why would you say that?!" Rose hissed incredulously. "We're not engaged!"

"I thought we were!" Henry whispered. "We agreed to be parents to the same child, and you said you wanted to talk to your father—"

"About my *tuition!*"

"Well, you might have *said* that!"

"What's this?" Rose's father asked, stomping to the doorway. "My daughter brought a fiancé to see me?"

"Henry Wainscott, sir," Henry said, holding out his hand awkwardly. "Uh ... I may have been a bit premature ..."

"You certainly were," Rose's father growled. "You haven't asked my permission yet. Don't just stand there, come in!"

Henry shot Rose a panicked look.

"You heard the man," she said tightly.

Henry removed his hat and ran his hand over his oiled hair nervously. He stepped into the parlor, twisting the hat around in his hands.

"You're engaged?!" Rose's sisters gasped, barreling down the stairs. One of them wore fluffy yellow and the other wore fluffy blue. They were only nine months apart in age, and nearly interchangeable.

"Hello, Sara. Hello, Louise," Rose said flatly.

Louise, the one in the blue dress, squealed and held her hands to her chest. "How did you meet? Was it love at first sight?"

Sara pretended to swoon, and Louise caught her.

"We met at the Museum of Natural History," Rose said.

"That place?" Rose's father asked sharply. "Were you wasting your allowance on those blasted bones again?"

Rose set her jaw. This was not a good beginning.

"I know, I know!" Sara cried. "One of them fell on a dragon skull, and it was love at first *bite!*" She made a chomping sound.

Louise giggled.

"I'm so glad that Rose has a beau!" their mother trilled, coming out of the kitchen with a platter of ham and onions that were all rather scorched at the edges. "Here I thought we'd never see her be interested in anything but those dusty books!"

"She's a terrible cook, by the way," Sara informed Henry. "She forgets there's something on the stove and burns it."

"I haven't done that in months," Rose objected. She didn't mention her roommates had nearly banned her from the kitchen.

"Hush!" Rose's mother said, shooing the girls away with a slightly panicked look. "Don't scare him away! Shoo! Shoo!"

Henry was chuckling in amusement when Rose's father loomed up behind him.

"So?" the man thundered. He snatched Henry's hat and tossed it at the hat rack. It snagged the hook and spun around slightly, then stayed put. "Why don't you tell me the reasons you think you should marry my daughter?"

Henry swallowed visibly.

Chapter 8
Engaged

Don't mention the dragon egg, Rose thought. *Do not mention the dragon egg. Just find a graceful way to get out of it, and then leave.*

"To tell you the truth, sir," Henry said, his fingers twisting nervously, "there's no good reason why I should marry your daughter. We've only known each other for a short time. I've liked her since we first met..."

Sara and Louise giggled.

"Shhhh!" Rose's mother hissed, waving them down and watching

Henry avidly.

"... but really," Henry faltered, "I couldn't blame you if you wanted to refuse me. I'll go now."

He tried to get to the hat rack, but Rose's father blocked his escape.

"Hang on now," the man said. "It would do Rose some good to be married. Teach her to be more realistic about things."

Rose's jaw clenched.

"Tell me about yourself, boy," Rose's father said. "What do you do?"

"Uh ... I'm a sophomore at City College. I study biology."

"That's a good field to be in," Rose's father said. "Good way to earn a living."

Excuse me? Rose thought indignantly. *You wouldn't let me take the class I wanted to about it this semester!*

Henry murmured something noncommittal.

"You should go into medicine," Rose's father said firmly. "There's always work for doctors."

"My father says the same thing," Henry said wearily.

"Smart man," Rose's father approved.

"Yes, I think the two of you would get along," Henry sighed.

"To the table, to the table!" Rose's mother said, gesturing. "We're already late with starting! Who wants to say grace?"

"I will!" Louise volunteered. And then she said something so short and covered in giggles that nobody could understand a word of it.

"... Right," Rose's father said, after a pause. He cleared his throat and reached for the butter knife and a roll. "So, how do you plan to support my daughter?"

"I ... have no plans, sir. I know that must be a problem. We must have been too hasty. How about you forget what I said before, and I can come back later ..." He got up from his chair.

Rose's father grabbed his arm and shoved him back down.

"How are you paying for your rent now?" he demanded. "Do you live with your parents?"

"N-no, I have a stipend from my grandfather," Henry stammered.

"It covers my tuition and living expenses until I graduate."

"Ah." Rose's father sat back in satisfaction. "So you *do* have some means. Good. I assume that getting married wouldn't cause a problem there?"

Henry shook his head. "My older brother got married during his senior year, and it wasn't a problem. But, uh, sir—"

Rose's father plowed right on. "Now, tell me about your classes. I assume you're getting good grades?"

"I was at the top of all my classes this semester," Rose said sourly. "Thank you for asking, Papa."

"Oh, look at how fun this is!" Rose's mother put in bubbily. "It's so nice to have another man around! George loves a solid intellectual discussion, and he never gets them around here!"

Rose's fists tightened on her lap.

"Rose strikes me as quite intellectual," Henry said.

"That's why she's going into teaching," Rose's father said, wiping his knife clean of butter and taking a large bite out of his roll. "Or was. Won't be necessary now that she's getting married, eh?"

Rose's fists were clenched so tightly, her arms started shaking. If this meant her father tried to pull her out of college altogether, she would never forgive Henry.

"Oh, no," Henry said, some sharpness in his voice. "I'm sure she'll want to keep studying. In fact, I'd say it's a *necessity*. I certainly wouldn't want to marry a woman who gave up on her schooling."

Rose's father looked rather taken aback.

"When are you going to get married?" Rose's mother asked excitedly. "Have you chosen a date?"

"I'll have to discuss that with Rose," Henry said vaguely. He flicked a glance over at her.

Rose kept her face still, betraying no emotion.

"We should try for late spring," Rose's mother said, her eyes bright. "You know what they say about June brides."

"That's up to Rose," Henry said.

Rose fixed her gaze on the hideous cubist painting her father had bought last year. It was hanging on the wall where her mother's oil pastel picture of squirrels used to sit. Her mother's choice had been a trivial thing, amateur work, but Rose had loved it. The two squirrels fighting over one acorn while several more hung on a branch above them had reminded her of her sisters.

Then Rose's father had come home with a painting he had bought at a gallery, one with jagged edges, garish colors, and a hefty price tag. Now she was forced to stare at it every time she ate dinner with her family.

"Excuse me," Henry said, pushing back his chair. "Would you mind if I excuse myself for a minute? I'd like some air."

"You want to smoke?" Rose's father asked. "I have cigars."

"No, thank you," Henry said. "There's something I'd like to speak with Rose about. Rose? Would you mind coming with me?"

Rose pushed her chair back and got up, her face still and her voice silent. She followed Henry to the front door, which he opened. They went outside and stood on the front step, and he shut the door.

"I'm sorry," he said. "I really thought you were thinking the same thing. This is a sincere apology."

There was a rustle and thump on the other side of the door.

"Speak quietly," Rose said. "My sisters are listening in."

Henry eyed the door. "People do that?"

"*Constantly.*"

Henry rubbed his forehead, then his bare upper lip. He looked uncertain of what to say.

Rose stood there for a moment in silence, looking at him. He wasn't wrong that getting married was the logical thing to do. She simply hadn't thought about it. The thought of marrying a stranger was not terribly appealing, but the thought of splitting a child between two households wasn't appealing, either.

Then again, the thought of marrying purely for logic was ... fairly depressing. Besides, she'd already chosen to make one lifelong commitment today. Two was far too many. The man also had several annoying qualities. She wasn't sure she wanted him in her life permanently.

Not that it would be easy to avoid that in any case, since they'd both agreed to raise the dragon.

So the real question is, Rose thought, *do I think someone better will come along that I'd regret not being able to marry?*

Rose surveyed him silently. He wasn't unattractive. He seemed like a decent man, and one who respected her. There were things about him that were maddening, but that would probably be true about anyone. Unless some terrible secret came to light, he was probably as good a prospect as any.

Somehow, the thought of being engaged didn't seem nearly as daunting as the thought of parenthood had, and she had already agreed to that particularly terrifying change. She already had roommates. She supposed she could get used to the idea of having one permanently.

"I'll consider it," she said.

"Consider what?" Henry asked.

"Consider marrying you. It's not impossible."

Henry let out a long breath. "That doesn't sound very flattering."

"It's not, not really. It's practical."

"I was hoping to be something a little more than *practical*," Henry complained.

"We've barely met. You can't expect there to be anything more."

"I liked *you* from the beginning."

Heat rose in Rose's cheeks. "Well ... thank you. But that's the rose-tinted glasses of hindsight speaking."

"No, it's not," Henry insisted. "I did."

Rose glanced at the door, embarrassed to think of her sisters overhearing any of it.

Henry glanced at the door, too, and cleared his throat.

"So ... the answer's maybe?" he said in a lowered voice.

Rose nodded. "Maybe."

Henry rubbed his forehead. "Does that mean I should stop sabotaging myself with your father?"

"Did you think that was sabotage?" Rose asked with amusement. "No, by all means, keep going. He *loves* persuading people to do something they're reluctant to do."

Henry looked ill.

Chapter 9
Eavesdropping

As dinner wrapped up, Rose pushed away her half-eaten piece of cherry upside-down cake, which was soggy in the middle, and cleared her throat.

"Papa," she said. "May I have a word with you?"

Rose's father turned a deaf ear. "Henry, do you play cards?"

"Sometimes, when my roommates and I aren't too busy."

"Good lad. Come, play with me."

"Uh, don't you usually need four people?"

"We'll make do," Rose's father said. He thumped his arm around Henry's shoulders. "Do you know gin rummy?"

"No ..."

"Papa!" Rose snapped. "We need to talk!"

"I don't see what we have to talk about," Rose's father growled, barely glancing at her.

Rose drew in a deep breath, trying not to lose her temper. "Remember? Last week, I told you that we needed to talk about my classes next semester. You said we'd talk about it next week. It's next week now, and I have my schedule planned out. The first class I need to take—"

"Just a small wager between friends, eh?" Rose's father said to Henry.

"*Wager?*"

"Papa!" Rose shouted.

"Come with me. I'll teach you the game." Rose's father shoved his chair back and pulled Henry up to his feet. Henry flicked a panicked look over at Rose, then a panicked look back at Rose's father, as the man dragged him down the hallway.

"The first class I need to take," Rose shouted, following after them, "is—"

The door to her father's study slammed in her face. There was a clicking sound.

Rose stared at the solid oak door, fuming. He always did this. It was maddening.

"You're never going to get through to him that way, dear," Rose's mother said, passing by and carrying two crumb-covered plates. "He doesn't like to lose arguments. He likes to win."

"Then how am I supposed to convince him?" Rose demanded.

Her sisters scampered over, each carrying an empty glass. They each pressed their glass to the door and their right ear to the end of the glass.

"Have you two no shame?" Rose asked.

"Shhhh!" Louise said, putting her finger to her lips. "Papa's explaining the rules now."

"He wants him to make a wager of five dollars," Sara said. "Mr. Wainscott made a choking sound."

"Now he's saying he doesn't have any money on him at all," Louise said. "I bet he's lying."

"No wonder, if Papa wants him to bet a month's worth of groceries," Rose snorted.

"Papa's saying Mr. Wainscott can owe him," Sara said. She was silent for a moment. "Mr. Wainscott refused."

"Now Papa's *really* keen," Louise said. "He's offering ten-to-one odds. And a handicap. He's really confident, isn't he?"

"Papa usually is," Rose said. She'd heard him bragging to her mother once that he could beat his friends more often if he wanted to, but it was better to make sure they kept on coming.

"Mr. Wainscott still refused. Now Papa's saying they can do a practice round first, and then twenty-to-one odds."

"He should really take Papa up on that," Sara opined.

"He did!" Louise cried. "He's saying he'll bet five cents!"

"He should've done more than that," Sara said. "Papa will probably let him win the first round."

"Five cents is still a lot of money," Rose said. "That's a trip on the subway."

"Shhhh!" Louise said, putting her finger to her lips. She listened for a long moment, intently.

Rose's mother walked by with two more crumb-covered plates.

"Do you want help clearing the table?" Rose asked her.

"No, no, dear," Rose's mother said. "Would you like a glass so you can listen with your sisters?"

"I am not a nosy busybody," Rose said huffily, "unlike some people, who—"

"They're talking about you, they're talking about you, they're talking about you!" Sara gasped. She yanked her ear away from the glass and gestured at Rose. "Come listen, come listen!"

Rose hesitated, but her younger sister grabbed her and shoved her ear against the glass.

There was a muffled, echoing quality, but she could hear the sounds surprisingly well. There was noise as her father expertly shuffled the deck, partly drowning out Henry's words.

"—to thank you for not letting her take science classes," Henry was saying. "That's not really a woman's place, is it?"

There was a scuffing sound as Rose's father dealt out the cards. "Of course not. That would be ridiculous."

Rose's mouth gaped. *What in the world is he doing?*

"It doesn't matter that she's smarter than me," Henry said. "In fact, it would be embarrassing if people realized it."

"It's not so bad," Rose's father said. "Mabel's got a great head on her shoulders. She can balance a budget like no one else."

"But that's a useful skill," Henry said. "Not like paleontology."

Rose was mad as hornets. She envisioned the tongue-lashing she would give that liar at the first opportunity.

"Hear, hear!" Rose's father agreed. "What good does ancient history do anyone today, I ask you? Nothing!"

"Especially given the cost of college," Henry said. "It's just not worth it without the guarantee of a well-paying job afterwards!"

Ha! Rose thought, smirking. Hearing people say that was one of her father's pet peeves. It was his greatest regret that he'd never gone to college, even though he made plenty of money.

"Education does have value for its own sake," Rose's father said stiffly.

"But only when it's something useful," Henry said. "Not when it's something useless like geology or art history."

There was thunderous silence.

Rose bit her knuckle to keep from laughing. Her father had

dozens of art history books in his study. How had Henry missed those?

"Besides, it's not like she would actually follow through and get all the degrees that would be necessary," Henry went on blithely.

"Watch your tongue," Rose's father growled. "Follow-through is not that girl's problem. Abominable stubbornness is."

"That's only if she wants to get the degrees," Henry said. "She doesn't really, you know."

What? Rose gaped indignantly.

"Then you don't know her at all," Rose's father snapped. "She hasn't shut up about it since she was nine years old. Wish I'd never bought her that book about dragons."

"That's just it. She didn't originally realize how much work it would be. Now she can't back down because her pride is at stake. Think about it: why hasn't she applied for a scholarship, if she's so stubborn and she wants to do it?"

Because I don't want to take the money away from students whose parents can't afford their tuition! Rose thought furiously. *My father can pay, so he should do it!*

"Hmmm," Rose's father said. There was a flipping sound. "I win."

"Do you want to play again?" Henry said. "I'll up the bet to ten cents."

Sara squeezed between Louise and Rose with a fresh glass in her hand. "What did I miss?"

"He lost the first round, and now he's upping the bet," Louise informed Sara. "I don't think Papa likes him. He beat him in the first round."

"Ooh! If Papa doesn't care if he comes back, he'll squash him in every round. I wonder how long he'll last," Sara grinned, putting her glass against the door and pressing her ear to it.

"No, thank you," Rose's father said stiffly. There was a scraping sound, then several pounding footsteps. Rose dropped the glass and scrambled out of the way just in time.

Her sisters didn't. They tumbled into the room as the door swung open.

"Hello, nosy twits," Rose's father rumbled.

"Hello, Papa," the girls chorused innocently.

"Rose!" her father snapped, looking around. "There you are. Let's talk about those classes you want to take."

Chapter 10
Effrontery

"Please tell me that worked," Henry said, as Rose stepped out of her family's house, half an hour later, in something of a daze.

Rose spun around and shot him a glare. How dare he loiter around after her father had kicked him out of the house? Had he no sense or dignity?

"Hold on," Henry said, putting his hands in front of him. "I'm sure your sisters told you what I said—"

"They didn't have to," Rose said coldly. "I heard it myself."

Henry stared at her for a moment. "Eavesdropper!" he cried.

"Talking behind my back!" Rose shot back.

"All right, I was," Henry said, his mouth twitching. "But did it work?"

"Did what work?" Rose asked suspiciously.

"Did he agree to let you take the classes you want to take?" Henry asked, slowly and patiently.

Rose stared at him for a long moment. Her anger dissolved. "You did that on purpose?"

"Of course I did," Henry said. "I didn't mean any of that nonsense. Wasn't it obvious?"

"No, it wasn't," Rose said slowly. "But I suppose if it had been, it wouldn't have worked."

"So it *did* work?" Henry asked, his eyes brightening.

Rose glanced back at the house nervously. She indicated with her head and started walking back in the direction of her apartment. She hoped her sisters hadn't been listening at the windows. Henry followed at a loping pace.

Once they were a safe distance away, Rose picked up the conversation again as they walked.

"He immediately started arguing with me about all the things you said. I kept protesting, because he kept trying to rebut arguments I'd never said or even believed, but that just made him more vehement. It was rather bizarre to have him insisting that I do something I've been begging him to let me do for ten years."

"So you're taking the classes you want to next semester?" Henry grinned.

"I hope so," Rose said, twirling her finger through a bracelet on her wrist. "He's insisting on helping me rearrange things ... because apparently I can't possibly choose the ideal class schedule on my own ... but I think that's just because he wants to feel useful." She glanced over at Henry as they kept on walking. "That was a rather brilliant idea."

"It was your idea," Henry shrugged. "You said he liked to talk people into things. I figured that meant it would be helpful to put him on your side, instead of against you. I was just hoping it wouldn't backfire horribly."

"You mean, like the effrontery at the museum?" Rose asked.

"Exactly."

"And like telling my family we were engaged when we weren't?"

Henry's face twisted. "Yes. Like that."

Rose smiled.

"In all seriousness," Henry said, looking over at her, "what *are* we going to do about the egg? We can't just leave him sitting there forever."

"I think," Rose said seriously, "we need to first arrange a place to bring him. Then we can worry about relocating him."

"I was thinking I'd take him home," Henry said.

"Do you have roommates?" Rose asked.

"Yes."

"Did you ask them how they'd feel about you bringing in a baby with a capacity to scream telepathically?"

Henry hesitated.

"I thought not," Rose said. "I doubt my roommates would be any more enthralled about the prospect."

Henry paused. "Marry me," he said.

Rose stared at him. "Excuse me?"

"Marry me," he repeated. "If you marry me, we can move in together, and we'll have a place to put him."

"That's not very romantic," Rose said.

"It's not romantic," Henry said, "it's practical. But I hope it could be more, in time."

"My father hates you, you know," Rose said. "You really *did* sabotage yourself this time. I doubt he'd give his permission."

Henry winced.

"But maybe," Rose said. She paused, and smiled. "Probably."

THE NEXT DAY was a quiet one. Rose and her roommates went to church in the morning, where Penelope sang off-key and Natalie made a big show of putting two dollars in the collection plate. Then, as soon as they got home, Natalie turned on the radio and Penelope pulled out stacks of homework, both seeming to forget their earlier piety.

Rose didn't tell them about Henry, or the dragon egg. How could she? It was still too new, too private. She stayed in her room for most of the day, thinking.

Monday afternoon, she met Henry outside of the Museum of Natural History fifteen minutes after lunchtime.

"Are we ready for this?" Henry asked. "They might kick us out again."

"If you feel a snide remark coming on, keep your mouth shut," Rose told him.

"I wasn't trying to be rude before!" he protested.

"I remind you of a certain long string of epithets."

Henry hesitated. "Fair point."

"Have you spoken with your professors about using the empty laboratory?" Rose asked.

"I spoke to the dean. He gave me two weeks. I have the key." Henry pulled a long string out from under his shirt, with a key dangling from it. "I know it's not ideal for you, because City College is an hour and a half walk away ..."

"You want to be a parent more than I do. It's only fair that you have closer access than me."

They stared up at the building.

"Of course, this is all predicated on whether or not we can get him out of there," Rose said. "It might take months before they're willing."

"And by then, we'd be married," Henry said.

Rose bit her lip. She'd given him a tentative *yes* this morning, but her stomach still clenched whenever she thought about it. She hoped she'd be more willing to consider setting a date soon, because two weeks wasn't long. They should probably be looking for an apartment already.

Henry took her hand. She looked down. Then she nodded, and they walked up the stairs to the museum.

Nobody stopped them from entering the doors, so they headed straight for the stairs. They were nearly on the third floor when they spotted Director Campbell on his way down.

"Oh, no," Henry moaned. "Here we go again ..."

"You!" the director shouted, pointing at Henry. His eyes were bloodshot and wild. "Get upstairs! Get upstairs right now!"

"What?" Henry looked dumbfounded. "I thought you were going to kick me out."

"Do you know how long it's been since I've slept?!" the director shouted. "*Thirty-six hours!* It's asking for you. It's screaming for you. It won't *stop* screaming for you. Make it stop!"

Henry didn't need to be told twice. He raced up the stairs, two at a time.

Rose hesitated. "Are you all right, Director Campbell?" she asked. There were circles under his eyes that were dark enough to use as inkwells.

"That thing has to get out of my museum," the director said wildly. "No one can go up to the fourth floor. I keep trying to calm it down. It won't calm down! It needs to leave!"

"Can we get that in writing, sir?" Rose asked tentatively.

The director fumbled through his pockets, yanked out a notebook and pen from an inner pocket, and scribbled something down. He ripped off the piece of paper and handed it to her. *Director Campbell authorizes taking the living dragon egg out of the museum*, it said, with a signature at the bottom.

Rose sighed with relief. It wasn't everything they would need—it wasn't even permanent custody—but it was enough to start with.

"Thank you, sir," she said politely, nodding her head.

Then ran up the rest of the stairs to help her fiancé with the screaming baby.

Chapter 11
Everything

"You know, I never really thought I'd be looking forward to the day my first child hatched," Henry said, running his hands over the leathery surface of the egg. According to Mr. Teedle, it felt softer to touch now than it used to. The other eggs were all hard and slick. Rose couldn't compare herself because she hadn't been allowed to touch them.

"It was your idea," Rose said, paging through her textbook. She was doing her homework here because it was a better use of time than sitting around doing nothing, and the egg didn't care what she did, as long as she was here as long as possible. "Don't complain."

"Oh, I'm not complaining," Henry said. "It's just ... sometimes it's still surprising. You know?"

"I know," Rose said. She wrote down a note in the margin of her textbook, and turned the page.

"I want to give him everything," Henry said longingly. "I want to give him the world."

"You don't own the world," Rose said tartly. "But there is something that we probably ought to give him."

Henry sat up straighter. "What?" he asked.

"A name. We can't keep calling him 'the dragon' or 'the baby' forever."

"Good point," Henry said. "We do know the gender already."

Rose shut her textbook. "What do you say, dragon?" she asked. "Shall we give you a name?"

A name! He didn't know what a name was. Was it something to eat? He looked forward to learning how to eat. Crunch crunch!

"What kind of name would suit him?" Henry asked thoughtfully.

"I suppose we could go with something descriptive," Rose said. "Spiny or Spiky or ... no."

"No," Henry said.

"No. That sounds too much like a pet's name."

"A human name, then," Henry said. "Are there any you like?"

"James. Or John. Or William. How about you?"

"Commodore, Virgil, and Bartholomew," Henry said promptly.

Rose stared at him. "You have strange taste in names."

"The girl names I like are Louvenia, Glendora, and Pleasant," Henry added.

"I can't tell whether you're serious or joking."

"Oh, I'm perfectly serious."

Rose wrinkled her nose.

"How about we use one of your names, and one of mine?" Henry asked.

"Virgil's not bad," Rose said. "That could be a first name. How about for a middle name?"

"I guess the least boring one is ... James?"

"All right," Rose said. "Virgil James ..."

"... Wainscott," Henry added.

Rose shivered. Somehow, adding in the last name made it seem real.

"What do you think?" Henry asked the egg, running his hands along its orange-and-brown surface. "Are you Virgil James?"

He was something. He was happy. He was hungry. No, he wasn't hungry. He didn't know how to be hungry. He was going to wiggle his toes.

There was a knock on the door to the laboratory. Rose got up to answer it.

Mr. Teedle stood there, his face pale. He held a rolled-up newspaper in his hands.

"Have you two seen this?" he asked in a shaking voice.

"Has news gotten out about Virgil already?" Rose asked, alarmed.

"Virgil?" Mr. Teedle looked confused.

"We named the dragon," Henry said.

"Oh. No, news has not gotten out about this dragon egg. The museum's still not planning to release a press statement until he's been hatched. But look."

Mr. Teedle unrolled the newspaper and thumped it on the table. On the front page, in bold letters, it declared, *DRAGON EGG HATCHES AT MUSEUM!*

Rose stared at the paper blankly. There was a picture of a *Deinonychus antirrhopus* dragon egg with a tiny snout just starting to protrude from the top. She glanced at the caption underneath the picture. "The Dragon National Monument?" she said slowly.

"Where the eggs were found," Mr. Teedle said, breathing heavily. "They have sixty of them on display. A vacationing couple passed by one of them, and ... *crack!*"

Virgil liked that noise. He repeated it. Crack! Crack!

Rose stared at the picture. She stared at the egg. She stared at Henry.

"Then that means," she said slowly, "that it's not just *one* dragon egg that's alive ..."

Mr. Teedle nodded. "*All* of them are."

Author Note:
Parenthood is hard. It's especially hard when the child is very different from their parents' expectations.

In my case, it's autistic children.

In this case, it's a dragon.

DRAGON'S DAWN

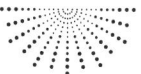

*R*ose unlocked and turned the handle of the empty laboratory where they had been permitted to store their child. In a box in the corner, a *Deinonychus antirrhopus* egg was snuggled with a blanket, warm and hidden from prying eyes.

"Hello, Virgil," Rose said, walking over. She sat down beside the egg and brushed aside the absurd teddy bear her husband-to-be had brought for him. According to Henry, a child should have a toy to cuddle with. According to Rose, the child was currently inside an egg.

She felt a stirring in her mind, a sensation she was gradually becoming more used to. *Deinonychus* dragons were, they had discovered, telepathic. This was good, because there was no way they could have communicated with the fetus otherwise, nor even known that he was intelligent.

"Are you asleep now?" Rose asked.

Warmth. Comfort. Sleepiness. Gone.

Rose reached into the bag she had brought with her and removed her textbook and notebook. Carefully, she smoothed down the pages and began taking notes. She had splurged and spent the five cents on the subway because she had a great deal of studying to do before next week, and she had not wanted to spend an extra hour walking. Quiet would suit her perfectly.

Try as she might, though, she could not ignore the fact that her wedding was tomorrow. Her wedding to a man who was still little more than a stranger, in order to parent a child who was not even their species. Her mind skittered away from the notes she was taking, and terror squeezed her heart.

What am I doing? Rose thought frantically. Her fingers tightened around the edge of her notebook. *Almost all of the women in college are single. Even though it's 1920 now, not the eighteen hundreds, I know no women with a baby and a career. I'm determined to become a paleontologist, which is a difficult field to break into in any case. Am I destroying my whole future?*

Her fingers tightened around the notebook, crumpling the paper.

And then there's Henry. What if I'm wrong about him? What if he becomes chauvinistic once we're married, like my father? He's already shown signs of inflexibility!

Her fingernails dug into the paper, opening a tear. Heedless, her thoughts kept on spinning into further and further fear.

And then there's Virgil! We haven't told the city that he exists yet. How will they react when they learn that not all dragons apparently died millions of years ago? He'll be seen as a miracle. He'll be seen as a monster. He'll be seen as a pet, or animal, or source for curiosity. How will we make people understand he is a person?

She wanted to cry. Her shoulders heaved.

The equivalent of a matching howl came from the egg. He was tight and he was uncomfortable and his tail was squashed and his toes were squished and he couldn't move and he hated it! He hated it, he hated it, he hated it!

Rose was in no mood to put up with a tantrum. She slammed her notebook shut.

"You're going to hatch soon," she told him sternly. "You'll be fine."

He didn't want to hatch, he wanted to stay right here, where he was warm, and comfortable, and SQUISHED! He hated it! He didn't want to be squished anymore! SQUISHED SQUISHED SQUISHED SQUISHED!

"*You* were the one who told us you were close to hatching. *You* were the one who looked forward to it eagerly. Remember?"

Nooooo! He didn't want to, he didn't want to! He was going to kick the side of the egg!

Whump. Whump. Whump. Rose could actually see the egg moving.

"If you do that, you're going to hatch right now," Rose said dryly.

The dragon sent out a burst of terror and a kaleidoscope of panic. He didn't want to hatch! He didn't have to! He would just stay here forever!

The doorknob unlocked and turned, and Henry walked in.

"Perfect timing," Rose said. "Virgil's throwing a fit. He says he doesn't want to hatch."

Whump! Whump! Whump! Whump!

"Whoa," Henry said, walking over and putting his hand on top of the leathery egg. "No one's going to force you to do anything before you're ready, Virgil. You don't have to feel rushed. You can do things at your own pace."

The egg stopped moving. The panic stilled.

Virgil's father was nice. Virgil liked his father better today.

"Thank you," Rose said with annoyance.

Virgil's mother was scared, too. She had woken him up. Virgil hadn't liked that. He'd share his memory of it.

Rose winced as her own emotions from moments before flooded back over her again, this time filtered through the dragon's perception. Henry raised his eyebrows at her.

"You're having second thoughts about the wedding?" he asked.

Rose hesitated. It wouldn't be much use to deny it, given that their son apparently could tattle on her. "Not so much second thoughts as ... doubts. Fears."

"Ah." Henry sat down beside her and tucked the teddy bear back in with the egg. That ludicrous teddy bear. "Well, I'll tell you the same thing I told to Virgil. I'm not going to force you to do anything before you're ready. If you want to wait, we can wait."

Rose drew in a deep breath. "But we have to get married as soon as possible. We've paid for the apartment. I've moved most of my clothing there. My roommates have found someone to replace me. We can't possibly delay it."

"We most certainly can, if you want to," Henry said. "We'll find a way." He made a face. "Even if your father makes my life miserable for it."

Rose laughed. Her father was a difficult man even when he liked a person, and he wasn't fond of Henry.

"I mean it," Henry said seriously. "I don't want to start a marriage with you having second thoughts. If you to delay, we can delay."

Rose gave that serious thought. Did she want to delay?

Henry had promised not to stand in her way of her dreams, despite the fact that her ambitions were unusual for her gender. He had always treated her with respect. He was undoubtedly a better father than she was a mother. In many ways, he was the ideal match, and Virgil was a better child than she deserved.

The timing might be rushed, and that was frightening. But this was the right family.

Rose reached out to put her hand on top of Henry's.

"No," she said softly. "Tomorrow. Tomorrow will be fine."

It no longer seemed like a source of fear.

AUTHOR NOTE:
I wrote this short story to go in between the first and second books in the Dragon Eggs *series, and it was very well liked, so I'm including it here.*

DRAGON'S HOPE

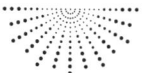

Chapter 1
Hall

She wasn't really clear on why she was here, in the Hall of Saurischian Dragons, rather than getting ready for the day that was supposed to be the most important of her life. After all, she had a very full schedule today. Her roommates would be incredulous if they discovered where she'd snuck off to.

But something had drawn Rose back to the museum.

The crowd oozed past Rose as she watched the eleven *Deinonychus antirrhopus* dragon eggs that now remained in the display case. They lay there silently. Still.

"You're not dead," Rose murmured under her breath. "If Virgil wasn't, if another dragon out in Utah wasn't, you're all living, too. So wake up."

A cluster of children passed her, following a harassed-looking nanny. "Would you two stop poking each other?" the woman complained, separating a boy and girl who were jabbing fingers into each others' ears. "And you—!"

The milling mob of children passed in front of her, momentarily blocking the display case. As her view cleared, Rose held her breath, wondering if another egg had woken. But no. The mob was past. The nanny was gone.

Rose let out a long sigh.

She wasn't sure why it seemed so important to her that the other eggs awakened. She certainly was not looking to adopt a second child; she barely knew what she and Henry would do with the first one. Why was it that it mattered to her, then?

Rose stood there, lost in thought, troubled by the fervency of her desire. What was it? What was the reason?

The eggs did nothing. The crowd kept passing in front of her, sometimes jostling her, sometimes blocking her view, but always the eggs remained the same, still and in deep hibernation. Hibernation, because surely they must still be alive.

Why? Why did it matter so much?

Of course there was the obvious answer. As a prospective paleontologist, she had every reason to be fascinated by the prospect of living dragons. The fact that one had chosen her to be his mother bore no weight: she could not treat her son as a research subject. She, in fact, dared not. Another person's dragon child, however, she could treat with scientific objectivity. She would dearly like to have such an opportunity.

Then, too, there was the fact that Virgil was currently the only living dragon in this part of the country. Were he to be the only member of his species within his lifetime, it would be difficult to play with other children safely, or to feel like he had any place in the world other than as a relic, a living fossil of an ancient and long-dead age.

No child deserved to feel that way.

A raucous little boy burst out laughing as he ran toward the *Tyrannosaurus rex* skeleton displayed prominently behind her. "Its wings are tiny!" he shouted. "Its arms are even smaller! It looks so dumb! Ha ha ha!"

Rose closed her eyes. Mockery of a skeleton was one thing. But would her son have to deal with similar thoughtlessness from other human children his age?

Please hatch, Rose thought, blinking back tears. *Not for my son's sake. I'm more selfish than that. I don't want to be the only mother to a dragon in New York City. I don't want to be the only one going through this.*

Oh, there was Henry, of course. But Henry's cheerful optimism and unflagging enthusiasm seemed to belie any real understanding of the challenges they were going to have to face. When Rose attempted to speak to him of all her worries, he simply turned a deaf ear, or else changed the subject to something more positive.

Perhaps he did it because he saw no value in borrowing trouble that might never surface. Perhaps he preferred to focus on the prospect of fatherhood, in which he seemed to take unending delight. That was valid. But to Rose, who felt far more terror than joy at the prospect of parenthood, it was also isolating.

If another dragon hatched, she thought, *there would be another woman in the city who would understand how I feel. Perhaps it wouldn't even matter who she was.*

All the professors and paleontologists and zoologists who had quietly and confidentially assembled to study the dragon were men. Rose wanted their respect, not their dismissal, so she dared not speak to any of them about feelings. One day, after all, she hoped to be among them, and to act like an emotional woman in front of them would only sabotage this.

Please hatch, Rose thought to the eggs, knowing that they could understand her meaning without her speaking aloud. *Please wake up. Please choose parents. I don't want to be alone in this.*

The eggs did nothing. Well, perhaps she couldn't really blame them. They were fetuses. They couldn't be expected to understand an adult's concerns, even if any of them were on the verge of waking.

Rose swallowed her emotions, as she had grown used to doing, and tried to leave. Then she turned back and spoke aloud.

"If not for me, then for yourselves," she said. "Perhaps you do not understand this. Perhaps it is ridiculous to even say it to you. But I will say it, nonetheless. You are not mere refugees from the past. You are the future of *Deinonychus antirrhopus*, a future that can only exist if your species becomes viable. The more individuals who hatch, the better that chance."

The eggs did nothing. Rose spoke again, this time forcefully.

"I do not know what mechanism you've used to hibernate. Whatever it is, it is extraordinary, to have preserved you so long and so well. It defies our current understanding or capacity for explanation. But one thing is clear: as long as you were all asleep, it was in your best interests to remain that way together. But now that even one has wakened, it is in your best interests to follow, so that you may be of compatible ages. Perhaps you are too young to consider your own offspring, but nature is not so merciful that you can ignore it. You *must* hatch now, if you want your species to have the best chance to survive."

The eggs did nothing. She had not really expected them to. Important as her words were, it was too much to expect not-even-infants to understand them.

Rose sighed heavily and turned away from the display case. A little girl with a sticky face was sucking on her fingers and watching her, and a whole family was staring at her oddly. Embarrassed, realizing she probably should not have said so much aloud before any announcement had been made, Rose walked briskly away towards the stairs.

She had spent far too long at the American Museum of Natural History today already. Her roommates would wonder where she had been.

Ducking through the crowd, not stopping to walk through the Hall of Ornithischian Dragons despite the fact that it had been weeks since she'd been there, Rose headed down the stairs, out the entrance, and into the street. Breathing in the odoriferous air, she settled into the walk through Central Park to reach her apartment.

It was a lovely Saturday morning, half-past ten, and there were families and nannies all over the park.

Will this be Henry and me in a few weeks? Rose wondered. *Or will we be too much celebrities once our son hatches and the newspapers are given the story?*

They hadn't even told their families about the dragon yet. She and Henry had discussed it at length, and he had said he didn't think his brother could keep a secret, while she had expressed concern about her nosy sisters and their love of gossip.

It wouldn't be long before they knew now, though.

Rose checked her wristwatch, and then picked up her skirts to walk more quickly. She had definitely stayed at the museum much longer than she should have.

She didn't want to be late to her wedding.

Chapter 2
Here

"Where were you?" Henry demanded as she bustled past him into her parents' house, closely followed by her roommates, who had griped most of the trip that she hadn't left them any time to do her hair up nicely.

"Delayed," Rose said perfunctorily. She didn't want to explain where she had been, lest it exasperate him. There wasn't time to speak with him privately about dragons, anyway. "I lost track of time. I'm here now."

"Rose!" her mother shouted, rushing in from the living room. "Where have you been? We've only half an hour before the minister arrives!"

"And my sister-in-law isn't getting along very well with your father," Henry added.

Rose felt weary.

"We tried to get here in time, but she didn't come back until half past ten," Natalie said in her usual bossy tone. "She said she'd been off on a walk. I think she was trying to run away."

"Natalie!" Penelope hissed, scandalized.

Henry caught Rose's eye, glancing over at her roommates as if to ask whether there were any truth to this. She shook her head in irritation. He looked relieved.

"Upstairs!" Rose's mother ordered, making shooing motions. "We need to get you ready!"

Rose gladly obeyed, mounting the stairs with haste. Her mother followed swiftly at her heels.

The dress was laid out on her bed, waiting for her. Rose suppressed a sigh. It wasn't really one she would have chosen for herself. It was lovely, with a scoop neckline and an elegant train, but it didn't feel like her. It was too soft, too gentle, too womanly. Her mother had worn it twenty-two years ago, and it had suited her mother perfectly. Had Rose chosen her own, she would have gone with something much more simple and plain.

But practicality was practicality. There had been no time to have her own dress made, nor would there have been the money. Rose's father had chosen to show his intense dislike of the groom by tightening his purse-strings.

Fair enough. It was sufficient that he had consented at all. At first, he had seemed likely to refuse outright, but then Rose's mother had taken him aside and spoken with him, and he had come back with a surly expression and an agreement that a wedding could be held in their home, but there would be no money paid for non-necessities.

Rose didn't know what her mother had said, but she had a nasty feeling that her parents, and most likely all of her and Henry's relations, were assuming she was pregnant. What other conclusion could they come to, when the two of them had announced the engagement so suddenly and insisted that the wedding be only two weeks away?

In fact, that conclusion wasn't far from the truth. There *was* a child on the way, a child that made their marriage the most sensible thing.

Still, it rankled to think that such assumptions might be spreading, even if they could be corrected later. Rose strongly suspected that her roommates had spread rumors about her to all their acquaintances.

"You look lovely," Rose's mother said, buttoning the dress up the back. There were dozens of tiny buttons.

Rose held her tongue and did not complain, though the dress was slightly too tight at the waist and squeezed her ribcage. "Thank you, Mama," she said politely.

"We'd best do something with your hair, too," her mother said, fingers moving busily.

Rose stood still, watching her reflection in the mirror as her mother bustled about. *Poor Mama*, she thought. *It must be such a disappointment to her that this is all the wedding she'll get from me. I suppose Sara and Louise will have to make up for it in lavishness, when their turns come in a few years.*

They were soon heading downstairs, and the next hour passed in a surreal blur. It was a ceremony just like any she had attended for cousins or her mother's acquaintances, only this time it was her standing before the minister, speaking the traditional words, and accepting the kiss from the young man who, in other circumstances, might have been a favorite beau, but instead was little more than a stranger. As family members rose from their chairs to share congratulations, Rose felt a curious sense of unreality.

This is it, then, she thought. *It's official.*

She wondered how Virgil was doing. When they had left him last night, he had been complaining about feeling tight within the egg, which meant he must be close to hatching. How much longer would they have? One week? Two?

Rose's mind raced as she thought about the preparations they had made. Every person had had different theories about what a *Deinonychus antirrhopus* infant might eat, or what might be the closest equivalent in their era. There were now four leading theories, and one of Rose's prevailing worries was that none of them would be adequate.

Of course all of them had asked Virgil, but his responses had been confusing and less than optimally helpful. It seemed clear he didn't understand what they were asking, and perhaps he didn't even have enough relevant memories from his parents to share in the first place. And of course, all of the prey species his parents had devoured were now extinct.

Mr. Teedle had immediately sent a telegram to the Dragon National Monument to inquire what they had fed their dragon hatchling, upon reading the news that one had hatched there, but there had not yet been a reply.

Rose rather suspected that he had failed to communicate any sense of urgency, and thus it had been buried in a pile of other inquiries from curious scientists and eager journalists.

Thus it was that there were now stockpiles of rats, frogs, insects, pigeons, and chickens filling an icebox that had been lugged into the laboratory where Virgil was currently settled. Every day, one of the professors brought a new bag of ice to keep the potentially-needed ingredients fresh.

Rose quailed at the thought of all the effort that was being put into the preparations to keep their son alive. Quite honestly, she would have preferred to leave him to the care of the dozen capable specialists for several more weeks. But no: the deal was that as soon as they were married, they were to take the egg home so that the empty laboratory could be used for scheduled classes again.

Presumably this meant that the whole icebox would be moved to their apartment, and that the researchers would continue visiting their home on the same constant schedule that they currently maintained in the laboratory they were borrowing.

And she was less than thrilled that the apartment Henry had rented for them was within an easy walking distance of City College, but over an hour's walk from Hunter College. He hadn't even asked her opinion before he'd taken it.

I'll have a long walk to school on Monday, Rose thought, feeling sick. Her roommates had already found another student at their college to replace her, and one of her professors had made an offhanded comment that implied he thought she would drop out of school before the semester was finished. It was as if nobody thought her education mattered.

"Congratulations," Henry's grandfather told Rose stiffly, shaking her hand. He seemed like a very formal gentleman.

"Thank you," Rose said politely, snapping back to the moment. This was her first introduction to most of Henry's family members. She should really make an effort to pay attention to them.

Then she looked over at Henry, and realized with a start that Mr. Teedle was standing next to him.

What? Rose thought, startled. *Did we invite him?*

She barely had time to wonder before the man opened his mouth and blurted out words that were both quick and rather too loud.

"The egg is hatching! You need to come right away!"

Chapter 3
Hurry

Outside the door, a cab was waiting. They rushed out to meet it, heedless of their family and neighbors shouting out and murmuring after them.

"Where do you think you're going?" Rose's father thundered, with an air of extreme offense.

Rose didn't stop to answer. It would only provoke an argument, which would delay their exit longer. She was not going to miss the hatching.

"Henry?" an elegant woman with an arrangement of curls protested. She had been introduced as his mother. "Henry!"

He made no move to stop, either. The two of them scrambled up into the cab, Mr. Teedle following after them. Scrunched in between the two men, Rose wound her train around her arm in hopes that it would not get caught in the enormous wheels on the way.

"Where are you going?" Rose's mother shouted as the the cabbie flicked his reins and the horses began moving forward. "Rose! *What egg?*"

The cab jostled around them as they drove down the city streets. There was a tense silence as they waited to arrive.

"I take it you haven't told your families?" Mr. Teedle asked.

"My mother is a gossip," Henry said briefly.

"So are my sisters," Rose added.

Mr. Teedle nodded silently.

"I think we should tell them before any announcements in the papers, mind you," Henry put in.

"Oh, well, obviously," Mr. Teedle agreed.

Rose wound the train around her arm more tightly, wondering

when that would be. When she thought of telling her parents, of introducing them to the egg ... no, soon to be the hatchling ... her mind rebelled to even imagine it. How would her father react to the news that there were dragons alive? What about her mother and sisters?

She had only just made Henry's family's acquaintance. They lived just far enough out of the city to make traveling inconvenient, so she had only met them today.

They would be even more of a mystery.

When they reached the City College campus, Mr. Teedle directed the driver down the streets until they reached the appropriate building. Mr. Teedle was quick to dismount. He offered Rose his arm to help her get down, and then went to pay the cabbie as Henry hopped out. Henry made no move to wait. He strode straight up the stairs towards the entrance.

"Mr. Teedle," Rose said anxiously, "do you mind if I ...?"

"Go ahead," Mr. Teedle said, waving his arm.

Rose hurried up the stairs after Henry, with some difficulty because of her dress. Henry held the door for her at the top, and she followed him in.

"Five dollars!" Mr. Teedle expostulated behind them. "That can't have been more than five miles! You must be joking!"

They ran down the hallway, Rose's heels clacking loudly against the floor. Unlike most days, when they had to dodge students, the building was empty.

It's rather nice not to receive odd looks for being here, Rose thought briefly. Since the school was for men only, she had had to pretend to be looking for Henry if anyone asked. One of his roommates had stopped her once, to chide her for going into a building where "women had no business being."

As if women can't study sciences, too! Rose thought, remembering the indignation she had felt that day.

They reached the door to the laboratory that was not currently being used for classes. The window was blocked so that no curious onlookers could peer inside, and Henry patted his pockets for the key. He stared at Rose in distress.

"I didn't bring mine, either," she said. "Knock."

Henry knocked on the door. "This is Henry Wainscott," he called. "Rose Palmer is with me. Would you please let us in?"

There was rustling, then footsteps, and the door opened. There were six men inside, all scientists that Rose recognized.

"Are we too late?" she asked breathlessly, rushing inside as the man held the door for her. Henry followed after her. "How is Virgil?"

"See for yourself," another of the men said, drawing aside. The egg was on the floor, nestled within a nest of blankets. Off to the side was the teddy bear Henry had bought for their son, a ridiculous gesture that Rose had objected to.

At first, the egg seemed the same as always. But then she noticed there were tiny cracks at the edges. She walked around, and saw that the cracks were much larger on the side that hadn't been facing them.

"Is he all right?" she asked anxiously. "He's not saying anything."

"He has been," one of the professors said. "It's just—"

The egg jostled, a noticeable jump. He was very, very upset that nobody was helping him!

"That," the professor said. "That's what he's saying."

Henry started to move forward. One of the men, a zoologist, put out his hand to block him.

"No," the man said. "The dragon's shared no memories of any ancestors being helped with hatching. I don't think he's supposed to be helped."

"But—" Henry protested.

"If you help a chick hatch out of an egg, it'll die," the man said firmly. "We don't know if that's true for dragons, but it wouldn't be wise to risk it. He must do this himself."

Another crack spread across the egg. It jostled. He was very, very, very upset!

Henry let out a small moan.

Rose unwound the train from her arm, anxious to do something. She had been horrified to think of him hatching without her, but now it was unbearable to stand here waiting.

The egg jostled again. No new cracks spread across it.

Virgil was miserable. He was very, very miserable. He was stuck and he was miserable and he just wanted to sleep. Nobody was helping. He was very unhappy.

"How long will it take?" Henry asked pitifully.

"There were cracks on that side of the egg when I came," one of the men said. "That was two hours ago."

"My wife took more than eight hours to deliver our son," another man said.

Rose shuddered. That wasn't something she wanted to think about.

There was nothing from the dragon for a long time. Rose wondered whether he really had gone to sleep. Was that normal for a dragon? She didn't think it was normal for most other creatures. She was just about to ask when the egg wriggled vigorously.

He was stuck and he was uncomfortable and he was STUCK STUCK STUCK! He wanted to get out, he wanted to get out, he wanted to get OUT! *OUT, OUT, OUT!*

One of the cracks spread further as the egg bounced.

"You can do it," Henry gasped, clenching his fists. "You can do it. Please!"

The door rattled behind them, and Rose spun around to glance back. Mr. Teedle shut the door behind himself and put away his key. "Five dollars, indeed," he was muttering.

"Ooh!" one of the men shouted. "That's another crack!"

Furious with herself for getting distracted, Rose spun back. The crack was stretching further ... further ... further ...

"He's going to do it," Henry gasped. "He's going to do it!"

"Let me see!" Mr. Teedle said, elbowing one of the other men off to the side so that he could get through them.

Virgil was scrunched and stuck and miserable and he was VERY, VERY, VERY UPSET!

There was a cracking sound, and something tiny and sharp poked through the center of the fractured web.

"It's an egg tooth!" the man standing next to Rose shouted.

Everyone rushed to their side of the egg. Rose was so crowded in among them that she could scarcely breathe, but she didn't care. Almost as one, they all held their breath.

The tiny egg tooth chipped away, and small glimpses of green began to come into view.

"Is he green?" Henry murmured.

"Were *Deinonychus antirrhopus* dragons green?" another man wondered.

"We have no way of knowing," Mr. Teedle said reverently. "This is our first time finding out."

It's not true that we have no way of knowing, Rose thought. *He's shared some of his parents' memories, including how they saw each other. His father was blue, and his mother was green ...*

A whole snout burst through, and there were shouts and cheers around them.

Virgil was angry! Why were they making noise instead of helping him? They were right there!

"You're almost out," Henry said eagerly. "You're almost out, Virgil. Come on! You can finish! I know you can!"

A huge section of egg broke free and shattered across the floor. Behind it they could see a glimpse of a tiny face, and a tiny claw gripped the edge of the opening.

The dragon's head shot out, dripping and shiny, with tiny nubs where horns would soon be. The egg toppled forward, and his head smacked the floor. Virgil struggled further, and another claw emerged from the egg. Then another. Then a whole arm. Then a leg.

At last, only the tail was still left within the egg. It tapered down into a wet and sticky mess behind him.

Virgil was sad. Virgil was very tired.

Virgil was hungry.

Chapter 4
Hungry

"Food," one of the professors said out loud. "We have to feed him. What are we going to start with?"

"I want to be the first to feed him," Henry said immediately. "Unless ..." He looked over at Rose, his expression guilty. "Do you want to be first?"

"No," Rose said. Quite honestly, she didn't even want to be the second. "You can be first."

"Do we have anything prepared?" Mr. Teedle demanded, looking around at one of the other men.

One of the other professors cursed, with rather shocking language. "I'm sorry. I meant to get something started, once the egg was hatching ... but in all the excitement ..."

"Do we have anything even *thawed?*" Mr. Teedle demanded.

"Rheinhold was going to do that, and he's not here," a professor said uncomfortably.

Are they really going to waste time assigning blame? Rose thought incredulously. "Then start with insects," she said briskly to the biology professor who stood near her. "Pull them out and cook them over a Bunsen burner until they're thawed. Then cool them down however necessary, so they won't burn his mouth. And you," she added, turning to the man next nearest her, "you do the same with the meats."

The men nodded and hurried to the icebox. Two other men started to set up Bunsen burners.

"What else do we need?" Henry asked. "Do we have a ... prepared recipe?"

"We'll have to develop that as we see what he accepts and rejects," Mr. Teedle said.

Rose said nothing. She knew what they were all thinking. *If he rejects everything, if the only things he could eat went extinct millions of years ago, he'll starve to death. We'll have no way to save him.*

Surely that wasn't going to happen, though. Surely their son would be all right. Surely the baby would eat.

Please eat, Rose thought. *Please don't put us through what Mama went through with her daughters. We can't hire a wet nurse, like she had to. Please eat.*

Virgil was sleeping on the floor. Rose crept closer to watch him. His chest moved in and out as he breathed, and his tail twitched in the slime of the egg. She wanted to move forward, to clean him off, but she wasn't sure if that would wake him. She didn't want to wake him, not before they had food ready.

Please eat, Rose prayed. *Please ... be able to eat what we have prepared.*

Three men were clustered around each of the Bunsen burners.

"Don't cook the crickets too much," one of the men opined. "They must have eaten raw food."

"How do you know?" another man challenged. "They breathed fire. One of the prevailing theories is that dragons cooked their food."

"Cook some of the crickets and leave the rest as raw as you can," Mr. Teedle said, moving over to them. "It's very likely that adult dragons preferred roasted food, or at least didn't mind it. They presumably used their fire for hunting. But we don't know about infants."

"Cooking meat makes it more digestible," another man said. He was holding a frozen chicken while another man set up a tripod to put it on. "That's why we do it."

"So cook most of the chicken," Mr. Teedle said. "We'll try it with various pieces at varying levels and see what he'll accept. What about the rats? Who's thawing a rat?"

"I'm going to do it just as soon as I'm done with these insects," one of the men over a Bunsen burner grunted, stirring something in a small bowl that was set over the tripod. "Yes, I think these are close to thawed. Here, you," he said, turning off the Bunsen burner and picking up the bowl gingerly in his gloved hands. He set it on the table on a mat that had been laid out for it. "Crush these into a paste. We can be reasonably certain that the babies didn't eat their food whole."

Henry nodded and picked up a pestle.

The door rattled, and two men rushed in. They were both paleontologists who worked with Mr. Teedle.

"Did we miss it?" one of them asked.

"Traffic was horrible on Broadway," the other one added.

"He's over there," Mr. Teedle said in a low voice. "He's sleeping."

The two men looked crushed, but then they crept over to that part of the room, and one of their faces lit up. The other just looked fascinated.

I know, Rose thought, smiling slightly. *I know.*

"Can we touch him?" one of them asked.

Henry's head shot up.

"We don't know yet," Rose said. "Better not to risk it. We'll wait until Henry feeds him."

"Do you think he might catch a chill?" one of the men asked. "Maybe we should put a blanket on him."

"He might be temperature insensitive," the other one said. "Dragons breathed fire, after all."

"It's doubtful that the infants did," the first one objected. "We don't want him to get ill."

"The egg didn't need incubation," Rose spoke up. "Not in the past few weeks, and not in his parents' memories. The mechanism that produced fire must at least be sufficiently active to keep him warm."

The men fell silent, and all three of them watched the dragon.

The mechanism that produced fire, Rose thought. Her veins tingled in excitement. Dragon fire was one of the great mysteries in paleontology. Where it had come from, what had produced it, what the many dragon species had used it for ... those were all subjects of intense debate.

One of her goals had long been to be the paleontologist who discovered the answers to those mysteries. And now, perhaps, the answer to all of those questions was lying in front of them, sleeping.

It was both exciting and frustrating. Exciting, because she could hardly wait to find out all the things Virgil would teach them about his species. Frustrating, because she had promised herself not to think of him as a subject of research. How would she do that? How could she possibly reconcile her curiosity with the fact that he needed a mother who looked at him lovingly, not clinically?

Rose glanced over at Henry, who was grinding crickets without complaint.

If I fail, at least he'll have Henry to be affectionate, she thought. *The man was almost built to be a parent.*

But with that thought came some jealousy. Why did it come so easily to him? What did he have that she was lacking?

"Should I pour some water in this?" Henry asked. "Presumably he'll have to get water from someplace."

"Yes, tentatively, but let's try it without first," the man next to him said. "I really should have thought to remove the hair from this rat before we froze it," he added.

Henry wrinkled his nose. "I hope rats aren't the thing he likes best. I don't favor the idea of capturing them."

"I don't think you *should* capture them, even if he does favor them," the man said. "Rats often carry disease, and they're often poisoned. You don't want that being ingested by the dragon."

Rose shuddered at the idea.

"So we'd have to buy them?" Henry asked. "Presumably from the same people who supply them to laboratories?"

"That would be my recommendation," the professor said.

Henry looked less than thrilled.

"Wouldn't insects have the same potential problems?" Rose spoke up. "Presumably pigeons, as well?"

"Oh, yes," Mr. Teedle said. "Better to only stick with food you can buy."

Henry looked even less thrilled.

Rose sighed. He had refused to show her his finances, but she assumed he was worried about the expense. No wonder, since his budget would now have to stretch to feed three.

He had insisted that the money wouldn't be a problem, and that she didn't have to worry about it. He'd claimed the stipend from his grandfather would be sufficient for whatever they needed. But she wondered. Full-grown *Deinonychus antirrhopus* dragons were twice the size of humans, and the speed at which they had grown to adulthood was still a mystery.

Please eat, she thought to Virgil. *And please don't eat so much that we can't afford it.*

The tiny dragon stirred, and his eyes opened. His tail flicked one of the eggshell fragments, which skittered across the floor. Everyone in the room stopped what they were doing, fixated on the sight of the small dragon.

Virgil was hungry. He wanted his parents to feed him.

Chapter 5
Health

"Crickets first?" Henry asked, looking very nervous.

"Crickets first," Mr. Teedle confirmed.

Henry moved forward, carrying the bowl with him. He held it in his bare hands, which implied that it had cooled enough to be handled comfortably. Hopefully that meant the contents were also sufficiently cooled ... if that even mattered in the case of dragon infants.

Henry's arms shook as he sat down on the floor beside the dragon. "Hello, Virgil," he said. "I'm your father. Do you remember me?"

Virgil recognized his father's mind, but his father looked strange. Where were his horns and claws?

"I don't have horns and claws," Henry said. "I've tried to explain this to you before. We're human. We're a different species."

Virgil didn't understand. Virgil was hungry.

"Okay," Henry said. He swallowed several times, visibly. "I have some food for you here. Try this."

He reached into the bowl and pulled out a mashed-up bug. He held it out.

The tiny green-scaled dragon just stared at it. He felt very reproachful. That wasn't food. His father should know what food was. Why was his father giving him not-food?

"All right," Henry said. His voice was steady, but his hands were shaking. "Would you please explain what food is?"

Food was food! His father was supposed to feed it to him! He should open his mouth, and then Virgil would eat from it!

"You want me to ... uh ..." Henry stared down at the bowl. "No, I'm not going to put crickets in my mouth. Sorry."

Virgil didn't want that not-food! Virgil wanted *food!* His parents should give him food! Virgil was getting very, very upset!

"What do I do?" Henry asked the rest of them, looking panicked.

Let me try, Rose thought, but she didn't say it. If she failed at this ... if she failed ... she wasn't used to failing, and the thought of failing when a child's life depended on their success terrified her.

"Let me try," one of the men said. "I've nursed a baby pigeon back to health once. My wife has a soft spot for them."

Looking angry, and embarrassed, and relieved, and unsure of himself, Henry hesitated and then handed the bowl over. The man took them and knelt down by the hatchling.

"There's nothing to be afraid of," he said coaxingly. "Just try this little bit. If you don't like it, we can try something else. We just have to see if this will work."

Virgil opened his mouth and let out a high-pitched, piercing shriek.

Rose reflexively covered her ears as the high pitch grew louder and louder. She saw most of the men in the room had done the same thing.

Virgil was very, very angry and offended! He would tell them that while he was breathing! Now he would scream again!

"No, please don't—" Rose began.

The unbearably high pitched scream started up again.

"Virgil," Henry said in distress, moving closer to the dragon. He put his hand on the nubs where his horns would be. "Virgil. It's all right. If you want me to feed you, I'll feed you."

The shriek stopped.

Virgil was sad. Virgil was angry. Not-parents couldn't give him food! Only parents could give him food!

"All right," Henry said anxiously. "All right. I'll even put it in my mouth if you want."

He took the bowl from the man who held it and plunged his fingers in, then hesitated for a long moment, his fingers hovering over the mashed crickets. He looked like he was trying to force himself to move.

No! Virgil didn't want that! That wasn't food! Virgil wanted the food his mother and father had already made for him! In their mouths!

"Uhhhhh ..." Henry said. "What?"

In their mouths! In their mouths, in their mouths, in their mouths! Virgil was hungry! Virgil was getting upset again!

"Oh, no!" a man across the room cried. His face had gone pale. "Crop milk! He's talking about crop milk. I don't know how we're going to replicate that!"

"Crop ... what?" Henry repeated. His arms were tight with tension. "What are you talking about? Dragons aren't mammals!"

"Neither are birds, and crop milk is a way some birds feed their young," the man explained. "I can't believe it never even occurred to us that ..."

"It occurred to me," Mr. Teedle said, running his hand through his well-oiled hair in agitation, "but I didn't think it would actually be a concern. There's a theory that dragons were the evolutionary ancestors of birds, but I've never put much stock in it, as the wyverns like *Pterodactylus antiquus* would make so much more sense as ancestors, being four-limbed just like birds are, whereas dragons are six-limbed, unlike any other living creature in the world today—"

"Excuse me," Henry broke in, his face turning red with anger. "Can we get back to my son? How do we feed him if we can't replicate the equivalent of mother's milk for him?"

Virgil was getting very hungry. Virgil was getting very tired. Maybe he would scream again.

Two men's hands flew to their ears.

"We feed him what we can," Rose said firmly.

She walked past the two men standing beside her, knotted the train of her dress around her waist, and knelt down on the floor by Virgil. Perhaps this would make her dress filthy, though she hoped she could avoid that, but right now, the baby mattered far more.

"Virgil," she said, "we don't have what you're asking for. I'm sorry. We'll have to try whatever we can. It might make you sick. But it's far better than not trying."

Virgil was confused. They'd agreed to be his parents. They should have started to make food then. Why hadn't they made him food? Didn't they love him?

Beside her, Rose saw Henry's fists clench.

The little dragon's tail twitched. He was starting to look lethargic. His eyelids drooped, and he let out a pitiful memory of hunger.

"Henry," Rose said, "open your hand."

"But he won't take—" Henry began.

Rose seized Henry's hand, scooped up a small handful of cricket mash, and slapped it in his palm. Then she put his other hand on top, connected at the wrists and open in front.

"Virgil," she said, "there's a mouth here. Eat the food in it."

Virgil's eyelids drooped. He raised his head and pushed at the hands with his nose. His snout somehow found his way into them. His tongue snaked out and licked the cricket mash.

Virgil's eyes flew open, and he jerked back. He let out a long, high-pitched scream.

Hands flew up to cover ears all over the room.

Virgil's mother had betrayed him! Virgil's mother had lied to him! That wasn't a mouth! That wasn't food! That was something! That was not-food! That was *something!*

"Yes," Rose said sternly, her hands in her lap. She made no move to cover her ears. "That was *something.* Something that might possibly work as food."

That was not-food! That was something! That was not-food! Virgil was very upset!

Henry bit his lip. He looked on the verge of tears.

"Yes, it was very unfortunate," Rose said coldly. "But it might also keep you alive."

Virgil was very upset! Virgil was very upset! Virgil was very, very, very *UPSET!*

Rose said nothing. If she let herself feel bad for him, she wouldn't have the firmness of will to force him to eat until they found something that he would partake of willingly.

"Perhaps it would help to buy lemon juice, and use that as a marinade," one of the professors said into the silence. "That can help break meat down. Make it easier to digest. He might need something like that, since presumably he's not supposed to be eating solid foods yet."

"Good idea," Mr. Teedle said. "We might also ask a butcher to save us intact stomachs. The juices in there might be helpful to break down food."

There seemed to be no question that they were all staying. Though Mr. Teedle did order one of the men to go to a butcher and buy cow, pig, lamb, turkey, and any other meat available that they did not already have on hand, as well as any intact stomachs that might be available.

"A whole bird, such as a chicken or turkey, if necessary," Mr. Teedle added.

The man nodded, then left.

Virgil's reproach had given way to his sleepiness, and he was dozing again.

And now we wait, Rose thought. *We wait to see if he survives this.*

Chapter 6
Handle

The crickets did not agree with Virgil. Fortunately, it turned out that dragons could vomit.

Unfortunately, the mess turned out to be so acidic that it was too dangerous to handle without thick gloves. For some inscrutable reason, Henry had attempted to clean it with only a small cloth, and the skin on his palms was now red and rashy, despite his having yelped and run to the sink to run his hands under the faucet for several minutes.

This is not a good beginning, Rose thought. *I hope his feces will not be as toxic.*

They had not yet had occasion to find out, and insightful as it would no doubt be about *Deinonychus* digestive processes, Rose was not looking forward to the necessities inherent in that particular discovery. After all, she and Henry would not be the ones collecting samples and running tests on them. They would be the ones cleaning the baby.

They skipped the rat altogether, and for Virgil's second meal, they tried well-cooked and finely chopped-up chicken.

"If dragons are related to birds, that's probably closer to the kind of meal his parents would have brought home," Mr. Teedle explained to everyone in the room.

Rose concurred.

To her intense relief, the chicken seemed to agree rather better with Virgil, even though he still complained about a tummyache afterwards. To Henry's obvious intense relief, the dragon did not vomit again.

Less than an hour later, the man who had been sent out returned, having visited a butcher's shop. He also carried a rather ugly, worn carpet bag, which he dropped on the floor beside Rose.

She looked at him questioningly.

"I raided my wife's closet," he said. "I presumed you wouldn't want to be wearing that dress for the rest of the day."

"Oh, thank you," Rose said, touched by his thoughtfulness. "Where is the best place for me to change?"

"There is a restroom down the hall," he said, pointing.

"Thank you," she said, picking up the carpet bag. Then she paused, remembering a complication. She hated to mention it in present company, but there were very few other options. "I'm afraid I can't undo all of the buttons on the back on my own. This dress wasn't designed for practicality."

Most of the men in the room looked hideously embarrassed. Henry held up his red, rashy hands, grimacing.

"I'll help," Mr. Teedle said briskly. "You're nearly my daughter's age. Turn around and tell me which ones you can't reach by yourself."

It was with relief that Rose was finally able to shuck the wedding dress off in the restroom several minutes later. She sorted through the carpet bag and found that Professor Anton's wife was, as she might have suspected if she'd thought about it, several sizes larger than she was. The woman was presumably her mother's age, after all, and he had mentioned that they had four children.

Still, she was able to make do, though the brown house dress he had selected for her was quite unflattering, and hung off her arms like a dangling sack.

Never mind, Rose told herself. *Nobody here will mind if your appearance is less than presentable.*

She sighed as she tucked the wedding dress away into the carpet bag, folding it carefully, though the yards of train did not fit and had to be piled over the top between the handles. It was quite a large carpet bag, but this was not a small dress.

The thought of going back to that laboratory, and facing the stress and newness and anxiety, was difficult to persuade herself to do. But she took a long breath, in and out, and then set forth back down the hallway.

"Thank goodness," Henry said as she walked in the door. "Virgil's awake. He wants you to feed him."

Rose breathed in deeply again, and then moved to the spot on the floor where the slime from the egg had still not been cleaned up. The thin layer coating Virgil had dried into a thin, flaky crustiness all over his scales.

We need to give him a bath, Rose thought. *Can we do that safely? Do dragons bathe?*

"Hello, Virgil," she said. She reached out hesitantly, then stroked the nubs at the top of his head where horns would grow in. It was an affectionate gesture she was fairly certain she'd seen in one of his parents' memories. "Do you want to eat the same thing your father gave you before?"

Virgil wanted to have food. Virgil wanted her to feed him by mouth.

"I know you do," Rose said. "But you'll be eating out of our hands, just as before."

Virgil was sullen. Virgil was pouting.

The querulous emotion that she associated with a toddler sticking out their lower lip pushed into Rose's mind. It was all she could do to keep from laughing at the incongruity. The little dragon showed no facial expressions, nor did he have lips, but apparently some things transcended biology.

"We're going to try something different this time," Rose said. "We're going to add some stomach juices, to see if that helps you digest better."

Virgil didn't understand what that meant. Virgil wanted her to feed him by mouth.

"I know," Rose said, "but we're doing what we can do."

Virgil struggled and griped, but at last accepted the chicken with ill grace. He nearly choked at one point, and she had a brief second of panic. Then he managed to swallow, and he let out a small moan of protest before nibbling another bite out of the tiny bits of chicken in her hands.

"We need to add more water," Henry said from behind her. "If he almost choked, that means it was too dry to swallow."

"We can add a little next time," Mr. Teedle said, "but so far he hasn't complained about being thirsty, and we don't want to overdo it. Too much water can be as bad as too little."

"He not be able to tell the difference between thirst and hunger yet," Henry challenged.

"True." Mr. Teedle looked troubled.

Virgil's eyelids drooped, and he stopped eating. He curled his tail around his body and nuzzled his head on top of it. In a moment, he was still, except for breathing.

Tentatively, Rose reached out and ran her finger along his back, hoping that it wouldn't bother him while he was sleeping. He didn't stir or even seem to notice, so she kept doing it.

The texture of his scales was slick yet soft, like snake skin. But unlike snake skin, the dragon scales seemed firmly in place, so there was no danger in rubbing against the grain, no matter what direction her finger moved in. She wondered how many dragon species had had scales like this, or if it had been a unique feature of *Deinonychus*.

She reached a part where the sticky, crusty egg slime was particularly thick, which reminded her of something she had been thinking about earlier.

"Can someone bring me a wet cloth?" Rose asked. "I'm going to clean him off."

Henry did so, and she carefully wiped the dragon's scales clean, at first very gently, and then harder and more firmly as she reached the places that held thicker layers of dried crustiness. It didn't appear to hurt Virgil; he continued to sleep soundly.

"He doesn't seem to be delicate," Henry said. "That's one thing we can be grateful for."

"But we should treat him very carefully, anyway," Rose said. "There might be areas that are unexpectedly vulnerable, like the soft spots on the heads of human babies."

Henry nodded, looking nervous.

Two hours later, they had the opportunity to deliver some insightful samples about *Deinonychus* digestive processes to an eager zoologist and two hovering biology professors. They also had the less-than-delightful opportunity to clean up the rest.

"He is going to be wearing diapers," Henry said.

Chapter 7
Haggard

After thirty-six hours, they had fallen into an exhausting rhythm. Every twenty minutes, Virgil woke up wanting to eat. He nibbled a few bites, complained again about how it wasn't the food he wanted, and then curled his tail around himself to go back to sleep.

The men left after just a few hours, Mr. Teedle promising to return in the morning. It was only after they'd left that Rose realized she hadn't eaten anything since breakfast. She nibbled a few scorched bites of the chicken, too dry and charred to offer to the infant, and offered some to Henry, too. They munched quietly until Virgil woke up again.

There seemed to be no question about going to their new apartment tonight. Trying to contact their families wasn't mentioned, either. All that mattered right now was feeding Virgil.

As night drew near, Rose yawned. She usually kept herself on a strict schedule, and her body was informing her that it was bedtime. The day had been emotionally wearying, which didn't help matters. She still felt inadequate, though Virgil's complaints had grown less vehement, and he seemed reasonably healthy.

Henry noticed her yawn. "I'll feed him for the next four hours. I'm used to staying up late to finish homework at the last minute. You go get some sleep."

Rose nodded, grateful. She picked up the carpet bag and moved to the furthest corner from the egg, where Virgil's telepathic cries would not awaken her. She settled down on the hard floor, using the bulging carpet bag as a pillow and the dress's train as a makeshift blanket across her feet.

All too soon, Henry awakened her.

"It's your turn," he said. His eyes were bloodshot, and he rubbed his neck as if it was sore.

Rose nodded, reluctantly, and stood up. She walked over to the side of the room with the egg, and found that there was no more food prepared. She sighed and started shredding chicken into the smallest pieces she could manage.

Glancing back, she saw that Henry was using the carpet bag and the dress much as she had. She tried not to be annoyed by his use of the wedding dress. It was one thing when she did it, but ...

There are more important things to worry about right now, Rose told herself firmly.

The next few hours were agonizing. It was all she could do to stay awake while feeding Virgil. She started to doze in small spurts in between his awakenings. After four hours, she stumbled over to wake Henry, but he kept on sleeping soundly. In furious misery, she stormed back to her duty.

After seven full hours, Henry finally yawned and sat up. He glanced at his watch blearily. "You should've woken me up three hours ago," he mumbled.

"I tried," Rose snapped. "You kept sleeping."

"Oh. I'm a sound sleeper. Sorry. I've missed some morning classes that way. Just pour cold water over me or something."

"Don't tell me that," Rose said irritably. "I actually will."

"Feel free," Henry shrugged. "My father used to do that to wake me up for school. One of my roommates put ice in bed with me once when he knew I had to get up for a test."

Rose was beginning to infer a major disadvantage to living with Henry.

The tiny dragon stirred. Virgil was hungry! Virgil wanted food!

Rose groaned audibly.

"Is that him again?" Henry asked, pushing the dress's train off his legs. "I'll take care of it. You go back to sleep."

Rose should have been grateful, but she just felt grumpy. She stormed back to the corner, relieved when she passed beyond the range of Virgil's complaints. As soon as her head hit the carpet bag, she fell back asleep.

An hour later, the door squeaked open, which woke her up again. Mr. Teedle stood there, putting away his key.

"How are you doing?" he asked. "It occurred to me you probably haven't had anything to eat. I brought breakfast."

Rose peered around to the side, and saw that he was holding a basket of muffins. Her mouth watered, and she stumbled up to her feet.

"Thanks," Henry said, walking over to help himself. "We ate some of the burnt parts of the chicken, but that was it."

Rose took two muffins to assuage the hollow feeling in her stomach. She polished them off rapidly.

"How's he doing?" Mr. Teedle asked, nodding towards the sleeping dragon.

"Fine," Henry said, "I think."

Rose helped herself to another muffin. There were apple chunks in it which had not been cooked sufficiently, so they were rather chewy instead of soft, but that didn't matter. She chewed and swallowed rapidly.

Mr. Teedle hesitated. "You know," he said, "the offer still stands. The Central Park Zoo would be happy to take care of him. It would be close to the museum, and within reasonable walking distance of your home, so you could visit him frequently, just as you have here—"

"No," Henry said shortly.

"He won't take food from anyone but us," Rose reminded him.

"True," Mr. Teedle said, "but there's no reason to assume he couldn't be trained—"

"No!" Henry said vehemently. "I will not relinquish his care to strangers! He is *ours* to take care of!"

Mr. Teedle looked like he would very much like to disagree.

"Mr. Teedle," Rose said quietly, "we appreciate all you have done for us, and we'll continue to appreciate whatever help we can receive. But Henry does not think it would be best for Virgil to be separated from us."

She didn't add that she would personally have loved to take him and the zoo up on that offer. She was tired and worn out, and did not know how they were going to manage their classes tomorrow morning. It was just as well Virgil had hatched on a Saturday.

But Henry's feelings were important, and he wasn't wrong about it. If they allowed Virgil to be taken in by strangers now, they would never truly be allowed to raise him. There were too many other people who'd consider themselves more qualified, too many other people who would have high motivations to wean him away from the parents he had chosen. Too many other people who would be more interested in his development as a research subject than as a child.

And that was not what Virgil needed.

Mr. Teedle sighed. "Well, in either case, we'll have to bring a journalist and photographer here later today. Will you be ready for that?"

Henry looked down at the rumpled grey suit he had worn to the wedding. He had long since removed the bow tie, and the front of the ruffled shirt was stained.

"I would like a change of clothing," he said wryly.

"As would I," Rose added. "Something from my own wardrobe, if possible."

"I can fetch clothes for you if you give me the key to your apartment," Mr. Teedle said.

Henry nodded and fumbled through his pockets. He pulled out his key and handed it over.

Rose realized with a start that she still did not have her own. She had moved most of her things to the apartment, but it had always been when Henry was home, and always when her mother or one of her roommates had been beside her, helping carry bags and acting as chaperone. Now that place would be her home, and she did not have a key.

She wondered what else they'd find they had forgotten.

"I'll fetch you something appropriate for photographs," Mr. Teedle promised. "Have you any preferences?"

"Something clean," Henry said.

"My crimson dress with the high collar and the long sleeves," Rose said. "Also fresh stockings. And my black shoes."

She was still wearing the white high heels that had been made for her mother's dress, and white was inappropriate to wear outside of weddings after Labor Day.

"Understood," Mr. Teedle said. "Would you like anything else to eat for lunch?"

"Yes," Henry said. "I want eggs. Hard-boiled eggs."

"Eggs might be a good idea," Mr. Teedle said thoughtfully. "There's every chance that he might respond well to them, too." He nodded at the dragon. "We can try to add some to his diet tomorrow."

Rose looked over at Virgil, who was still sleeping. The tip of his tail was tucked underneath him, and the large, curved claw on each of his back toes was resting against the floor.

"When can we take him home?" she wondered.

"Tomorrow morning," Mr. Teedle said. "Or tonight, if you can sneak him across the city and up to your apartment without anyone seeing. We don't want rumors spreading before the papers come out, but if you can manage that, it might be better."

And when can we tell our families? Rose wondered.

If they failed to tell their families personally, it would likely cause hurt feelings. If they spoke too soon, it would risk rumors spreading early.

"Do me a favor," Henry spoke up. "Call my family and tell them to watch for the paper tomorrow. Then they'll know why I had to leave the wedding early."

Or that's another way to handle it, Rose thought.

"Do the same for mine," she said.

Even though she suspected her mother would not be pleased at such a third-hand relaying of information.

Chapter 8
Haze

Voices were speaking on the other side of the door. Rose heard them through her tired midafternoon haze. She wished she had been able to snatch more than six hours of sleep; she did not feel she was operating at peak efficiency.

The doorknob rattled as it was unlocked, and Mr. Teedle appeared, as well as both of the paleontologists and three of the professors who had been here yesterday. Following after them were two men that Rose didn't recognize. The journalist and the photographer, presumably.

She rose. "Good afternoon, gentlemen." She had taken a seat to alleviate the ache in her feet, but she had every desire to make a good impression on them. "I'm Rose Palmer. This is Henry Wainscott."

"Mr. and Mrs. Wainscott," Henry said, walking forward to shake the strangers' hands. "You must forgive her for forgetting. We were only married yesterday."

Allow me to speak for myself! Rose thought with irritation. But it was true she had forgotten.

"Where is this thing you mentioned?" one of the men asked, craning his neck. "The dragon?"

"This way," Mr. Teedle said, guiding them around a table.

Rose watched silently, her heart pounding.

Virgil was lying on the floor, fast asleep. His snout wiggled as if he was dreaming about eating, and his tail twitched.

The two new men stared at the dragon. One of them opened the large, boxy camera he held, his hands trembling.

"This is a hoax, right?" the other man asked skeptically.

Mr. Teedle drew himself up to his full height, which was not very tall. "Young man," he said stiffly, "I am the curator of the Dragon Collection of the American Museum of Natural History. I do not perpetuate hoaxes. This is a real, live, bona fide *Deinonychus antirrhopus* dragon, hatched from an egg that we had in our possession. We do not understand the mechanism by which this egg was still alive after millions of years—it defies our current comprehension. But alive it most assuredly is."

The cameraman pressed the bulb to take his first picture. He looked very excited.

Virgil stirred and opened his eyes. He stared up at the strange men all around him, looking confused.

He wanted food. Where were his parents? He wanted food again. He was hungry. Who were all these strange minds around him?

The journalist man jumped back. "It talks!" he shouted.

"'It' is a he," Henry said waspishly. "And he's a person, just like we are. Don't you know anything about *Deinonychus* dragons?"

Do YOU know anything about Deinonychus *dragons?* Rose wanted to challenge him. As far as she was aware, Henry had had no clue that there were theories the species had been intelligent, until Virgil had awoken.

The little dragon's wings flapped slightly. His curved back claws scraped the floor.

Virgil was hungry! Virgil was getting very upset!

"Sorry, sorry," Henry said quickly, kneeling down with the bowl. "Here. Have some food."

Virgil poked his snout in Henry's hands and took a few small munching bites. Then he pulled back warily and eyed the camera, which was being readied to take a second picture. The cameraman scrambled to take it while the dragon was facing him.

Virgil didn't understand why the stranger was staring at him. Virgil didn't know what the box was. Why did the stranger think it was looking at him? The box was scary. It didn't have a mind.

"It's all right, it's all right," Henry soothed. "It's a camera. It's like a rock. It's not supposed to have a mind."

Virgil didn't like that the stranger thought it was looking at him. Virgil didn't like the stranger. Virgil wanted him to go away.

"Errr ..." Henry said awkwardly, looking up. "Sorry, but ... would you mind ...?"

The cameraman was already moving backwards, an abashed look on his face.

"This is incredible," the journalist said. His eyebrows furrowed. "In the sense that I don't believe it. How do you make it do that?"

"I don't 'make' it do anything," Mr. Teedle said impatiently. "It is a living creature, which communicates what it thinks when it wishes."

"And 'it' is *he*," Henry added sharply. "He's a child, not a creature, and my wife and I have adopted him."

The journalist seemed very interested in this angle of the story. He began asking Henry questions and completely ignoring Rose. This irked her, so she moved over to where Henry was sitting and began to answer some of the questions herself.

"Yes, he could communicate while still in the egg," she broke in, as the journalist asked a question which she was perfectly qualified to answer. "As you can tell, his method of speaking is telepathic. That is fortunate, because it is doubtful that he could pronounce most of the sounds humans use to speak."

"'Couldn't pronounce sounds humans use to speak,'" the journalist murmured, scribbling that down in his notepad. He looked back up at Henry. "And what else can you tell me about the creature?"

Henry's eyebrows furrowed. "Well, for one thing, he's not a creature. He's a person. *Deinonychus* dragons are as intelligent as humans."

"'Very intelligent animal,'" the journalist murmured, scribbling in his notepad. "Very good, very good. What else can you tell me?"

Henry looked like he wanted to hit the man.

Assuming that would not be a wise idea, Rose said quickly, "Mr. Wainscott is a student at City College. He's studying biology. I am a student at Hunter College, studying paleontology."

"'Biology and paleontology,'" the journalist murmured, scribbling. "What's paleontology again?"

"The study of fossilized animals and plants," Rose said.

"The study of dragons," Henry said at the same time.

"Ah." The journalist's confused expression cleared. "That must come in handy here." He indicated Virgil, who had finished eating and settled back to sleep with his tail curled around his feet.

"Yes," Henry said.

"Paleontologists don't just study dragons," Rose said. "They also study plants, wyverns, prehistoric mammals—"

The journalist did not write any of this down.

Soon enough, the man moved on to interview Mr. Teedle and the other experts in the room, and the photographer crept closer.

"Do you think it would allow me to take pictures again?" he asked hopefully.

"*He*," Henry said. "And I imagine he won't notice. Please do."

The man looked relieved, and set his camera up again. He took a dozen pictures of Virgil from different angles, and then took several with the three of them together.

After that, Virgil woke up again, and this time Rose fed him. The journalist drew Henry aside to ask him more questions.

Does that man think I am not capable of speaking, or something? Rose thought with irritation.

Virgil's snout moved through her hands, licking up tiny pieces of chicken that had been moistened with water. His tongue was surprisingly dry. She wondered if that was normal, or if it was because he wasn't getting enough to drink.

Virgil raised his head up from her hands. His eyes blinked blearily, and one of his front claws scratched the floor beneath him. He looked sleepy, but curious.

His mother was annoyed. Why was his mother annoyed?

"Many reasons," Rose said, "but none have to do with you."

Virgil was sleepy. Virgil was going to take a nap.

"Please do," Rose said.

When the journalist and photographer finally left, it was quite a relief.

IN THE MORNING, Rose and Henry and an escort of three professors tucked Virgil into a large picnic basket and walked across campus to their new apartment. They had to stop twice for Henry to feed him, which he did by putting his hand into the picnic basket to avoid the swarm of onlookers that would no doubt gather if the dragon emerged. The professors left, and Henry slumped onto the couch, holding his eyes.

"I just want to sleep," he mumbled. "I wonder how many days I can skip class before it affects my GPA ..."

"I'll be going to class," Rose said.

Henry took his hand off his eyes. "When? Obviously not today."

"Of course today. It's Monday."

Henry gave her an incredulous look. "You want to go *today?*"

"Yes. I have class today. School matters to me. I've told you that before."

"Our son *just hatched*," Henry said. "Take a few days off."

"I will be leaving in an hour, and I'll be back at four pm," Rose said. "If you prefer, I will take Virgil with me."

"You're not going to take him away from me!" Henry exploded. "And you're not going to leave me alone for eight hours, either!"

"I don't ... skip ... class," Rose said coldly. "What did you think was going to happen? Did you think I was going to drop out? Is that why you got an apartment that is so near to your college and so far from mine?"

Henry appeared to be struggling with rage. "All right," he said. "Then go. Go to class!"

"I don't have to leave for another hour," Rose began.

"Just go!" Henry shouted.

So she left.

Chapter 9
Her

It was very difficult to concentrate in her current state of exhaustion, so she took copious notes and hoped that those would compensate for her damaged attention.

After class, she started to walk back to her new apartment, and then veered off to the left through Central Park instead. She had no desire to go home right now, not after the altercation with Henry.

If she was honest with herself, she had no desire to see Virgil right now, either. The child had drained her to her last shreds of patience, and she felt like she had no more to give.

So she walked to the American Museum of Natural History, more out of habit than anything. She walked through the Hall of Ornithischian Dragons, where she had not been in weeks, admiring the *Stegosaurus* on display with its wings outstretched and the *Corythosaurus* behind glass with its wings folded.

When she reached the end, she hesitated. Hadn't she had enough of carnivorous dragons over the last few days? But it felt disloyal to not walk through the Hall of Saurischian Dragons while she was here. So she walked briskly through, intending to finish and go back home as swiftly as possible.

The *Deinonychus* eggs exhibit was the same as always, except that there were far more people surrounding it than usual.

Of course, Rose thought. *Because the newspaper will have come out by now. I really ought to look at it when I have the chance.*

She started to walk by the crowd, but then a familiar sensation hit her. The brush of a dragon's mind.

Hello! Her name was Violet! Her new father had named her! Had they met her new father yet?

Rose stopped abruptly. Her pulse quickened. Another dragon had woken up. Another dragon had woken up—

—*now*, of all times?

She shoved through the crowd, making liberal use of elbows, to the annoyance and dirty looks of those she pushed through. Rose paid that no heed. Near the front of the crowd, standing close to the display, was a filthy man with unkempt hair. He looked and smelled like a hobo.

No, Rose thought. *Surely not him.*

Violet hadn't wanted to wake up. Violet had been very sad. Violet's parents had died, along with everyone else she had known.

Rose gasped as a horrifying memory washed over her mind.

There had been a giant shaking feeling. Then all the minds around her screaming, and then silence. She screamed herself, as far as she could possibly reach, and yet nobody came to save her. She was going to die.

Some adults found her. She was carried to the orphan cave. There were hundreds of other minds there, minds like hers, minds that were young, minds that were still eggs. They were all screaming for their parents. Everyone was dead. Everyone was dead. Everyone was dead. There were hundreds of them. There were thousands. More kept coming.

There were very few adults left. All they did was bring more eggs. They didn't come to adopt any of them.

That wasn't right! That was wrong!

She seized on two of the adults when they came near her, and they said no. They were very, very sad. They said the world was wrong. They said there was no food now. They said they would come back when the world got better. They said all they could do now was save any eggs they could find.

She didn't understand. She needed parents!

She needed to not hatch right now, they said. She needed to

hibernate. The babies who were hatching were dying. The eggs could only live as long as they stayed eggs, as long as they did not hatch, as long as they did not leave.

She screamed and screamed, but no one answered her. There were fewer and fewer adults. Soon, there were no adult minds at all. Only the other eggs. Only the eggs all crying.

The other eggs all started to fall asleep. She struggled to stay awake. She wanted parents. She wanted to hatch now. She wanted parents. Where were the parents?

At last, the emptiness overwhelmed her, and she too fell asleep.

Rose came back to herself. She burst out sobbing, as did others around her. The loneliness had been so absolute, the dragon's memory so desolate.

Was she alive for the extinction event? Rose thought. She tried to clean her face with her gloved hands, but more tears kept on coming. *Is that what that was? Is that what she experienced?*

Violet's father had been through awful things, too. She would show them.

The crowd burst outward, as if everyone in it was desperate to escape. For those in the front, including Rose, there was no time to get out of range.

Horrible visions exploded through her mind. There were diseases and gunshots and screaming and dying. All of his friends were killed in one day. It was so senseless, so stupid. It was the apocalypse.

Rose came back to herself, too stunned to even cry. She'd never seen anything like that. She hoped she never would again.

"That's enough of that, Violet," the hobo growled. "My memories are my own."

Rose stood where she was, too devastated to move. She had heard rumors about the Great War in Europe, had even known two neighbors' sons who had been drafted and died out there. But she had never dreamed that she would be forced to experience any of it.

Most of the other onlookers were fleeing. One mother was trying to comfort several sobbing children. One man looked like he was going to be sick.

Violet didn't understand why all the minds were leaving. Violet was sad. What had she done to make them so unhappy?

Rose breathed in and out, deeply. This wasn't what she had intended when she'd asked the other dragons to hatch. She turned to walk away.

Oh! Violet remembered her! This was the adult who had told her to hatch! This was the grown-up who had said it was time to choose parents! That was why Violet had woken up! She was so happy!

Rose turned around slowly. The filthy man was staring at her.

"You were in the paper, weren't you?" he said slowly. "You and that man. The ones with the dragon."

There seemed no point in denying it. "Yes," Rose admitted.

The man walked over and clapped his hand on her shoulder. It was all she could do to keep from flinching. "Thank you for doing that article," he said. "Gave me the gumption to come here and talk to 'em. And now I've got Violet. Ain't she a gem?"

This close, his breath reeked.

Are you aware that alcohol is illegal? Rose thought. *And you can't possibly be married. What will Violet do for a mother?*

Oh, Violet didn't need a mother! Violet was perfectly fine with just her father! Violet was so happy she had found someone who understood what she had gone through!

"Yes, you *do* need a mother!" Rose snapped out loud. "Do you have any idea how much work it takes to keep a baby dragon alive? I do! One person cannot possibly do it alone! It's not physically possible!"

The filthy man withdrew his hand, looking confused.

Violet didn't like her anymore! She didn't like Violet's father! Violet was going to take a nap.

The hobo gave Rose and angry, suspicious look. "What did she mean, you don't like me?"

Rose cringed. It was embarrassing to have been caught out.

"It's not that I don't like you," she said hastily. "It's just that ... after all we've been through to keep Virgil alive these past few days, I don't see how one parent can do it alone. I simply don't."

"Oh." The man's expression cleared. "That's simple enough. The museum director came to talk to me this morning, after Violet first woke up. Nice man. He's arranged for her to be transferred to Central Park Zoo, where they'll pay for the food and take good care of her. Good for everyone, eh?"

Rose stared at him. She knew all the practical reasons why the zoo would work, but faced with a parent who had actually chosen that path, she was speechless.

"Name's Harrison," the man said, holding out his hand. "Pleased to meet you."

"Pleased to meet you," Rose murmured, shaking his hand gingerly. She was grateful to be wearing gloves, and hoped to wash them as soon as she got back home.

Home. Where Henry and Virgil were waiting.

"I must go," Rose said quickly, extricating herself. "My husband and son are expecting me. I didn't mean to stay here so long."

Husband and son. The words sounded strange as she spoke them, even as she knew they were true. Her life had changed so drastically overnight, it still astonished her.

"Go on, then," the man said cheerfully. "Maybe we can have our babies play together later. Eh?"

Maybe if you bathe yourself and don't drink your entire breakfast at a speakeasy! Rose thought.

"Perhaps," she said politely.

As she walked rapidly home, attempting to make up for lost time despite her exhaustion, her mind kept spinning around the filthy man and the new dragon. He seemed so clearly unsuitable to be a parent, and yet he had been chosen. Chosen and loved, despite all his obvious deficiencies.

Perhaps, Rose thought, *perhaps I am not so inadequate to the task as I have worried.*

Chapter 10
Henry

Henry was asleep on the couch when she walked in. His hand was dangled on the floor next to Virgil's head, and it was filled with a large clump of watery, shredded chicken. Some had dripped on the floor and scattered along the carpet.

That seems a fairly good solution, Rose thought, setting aside the shoulder bag she had used to carry her notes and writing implements. *Has Virgil been helping himself while Henry sleeps?*

As if on cue, the little dragon stirred. His front claws dug into the carpet, and he raised his head, his eyes wide open.

Virgil wanted food now. Virgil wanted his father to wake up so that he could eat. Virgil wanted his father to wake up so that he could eat. Virgil wanted his father to wake up so that he could eat. Virgil wanted his father to wake up so that he could eat.

Henry groaned and stirred. He sat up, his eyes still shut, and held out his hand. Their son's scaly head darted forward.

Apparently he has not been able to sleep while Virgil helped himself, Rose thought. *A pity.*

The hatchling's head jerked away from the food.

Virgil's mother was home! He hadn't noticed! Could she feed him, too?

"Oh, are you home?" Henry murmured. His eyelids cracked open. "Good. Does that mean I can sleep?"

"Go ahead," Rose said, though her eyes ached and her legs felt leaden. "I'll feed him for awhile. Is there anything prepared?"

"Bowl in the kitchen," Henry muttered, staggering to his feet. "Your parents called. Read the newspaper."

"What did they say?" Rose asked, her heart hammering.

Virgil was still hungry! The food was gone! Virgil wanted his food! Virgil's mother needed to give him food!

Henry rubbed his eyes, then stopped and stared down at the hand covered in chicken, which he had just smeared all over his face and dropped down the front of his shirt. He muttered something unintelligible that was likely profane.

"Language," Rose said, just in case.

Henry looked grumpy. "Your mother said they wanted to meet the dragon. Your father said, 'Is this real?' One of your sisters, I'm not sure which, said, 'Trust Rose to find a live dragon!' Then the other said, 'Can we get one?' — "

"He's not a pet," Rose said peevishly.

"I'm aware," Henry began.

Virgil was very, very, very hungry! Virgil's parents needed to feed him! He was going to scream!

Rose yanked off her gloves and lunged for the chicken still on Henry's hand. She got her hand down to the floor just as the earsplitting screech began. She waved her hand up and down frantically until the little dragon noticed.

Virgil thought that was better. Virgil was going to eat now.

A rough, dry tongue began to gather up bits of watery chicken from her hand, the little dragon emanating indignation.

"What else did they say?" Rose asked.

"Not much," Henry said, shrugging. "I told them you went to class. Your mother didn't believe it at first. Your sisters thought it was hilarious. Your father said, 'Why am I not surprised?'"

Rose took a little pride in that.

"Speaking of which," Henry said, "we need to come up with something to make our schedules compatible. We really do."

Rose swallowed. She hadn't forgotten how angry Henry had been this morning, and she supposed he hadn't, either.

"I'm sorry," she said. "I should have thought to mention it before, but with all that happened so quickly — "

"No," Henry said, his jaw twitching. "Don't apologize. I'll just get mad all over again. I'm tired and I'm not thinking straight. Just ... we need to think of something. That's all. I'm not going to quit school, either. You understand?"

Rose nodded vehemently. She would never want a husband who hadn't finished his education.

"I only have one class on Tuesdays and Thursdays," she said. "It's still early in the semester. I imagine I can drop it, or attempt to find another time it's held between the classes I have the other three days."

"That's a start," Henry said. He yawned widely. "Got to sleep now. Good night."

"Good night," Rose said, though it was midafternoon.

He staggered off to the bedroom, leaving her alone with the dragon. Their son, the dragon.

"Hey, Virgil?" Rose said quietly. "Thank you for choosing us."

A scaly face with yellow eyes looked up at her.

Virgil was glad he'd chosen them, too. Even though they looked strange. And they didn't feed him real food.

Rose hesitated, because she wasn't prone to bursts of affection, and then leaned forward and kissed the top of the tiny dragon's head.

Virgil paused in his eating. Why had his mother done that? There was no food on his head.

"It's a way that humans show affection," Rose said. "I'm getting used to you."

That was good. Virgil was used to her, too. Where was more food? He had finished. Where was more food?

Rose got up and went to the kitchen, where she found the bowl Henry had mentioned. She scooped some of the contents into her hand and walked back to the living room, where the dragon was digging into the carpet with his curved back claws.

"You're destroying the carpet," Rose said. "Please stop."

Virgil was hungry. Virgil didn't know what a carpet was. Where was Virgil's food?

She bent down and gave it to him. While the dragon was eating, she checked the thick cloth they had wrapped around his nether regions. It was, unfortunately, sopping wet.

Once he was asleep, she got up and walked to the kitchen, where she found a replacement small towel in a bottom drawer. Then she clumsily undid the safety pins and wrapped the new towel around his bottom and the top part of his tail. She carefully fastened the safety pins back again.

Rose breathed out a sigh of relief.

I can do this.

She stood up and took the disgusting, soaked towel to the kitchen, where she proceeded to wash it with soap in the sink. Then she wrung it out and hung it to dry over the top of a lower cabinet door.

She walked back to the living room, where Virgil lay curled up with his tail around him. His snout wriggled as his curved back claws attacked the carpet.

I can do this, Rose thought.

She sat down, intending to start on her homework, and then Virgil raised his head and looked at her.

He was hungry. Where was his food? He was hungry.

I hope I can do this, Rose thought with a sigh, returning to the kitchen to get him more chicken.

Chapter 11
Hello

"Look at that little tail!" Rose's mother exclaimed. "It's so long and thin and scaly! Does he use it for balance? It seems to be so flexible. Oh, that dragon is so sweet!"

Virgil wriggled and squirmed in a circle, trying to catch sight of it. His legs couldn't support his weight, so all he could do was scoot around and leave claw marks in the carpet.

Why was this person so excited about his tail? What was so special about his tail? He wanted to see.

Rose's father let out a snort that sounded like an attempt to disguise laughter.

"Why does he have those things?" Louise demanded, pointing at the long, curved claw that defied the length of all the others on each of his back feet. "You should trim them. They look dangerous."

"I'm not going to trim them; that's normal for his species," Rose said. "*Deinonychus* means 'terrible claw.' That's where the name came from."

"I want a pet dragon," Sara sighed wistfully.

"He's *not* a *pet*," Henry growled.

"But there were lots of other dragon species, too, right?" Louise asked excitedly. "What if somebody found live eggs from them? Then there could be such a thing as a dragon pet!"

Rose was highly disturbed at the idea. It was one thing to find that one species had survived, especially an intelligent one. But a dozen other dragon species ...? The ecological niches those species had filled were now taken, and the world did not need invasive species to threaten the ones that were now living.

Although perhaps, Rose thought, a little shaken as she followed her own line of reasoning, *perhaps humans have filled the role that* Deinonychus *once held. Perhaps, by encouraging them to live and grow and procreate and eventually restore the species, we may be encouraging our own extinction?*

The thought was chilling. She shivered.

Please hatch, she had asked the other eggs, and one of them had awoken. Surely the others would soon be forthcoming. What if New York City, in a few generations, would be overrun by terrible claws who wished to wipe out humanity?

She stepped on the thought firmly. So there was danger. What of it? There was hope, as well. If it came down to it, their species could learn to coexist. Nature was vicious and cruel, but people need not be.

For now, and for the future, she would focus on hope. Hope for her son's future. Hope for the future of *Deinonychus.*

"You know, when my wife told me she thought there might be a child in the picture," Rose's father broke in, "this wasn't exactly what I envisioned."

Rose's mother gave him a furious look. It was clear that this had not been a conversation she had wished repeated.

I knew it, Rose thought, her fists tightening. *I knew that was what our relations had to be thinking. I certainly hope we can disabuse them of that notion swiftly. Without, of course, mentioning the subject directly.*

There were some things that one just didn't do. Unless one was Rose's father, apparently.

Henry's face turned red. It didn't look like he had considered the possibility of rumors at all. "S-sir," he sputtered, "I assure you ..."

Rose's father watched him squirm with evident amusement.

"Is he healthy?" Rose's mother broke in, rubbing the top of the dragon's head. "Is he eating well?"

Rose smiled at the concern in her mother's voice. It sounded like her mother had accepted Virgil as family. "He seems to be all right, so far. We've added chicken fat and egg yolks to the chicken mixture, and that seems to be beneficial. He's now sleeping an hour between feedings, rather than fifteen minutes."

A trend she profoundly hoped would continue. Since tomorrow would be her first day alone with Virgil, now that she had changed her schedule, she very much wanted the time to do her homework.

Virgil's stomach hurt. Virgil was uncomfortable.

"Uh oh," Henry said, diving to the floor. "You might, uh ... want to leave now. I expect we're going to have to clean up a mess."

Virgil's stomach hurt now!

"Understood," Rose's mother said hastily. "We'll leave you to it. Virgil, it was nice to meet you and say hello."

Virgil's stomach hurt! Hurt, hurt, hurt!

Rose's mother rushed to the door, her father following at a rapid pace. Rose's sisters hovered in the doorway curiously to watch as Henry gathered up the baby.

"Thank you for visiting," Rose hinted strongly. "It's a shame you have to leave now."

"Louise! Sara!" their father barked from all the way down the hallway.

Looking reluctant, her sisters turned away.

"I want a pet *Brontosaurus*," Sara said to Louise. "Those have the best wings."

"It's *Apatosaurus*," Rose shouted after them, "and no, you don't!"

Do they have any idea how large that dragon used to be? Rose thought with exasperation, locking the door firmly after her family.

She found Henry in the bathroom, where he had placed their son in the bathtub. The hatchling seemed less than thrilled about this.

Virgil was sleepy. Maybe Virgil would take a nap. He needed to get out of this box now.

"Oh, no, you don't," Henry said.

Virgil didn't like this box! It was white and cold and there was nothing to claw!

"How very unfortunate," Henry snorted.

Virgil liked that noise. He was going to snort, too. Snort, snort, snort, snort—

A roar of flame burst from his nostrils and reached the towel on the rack across from him.

Henry's mouth fell open.

Rose leapt forward, seized the towel, and dunked it in the toilet, which doused it. She pulled it out, dripping. A huge black hole was now eaten in the once-serviceable object.

Virgil's stomach felt better now.

"Well," Rose said after a moment of silence, "at least we know when *Deinonychus* dragons start breathing fire. That's been a mystery for centuries."

"This is going to be so much worse than potty training," Henry groaned.

Author Note:

There are six books in the Dragon Eggs *series. I decided to include the first and second in this collection because I think they form a good arc.*

The funny thing about the Dragon Eggs *series is that it's technically historical hard science fiction, because everything about the worldbuilding can be explained in terms of science, and it's all been exhaustively researched ... but try saying that to people! It has dragons and a historical setting, therefore it's fantasy!*

One of those examples of where genre lines are very hard to define.

DRAGON'S YOWL

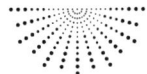

Henry awoke to a telepathic yowl.

He rolled over and looked down to see their dragon son, the culprit, lying on the floor beside their bed and emanating piteousness. He had apparently escaped the bathroom, where he was supposed to sleep.

Virgil had had a bad dream! He wanted to sleep with his father and mother tonight!

Henry's wife muttered, "No. The bed is flammable. You know that. Go back to your bathtub, Virgil."

But Virgil was lonely! Virgil was sad! Virgil had had a bad dream!

And that was how Henry ended up sleeping in the bathtub that night.

AUTHOR NOTE:
This is the only thing in the Dragon Eggs *world I wrote from Henry's point of view, rather than Rose's. I should have given him a point of view thread. He deserves it.*

ONE MIDSUMMER'S NIGHT

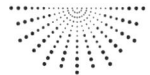

One midsummer's night
    With a moon you could see,
        The wild fairies came
            To take something from me.

They offered me beauty.
    I said, "I don't need it."
        They offered me wisdom.
            I said, "I won't cede it."

They offered me power.
    I said, "Don't need ranks."
        They offered me humor.
            I said, "Nah, no thanks."

They offered me friendship.
    I said, "Are you crazy?"
        They offered me money.
            I said, "That's just lazy."

They offered me magic.
    I said, "Still no way."
        They offered a pet dragon.
            Hmm ...

AUTHOR NOTE:
When I write a story as a poem, it's because the form adds something to it.

In this case, it's part of the humor.

THE RISE OF STARLIGHT

"And the winner of the Magical Girl Team of the Year Award is ..."

Girls all over the auditorium took deep breaths. Some jerked out of their poses, even though they weren't supposed to. The audience sitting in front of the stage had their attention fixed on the man with the man with short hair wearing a business shirt and tie. All eyes in the immense hall were fixed on the announcer.

"Oh, please, please, please, please ...," a girl in a team pose was whispering.

"... Victory's Bloom!" the man shouted.

"YES!" screamed the girl in the pose. She leapt down from their team pose on top of three boxes and flung her arms in the air, jumping up and down. "YES, YES, YES!"

"Now, let us introduce our three special winners to you!" the announcer cried. "Victory's Bloom, come forward!"

The three girls of that team ran up to the stage. One was a girl with pigtails in a dark magenta cute-and-funky outfit, one had short dirty blonde hair and a green dress that was trying too hard to look cute, and the third had long blonde hair and wore a elegant grey and blue dress with a skirt that looked like tulip petals.

"Let's introduce them one at a time!" the announcer called, walking over to the girls as they reached the top of the stage. The girl in green was slightly pudgy and still panting for breath after running up the six stairs to get up to the stage. Naturally, he chose her first. "There's Geranium, the avatar of courage, with the magical power of sound!"

The girl panted and looked back and forth, seeming panicked. Noticing the audience focused on her, her cheeks glowed pink and she gave an awkward and jerky wave.

"Demonstrate your power for us," the announcer urged.

The girl's face flushed deeply, but she took a deep breath and sang into the man's microphone. The note was clear and in perfect pitch, and it shot a targeted shockwave across the room.

"Wonderful!" the announcer praised. "Such a versatile power!"

The audience applauded.

The announcer moved on to the next girl, the one in the elegant grey and blue dress. She was slender and expressionless. "There's Primrose, the avatar of hope, with the magical power of illusion!"

Without prompting, Primrose raised a baton and waved it around herself. Her costume changed color.

"Ooooh ..." several people in the audience said.

"And that brings us to the final member!" the announcer called, drawing out his words for effect. "Best of all ..."

Excitedly, Geranium patted her hands in the air, creating a drum-roll effect.

"The leader of the team ..."

Expressionlessly, Primrose twirled her baton and created sparkles to surround their team leader.

"Mistletoe, the avatar of love, with the magical powers of clairvoyance, healing, singing, farseeing, telepathy, shapeshifting, teleportation, and of course her Valentine Finishing Blow!"

The audience gasped, and there was an excited babble across the room.

"That's an amazing assortment!" the announcer said into his microphone. "I'm sure we're all curious about your original power!"

"Clairvoyance!" Mistletoe said happily.

"Amazing!" the man said. "How strong are those powers?"

Mistletoe giggled. "Pretty powerful, I guess. Do you want to see all of them?"

"Yes!" the audience shouted.

"We can't hear you!" the announcer called into his microphone.

"YES!!" the audience roared.

Mistletoe grinned and waved her hand. A heart-shaped ring with diamonds and ribbons affixed appeared in it. It was evident that her focus item had developed frills of justice several times.

"Love's Miraculous Teleport!" Mistletoe called, holding the heart-shaped ring over her head. A shower of pink hearts appeared out of nowhere, scattered around her, and she vanished. Then she appeared in the same place.

The audience screamed and applauded.

"Love's Beautiful Song!"

Light shaped like a heart glowed at Mistletoe's throat, and she sang a verse of a hit pop song.

The audience cheered again.

"Love's Healing Wind!" Mistletoe cried, pointing at a platform across the room that Geranium's shockwave had destroyed.

The platform immediately glowed and reassembled itself.

"Love's Mind Ray!" Mistletoe put the heart-shaped ring to her forehead and scanned the audience with squinted eyes. "That boy! He has a crush on me!"

A boy in the audience blushed furiously and hid under his seat. The audience laughed.

"Love's Alternate Costumes!" Mistletoe switched between four different variations of her magical girl outfit.

The audience applauded and whistled.

"Love's Farseeing Ray!" Once again, Mistletoe put her focus item to her forehead. "And the furthest away boy who has a crush on me is ... one of Queen Hemlock's minions!"

The audience burst into titters.

Missy was having the time of her life. Her teammates never wanted to see her show off her powers. Gerry was always polite and just said she'd seen them all before, but Rose could be downright rude. It was a shame she was almost done. She would've loved to stand here all day.

"Love's Sleepy Clairvoyance!" Missy proclaimed, touching her heart to her forehead.

The audience leaned forward.

"I have to fall asleep before it'll work," she added sheepishly.

The audience burst into laughter.

"And finally ..." Missy said.

Gerry obligingly started a drumroll behind her.

Missy spun around, tossed her heart in the air, caught it, made a complicated overhand and underhand pass, thew it up in the air again, and caught it in a crouched position. "Valentine Finishing Blow!"

An explosion of magenta light blasted out and bathed the auditorium in a warm fuzzy feeling.

Someone in the audience screamed and burst into flames. The rest of the audience yelped and screamed out of their seats.

"It's okay!" Missy called. "It only works on evil! That means he was an undercover minion here to spy on the winning teams!"

One of the audience members tentatively prodded the man who had screamed. The dead minion's skin was charred, but his clothes were untouched.

"He's wearing a villain costume under his coat!" the audience member reported. "I see spikes!"

Everyone relaxed, and went back to happy chattering.

Missy turned around and gave her teammates a brilliant smile. "I saved us all, and didn't even know it!" she mouthed.

Gerry applauded quietly. Rose just shrugged.

"That's an amazing power!" the announcer said into his microphone. "And what a privilege that we were able to see it in action today!"

The audience whistled and applauded with almost deafening volume. Missy basked in the attention.

"Why don't you tell us about how you got your powers?" the announcer man asked, holding his microphone out in front of her.

Missy giggled. She still couldn't believe that she had made it, that she was standing here and being interviewed. It was such a dream come true! Literally, since she had dreamed about this. "Oh ... well ..."

She could remember it all like it was yesterday. That had been the most important days of her life. That had been the day she had become Mistletoe.

"It all began one night when I had a dream about becoming a legendary warrior," she said. "When I woke up, I had the talisman I'd dreamed about in my hands. What's more, the dream I had the next night showed me I needed to choose two teammates. Of course I gave one of *those* talismans to my best friend!"

She waved back at Gerry, who flushed pink and gave a tiny wave in response.

"That's quite an unusual beginning," the announcer said. "You dreamed about having magic before you got it?"

"Yeah," Missy said.

"But how is that possible?" he asked. "Most magical girls don't get their focus items until after they've decided to be magical girls. In fact, I can't think of a single one who's gotten a focus item first."

"Oh ... well ..." Missy giggled, embarrassed. "I think I might've been a magical girl before and just forgotten about it. My mom says when I was five, I used to run around with a toy I said was my focus item. She never saw me transform, so she figured I was just playing pretend. I guess I wasn't, though."

"Perhaps that would explain why you have so many more powers than your teammates!" the man said. "If you've had ten more years to develop them."

"Oh, no, no!" Missy giggled. "I only started with clairvoyance. I've gotten all the rest through power-ups in the past three years."

"But ..." the announcer said, faltering. "How many power-ups have you had?"

"Only four," Missy said, waving her hand. "The first one got me farseeing. The second one got me singing and shapeshifting and my

Valentine Finishing Blow. The third one got me telepathy. The fourth one got me healing and teleportation. My focus item didn't even change how it looked with the last power-up!"

The announcer swallowed. He looked over at the other judges, who were standing offstage. The other judges were murmuring.

Is something wrong? Missy thought, worried.

The announcer quickly recovered and handed her the microphone. "So tell us more about the start of your team!"

Missy giggled, taking it. "Oh, well, like I said, the other two talismans appeared in my hands when I woke up after the second dream. I gave one to Geranium because she was my best friend. Then we discovered that the new transfer student in our class had tremendous magical potential, which meant we had to make her our third teammate. She was overjoyed by the news!"

The judges' flurried discussion had resulted in one of the judges running up to the stage. She was a woman with her hair back in a severe bun.

She took the microphone from the announcer.

"Let me clarify something," the woman said. "You say *their* focus items appeared to *you?*"

"Yeah," Missy said. "Because we were meant to be a team."

"*Their* focus items appeared to *you?*"

Why did she keep repeating that?

"Like, that's normal, isn't it?" Missy asked. "I mean, I'm the team leader."

The woman looked speechless.

"Is that *not* normal?" Rose asked sharply from behind them.

The woman judge shook herself. "No, it's ... not normal. There's really only way that could happen, and it's very unusual. If you're not aware of what's going on, you ought to be."

Missy stared at the woman in alarm. Why did the judge look so serious?

The announcer leaned forward and whispered, "Is this the time or place?"

The judge waved him off with a sharp gesture and said into the microphone, looking at Missy's two teammates, "Mistletoe has a segmented focus item. That means it comes in multiple pieces. That's unusual except with things like earrings that are naturally in pairs, but it's not unheard of. What's *very* unusual is what you three have done."

Gerry looked baffled. "What did we do?"

"You took segments of her focus item," the judge said, "and made them *your* focus items. That means your magic is permanently linked to hers. All of your power-ups go to her. All of your costume changes go to her. That might explain why two of the costumes she shapeshifted between look like frills of justice versions of yours."

Rose's face had gone completely blank.

"That's not true!" Missy burst out. "I've never taken anything that belongs to them! I've just powered up more because I'm the main magical girl!"

"You've powered up more," the judge said sharply, "because you're the only one of the three who *ever will*. And if the other two aren't aware of that, they really need to be!"

The announcer finally wrestled the microphone away from her.

"Ha ha!" he said uncomfortably, looking rather desperate. "Well, that's our Magical Girl Team of the Year! Who knew that they were so closely connected, eh? What a special and unique situation, choosing to share powers that way! Now, let's move on to the closing ceremonies—"

"No!" Missy burst out. "You're trying to make us sound horrible! That's not how it is at all! Things were right from the moment we first battled together. We're an invincible team; no villain has ever been able to stand against our triple teamwork. We're *friends!*"

"So how *do* you three work together?" the announcer asked, holding the microphone out to her. "How have you been winning your most recent battles?"

"Well ..." Missy said. "Recently, Geranium's been scouting ahead to figure out the terrain. Primrose distracts any of Queen Hemlock's minions that lie waiting for us. And then, when they least expect it, we join forces and defeat them!"

Two voices murmured behind her.

"Join ..."

"... forces?"

"Sounds like a successful battle strategy!" the man said.

"Oh, yes!" Missy agreed, relaxing. They were back to talking about how wonderful her team was. "Of course, our current archenemy, Queen Hemlock, is particularly nasty, so our teamwork has to be impeccable—"

"*Impeccable?!*" an outraged voice shouted from behind her.

Startled, Missy turned to face her teammate who had spoken. Why did Rose look mad?

"Primrose?" Missy asked hesitantly. "What's wrong?"

The third member of their team looked like she was about to explode. "What do you think? I'm not your teammate—I'm your *sidekick!* Everything we do is all about *you!*"

"Ooooooooooooooooooooooooooooooooooh ..." the audience murmured, chatter rolling across the people in the seats.

"About *me?*" Missy asked, rather panicked. She put her hand to her chest. "But we do everything together!"

"Together?" Rose sneered. "Yes. But when have we three ever been equals?"

The announcer stirred, looking concerned. He raised his microphone to speak more, but Rose kept talking and cut him off.

"Your transformation scene is three times longer than ours."

"Geranium's has more sparkles—"

"You get *all* the power-ups."

"But that's just because I always defeat—!"

"No, it's *not!* We just *learned* that it's not! Singing and healing were clearly meant to be Geranium's powers, and shapeshifting and teleportation were clearly supposed to be mine!"

"It appears this team wasn't aware just how closely tied they were," the announcer said with a nervous laugh and a look at the audience. "So, let's talk more about your beginning! Who was the first archenemy you three fough—"

But Rose just talked more loudly. "And *every single boy we meet* seems to fall in love with you, *including* half the villains!"

Missy rubbed her head sheepishly. She'd noticed that fact. She suspected it was a passive power she'd gotten at some point. "Eheheh ..."

"About your first enemy—" the announcer tried desperately.

"Did it ever occur to you that we might want to help save the world, too?" Rose demanded. "That that might be the *reason* we joined your team?"

Gerry raised a hand hesitantly up near her face. "Umm, I just joined because Mistletoe was my friend ..."

"We distract villains," Rose snapped. "You save the day. What part of that is *teamwork?*"

"B-but you've saved us from things before!" Missy protested. "Alone! Like that evil alarm clock last year!"

"Yeah, when you had a fever of a hundred and two and couldn't get out of bed," Rose snorted. "Big deal."

Missy was starting to feel panicked. This was supposed to be a glorious victory. Why was everything falling apart?

"We're a team!" she said desperately. "We're best friends in the whole wide world! We're—"

"We're throwaway minions to you, just like the ones Queen Hemlock uses!" Rose shouted.

"But Primrose, that's not fair!" Gerry burst out. "She's the one who *gave* us our powers! And, anyway—"

Missy burst into tears and ran off the stage.

"Ummm ..." the announcer said slowly into the microphone. "I suggest we take a ten minute break ..."

———

HUDDLED BACKSTAGE with a bunch of boxes and her silent teammate who had just had a complete meltdown, Gerry was at a loss for words.

"Rose?" she said tentatively.

Rose said nothing. She just sat in silence, still transformed as Primrose, with her bangs over her face.

The silence stretched on, and on, and on. For all that Gerry was timid, she couldn't take it any longer.

"*Why?*" she burst out finally, clutching her wand to her chest. "Why did you say that in front of a live audience?"

Rose didn't move.

"Surely you didn't really mean it! And now Security has to search to find Mistletoe!"

Rose moved slightly. Her head was still ducked so the bangs covered her face. "I'm sorry, Geranium. I didn't mean to blurt everything out in public like that. But I *did* mean what I said."

Gerry swallowed, and swallowed again. If Rose was that unhappy ... if Rose was that unhappy, then ...

Wait! A solution occurred to her!

"Well, I guess if you really feel like that, Mistletoe and I could find some way to make sure you get the next power-up," Gerry said with relief. "Now that we know what's going on, we should be able to shift the next one over you or me. I don't mind not getting any, so you can get all the rest from now on ..."

"That's nice of you, Geranium, but no," Rose cut her off. Her head was still ducked, the bangs still covering her face. "I'm sick of everything. I'm leaving."

"You ..." A spike of panic shot through Gerry. "You just mean, like, the competition ... right?"

Rose was silent for a long moment. "Wrong."

She stood up slowly and picked up her focus item, the grey and blue baton with purple sheer tulle draping from it. She held the baton above her head, and a circle of sparkles engulfed her, swishing down from her raised arm to her toes.

She was now only Rose, standing there in a pair of jeans and a blue T-shirt.

"Prim—" Gerry began.

Rose's silence was eloquent. So much that it shut Gerry up.

Gerry tried to summon up the courage to say something. Anything. Something that would fix this. Anything that would stop her friend from leaving.

Rose set the baton on a box and walked towards the exit. "That's the last time you'll ever see me transform."

"*PRIMROSE!*" Gerry cried, finally capable of speaking again.

But Rose was already out the door.

SLAM!

Geranium sat there, frozen, her arms outstretched from where she had been reaching out for her lost teammate. Slowly, she pulled them back in. She fell to the ground in blackest despair.

Memories engulfed her. Memories of everything she'd had and now lost.

Missy holding out the two cute talismans to her after school. *"Pick one!"*

Gerry had been so flattered, so excited, so pleased to be chosen despite being pudgy and shy and nobody's idea of an ideal magical girl.

She remembered Missy chasing down the new girl at school. *"I'm sure you have tremendous magical potential! I'm very, very, very sure! I saw it in a dream! You have to be our teammate!"*

She remembered the look of horror on Rose's face, which had been so hilarious at the time because Missy had completely missed it.

She remembered Missy's silly theory about their powers. *"Do you think our powers come from things we're* weak in? *I mean, courage for Geranium, who's so shy, hope for Primrose, who's sort of cynical ..."* And then a long pause that became increasingly sheepish. *"Er ... love ... er ... which I hope I'm not weak in ..."*

Missy's excited face a few weeks ago. *"Guess what? I've entered our team in the biggest magical girl competition!"*

Their team pose less than an hour ago, which they had done a thousand times before. *"We're Victory's Bloom!"*

And now it would be the last time they ever did.

Gerry started to sob, mourning over her lost team, her lost friendship, her lost dreams. Everything was gone now. Everything was ruined. Why had they become friends, only to have it end this way?

"Victory's ... Bloom ..." she sobbed, lost in grief.

"Look! It's Geranium!" an unfamiliar voice shouted.

Gerry looked up, startled. She saw a pigtailed child standing at the entrance to the backstage. "Wh—What?"

"Can I get your autograph?!" the little girl squealed. "You guys are, like, my favorite team ever! You're always fighting bad guys in my town, so I bet you live where I do! I was hoping you would win the whole time!"

Gerry fumbled, lost in social situations to begin with, but especially too shattered to deal with this one. "B-but ... our team just ..."

"I brought you a piece of paper!" the little girl cried, yanking a crumpled piece of paper out of her pocket. She held it out. "Sign it for me! Say, 'To Chelsea!'"

"CHELSEA!" another voice yelled from behind them. "What did I tell you about running backstage?!"

Gerry's head whipped over, and she saw a woman with two buns at the back of her neck glaring at the small child. Gerry looked back at the child, who stuck her tongue out at the woman, and then she looked back at the woman. The child's mother?

The woman leaned against the doorway in exhaustion. "I'm so sorry ... I don't know what possessed her to run back here like this. Especially given what you're probably going through ..."

She glanced down at the baton sitting on the box. Gerry had the feeling the mother understood what had just happened, even though the daughter didn't.

"Autograph! Autograph!" the little girl shouted. "And then I'll give you *my* autograph! So when I'm a Victory's Bloom, it'll be worth a fortune!"

The woman got a pained look on her face. As if to explain the child's audacity, she said, "My daughter idolizes you ... She keeps saying she wants to be one of you when she grows up ..."

"Autograph, autograph, autograph!" the little girl squealed, holding out the paper and jumping up and down.

A strange idea rose in Gerry's mind. It was a ridiculous idea. A crazy idea. And yet ...

Missy wanted teammates, didn't she? Two teammates, in fact. If she hadn't wanted teammates extremely badly, her focus item wouldn't have segmented itself into three. True, the consequences hadn't been what Missy had intended, but Gerry didn't mind it. Maybe ... maybe if they had another teammate, one who wouldn't mind using a segment, that would be enough for Missy.

Slowly, Gerry looked up.

"One ... of us?" she murmured.

Gerry wanted Rose back. She wanted Primrose so badly that she could barely contain the ache. But Primrose was gone. She wasn't coming back. And Victory's Bloom couldn't be Victory's Bloom without a third teammate.

Mistletoe couldn't be Mistletoe without a third teammate.

I'm not useless, Gerry realized with amazement. *My being a magical girl is what makes Mistletoe so powerful. She wouldn't power up nearly as much without me. I'm not just a scout to check the terrain — I'm essential!*

It was a wonderful realization. And that hardened her resolution.

Gerry got up and seized the baton from the box. It was as intact as ever, despite the fact that Rose had abandoned it. Of course it was. It couldn't have crumbled. It wasn't just Primrose's focus item — it was Mistletoe's, too.

And now it would belong to somebody else.

"Know why we're strong?" Missy had proudly told the two of them once. *"Because we weren't one of those teams that a bunch of mascots picked out. We three* chose *each other!"*

"I'm sick of everything." Rose had been so sure, so certain. She hadn't even looked back. *"I'm leaving."*

The woman was still talking. Perhaps she had been talking all this time, and Gerry just hadn't been listening. "She even has pajamas that she puff-painted your team symbol on — "

"Mommm!" the little girl protested. "You weren't supposed to *tell* her that!"

Gerry took a deep breath. She had to figure out a way to ask. It wasn't too much to ask this girl, surely?

"I'm sorry ..." the woman said quickly, noticing her deep breath. "I'll get my daughter out of your hair ..."

"No. Wait," Gerry said softly, summoning her courage. "Let me find Mistletoe. I have something I want to ask her."

Rumors had been flying and buzzing around the auditorium, between the members of the audience and the girls of the one hundred and seven losing teams.

Everyone had opinions.

Everyone thought they understood the implications.

"Should we rescind the title?" one of the judges was saying.

"We can't do that," the announcer said.

"Why not? We have rules about cheating," a woman challenged. She was the judge who had gone up on the stage to tell everyone about Mistletoe's segmented focus item.

"They weren't technically cheating," the announcer argued. "There was nothing in the rules about this situation."

"But it's an embarrassment," a male judge complained. "That one girl, Primrose, is probably going to quit. Can you imagine the headlines tomorrow? 'Magical Girl Team of the Year Dissolves On Stage!'"

"And whose fault would that be?" the announcer muttered, eyeing the woman judge with dislike.

"I refuse to apologize for telling those two girls exactly what they needed to know."

"You could have waited until *after* the competition!"

"Why would I do that? It was good for the audience to hear. We don't want more teams seeking to emulate Victory's Bloom's gross power imbalance next year."

"You voted for them! Knowing their 'gross power imbalance'!" a male judge cried.

"I assumed that two of them were high-powered specialists and one was a low-powered generalist," the woman said coldly. "It was the natural assumption to make. That's an unusual team composition, so it made them the most interesting team here. Besides, I might add, it turned out that they *were* the most interesting team here, just for all the wrong reasons."

"If we rescind the title, we could give it to someone who really deserves it," the male judge argued. "Like Seasonal Spices."

"I'm sure the Seasonal Spices girls are lovely," the announcer said, "but have you thought about what that would mean? There are ten minutes left in the show. We wouldn't have time to interview anybody. And if they won, they'd be ineligible to win it next year, which they have a real chance of doing. Why would you deny them the chance to win the spotlight for real, rather than being an afterthought?"

"Look, whatever we do," a second woman judge said, "there's no damage control we can do here. We can't just play this off as a publicity stunt if their team fractures. Let's just wrap this show up and get it over with."

A woman with two buns at the back of her neck rushed over. She talked to the judges in rapid whispers.

The judges reacted with surprise. The female judge was incredulous. The announcer's eyebrows raised.

"Well, that would be a solution," he said.

TEN MINUTES LATER, when the program was scheduled to end, people were getting out of their seats and picking up programs and starting to murmur as they headed toward the doors. The announcer ran up on the stage and waved his hands frantically.

"Welcome back, guests!" he called loudly into his microphone. "We have an unexpected development! We hadn't realized this, but the team had been planning to disband, anyway. And it seems that Victory's Bloom has chosen this moment ... to unveil their brand-new teammate, Peony!"

A little girl came prancing onto the stage. She had her hair in pigtails with ribbons around them, and wore an outfit that was ... sort of similar to Primrose's, except that it looked silly and had tomboyish shorts instead of an elegant tulip-like skirt.

"I AM PEONY!" the girl exclaimed. She spun around and tried to flip the baton up in the air, which fell to the ground and clattered. Undaunted, she grabbed it. "I'm a Victory's Bloom! I'm amazing!"

"Um," the announcer said, "I think you mean you're a member of Victory's Bloom ..."

"I'm one of the Victory's Blooms!"

"A team name's not used that wa—never mind. Mistletoe, Geranium, come tell us what you think of your new teammate!"

Mistletoe moved forward gingerly. She had a rather shellshocked and uncertain look on her face. She took the microphone that was offered and said, "W-well, Primrose was planning to leave after the competition, and we'd already chosen Peony to replace her, so, like, this was planned all along ..."

SOMEONE PUSHED a button on the remote, and the broadcast of the Magical Girl Team of the Year competition winked out and died.

"I love it," a woman declared. She was dressed in a miniskirt and cape, with low-cut cleavage showing. There were spikes all over her costume, and an upside-down crown on her head. She held a scepter in her hand, which she also held upside-down. "It was past time, but I love it."

Beside her was a silent girl with long blonde hair. Bangs covered her face.

"And when I say that it was past time, I mean it was *really* past time," the woman continued relentlessly. "How many months has it been now, Nightshade?"

The girl said nothing.

"Say something!" the woman snapped. "For crying out loud!"

"Well, Mom, I quit," the girl said dully, not looking up. "I broke our championship team. Just like you wanted."

"Yes, only five months after I ordered you to," Queen Hemlock snorted. "Honestly, Nightshade, I was beginning to wonder where your loyalties lay."

"We were teammates for *three years*, Mom!" the girl exploded. "And on your orders, no less! They thought we were friends."

"Which *will* work to our advantage in demoralizing them, true," Queen Hemlock said, drumming her fingers along the edge of her upside-down scepter. "And breaking your team in front of that live audience *was* a master stroke. But we're still behind in our plans. So, when you go back to reveal yourself as Queen Hemlock's daughter—"

"Wait ..." Nightshade said slowly. Something had finally penetrated. "You expect me to go *back* to my old teammates as a villain?"

"Don't be stupid, Nightshade," her mother said, folding her arms. "Why, exactly, did you think I ordered you to join when their leader recruited you?"

"As an infiltrator," Nightshade said.

Nobody would ever expect a minion to be capable of being a magical girl. You had to be both young and innocent, and minions were usually adults and anything but. But Nightshade had been a special case. Nightshade had been only three months old.

Nightshade was a homunculus. A special kind that had taken a lot of her mother's magic to create. One with a will of its own.

"As an infiltrator," her mother confirmed. "And what do infiltrators do?"

"Get information."

"In order to ...?"

"I don't know." She'd tried not to think about it. She'd tried never to think about being a villain whenever she'd been with her friends. She liked them better.

Or rather, she *had* liked them better before she'd learned that Mistletoe had been using her. Now she just felt broken inside.

Queen Hemlock snorted. "Your infiltration will have taught you all their weak points—*and* the weak points of solo magical girls and magical girl teams in general, too. You know that. You've crushed hundreds by now. You're going to defeat Victory's Bloom next, and it's going to be easy."

"Defeat them," Nightshade said numbly. "You expect me to face my former teammates and ... defeat them."

It was bad enough to have to face them. She had planned to never return to their school.

But defeat them? Break their focus items, or slaughter their magical girl forms? How could she do that? How could anyone?

She'd expected her mother to understand. She'd known her mom would pulverize the team eventually once she left it, which was why she had resisted quitting, but she'd expected that her mother would send different minions. Hired minions. Maybe disposable minions. Not Nightshade. Not her strongest one. Not her best.

Didn't she understand that everyone had limits?

"Not just *them!*" Queen Hemlock said gleefully. "Destroying Victory's Bloom will be only the *beginning!* That competition gave us some fantastic leads on where to focus on next. Once we've eliminated every major team finalist, the path will be clear for us to *easily*—"

Her tirade was interrupted by a loud *Beeeep!*

"Oh, that's another of my hired minions coming back from defeat. Excuse me while I go chew him out."

The door slammed on her way out.

Nightshade said there silently.

If Queen Hemlock was going to seriously attack Victory's Bloom, they wouldn't stand a chance. Of that, she was completely certain.

Mistletoe had no concept of battle strategies. She threw around flashy magic as if that alone was enough, and half the time didn't even hit the minions she was aiming at. Geranium was the worst scout ever. She never noticed any minions before they snuck up behind her to attack. Primrose had been using illusion to hide their incompetence from both of her teammates, and her mother, for years.

If her teammates had known they were incompetent, they wouldn't have thought they deserved power-ups, and so wouldn't have gotten them. She'd figured power-ups were their only chance to become strong enough to survive.

If their team's many enemies had realized that two of them were incompetent, they would have sent their best fighters at Primrose every time, thereby nullifying the effectiveness of her power, which was focused on stealth. Worse, if she'd been forced to fight openly, it might have caused her teammates to question why she was so much better at fighting than them.

But most importantly of all, if Queen Hemlock had noticed they were incompetent, she would have canceled the experiment and pulled Nightshade back right away. Which was the one thing that

Nightshade, a.k.a. Primrose the magical girl, a.k.a. Rose the normal girl with friends, could not have allowed to happen.

But now the point was entirely moot. Because it turned out their friendship had been as much of a sham as her mother had wanted it to be all along.

Why don't I just let her do it? Nightshade thought bitterly. *Why don't I just let Mom squash them? Mistletoe deserves it. And even Geranium didn't balk at replacing me right away.*

But the thought of doing it herself ...

She wanted to forget the whole thing and pretend Primrose had never existed. She wanted to bury herself in Nightshade, the minion who never showed any emotion, who never felt anything, who just did her job because it had to be done.

Because it had to be done ...

How many magical girls have I destroyed because I made sure I never felt anything?

Nightshade looked up at the wall above the TV. There was a banner high above that said "Defeated Magical Girl Trophies." Underneath were focus items. Dozens of focus items. All of them from magical girls she'd killed.

Most focus items crumbled when a magical girl quit or had her magical girl form killed, because both owed their entire existence to magic. But those that had been physical objects beforehand survived to become lifeless and magicless objects, as they had been before. Those were the ones Nightshade had scooped up and taken home as trophies. She hardly knew why.

Her mother had loved the habit, gleefully creating her a wall to hang them on. She had shown the wall off to her villain friends many times, proudly proclaiming that it was a magnificent way to gloat and rub those former magical girls' faces in the fact that their magic had been destroyed. Those human girls who could no longer transform would not even have a memento remaining.

But that wasn't why Nightshade had taken them.

Perhaps I thought, she realized slowly, *that they might give me a way to escape.*

Nightshade had been able to become a magical girl because she was innocent. And innocent she had been. She hadn't recognized the difference between friendship and malice. Between kindness and cruelty. Between loyalty and slavery.

Mistletoe: *"I love you both sooooo much!"*

Queen Hemlock: *"Stop complaining and obey me!"*

Neither of them had truly deserved her loyalty. But one came a lot closer than the other:

The one who hadn't *purposefully* made her in order to use her.

Nightshade rocketed up to her feet and seized two of the trophies: a sword and a dagger that had probably belonged to intelligent magical girls who hadn't thought a hairbow or a genie lamp would be much better choices of weapons.

She'd become a magical girl because she was innocent. And she was no longer innocent. But there was something else that worked just as well to become a magical girl.

She could be *good*.

She had quit being a magical girl. By all accounts, that should be the end of it. But sometimes the magic system would allow a girl who was young enough and innocent enough, or good enough, to become one a second time. She had seen it before with girls whose magical girl forms she'd killed.

The magic system had been patient with her before. It had even let Nightshade transform invisibly on the battlefield and use Primrose's illusion powers for villain work.

Surely it would give her a second chance. Surely it would let her become a magical girl again if she intended to use magic for the right thing this time.

Please. Please. Please. Please ...

QUEEN HEMLOCK STOMPED down the corridor, irate.

"And no more excuses, slackers!" she yelled over her shoulder. "Next time, you'll all go *together* to defeat the Wings of Justice!"

What was she hiring minions for if they were just as useless as the ceramic ones? She'd sent one of the hired ones to fight that particular throwaway team right after the competition because Nightshade had been busy. What did he mean, "They're much more vicious than they used to be?" Imbecile! Magical girl teams didn't suddenly get better for no reason!

Maybe I ought to make some more like Nightshade, Queen Hemlock thought, storming down the hallway. *She's much more useful than those idiots. Saving up magic for another three years without using any would be a drag, but ...*

She stormed through the doorway to the room where she had left Nightshade.

"Right, then," she said, picking up where they had left off. "I'm going to send you back in three weeks. Just enough time for them to have gotten used to the idea that they will never see you again, and not nearly enough time for them to have practiced much with their new teammate—"

She stopped abruptly. Nightshade was not where she'd left her. The girl was now standing near the doorway with a sword in one hand and a dagger in the other. And of all things, she was wearing a dark blue costume with a pleated skirt and stars all over it.

"Nightshade, what are you doing?" she asked impatiently. "That's a terrible costume. It looks like something a magical girl would wear. If you want a new minion costume, we can go to Rhea Korstanos Designs. We'd have to pull a heist or two to pay for it, though."

Nightshade said nothing.

Said nothing.

Said nothing.

"I'm betraying you," she said finally, with exasperation.

"*WHAT?*" Queen Hemlock shouted, snatching the scepter from her side and flipping it upside-down. "You can't do that!"

Paralysis mist burst from the scepter, but Nightshade was already moving. She dashed forward, avoiding the paralysis mist, lifted her mother up, and slammed the dagger into the wall. When she darted away, Queen Hemlock was dangling by the top of her cape that was pinned to the wall.

"Don't try to follow me, and no one gets hurt."

"You can't double-cross your mother!" Queen Hemlock screamed, squeezing her hands into fists. "I created you!"

"Yes, and now I've outgrown you," Nightshade said coldly. "*You're* the one who taught me how to double-cross!"

Blast! Queen Hemlock had forgotten this was one of the risks of creating intelligent homunculi. She'd been warned that things like this could happen, but Nightshade had always been so loyal that there'd seemed no need for worry.

Well, it was fine. She'd equipped the minion with a kill switch for this very reason. Queen Hemlock flipped her scepter right-side-up, spun the gemstone at the top upside-down, and a button appeared. She slammed her finger into it.

Nightshade stood with her arms folded, completely unaffected. "You know, the thing about a kill switch is that it's only useful if the target's not transformed into a magical form that doesn't have to have anything in common with the original body."

With a sinking feeling, Queen Hemlock realized she'd made a slight miscalculation. So *this* was why intelligent homunculi weren't used more often to become magical girls. Still—

She slashed the sharp edge of the gemstone across her cape, which sliced, ripped, and set her free.

She flipped her scepter to the side and aimed it. Forget paralysis or kill switches. She had more than a month's saved magic in the storage section, which meant she had more than enough to coat the entire room with corrosive acid. She spun the scepter, and the gemstone glowed—

She was knocked off balance by a whirlwind of bladed stars.

CRASH!

She watched in horror as Nightshade slammed the scepter into the floor, shattering it.

"My scepter!" Queen Hemlock screamed.

"Magical girls aren't the only ones who lose their powers without their talismans, are they, Mom?" Nightshade asked with a chilly smile. "Now you only have access to the magic you generate second-by-second, which isn't much."

Queen Hemlock let out an incoherent scream of rage.

"Well," Nightshade said, tucking the shattered scepter into a hidden pocket in the costume's skirt. "Bye, Mom."

She turned to walk away.

"You can't switch allegiances *now*, you fool!" Queen Hemlock snapped. "Victory's Bloom won't ever take you back!"

Nightshade paused. Then she turned around. "True enough, after everything I said at the competition. But who said I still *want* to be part of a team?"

"You're a fool if you don't."

"No, I'm a fool if I do. I wasn't lying when I told them I quit. But I can fight perfectly well by myself. As you should know—you trained me."

"I'll make a new scepter soon!" Queen Hemlock snarled. "And then I'll come after *you!*"

Nightshade paused to consider this.

"I'm sure you will. Then I'll defeat you again. Goodbye, Mom."

She walked out the door and headed for the exit.

Queen Hemlock was left in smoldering frustration and rage.

THE GIRL with blonde hair stepped into the bright sunlight. She paused to take a deep breath. She didn't think she'd ever gone anywhere outside the lair without her mother's express orders.

"Hmm, I think I'll enter next year's solo magical girl competition as Starlight, Princess of Determination," she mused. "I wonder if I'll stand a chance to win?"

Prancing down the hill, she headed off in a random direction. It didn't matter where she was going. Anywhere where she could be by herself would do.

From now on, her life would be her own.

AUTHOR NOTE:
I'm very fond of magical girl anime. Why? Well, remember how I mentioned

the need for tough female characters who are super girly? That's the genre where I've found most of them.

So naturally, I decided to take all the most common tropes of magical girl anime and combine them into a cohesive universe.

I originally told this story in manga form, as "The Competition." It was the first thing I set in the magical girl world I'd created.

The second thing was my webcomic, To Prevent World Peace. The third was the prose adaptation, the Magical Mayhem series, which this story is part of.

TO PREVENT SIMILAR VIEWS

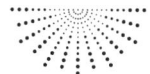

*K*endra was getting antsy. Cleaning up the clutter in the dungeon was dull, which gave her way too much time to think for herself. Now that her goal was met, and she was officially part of a villain team, it was hard to withhold her misgivings.

Not that she'd show those doubts in front of Chronos, of course. Oh, no. The soothsayer would likely use that as an excuse to break up the team.

But that was part of the problem. Even as a villain, Kendra needed teammates she could count on. How could she rely on Chronos, who'd only reluctantly agreed to be her boss, to put forth any effort to help her—or restrain her, if needed? How could she trust the psycho brat named Tiffany to not stab her in the back at the first opportunity?

She missed Florence. She missed having a teammate she could rely on, but mostly she just missed her best friend badly.

"Time to teleport this box upstairs!" the psycho little twerp called, holding up a tiny box. Then she glanced down and started rooting through it. "Oh, wait, Porter the Poster Tube should be with his friends over in that box ... and Freida the Fluffy Shirt doesn't look pretty next to Susan the Squeaky Boots ..."

And Tiffany proceeded to start pulling everything out of the box she had just spent fifteen minutes packing.

Kendra snapped. "It's all random clutter! Just throw it all out!"

Tiffany stared at her in horror. "They aren't junk! These are my friends!"

Chronos looked sympathetic.

"Oh, for crying out loud!" Kendra exploded. "Those are not friends! Those are stupid things you don't need that you've stolen in the first place!"

The spoiled little villain burst into sobbing crocodile tears.

And Chronos, who for some reason didn't seem to notice that the tears were fake, looked like she was on the verge of crying, too.

Is she buying the act? Kendra thought incredulously.

"Do you want the box upstairs, or not?" Kendra snarled.

Tiffany immediately stopped crying and beamed. "Yes! Just as soon as I put my friends in the right places! Porter the Poster Tube goes over here ..."

She resumed dismantling the contents of the box.

While she was waiting, Kendra stomped around the dungeon, picking up random junk and flinging it into an empty box. She filled six large boxes and teleported them all upstairs before Tiffany was finished rearranging the contents of her small one.

"There!" Tiffany beamed, holding up the tiny box in triumph. "Now you can teleport this upstairs!"

"Oh, can I?" Kendra asked acidly. "What a privilege."

Tiffany yelped, looking around frantically. "Where did Bobby the Blow Darts go? I left him right there to be with Freida the Fluffy Shirt! Now they're both gone!"

Kendra hastily teleported the box upstairs, dumped it out, and teleported back into the dungeon. Tiffany was still throwing a fit.

"And Porter the Poster Tube is missing, too!" Tiffany was wailing, not packing up anything.

Taking advantage of this opportunity, Kendra strode around the room to pick up more clutter and dump it into the box. Once it was full, she teleported upstairs and dumped it out. Then she teleported back down the dungeon.

Good. Using this method rather than the brat's insane one, we might have some chance of finishing before the end of the decade.

Tiffany was gone.

Kendra's head whipped around. "Where did she go?"

Chronos looked exasperated. "She said that the boxes couldn't go upstairs until they were ready, and she went upstairs to gather all the things you've taken up there to bring them back down again."

Kendra stared at her. "You're kidding."

"I wish I were."

"She's completely off her rocker!"

"Yes, she is."

"She's out of her gourd! She's nuts!"

"I'm not disagreeing."

"And you call *that* a teammate?!"

"Well, what would you prefer?" Chronos asked with annoyance, folding her arms. "Would you prefer that I return her to the family she was glad to be kidnapped from? Or keep her as a prisoner forever? Or sell her to some other villain who might be far more unscrupulous than we are?"

"Yes," Kendra said. "To all of the above."

Chronos gave her an indignant stare.

"The kids can take care of herself," Kendra explained. "She told us that she'd killed one of her previous 'masters,' right? Let's make sure that doesn't happen to us."

"She didn't ... actually admit to having killed him ..."

"She said he accidentally got killed by his own gun after he tried to sell her for ransom money," Kendra snorted. "And the kid has the magical power to sabotage things. Read between the lines."

Beads of sweat stood out on Chronos's forehead.

"Okay!" Tiffany cried, prancing down the stairs with an armload of clutter. "Now we can pack the next box!"

"Or we can leave and find a new lair," Kendra muttered to Chronos, sidling closer. "One unencumbered by a ten-year-old sociopath."

"She's not the one I want to get away from," the oracle hissed, and stormed over to help Tiffany.

Kendra sighed. Was Chronos still grumpy about being forced to join a villain team against her will? Kendra had even put the oracle in charge of the team. What more could she want?

Other than having me leave her alone, which is out of the question, because I need her power to see the future, Kendra amended.

Gloom settled over her. She'd never wanted to be a villain, either. It was, in fact, the opposite of all of her goals.

A few days ago, Kendra had been a magical girl, secure in her power and confident that everything she did was for justice and was helping to save the world.

But then Chronos had shown Kendra her future, in which she would have become so sure of herself and her own righteousness that she would have destroyed the world.

It was a bitter memory, so bitter that Kendra clenched her fists. Her fingernails dug into her palms.

She hadn't even said goodbye to her friends.

She hadn't even tried to explain the reasons.

She had just left, teleporting away after announcing her defection to villainy.

She'd done it that way to burn her bridges. To destroy the future she would have had. To stop herself from being tempted to stay a corrupt hero, to make sure she could never go back.

But now ...

Now she wondered ...

Would they have understood? She bit her lip. *I just assumed they wouldn't. But what if I had explained it? Would they have stayed my teammates? Would they have helped me save the world through villainy?*

She probably wouldn't have been able to convince Felicity. The third member of Wings of Justice, who went under the name Green Fairy, was not particularly bright. Subtle moral nuances would have gone over her head.

But Florence, also known as Pink Dragon ...

Florence was Kendra's best friend. And she was always thinking about ethical questions. Perhaps, if Kendra had explained everything to her, Florence would have understood.

No ... for *sure*, if Kendra had explained everything to her, Florence would have understood.

Could she have even helped me choose some other future? Kendra thought longingly. *Could there have been a way for me to remain a magical girl and NOT be fated to destroy the world?*

She shook her head vigorously. No. No. She couldn't afford to think like that. In her original future, Florence had been there, yelling at Kendra for doing the wrong thing. That scene Chronos had shown her was seared into her memory. If Kendra had stayed a magical girl, Florence wouldn't have been able to stop her.

But she would have tried.

Kendra chewed on her lower lip.

She *had* made a mistake in not explaining things to Florence. Florence would have come with her. Florence had been loyal to her even in that nightmare future, even when she'd disagreed with what Kendra was doing.

Florence was the only good part of that future, Kendra realized. *I shouldn't have left her behind.*

In retrospect, it was obvious. She'd forced Chronos to become her teammate because she needed an ally. Somebody to help her. Somebody to force her to stop when she was wrong.

She should have asked Florence.

She should have put Florence in charge of the team.

And Kendra had blown it. Because she hadn't explained.

Tears stung in her eyes and blinded her vision.

"No, see, Betsy the Batteries and Floyd the Flashlight are fighting," Tiffany was explaining to Chronos, insistently unpacking the one and only box the two had prepared in all this time. "So they can't be put together."

"I see ..." Chronos muttered, looking rather tired and very much like she did *not* see.

Kendra quickly shook herself. She wouldn't show weakness in front of the psycho.

"Now you can help me!" Tiffany said excitedly, looking over at her. "I have Matty the Mattress, and Benny the Boxes, and Barry the Bars from the cages—"

"Pass," Kendra said immediately. "I've got things to do."

Chronos frowned. "What kind of things?"

"None of your beeswax," Kendra snapped, and teleported away.

She didn't go far. Just on top of the roof of the building. Really, she didn't have anywhere else to go or anyone else to see, but she needed some space to herself. She needed to ... she needed to ...

Without thinking, Kendra summoned her halo and threw it over her head.

"Cream Angel ... *FLEDGE!*" she shouted.

Nothing happened.

Nothing at all.

Her transformation was truly gone.

Kendra's arms dropped to her sides. She felt numb.

Suddenly furious, she flung her halo away, making it disappear. She could still summon it, but it was useless. It would never help her transform into a magical girl again. And she had lost her only chance to keep her best friend with her.

Kendra screamed into the sky until her throat was raw.

... Or had she?

It's not too late, she realized. *I can just explain it to her now. If she would have understood then, she'll understand now.*

Kendra stood up, resolve filling her heart. She understood now. She saw the path to a better future than the one she had currently. And the path was Florence. All she had to do was convince her best friend to be a villain, too.

Kendra squeezed the watch on her wrist and teleported straight to Florence's bedroom. It was, unfortunately, empty—looking at the alarm clock on the dresser, Kendra saw there was an hour left before track ended. She sighed, tapping her foot impatiently.

She was going to have to wait here. She couldn't teleport directly to their high school, because somebody would see her in her villain outfit and call the police. Besides, Florence wouldn't appreciate it if Kendra started talking to her about magic in front of other people. She was unreasonably obsessed with keeping a secret identity.

Well, there was something practical Kendra could do while she was waiting.

She teleported over to her own bedroom. A rush of loss and homesickness slammed into her, but she clamped down hard on her feelings and grabbed the duffel bag from the top of her closet.

It still held the clothes from ballet lessons when she was a kid, neatly pressed and folded. She unzipped the duffel bag, pulled out the leotard and tights and shoes, tucked them neatly onto a shelf in the back of her closet, and then went through the drawers of her dresser looking for necessities.

All her underwear and socks, obviously. Two changes of sneakers. Three pairs of jeans, eight T-shirts, two long-sleeved shirts, and all of her belts, especially the one with the double buckles. She liked the one with the double buckles.

She didn't own a lot of jewelry, but she liked the ones she had, so she unzipped the side pocket and threw those in, too.

Kendra hesitated. *Is that it?*

No, there was one more thing she should bring.

She teleported to the bathroom and grabbed her toothbrush. She grabbed a washcloth and tucked it neatly inside, so it wouldn't get dirty, and teleported back to her bedroom to tuck it on top of the clothing.

Then Kendra hesitated. She wanted to stay. She didn't want to go back to the lair, not now that she was back home again. She felt her resolve faltering.

Surely the world didn't need her to give up her whole life in order to save it. Surely she could stay and see her parents instead. Surely she could just be Kendra, even though she could no longer transform. Surely ...

NO!

Kendra grabbed the duffel bag and teleported back to Florence's room. Her heart was hammering, and she was furious with herself for starting to waver.

No weaknesses. She must show no weaknesses. Even to herself.

Neither of her parents would understand. They'd try to talk her out of this path she had to be on. They knew her so well, they might even succeed. And then no one would be out there to save the world from the next corrupt magical girl who came along.

But Florence ...

Surely she could convince Florence.

Restlessly, Kendra got up and paced around the room. Why wasn't Florence home yet? Didn't she realize her future was here, waiting for her?

She walked over to Florence's closet. Maybe she should pack a bag for Florence. That would be thoughtful, and it would give Kendra something to do with her time.

She searched for a bag in the room, but she couldn't find one, and she didn't dare search any other rooms in the house. If Florence's parents saw her, it would be trouble. Florence's father was a pastor. There was no way he'd take kindly to Kendra coming to convert his daughter to villainy.

Kendra sighed, sitting down on the bed and drumming her fingers on the bedspread.

If I could just get up to the attic safely ...

Oh, wait! I have the watch!

Teleportation was such a great power. Kendra should have built her magical girl form around that, instead of flying, in the first place.

She teleported up to the attic, where she stepped silently across the floorboards, aware that anyone beneath could hear her footsteps if she wasn't careful. Fortunately she was naturally graceful, and had spent years combating villains, so it wasn't difficult to move carefully.

There were boxes and boxes and boxes. There was one that looked like it was filled with nothing but sweaters. But at last, Kendra found an old and battered suitcase. Satisfied, she picked it up and beat the dust off. It didn't look nearly cool enough for a departure into villainy, but it would do.

She checked her teleporting watch for the time. *Still five minutes before track ends. So I probably have fifteen minutes before she gets home, if she walks quickly.*

Florence generally did walk quickly, especially when Kendra was walking beside her and telling her about how great it would be to volunteer with law enforcement again.

It was Florence's fault they'd had to quit as FBI aides. She'd been peeved when Kendra had deliberately killed their arch-nemesis instead of capturing him so that he could be sent to prison.

But, hellllloooo, the guy had already escaped from prison once, Kendra thought, rolling her eyes. *Obviously he had to die.*

She teleported back to Florence's room and moved soundlessly, opening drawers and sorting through the contents within.

She selected all Florence's favorite clothes, re-folded them because Florence always folded them wrong, and tucked them into the suitcase in tidy piles.

She checked her watch. Ten minutes until Florence was due home. *Maybe I should assume she'll be five minutes early, just in case.*

Kendra flopped down on the bed with a suitcase on either side, satisfied with her work. Florence would be touched at her thoughtfulness when Kendra revealed that she'd already packed a suitcase for her.

Well...

Come to think of it, Florence had ranted a few thousand times about Kendra's "control freak ways" over the past year. Maybe she should hide the suitcase until after Florence had enthusiastically agreed to join her. *Then* Florence would be touched.

Kendra chucked that suitcase under the bed, moving her own duffel bag in front of it to keep it hidden until the right moment.

She sat on the bed, heart pounding, rehearsing her words silently, and waited.

Florence would be here any minute now.

Any minute now.

Any minute now.

Any minute now.

Where was she?!

"Are you all right?" Florence's mother's voice said from the hallway.

"No," Florence's voice answered tersely.

She's here! Kendra straightened and made sure she was in the best possible pose: casual and cool and relaxed, as if she hadn't been waiting for over an hour for her best friend to appear.

The door opened, and Florence walked in with her eyes closed, breathing a long sigh. She looked weary and tired.

Well, of course she looked weary and tired. She was missing her best friend. Why had Kendra ever left her behind?

"Hi, Florence," Kendra said with satisfaction.

Florence's eyes flew open. Her mouth quickly followed. She let out an incoherent, high-pitched, "Urghha!"

"What took you so long?" Kendra said teasingly. "I've been waiting here for nearly an hour. You usually get home from track much sooner than this."

"*KENDRA!*" Florence shrieked, dropping her backpack, which thudded to the ground.

"Yep."

"You—what—why—where have you *been?!*"

"Turning villain," Kendra said. Why would Florence ask such an obvious question? "Just like I said I would. Did you think I was lying?"

"You ... but ... *WHY?*"

Kendra shrugged. It was hard to explain. She would have to, of course, but she would wait until Florence had calmed down. Florence sometimes had trouble processing things.

Sure enough, her best friend seemed to be on the verge of hyperventilating.

Don't worry, Kendra was about to say, but Florence interrupted.

"Who brainwashed you?" she blurted out.

For an instant, Kendra was confused. Then she realized that might have been an obvious conclusion for Florence to come to.

"I wasn't brainwashed," she said, crossing her legs. Her foot hit the duffel bag, and she hoped that Florence wouldn't notice there was anything behind it. "Sorry."

"Then where have you *been?!*" Florence exclaimed.

"I was turning *villain,*" Kendra said, rolling her eyes. Why did she have to say the same thing twice? "Duhhh."

Florence leaned forward and clenched her hands into fists. "KENDRA!! EXPLAIN!!"

Kendra hesitated. Okay, Florence was probably right that she should have explained sooner. She'd just, well, you know, been in shock. It was only now that she could really think rationally about the whole thing.

"It's ... complicated," Kendra said slowly, hunching her knees up to her chest. The words were hard to say, so she had to force them out. "I kind of had to do it. To save the world."

Florence stared at her blankly.

And now she had to admit that Florence had been right about something all along.

Kendra traced her finger in a circle around the knee of her jeans, not wanting to look at her. "I didn't want to quit. I really didn't want to defect. But ... I found out ... it's possible for magical girls to turn corrupt. One with sufficient charisma and arrogance could even lead the world to destruction. That would have been my future. A born mage showed me. So I ..."

"You listened to a *born mage?*" Florence exploded. "After all the things you said to me about Lute Deathwave? Are you crazy? *Obviously* he was lying!"

Kendra's head shot up. "No, she wasn't!" she snapped.

Why would Florence even bring that up? The situation with Lute Deathwave, Florence's boyfriend who had turned out to be the son of their second arch-nemesis, was nothing like this!

She planted an accusing finger forward. "I became a villain for the same reason we both became magical girls: to protect world peace!"

Florence looked dumbfounded.

This isn't going as well as I thought it would, Kendra thought, her mind racing. *I just have to explain it more. What are the right words? What will make her understand?*

"Kendra ..." Florence said slowly, " ... why are you here?"

That was it! Those were the right words. Those were the only words that mattered.

"Because you're my best friend." Kendra reached out her hand. "Will you trust me? Will you join me?"

Florence stared at her with a blank face.

"Join me in being a villain," Kendra explained. The words came so smoothly now. "Join my new team. Join me in saving the world."

Florence's eyes grew slowly bigger.

She understands now. Kendra felt a great warmth flood into her heart. *She sees why this is so important. It's hard to get over the shock, but I will help her through it ...*

Florence took a step backwards. "Dad's always taught me that right and wrong ..."

A spark of flame appeared at her wrist, and then spread into a swirl of fire going past her elbow.

"... are more important than friendship."

Kendra froze inside. *What?*

Now wearing her focus item and able to transform, Florence lifted her arms high. "Pink Dragon ... *flare!*"

She whooshed up to the ceiling, spinning around at a fast rate, flames burning away her clothing as her dozens of braids expanded and coiled into corkscrew curls at the bottom. Enormous bat wings burst from her back as the flames blossomed outward into a fluffy pink dress. She landed, with flames roaring all around her. They swirled and sucked into her bracelet like a vortex.

She looked determined and hurt and angry, and ... good grief, so very, very silly. She really had to come up with a better costume when she joined the villain team. The pink dress could stay, but she really ought to consider feathery angel wings, like the ones Kendra had had. The bat wings looked so stupid on an ally of justice.

Kendra sighed, leaning forward. "I'm trying to save the world, Flo. What part of that don't you understand?"

"What part?!" Florence sputtered. "What part *does* make sense? You know what villains are like, Kendra!"

"Of course I know what villains are like," Kendra said, amused by her best friend's ignorance. Kendra had spent the last few days surrounded by them, after all. "What I didn't understand was what magical girls are like. I didn't understand that we weren't all virtuous."

Florence said nothing. Kendra could tell she was thinking it over.

"That's why I have to be a villain," Kendra said. She sat up proudly, stating her purpose. "I have to purify the magic system. I have to cut out anyone who's corrupt."

"You have to *not be a villain!*" Florence shouted. "Are you listening to yourself? You sound nuts!"

Kendra was irritated. Why was that always the first thing Florence called her when they disagreed? "It doesn't matter. Any cost is worth it to save the world. That's what I'm doing."

"By becoming a *villain?*" Florence snapped incredulously. She swung her bracelet around in a threatening position.

A terrible realization crashed over Kendra.

I'm not going to be able to convince her. Her and her blasted inflexibility. She can't see past the obvious labels of "hero" and "villain" to see what needs doing. All she sees is what she thinks is "right" and "wrong."

Very angry, but trying not to show it, Kendra lifted up the blinds behind the bed and unlocked the window. "All right. I'll leave. I'm sorry I came."

"But ... your parents," Florence said slowly from behind her. "Felicity?"

Kendra turned around and looked at her. *Is she asking if I'll invite them to join, too?*

For a moment, she considered it. But then she noted that Florence was still standing there transformed, her bracelet within easy access.

Florence the conscience. Florence the loyal. Florence the best friend. Threatening her with a bracelet that could breathe fire, ice, or poison.

"No way," Kendra shot back. "If you don't understand, there's no chance they will."

Florence shoved her bracelet out. "I'll breathe ice at you!" she threatened. "I'll *make* you stay and face them!"

There was no chance Kendra was staying for that. She hopped down to the floor, picked up the duffel bag, and heaved it through the window.

"I will!" Florence cried.

"Just ice?" Kendra asked sardonically, sitting on the edge of the window to hop out. "Why don't you breathe fire or poison, while you're at it? I'm a villain. The law justifies killing me."

Florence cringed. She pulled her arm back slowly.

"Pulling back?" Kendra taunted. She was still mad. "Don't you know I'm a dangerous criminal?"

Florence swallowed. "But ... then ... why don't you attack *me?*"

Kendra blinked. What a crazy question. "Duh. You're my best friend. You'll never be my enemy."

Fire roared around Florence as she detransformed. Her bat wings slurped back into her back, and her fluffy pink dress dissolved into smoke that coiled back into her former clothes. Her head was ducked, her shoulders hunched. "Go. I won't attack you, either."

Kendra knew that. But she supposed saying *I know* wouldn't go over well right now.

"Thanks," Kendra said. "I hope we'll be on the same side again someday."

She swung her legs through the open window and dropped to the ground, landing right near the duffel bag. Then she grabbed it and teleported back to her room of the lair.

Almost immediately, she heard Chronos and Tiffany arguing over some kind of heavy thing they were trying to shove up the stairs.

"What is this mattress even *filled* with?" Chronos complained, grunting and straining. "It keeps sloshing around!"

"Walter the Waterbed always makes noises like that."

"You're making me help carry a *waterbed?!* Without emptying it?!"

Kendra silently put the duffel bag with her clothing in her new bedroom's empty closet and lay back onto her rickety, uncovered mattress. It was covered in holes and singe marks, as if the previous minion living here had worn spikes or thrown fire around casually.

She should have realized Florence would refuse her. She should have realized she'd been right all along. Florence was too rigid, too inflexible, too convinced her of her own morality to question whether right and wrong were really so extreme as she claimed.

That was just so typical Florence. My best friend really hasn't changed at all.

But maybe someday Florence would join her again. And in the meantime ... she did have two teammates.

Kendra stood up and clenched her fists, steeling herself.

Then she left the room to help that psycho Tiffany move.

Five hours later, Florence discovered a suitcase under her bed filled with a bunch of her clothes. It was obvious who had packed it because they were all re-folded the wrong way.

Florence clenched her fists. *You PACKED a SUITCASE for me? Why do you always think you can make decisions for me?! Why do you always think you can predict me?! What is wrong with you?!*

After a moment of silent fuming, her fists unclenched, and Florence pulled the clothes out and sighed.

That was just so typical Kendra. My best friend really hasn't changed at all.

But maybe someday Kendra would join her again.

Author Note:

In To Prevent World Peace *(and in the* Magical Mayhem *series), there's an important scene where Kendra tries to convince her best friend to join her on her path to villainy.*

One of my fans said that he wanted to see it fleshed out more, in order to get a good idea of what was going on in Kendra's head through that scene.

So I fleshed it out, discovered that it stood alone quite well, and made it a short story.

NOT QUITE A CURSE

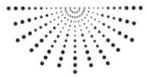

Chapter 1
Not Quite Aware

*L*ucy didn't realize she was cursed at first.

It wasn't like the day started out badly. In fact, it started out really well. For instance, there was the fact that she got asked out on three different dates by three different guys.

"Hey, Luce," George called, hurrying over as she shut her locker door. "Do you have any plans this Friday night?"

"Nope," Lucy said. "You?"

He grinned. "Well, I was hoping we might go out."

Lucy gave him an appraising look. She'd gone out with him a month ago. Too soon to go out with him again?

She'd found that when she went out with the same guy too many times in a row, he started to think they were going steady, and that just would not stand. She hated it when guys got clingy.

"Maybe," Lucy said, tossing her hair. "What time?"

"Dave's Pizza Buffet, right after school?" George asked. "We can double with one of your friends, if you want."

He knew her so well. Lucy loved double dates. They were so low-pressure.

Plus, then there would be *two* cute guys to stare at, rather than one. Her friends tended to have great taste in boys, too.

Not that, you know, she noticed or anything.

Anyway, at lunchtime, she passed by the really cute new boy who had just started school here a few days ago.

"Hi, Pablo," she said.

He did a double take, looking over at her. "Hi ...?"

"Lucy," she said.

"You know my name," he said with surprise.

"I know everyone's names," she said matter-of-factly. She put no effort into schoolwork, but she had memorized the names of everybody at school. She liked saying hello to people, even the shy ones. Being popular didn't mean you had to be a jerk.

"Sorry I didn't know yours," he said.

"That's okay," she beamed. "You'd've heard it sooner or later. Everyone knows me. I'm the cutest girl in the school."

He stared at her.

"What?" she asked with a mischievous smile. "It's true. Should I be falsely modest?"

"Most people would."

"I'm not most people."

He laughed. "So I see."

"Well, I'd better get in line before the cafeteria runs out of anything good," she said, turning and waving. "Bye, Pablo."

"Wait!" he said. "I can't believe I'm asking this, but ... do you have any plans this weekend?"

"Are you asking me out?" she asked with an impish grin.

"Am I asking out the cutest girl in the school? Well, it seems like a wise thing to do."

"Sure," Lucy said. "My weekend's not totally full yet."

"I'm not sure whether to be insulted or not."

She laughed. "You shouldn't be. You're cute."

He looked bemused. "You're not very shy, are you?"

"I tried being shy once, when I was three," Lucy informed him. "I figured it had to be fun, or else people wouldn't do it. It was boring, so I ditched it."

He snorted with laughter. "You do realize people aren't shy because they choose to be, right?"

"Well, I know that *now*," Lucy said, tossing her hair. "Seriously, people would have way more fun if they weren't afraid of what other people think. Anyway, what time and place?"

"Friday night?" Pablo hazarded.

"Sure, as long as it's not immediately after school. I have another date then."

"You just ... come right out and say that, do you?"

"I'm cute. I have dates. We're talking about scheduling here. I should be done by five, so maybe we could get together around five thirty or six?"

"Yes, your majesty," he said with a mock bow.

"Oh, yeah, and just so you know, me sitting in the bleachers watching you play basketball because you forgot you had practice that day is *not* a date," Lucy added, shaking her finger.

"That seems ... oddly specific."

Lucy tossed her hair. "It's from personal experience."

"I would never have guessed."

"Here's my address, so you can pick me up on Friday," Lucy said. She rummaged through her purse for a pen, then grabbed his hand and wrote her address and phone number on it.

"I have a notebook," he said.

"It was an excuse to hold your hand," she said teasingly. "See you on Friday!"

And then she bounced off to the lunch line.

Right after the last bell rang, Lucy was gathering up her books and sneaking glances at Jonas, the guy she'd had a giant crush on in elementary school and who still hadn't seemed to notice she was alive, despite the fact that it was ten years later and she was now the cutest girl in the school. It was maddening that he sat next to her in the most boring class ever, and yet had never relieved her boredom by picking up on one of her flirtatious winks. Such a dunce. But so cute, anyway.

Jonas actually looked up and noticed her, for once.

"You're ... Lucy, right?" he asked slowly.

"Yup!" she said, pleased.

He stared at her for a long moment.

She decided to help him out. "I'm free on Saturday. Just so you know."

Relief raced across Jonas's face, closely followed by panic. "Um, do you ... would you ... that is ..."

Lucy waited for him to finish.

He mumbled something unintelligible.

"I'd love to go out with you," Lucy told him, hoping she was guessing what he'd said correctly. "What time?"

"One o'clock?" he hazarded.

"Sure. Okay. Looking forward to it. Bye, Jonas!"

Lucy waved and gathered up her books, and left the math classroom with a bounce in her step.

AFTER THE BUS arrived at her stop, Lucy hopped off and waved goodbye to the driver. "Bye, Guster!"

"Bye, Lucy!" he said, waving.

She skipped up the front steps and let herself in with a key.

To her surprise, her mom seemed to be home from work early, and she was yelling at someone on the phone in the kitchen.

"That's *not* what I said, Alfie!" her voice traveled.

Oh. Uncle Alfie. Lucy shrugged and tossed her backpack on the floor. If she was yelling at him, he deserved it.

"Lucy?" her mother called from the kitchen. "Is that you?"

"Yeah!"

"Talk to your father!" her mom shouted. "We've got some really bad news!"

Bemused, Lucy headed to her father's study. Her mom always made her dad break bad news, and it was never anything all that important. What was it this time? Had they forgotten to make dinner reservations for their date this weekend? Had one of her teachers called about her bad grades? Had her mom's favorite soap opera gotten canceled?

That would be a drag, actually. She liked the show, too.

Lucy opened the door and strolled in. Her father was sitting at his desk, typing. When he heard the sound of the door, he turned around and looked at her. His face was very solemn.

"Who died?" Lucy asked flippantly.

"Aunt Aggie," he said.

Whoa. Someone actually had died.

For a heartbeat, Lucy thought, *Well, we barely knew her, anyway.* And then the world came crashing down around her as she remembered what this death meant.

If Aunt Aggie was dead, that meant she was cursed.

That meant she was Virgo.

Chapter 2
Not Quite a Name

"I'm cursed," Lucy tried saying, but the words wouldn't come. Horribly, that confirmed it.

"I'm sorry, Lucy," her father said. "That means you're Virgo."

"I know," Lucy snapped. "Did you think I couldn't figure that out? I'm not stupid."

Aunt Aggie hadn't had any kids. She'd been too much of a workaholic to even date. And her parents, siblings, and other nieces and nephews had all been born during the safe eleven-twelfths of the year. That meant Lucy had been her closest living relative born within the dangerous dates, and thus her heir to the curse.

One day, Lucy thought sourly. *One lousy day.*

If she'd been born on September 23 instead of September 22, she would have been safe. But no, she'd had the bad luck to be born two months early, just in time to inherit the Virgo curse. She'd been dreading it for most of her life, so she was used to the idea by now, but it still stank.

"We thought Aunt Aggie would live longer," Lucy's dad said. "She'd only been cursed for nine years."

"Wha—really?" Lucy goggled at him. She'd thought she'd be able to count on a lot longer than that. "What'd she do wrong?"

Lucy's father sighed. "I don't think she bothered to fight it after the first few years. The more you let it change you, the harder it'll be to fight, after all."

Lucy's heart clenched. That was the worst thing about the curse —even worse than dying. It tried to turn your personality into the ideal Virgo. Oh, and once it succeeded, you died. Talk about a double whammy.

"I'll fight it," Lucy assured him.

"Will you?" her father asked sadly.

"Of course I will!" Lucy snapped. How could he even doubt it? "I don't want to be anything like Aunt Aggie. Talk about a boring person!"

Her father started to say something, and then stopped.

"Well," he said at last, "you hold on to that feeling. You're going to need it."

Lucy shuddered. Something creepy was going to start messing with her mind soon. What would it feel like?

She would just as soon never know, if it meant she'd never have to experience it. Too bad that was no longer an option.

"She was selfish," Lucy said angrily. "She should've hung on longer. If she had, I wouldn't have been—" She couldn't say the word. Boy, she hated this curse. "This wouldn't have happened so early!" she finished finally.

"Well ... she probably was selfish," Lucy's father said slowly. "Selflessness was never one of Aggie's defining traits. But you have no idea how hard she struggled at first. I hope you'll find it easier to resist the curse than she did, but in case you don't ..." He hesitated. "Well, I hope you won't judge her too harshly."

Lucy felt irrationally angry at first. But she breathed in deeply and let it go. She'd never been one for big, emotional displays.

Hurray, I get to die young, Lucy thought sourly. *Lucky me! But at least there's one thing that won't be so bad ...*

"Do you know what my—" Lucy started to say, but she couldn't. The curse wouldn't let her.

"Do you mean your power?" her dad asked.

Lucy nodded, relieved.

Maybe not being able to talk about the curse wouldn't be so bad. Her parents knew all about it, after all. They'd been the ones to tell her about it.

"I don't know," her father said. "From what I hear, every cursed person has a different power. Your aunt could magically sort data. She used it all the time as a computer programmer."

Lucy made a face. *That figures. Boring person, boring power.*

She hoped she wouldn't get something so lame that a computer could easily do it for her. She wanted a power that was so amazing, it would almost make up for the fact that she was going to die within twenty years.

Man. She was going to die within twenty years.

Stupid curse.

"Okay," Lucy said, trying to sound in control, even though it felt like her whole world was tilting sideways. "So what do we do now?"

"Well," Lucy's father said, "your mother is warning her brother."

Lucy made a face. "How is that going?"

"He still doesn't believe that curses exist."

Moron. Lucy rolled her eyes. At least she didn't have to feel too bad about her heir who would inherit the curse from her. She couldn't stand the man.

Of course, she couldn't completely blame him. Lucy's father and his sister were the ones who'd grown up in a family who'd had eight cursed Virgos in four generations. Lucy's mother and her brother hadn't. But because Lucy's nearest blood relative who'd been born between August 23 and September 22 was on her mother's side, the curse was going to skip families next time it moved on. Lucky, lucky Uncle Alfie.

Apparently the curse skipped families a lot. The bloodline of whoever-was-the-first-Virgo didn't matter, only the nearest living relative to whoever-was-currently-Virgo, so it often hopped from one side of a person's family to the other.

All the zodiac curses did that. That was why nobody knew when the curses had started, or why, or how.

She didn't even know if her father's family had been from the original bloodline. Probably not.

Probably none of the families were.

"Who are the other—?" Lucy tried to ask.

"The other cursed?" her father asked.

Lucy nodded.

"I only know two of them," her dad said. "Sagittarius and Aries. I'll call them up tonight. I just wanted to tell you first."

"We're not related to them, are we?" Lucy asked cautiously. Her older sister, who was in college, had the zodiac sign of Aries.

"Oh, certainly not!" her father exploded. "I cannot understand for the life of me why two people from cursed families would ever marry! Talk about dangerous for your kids!"

"Has it happened before?" Lucy asked.

Her father nodded. "Aggie mentioned that the Aquarius and the Sagittarius married a few generations ago."

The Sagittarius. Lucy swallowed. She realized that people were going to start referring to her that way now. *The Virgo.*

That wasn't what she wanted to be. That wasn't who she *was*. As if it wasn't enough that the curse wanted to strip her of her life, her mind, her identity, it was already trying to strip away her name.

It wasn't okay. And she decided right then and there that she would never call anybody by one of those titles, no matter how convenient it might be. When she met the others, the first thing she would do was ask their names.

"Yeah, call them tonight," Lucy nodded. "We should set something up so I can meet them. As soon as possible, I guess. Oh, but not this Friday or Saturday, if those are the only times they have available," she added quickly. "I have dates."

Her dad stared at her. "Don't you think those could wait?"

"No," Lucy said. "Changing my plans is like saying this has my permission to change my life. It does not have my permission. I'm not changing my plans."

Her father looked like he was unsure whether he should be

amused or relieved or exasperated. "Well ... I'll find out when a good time for you to meet the others is, then."

"Good." Lucy nodded.

She marched towards the door and opened it. From the kitchen, she heard her mother shouting.

"Alfie! I'm telling you this because I care whether you live or die! Even though you apparently don't!"

"Uncle Alfie's going to be really surprised if he inherits the—thing—and he still doesn't believe in it," Lucy commented.

Lucy's father winced. "I hope it'll be a long, long time before that happens."

That seemed like an odd level of concern for Uncle Alfie. "Why? Because Mom would be sad?"

Her father just stared at her.

"What?"

Her father looked incredulous.

"*What?*" Lucy asked.

"Lucy," her father said, "do you honestly think I'm concerned about your mom's idiot brother?"

Oh. The obvious came crashing down on her. *Uncle Alfie won't inherit the curse until I'm dead.*

"Yes, let's spare Uncle Alfie for awhile," Lucy said lightly.

Chapter 3
Not Quite Concerned

School was a relief, because her mother's way of reacting to the bad news had turned out to be exasperating.

Her mom had spent all night making Lucy take personality tests and fill out notecards. Color-coded notecards. All about her current personality, so that she could compare herself to those notecards and tests on a regular basis and make sure the curse hadn't changed her without her noticing it.

"My personality objects to color-coded notecards," Lucy tried complaining. But her mom ignored that.

Her father had spent all evening calling up the two cursed people he had the numbers of, collecting the phone numbers of the others, and calling everyone possible to arrange a giant meeting so that they could fill Lucy in on the details.

As much as they possibly could, given that none of them would be able to talk about anything directly.

"Lucy, do you have any plans this weekend?" her dad yelled from the study at one point.

"Yeah, I told you I have dates!" she called back. "Two on Friday and one on Saturday!"

"Three dates?!" he hollered.

"Don't worry!" she called. "They're all cute!"

"And this should make me *not* worry?!"

"Sure! Wouldn't you worry more if I had such bad taste that I was going out with ugly boys instead?" Lucy called.

"No, not really!"

"Let's use a different color to symbolize a different feeling on each subject," Lucy's mother said, opening a drawer to pull out a package of twelve matching pens in various colors. "Then it will be easy to cross-reference each of the basic cards with all of the details on the white cards about specific subjects."

Lucy stared at the stack of notecards on the table. It had multiplied. They were like rabbits.

"Lucy, I'm going to set up the meeting for Saturday morning!" her father called. "Don't make any more plans during that time!"

"Got it!" she yelled back.

"And are any of those dates with young men I haven't met before?" he called.

Lucy made a face. She'd known he was going to ask that. "You've met George!"

"Then I'd better meet the other two before you go anywhere with them!"

Lucy groaned. She hated it when he met her dates.

"Now, first of all," her mother said briskly, pulling out a stack of notecards and tapping them against the table to make sure they were perfectly aligned, "what are your opinions on each of your subjects at school?"

"Blah, bleh, blug, and blarg," Lucy said promptly.

"Be serious," her mother admonished. "This information might save your life someday. We need to know exactly every nuance of your real personality."

Lucy sighed. *And taking things seriously DOESN'T go against my real personality?*

Reluctantly, she let her mother grill her, even when some of the questions were embarrassingly personal. Since psychoanalyzing herself in exhaustive detail was something Lucy never did, it wasn't long before she was squirming. But her mom just kept on going, asking more details and writing it all down in tiny, neat writing across notecard after notecard.

"Can we please do something else now?" Lucy pleaded. "I have math homework, you know!"

"You never finish it, anyway," her mother said flatly. She raised her voice and called, "Harry, would you find a Myers-Briggs test online and print it out for me?"

"Sure!" her father called from the study.

"Oh, could you also print me out a more detailed description of Virgo?" Lucy's mother added. "All I've got right now is *Logical, responsible, loyal, detail-oriented, shy, and deeply perfectionistic.* I'm sure there are other more subtle traits worth tracking, and I've got plenty of notecards."

"I'll print out several different descriptions!" her dad called.

Lucy put her head in her arms and moaned.

Overall, the whole night was an ordeal, and she was very, very glad to go to school the next morning.

She waved hello to everybody she met, she got asked out on another date by a guy named Evan she'd gone out with a few times, and she told him that he'd have to wait till next week to try again, because she was booked this weekend and she never planned things out more than a week in advance.

Maybe I should have told some of my friends about the curse I was going to get before it happened, Lucy thought. *They could have helped me keep an eye out for any personality changes.*

But that sounded icky-sticky touchy-feely, exactly the sort of thing Lucy hated. She didn't have friends so that she could sit around overanalyzing everything and angsting. She had friends so that they could hang out and have fun.

Nah, I don't want them to know, Lucy decided. *If they knew, they'd treat me differently. What I need is for everything to stay exactly the same.*

Which meant no stupid notecards. Seriously.

Ivan asked her out after school, and she told him the same thing she'd told Evan: to try again next week when her schedule wasn't totally full.

After school, she hung out with Carrie, Matilda, Jezza, and Natasia, accepted a ride home from Matilda who had just gotten her driver's license, and then arrived home two hours late without remembering to call her parents to let them know.

"You might have called!" her dad yelled. "We were worried!"

"Well, at least that shows I haven't changed at all," Lucy said pertly. "You wouldn't want me to suddenly go responsible, would you?"

That shut her father up quickly.

Lucy grinned as she skipped up the stairs two at a time. This might not be so bad, after all. Being flighty and irresponsible was the opposite of Virgo, which was exactly what her parents wanted for her. The less responsible she was, the longer she'd live! This was great!

She couldn't believe she'd missed such an obvious solution. All she had to do was behave in exactly the opposite way the ideal Virgo would.

Lucy grabbed her backpack and yanked out her just-barely-started math homework. She tore it into little shreds and scattered them around the room as confetti.

"Fly, homework! Fly!" she cried, and giggled.

Her mother knocked on her door. "Lucy, may I come in?"

"If you want!" Lucy called. "I don't care!"

Her mother came in, looking cautious. "Lucy, we need to talk."

"I don't want to talk," Lucy said, scooping up a sock from the floor. She lay back on her bed and tossed it up and down, catching it. "I'm never going to take anything seriously again."

Her mother sighed. "I was afraid you'd say something like that. Luce, you can't use your curse as an excuse for bad behavior."

"Can so," Lucy said.

"Cannot."

"Can so! You want me to stay alive longer, don't you?"

"Can I be frank?" her mother asked.

"Sure." Lucy tossed the sock in the air.

"No."

Lucy dropped the sock. She jerked up to a sitting position.

"*No?*" she asked, outraged.

"No," her mother said. "Not at the cost of you turning your life into something not worth living. It's possible to ruin your life in ways other than surrendering to a curse."

Lucy set her jaw.

"The solution isn't to abandon your self-control entirely, Lucy," her mother said. "You need to use it *more*. That's what you'll need to grow into a better version of yourself. It's also what you'll need to resist the curse."

Lucy gave her a furious look.

"I know you're scared," her mother began.

"I'm not scared!" Lucy snapped.

"Well, you should be."

Lucy realized with horror that she had a lump in her throat. She fought it back. She hated crying. It was messy and disgusting.

"So what exactly do you want me to do?" she asked rudely.

Her mom reached out and gave her a hug. "Remember who you are."

Thanks, Mom, Lucy thought sourly. *Here I was planning on completely forgetting.*

CHAPTER 4

Not Quite Polite

Friday took forever to come, and even after it did, it felt like the school day dragged on twice as long as usual. But when, at last, the final bell rang, Lucy exploded out of her seat and raced towards the door, joining her friend Jezza in shouting, "FREEDOM!"

The math teacher did not look pleased.

George met her at her locker while she was putting her books away.

"You ready to go get pizza?" he asked.

"Sure!" Lucy said. She dumped the rest of her backpack's contents into her locker. There was homework in there somewhere, but eh. She wasn't freaking out as much now about the curse's certainty of affecting her, but she hadn't bothered to do her homework since Monday, either. She'd tried a few times, but every time she'd looked at it, she'd thought, *Aunt Aggie was a workaholic*, and then she hadn't been able to stand the sight of it.

The fact of the matter was, the curse was definitely going to affect her and kill her eventually. No one had ever lasted longer than twenty years. But that didn't mean she had to help it.

If she was going to turn into a—gag, gag—workaholic at some point in the future, she might as well enjoy her life now, while she was still herself. Future-her would probably be furious about that, but what did she care? Future-her wouldn't really be Lucy. Future-her would be Virgo.

Ugh. The future was depressing. Lucy wrenched her thoughts back to today, when she had two bright, shiny, exciting dates waiting.

"Are we doubling with one of your friends?" he asked.

"Yup," Lucy said. "Carrie and her boyfriend will meet us there."

Caleb was a new boyfriend, one Lucy had never met before. Apparently he went to a different school. Carrie tended to commit to relationships with lightning speed, and then she tended to be just as quick about falling out of love with the guys and dumping them.

Which wasn't to say that Carrie never got dumped. She did, about a third of the time. When that happened, she'd cry for a day and eat a whole gallon of ice cream, and then she'd latch onto the nearest cute guy who asked her out and declare him her next boyfriend. It was a cycle that happened over and over again. Lucy'd learned to be skeptical whenever that friend of hers declared she was in love.

Still, that was exactly the reason Carrie was such a great friend to go on a double date with. She almost always had a boyfriend, so it wasn't hard for her to get a date on a moment's notice, and he was almost always brand new. No pressure, in other words. That wasn't always true for Jezza or Matilda.

Worst of all was Natasia. Lucy'd tried double dating with Natasia before, but she and her boyfriend Sean had been going out for over a year, and ugh ... those two were always holding hands or smooching or whispering in each other's ears or just generally being really uncomfortable to sit near.

So they ambled out of the school building, strolled half a block to Dave's Pizza Buffet, and Lucy waved and said hi to a dozen classmates. Finally, she noticed Carrie and a super cute guy with brown skin sitting in a booth near the back, already having helped themselves to two slices of cheap and low-quality pizza.

He's hot, Lucy thought impishly. *I'll have to see if I can get his number after Carrie dumps him.*

She and George each grabbed a plate and a slice of pizza. Then they headed over to the booth near the back.

"Hi, Caleb!" Lucy said cheerfully. "I assume you're Caleb. This is George, and I'm Lucy."

"Yo," George said.

Caleb's mouth was full, so he flicked a hand in what might have been a wave.

"We're Carrie's friends from school," Lucy said, settling into the other side of the booth. George sat beside her. "What school do you go to?"

"Freedom Prep," Caleb said, making a face. "It's a private school. My dad's really into the whole academics thing."

"And you're not?" George asked.

Carrie's new boyfriend shrugged. "I like sports better."

"And he's amazing at wrestling!" Carrie exclaimed, gazing at him with a besotted look on her face. "That's how we met!"

"That's how you *met?*" George asked, looking unsure whether to be confused or horrified.

"He beat Aaron," Carrie said, giggling. "That was back when I was dating Aaron. I'm not anymore, of course."

Lucy snatched a napkin out of the dispenser and stifled her snorts of laughter in it. That was typical Carrie. She got really into competitive sports, and she only liked winners. If a guy she was dating lost, she usually dumped him and went after someone from the opposing team.

George looked more confused than ever.

"How about you?" Carrie asked flirtatiously, leaning forward. "Do you play any sports?"

"I'm in the chess club. Does that count?" George asked.

Carrie leaned back in horror.

Lucy couldn't stifle it with her napkin any longer. She erupted into gales of laughter.

Carrie stared at her furiously.

Lucy just kept on laughing.

"I need to use the bathroom," Carrie announced.

Lucy ignored the summons, blowing her nose in the napkin and going back to laughing.

"You need to use it, too," Carrie hinted threateningly.

So Lucy got up to follow her, rolling her eyes at both boys while her friend's back was turned. Caleb burst into a wide grin.

As soon as they entered the ladies' room, both girls started talking at once.

"The chess club? Are you kidding me?!"

"Could you be more transparent, Carrie?"

"The chess club!"

"George is cute, and he's nice. What's your damage?"

"That's, like, the ultimate nerd thing, Lucy!"

"Yeah, and? He can be smart if he wants. It doesn't make him a bad date. It kind of makes him the opposite."

Carrie screwed up her face. "I didn't realize you had such terrible taste in guys."

I didn't realize I had such terrible taste in friends, Lucy thought about retorting. Carrie had always amused her before, but now the girl was ticking her off.

"He's *cute,*" Lucy repeated. She barely managed to keep from snapping it. "And he's nice. And might I add that he's not your date, he's *mine?*"

Carrie sighed heavily. "That's true." Then she brightened. "What do you think of Caleb? He's gorgeous, right?"

"Totally," Lucy agreed.

"I think he's the one!" Carrie said, giggling.

"No way!" Lucy squealed, not believing a word of it.

Carrie patted her hair, checking the mirror to make sure her makeup was still perfect. She pulled a little bag from her pocket and a tiny pencil from there. She started touching up her eyeliner. "He's totally in love with me, you know, Luce. It's, like, a match made in heaven."

Lucy had heard those words a dozen times. She was starting to get sick of them.

"I'm happy for you," she said cautiously, carefully suppressing rolling her eyes.

"You don't believe me," Carrie accused. "Don't be sarcastic! That's rude!"

And dissing my date was the polite thing to do? Lucy wanted to sneer.

"I wasn't being sarcastic," Lucy said out loud. "I really am happy for you." She tried really hard to sound sincere.

"Okay, fine," Carrie said huffily, shoving the eyeliner pencil back into her makeup bag. She stuffed it in her pocket. "Let's go back to the boys."

Lucy followed her back to the dining area, feeling rather irritated. What was wrong with Carrie? She was usually so fun to be around, but today she just seemed like an annoying twit.

Chapter 5
Not Quite a Friend

CARRIE WAS in a snippy mood for the next few minutes after they got back to the boys, but she soon got over it, and went back to behaving like her usual self. If this was her usual self.

Was Carrie always so loud and desperate for attention? Lucy wondered.

It was unsettling.

No, make that terrifying.

Because what if the curse was making her see Carrie that way?

Had the curse already changed her enough to look at everyone she knew differently? Would she start hating all of her friends? She liked her friends. She didn't want to hate them. They didn't deserve that, and she didn't deserve that kind of loneliness.

"Earth to Lucy!" Carrie said, snapping two fingers in front of her face.

Lucy snapped to attention. "What?"

"I *said*, what's your least favorite subject at school?"

That was easy. "Math," Lucy said promptly.

"Mine's English," Carrie said.

"Mine's P.E.," George put in.

"Art," Caleb said. "Mom made me take that. I'm ditching it next year."

"Okay, now, what's your *favorite?*" Carrie asked, looking around the table and pointing at Lucy.

"Music," Lucy said. That was her elective this year. "Yours?"

"Lunch!" Carrie said, and giggled as if she'd said something really clever.

"Mine's math," said George.

"Mine, too!" Caleb cried, giving him a high five.

Carrie stared at her new boyfriend with a look on her face that suggested she had just swallowed a sour lemon.

"I kind of love statistics," Caleb said. "I might major in that in college. I like stuff that's really useful, you know?"

"Oh, it's all about the theoreticals for me," George said, shaking his head. "Seriously, did you know there are an infinite number of sizes of infinity? Blows my mind!"

"Okay, what's your favorite sport?!" Carrie broke in desperately.

For once, Lucy found herself in full agreement with her friend. The last thing she wanted was a conversation about math for the next half hour.

"To play, or to watch?" Caleb asked.

"Both."

"To play ... wrestling, obviously. To watch ... baseball."

"How about you?" Carrie asked, pointing at George.

"Do videogames count?" he hedged.

Carrie's expression said they didn't.

"Then none."

"You have to pick something."

"Who said?"

"I did!"

"But I don't like any of them. I like games that require thinking, not games where there are no brains at all."

Lucy inched away from her date. He deserved whatever Carrie was about to yell at him.

"No brains!" Carrie exploded. *"No brains?!"*

"Okay," George said quickly, "maybe that wasn't the best—"

But it was too late. Carrie was already going on a loud and emphatic rant, pounding the table in several places and drowning out any attempts to stop her.

"Hey, do you all go to the same school?" Caleb broke in suddenly, talking at twice the volume Carrie was managing.

Carrie stopped, looking taken aback.

"Yes," Lucy said quickly, talking slightly louder than usual.

"Yeah," George said, looking grateful for the change of topic.

Carrie took a breath, opened her mouth ...

"Have you two been going out long?" Caleb added.

"I wish," George said with a wry laugh. "But Lucy is, like, pathologically non-exclusive."

"Don't you think maybe calling me pathological might be a bad move?" Lucy demanded with mock offense.

George mimed holding his hands over his head.

"Anyway, like I was—" Carrie began.

"How'd you two meet, anyway?" Caleb asked.

"Let's see," George said. "I think it was that math test she needed help with at the end of last year. The teacher told her if she didn't pass it, she'd fail the class and have to make it up with summer school. She got a C, by the way, which meant she just barely passed it."

Lucy moaned. "Did you have to tell him all the details?"

"You worked hard! You should be proud!"

"No, I should be embarrassed!"

"Awwwww, but you're cute when you're embarrassed," George said, grinning.

"I'm going to get more pizza," Carrie said sulkily, sliding out of the booth and taking her empty plate with her. "Anybody else want something?"

"Hawaiian," said George.

"Pepperoni," Caleb added.

"The barbecue ranch one."

Carrie stalked off towards the pizza buffet table. There was a rather long line at the end, since the room had filled up with lots of fellow students from school.

Caleb leaned forward quickly. "Hey, I know this is awkward and bad timing and stuff, but can I get your number?"

Lucy stared at him, dumbfounded. "What?"

"Hope you don't mind," Caleb added, looking at George.

He rolled his eyes. "Whatever. I knew you were going to ask."

"Well?" Caleb asked.

"Carrie!" Lucy sputtered.

"Yeah, what about her?" Caleb asked.

"You're her *boyfriend!*"

Caleb looked baffled. "Since when? This is our first date."

Lucy stared at him in consternation. *How often does Carrie start calling guys her boyfriend on the first date? That would explain a lot about her relationships ...*

She shook her head. No, no. It didn't matter. Carrie was her friend. You had to be loyal to your friends.

"I'm sorry," she said in a low voice. "As long as you're dating Carrie—"

"Okay, I'll break up with her right now."

Caleb hopped up and walked towards the buffet line.

"Get back here!" Lucy cried in horror.

George snorted with laughter.

Lucy gave him a furious glare and jumped up, but he didn't help her by moving out of the way, so that left her mostly trapped in the booth. She tried to edge past his knees at a snail's pace.

"It might be better if you leave them alone," George suggested. "If you get right in the middle of that …"

Lucy broke free of the booth and ran towards the buffet line, but she was too late. Or rather, she was just in time to see Carrie burst into sobs and collapse to the floor, empty tray clattering beside her.

Lucy stopped, frozen. This was the worst thing that could have happened on a double date.

Then Caleb made it worse.

"Can I get your number now?" he called to Lucy.

A few girls standing in line gave Lucy shocked and outraged glares, while a few guys whistled.

"No!" Lucy exploded. "No, you cannot get my number! What is *wrong* with you?"

From the floor, Carrie's head lifted and gave her a hateful look.

Lucy had the sinking feeling she had just lost a friend.

Chapter 6
Not Quite Escape

After that fiasco, Lucy still had another date to get through. Two dates in one day no longer seemed quite as fun as it had a few days ago. And she still had to find a way to get home so that she could change her clothes and meet Pablo there.

George, it turned out, did not have a car. Lucy didn't have her own car, either; she sometimes borrowed one of her parents', but she hadn't done that today. Under normal circumstances, this wouldn't have been a problem, since she could have just asked Carrie to drop her off at home in her ancient clunker that she was so proud of. But that ... obviously wasn't going to happen today.

So she had to endure the ultimate humiliation: calling her parents to ask them to pick her up.

Her dad was the one who drove to get her. When she got in the car, he asked, "So what was wrong with Carrie? Your mother said you said there was some reason she couldn't drop you off at home."

Lucy groaned and buckled her seat belt. "It's a totally long story."

"I'm a totally curious person, and this car doesn't have to go anywhere. We could just sit here for hours while I wait to hear what happened ..."

Lucy glared at her father for this transparent ploy to get her to talk about her personal life, but whatever. It wasn't like the story wouldn't end up all over the school by tomorrow, anyway. Practically half the school had been there watching.

"Carrie's boyfriend hit on me," Lucy said sulkily. "She totally hates me now."

"Did you apologize?"

"It's not my fault!" Lucy cried. "I didn't encourage him! In fact, I told him no way would I ever date him as long he was dating Carrie, and then he went and broke up with her!"

Lucy's father started snickering.

"It's not funny!"

He straightened his face with great effort. "Right. You're right. Of course not. Please continue."

Lucy sighed and slouched back against the seat. "That's it."

"Really?" her father said. "That doesn't seem like that long of a story. I was looking forward to a long story."

"It *felt* long!"

"Right." Her father nodded seriously. "Just like every time I have to watch you go out the door with another young man I've never seen before in my life, and then I spend my whole evening worrying. Speaking of which, who is tonight's model?"

"Pablo," Lucy said. "His name is Pablo."

"Is he cute?"

"Why would you care?"

"Just taking an interest."

"Well, don't. It sounds weird."

Her dad tried very hard to keep a straight face.

"Daaaaaad," Lucy complained. "Can we go home now, please? I need to touch up my makeup, and I want to change my outfit."

He glanced at her. "What's wrong with what you're wearing?"

"Nothing's *wrong* with it," Lucy said impatiently. "It's just that he saw me wearing this outfit at school."

"And ...?"

"And I don't want him to think I'm the sort of person who wears the same thing, like, all the time!"

"Heaven forbid," her father said dryly, looking down at his army uniform.

"Exactly! Oh, and if you try to scare him off by showing up at the door polishing a shotgun or something, then—" She shook her finger.

"Then what?" her father asked with interest.

"Then *hmph!*" She stuck out her tongue at him.

Lucy's dad grinned and started the car.

At last, they were heading home. As soon as the car stopped, Lucy flung her door open and bolted for the house. She had only forty-five minutes left before Pablo arrived, and she didn't want to be late and give her father more time to interrogate him. That would be the end of the world.

She kept a close eye on the clock as she decided what to wear, calculating in her head how long it would take to get ready so that she knew how long she had to choose the perfect outfit. After trying on four and discarding three, she kept a long purple blouse and a super cute denim skirt she'd bought with her last allowance. Then she loaded up her arms with dozens and dozens of bracelets that jangled while she moved. She liked the way the noise made her the center of attention when she wore them.

Lucy was just giving her ponytail one last spritz of hairspray when the doorbell rang.

"I'll get it!" she cried, tossing the bottle on the counter of the bathroom. It rolled and fell to the ground, but she didn't stop to pick it up. She just raced downstairs.

Have to get to the door before Dad ... have to get to the door before Dad ...

"Hello," her father's voice said. "You must be Pablo."

Argh! Lucy let out a silent scream as she jumped down the last few steps and bolted for the front door.

"Gee, thank you for coming, Pablo!" she said brightly. "You have reservations that we can't be late for, right? Right. Let's go!"

Pablo looked confused. "I don't—"

"Now, Lucy, you know how this works," her father said, clapping Pablo on the shoulder rather harder than necessary. "I'm Lucy's father. You can call me 'sir.' Before you take my daughter anywhere, there are some ground rules you need to know ..."

And thus began the usual torturous, embarrassing ordeal that Lucy had desperately wanted to skip. She practically had the whole speech memorized, so she wandered over to the kitchen, where her mom was busy filling in a spreadsheet on her laptop.

"Dad's giving one of my dates 'the talk' again," Lucy complained. "Can't he lay off, for once?"

Lucy's mom didn't even look up from her laptop. "Given that your cousin got pregnant in high school, no, I don't think so."

Lucy made a face.

"I've been typing up your notecards," Lucy's mom said, glancing up and tapping the side of the screen. "Want to see?"

Lucy wavered. On the one hand, it sounded kind of interesting, but on the other hand, yuck.

"I guess so, maybe," she said reluctantly.

Her mom turned the laptop so that Lucy could see the screen better. It was a color-coded masterpiece of perfectionism. Lucy instinctively, passionately loathed it.

"Gee," she said, trying to think of something that wasn't, *That's even worse than the notecards.*

"I'm working on a scoring rubric," her mom said. "That way, you can take a test every week, and we'll be able to quantitatively compare your scores with where they used to be—"

"Oh, I think Dad's wrapping up now! Gotta go!" Lucy cried.

She raced back to the living room just in time to catch the tail end of her dad's speech. Anything was better than agreeing to take extra tests every week. Talk about a curse, sheesh.

"Now, one last thing," Lucy's father was saying. "I may not own a shotgun, but I want you to know that I do own ... *this*. And I know how to use it."

He seized a well-thumbed volume from the bookcase and held it up intimidatingly.

Lucy groaned. Was he trying to humiliate her?

When at last the interminable lecture was over, Lucy went out to her date's car. Pablo held the door open for her, and glanced back at the front door where her dad was watching. Her father nodded curtly. Then Pablo got in the driver's seat.

"Sorry about my dad," Lucy said, shaking her head. "He is way overprotective. Talk about annoying."

As he turned the key into the ignition, Pablo remarked, "You know, I think the fact that your dad owns Sun Tzu's *Art of War* and knows how to use it is a lot more intimidating than a shotgun would be."

Chapter 7
Not Quite a Shock

Despite her dad's attempt to ruin the date by making her die of embarrassment, the date went very well after that.

They went to see a horror flick, they smuggled hot dogs into the theater and bought a giant tub of popcorn, they wound up throwing most of the popcorn at each other, and they walked out of the building cracking up as they made fun of the characters, who had been way too stupid to live.

She had such a good time that when he said goodbye to her at the door, she spontaneously leaned over and kissed him.

He blinked as she pulled back. "I thought you told me you didn't kiss on the first date."

She smirked. "Only if I make the first move."

At that point, the door flew open, and her father stood there with a gigantic scowl.

"Bye, Pablo!" Lucy said, ducking under her father's arm to get in the house.

"See you at school on Monday!" he called.

Her father shut the door and folded his arms.

"It's none of your beeswax who I kiss, Dad," Lucy said.

"Didn't you just meet him a few days ago?"

"Yeah. And I like him."

"Don't you have another date tomorrow?"

"Yep, and I like him, too."

Her father glowered.

Lucy proceeded to spend the rest of the night ignoring her homework and putting sticky notes in her favorite pages of some fashion magazines she'd bought a few weeks ago. If she used sticky notes, she'd hopefully remember where to find the pages, and could take the magazines with her next time she went shopping. It was a genius plan.

Her older sister Lila called, freaking out because she'd only just checked her messages and gotten the news that Aunt Aggie had died and Lucy was cursed now.

Once Lucy assured her that things were fine, and no she had no clue what her magic power was, and yes she'd call her when she found out, the two of them wound up gabbing for hours about just about everything. It was amazing how well they got along now that they no longer lived in the same house.

"Just take care of yourself, Luce," Lila said as they were about to hang up. "I want you to stay alive."

"That's not what you used to say," Lucy said with a grin.

Lila snickered. "What can I say? College has matured me."

By the time the call ended, it was well past her usual bedtime, so Lucy brushed her teeth and headed to bed. Her parents were already asleep and snoring. Since it wasn't a school night and she'd been talking to Lila, they hadn't put a limit on her phone time.

Lucy lay awake for a long time, wondering.

What *was* her power? Would it be something cool? She really hoped it wouldn't have anything to do with spreadsheets.

She fell asleep and had unsettling dreams about color-coded math tests and her father throwing books at all of her dates.

LUCY OVERSLEPT THE NEXT MORNING, and only woke up when her father called up the stairs.

"Lucy, they're here!"

Who's here? she thought, rubbing her eyes groggily. *My date with Jonas isn't till this afternoon.*

Then she remembered, and her eyes widened. She jumped out of bed, spurred by adrenaline, and dressed with rapid haste. In only a few minutes, with no makeup and her hair unbrushed, she was running downstairs to meet the other cursed.

"They" turned out to have been an overstatement. So far there was only one person, an old man with brown skin and grey hair. He was sitting on the armchair, talking with her parents. Lucy came in, and he held out his hand. She took it gingerly.

"Hello," he beamed, shaking her head. "I'm Aaron Watson. You can call me Aaron."

"Aaron," Lucy repeated. It was odd to hear someone her grandpa's age asking her to call him by his first name, but nice. She hated calling people by their last names. It seemed so impersonal.

"I was born on March twenty-sixth," he added.

Lucy's mind went blank. She knew he was trying to tell her what his curse was, but the date meant nothing to her. The only zodiac birthdays she knew were Virgo's.

"Aries," Lucy's mom said helpfully.

"Oh!" Lucy said. "How long have you been ... um ..."

"Five years," he said, smiling.

"Five days," she said, pointing at herself.

"So I've heard."

There was a sound of a car driving up, and the doorbell rang a moment later. Lucy's dad got up to answer it. He came back with—

"Alex Jaketon?" Lucy blurted out.

He was a guy from her school. He was *the* guy, in fact, who had taken her out on a date to watch him play basketball because he had forgotten he had practice that day.

He seemed similarly surprised to see her. "You're, uh ..."

"*Lucy*," she said impatiently. "We've been on two dates. The least you could do is remember my name."

"Sorry," he said.

Honestly, Lucy thought, rolling her eyes. *You're not getting a third date.*

"Hi, Alex!" Aaron called from his chair, waving. "Is Xander coming today?"

"No."

"Xander?" Lucy's mom asked.

"His twin brother," Aaron said. "Which means ..." He lowered his voice as if he were about to reveal something very significant. "... they were born on the same day."

"Ohhhhh," Lucy's parents said in unison.

Uh, yeah? Lucy thought. *That's what being twins means.*

"So Xander is Alex's heir," Lucy's dad said slowly. "Or is it the reverse?"

"You got it right the first time," Aaron said.

But Lucy had noticed something far more interesting. "What's Xander short for?" she demanded.

Alex sighed. "It's short for my parents not having much imagination and giving us really similar names."

"Yes, but what's it short *for?*"

"Alessandro."

"And your name is Alexander?"

"Yes, but call me Alex, please."

The boy was extremely polite and extremely distant. He sat stiffly on the sofa. Lucy found herself rather exasperated.

"Are any of the heirs coming?" Lucy's mom asked anxiously. "It will be much easier to talk about things if we have people who can, well, talk about them."

"I know Steven's bringing his son," the old man answered. "My granddaughter lives several states away, and she's only seven years old, anyway. Catherine was too busy to come today, and her nephew is in college across the country, so he won't be here, either."

"Who is which?" Lucy's father inquired.

"Let's see," Aaron said. "Catherine's birthday is ... I'm trying to remember ..."

"Late July," Alex said.

Lucy's mother thought for a moment. "Leo?"

"Yes!" the old man said, looking pleased.

"What about yours?" Lucy's mom asked, looking at Alex.

"June eighth."

"Gemini?" she hazarded.

He nodded.

"That's the sign for twins, isn't it?" she asked. "How appropriate that you actually *are* a twin!"

"Funny, I've never heard that before," he said flatly.

"So we're just waiting for the Sagittarius and his son?" Lucy's dad asked.

Lucy blinked. She'd assumed there would be a lot more people than that. "Why just—?"

There came a loud knock at the door. Since Lucy was the only one standing, she went to get it. When she opened the door, there was a middle-aged man standing there.

"Hello," he said, shaking her hand. "I'm Steven. And you are?"

"Lucy."

"So you're the one this meeting is about."

She nodded.

"Well, I'm pleased to meet you, even if the circumstances are no doubt not very pleasant for you." Steven stepped to the side. "This is my son, Caleb."

And in that moment, Lucy knew true horror.

Chapter 8
Not Quite So Good

Yes, it was him. Of course it was him. That was just the way her luck went, apparently. Not only was he standing right in front of her, she now had to converse with him.

"Hi, Caleb," Lucy said frostily.

Steven looked startled. "Have you two met?"

Lucy tossed her hair haughtily. "He broke up with my friend Carrie in order to ask *me* out yesterday."

"I was only following your suggestion!" Caleb cried.

"If you wanted to stop dating her without hurting her feelings, it wouldn't even have been that hard!" Lucy yelled. "She breaks up with any guy who loses a sports game!"

Caleb paused, looking incredulous. "Wow. Really?"

Steven's eyebrows quirked. "This sounds like an amusing story. But can we talk about it later? Caleb's the only person who'll be able to speak freely, so he needs to be here. Can we come in?"

"My parents can speak freely, too," Lucy said with ill grace, but she moved aside to let them enter.

"Hi, Alex," Caleb said, flopping on the sofa next to him.

"Hi," Alex said. "What's this about Carrie?"

"Where's Xander?" Caleb countered. "Hasn't he shown up?"

Alex sighed. "Why does everyone keep asking that? No."

"He really ought to have come," Steven said, taking a seat on the end of the sofa beside his son.

"Xander does what Xander wants to do," Alex said tightly. "I don't control him."

"He doesn't even control himself!" Caleb said, cracking up.

Alex looked mildly annoyed.

So Alex's brother is a jerk, Lucy noted. *We're probably lucky he didn't show up.*

"Okay, so," Lucy said, taking a seat cross-legged on the floor, since all the chairs were taken, "what do I need to know?"

"About what?" Caleb asked.

"About the—!" She couldn't say the word. "Well, obviously!"

"Okay, but where do you want me to start?"

Lucy gave him a frustrated stare. "If I could say specifics, I wouldn't have had to let you come in. Maybe you could explain why you guys are the only people here?"

Caleb shrugged. "The Leo's busy at work. The Pisces lives in London. The Aquarius ran away years ago. And the other five are missing."

"Missing?" Lucy repeated.

"Yep."

"What do you mean, 'missing'?"

"I mean 'missing.' We don't know who they are."

"*How?*" Lucy shouted.

"Why are they missing?" Lucy's mother exclaimed.

"How could you lose an entire cursed family?" Lucy's father asked incredulously at the same time.

"Curses jump families," Caleb said. "It's that whole 'closest living relative' thing, you know? Sometimes there's nobody closely related with the same zodiac sign."

"But even then, surely it's not *that* hard to go back a few generations and figure out who your closest living relative with the same zodiac sign is," Lucy's mother argued.

"Not every family keeps records back four or five generations, much less eight or nine," Steven said. "And sometimes ... well ..."

He glanced at Caleb.

"Sometimes someone's naughty and fathers an illegitimate kid nobody knows exists, including him, so the heir turns out to be someone random that can't be tracked," Caleb smirked. "Taurus and Libra were *both* lost in the sixties. Guess why."

"It's not that it happens often," Steven said, "but once is enough to lose track of that particular line permanently."

Lucy shuddered. It was horrible to think about how many people must have died without even knowing they had a curse. In fact, the ones who didn't know probably died more quickly than the ones who *did* know, because they wouldn't even realize that they ought to resist.

"Okay!" Lucy declared, smacking her hand on the floor. She was sick of thinking about gloom-and-doom stuff. "Now what about the good thing?"

"What good thing?" Caleb asked.

"The good thing!"

"What good thing?"

"The! Good! Thing!"

"I think she's talking about this," Steven said.

He waved his hands, and landscapes and cityscapes flickered wildly around them. Lucy's mouth fell open in awe.

"How does it work?" she squealed.

"I can't explain it," he said. "I can only demonstrate it."

"He can show places he wants to visit," Caleb said, looking bored. "Only places, not people. He doesn't use it much."

"Why not?" Lucy demanded. "That's awesome!"

"Because I want to live," Steven answered.

That seemed like no answer at all. Lucy was baffled.

"Because it makes Dad want to travel," Caleb said impatiently. "Which makes him more like Sagittarius. So he doesn't use it."

"That seems so unfair," Lucy said, feeling sorry for the man. "The good part just makes the bad part worse."

"Oh, grow up!" Caleb snorted. "You think the magical powers are a good thing? They're *all* like that."

"Like what?" Lucy asked, confused.

Caleb's voice dripped with condescension. "Whatever the curse gives you is meant to tempt you into becoming more like what it wants you to be. The more you use it, the more likely you are to surrender to it. *All* the powers are like that. Using your power is a good way to die quickly."

Lucy stared at him in horror. "No—wait—*what?*"

Lucy's mother gasped. "Nobody told us—"

"Aggie never mentioned—" Lucy's father broke in.

"There's no cause for alarm," Aaron said soothingly.

Lucy leaned forward, hanging on his every word. His voice was magnetic and electrifying. She instinctively trusted everything he said.

"He doesn't truly understand anything," the old man went on. "There's no risk to anybody at all."

Lucy nodded. Of course he was right. Why had she been worried?

"Knock it off, old man!" Caleb shouted.

Aaron sat back, his dark eyes twinkling. "I thought we were demonstrating what we can do for the young lady."

Lucy gasped, suddenly realizing what he meant. "Was that your—your—your thing I can't say—?"

"His power," Caleb said, folding his arms.

Aaron shrugged and smiled. "I try to avoid using mine, too. Quite apart from wanting to live, I'd rather not manipulate people against their will. It doesn't seem like a good thing to be doing."

Lucy's pulse raced, thinking of how easily that power could be misused. She was glad it seemed to belong to a relatively harmless old man, and not some wannabe dictator tyrant.

"So—so what you just said," Lucy's mother sputtered, "about there being no cause to worry—that was—"

"A lie," the old man said with an impish smile. "Listen to Caleb, not me. Especially if I sound particularly trustworthy."

Lucy whipped her head over to look at Alex. "What about you?" she demanded.

Alex looked uncomfortable. "I can't demonstrate mine."

"Can't or won't?" Lucy asked suspiciously.

"Can't," Caleb said. "He reads his brother's mind. That's his power. Stinks to be him, in my opinion."

Lucy made a face. She loved her older sister, but she'd hate to be inside her head all the time. "So you rarely use it?"

"No," Alex said. "Unfortunately."

"Some of the powers don't turn off," Caleb shrugged. "His is one of them. Lucky him, right?"

"What's your brother thinking now?" Lucy asked curiously.

"Even if I were capable of answering that question—which I'm not, for the same reason that Steven couldn't answer your question to him a minute ago—I wouldn't want to."

"Privacy?" Lucy asked.

"I really couldn't care less about his privacy," Alex said darkly. "But his thoughts should never be repeated in front of a girl."

"Lucy, you are never dating Alex's twin," her father said immediately.

"Dad," Lucy said, looking at him with exasperation, "I haven't even met that guy, okay? Quit with the overprotectiveness."

"What about you?" Caleb asked.

"What about me?" Lucy turned to look at him.

"Yeah. What's your magical power?"

"That's why I brought up the subject!" Lucy exclaimed. She looked around the room hopefully. "Do you know what it is?"

Chapter 9
Not Quite the Hope

"We have no idea," Steven said. "Have you tried testing it?"

Lucy was very annoyed. Of course she hadn't tried testing it. What did they think she was, her mother with the notecards and the color-coded spreadsheets?

"No," she said, a little rudely. "There's been nothing *to* test."

"I'm sure it'll turn up eventually," Aaron said kindly.

That was not what Lucy had wanted to hear. She'd wanted answers, not a bunch of shrugs all around. If they were going to be unhelpful, they could at least have been eye candy. Steven was her dad's age and presumably married, Aaron was ancient, Alex was boring as toast, and as for Caleb ...

Okay, Caleb *was* eye candy. He was totally gorgeous. His dark brown skin was a delicious contrast to his white T-shirt and faded denim jacket, and the long sleeves of the jacket didn't quite conceal the fact that he was well-built. Shame about him being a jerk.

"Look, what exactly do you have against me?" Caleb burst out.

Lucy sniffed. "The fact that you treated my friend like dirt might have something to do with it."

"I'm sorry, okay? I'll apologize to her! I'll even go out with her again if you really want me to, but *you're* the one I like, not her!"

A puzzled look flickered across Alex's face.

That was delightfully flattering, and if only he hadn't met Carrie first, Lucy would have thoroughly enjoyed hearing it.

"Well, I'm sorry," Lucy said loftily. "After yesterday, I don't think I could ever go out with you, even if you got back together with Carrie and she dumped you next time. She'd never forgive me."

"Are you kidding me?!" Caleb shouted.

Lucy's mother jumped to her feet. "You know, I nearly forgot to prepare that veggie platter that I wanted to make. I'll be right back."

"I'll help, too," Aaron said, getting up.

"And me," Steven said hastily.

Three of the adults escaped into the kitchen.

"I know we only just met, but I really want to go out with you!" Caleb cried. "It's so unfair that you won't give me a chance!"

Lucy had to admit that she was enjoying this. Just a smidge. "Nope," she said with a coy smile.

Alex rubbed his forehead.

Lucy's dad sat on his chair, folding his hands over his knees and smiling broadly.

"Harry! Come in here to help me!" Lucy's mom called.

"I'm supervising!" he called.

"Supervise from the kitchen!" she yelled.

With a grumpy look on his face, Lucy's father got up and headed out of the room.

"Do you want me to grovel?" Caleb demanded. "Is that it?"

"I don't want anything from you," Lucy said, tossing her hair. *Except to look at you, maybe,* she thought wickedly. *You're even more gorgeous when you're mad at me.*

"ARGH!" Caleb shouted.

Lucy's dad poked his head back into the living room to make sure they were still arguing, seemed pleased with what he saw, and disappeared back into the kitchen.

"Please," Caleb pleaded. "I'm going crazy. I'm crazy about *you*. You have to go out with me. You have to!"

Lucy giggled and shook her head.

Alex muttered something under his breath.

"Do you have something to say, Gemini boy?" Caleb roared.

"Only that I think we've found the answer to Lucy's question," Alex said with faint exasperation.

Lucy's heart leapt. "You mean my—" Of course she couldn't say it, so she phrased it indirectly. "You mean, the good thing?!"

"Mmm. First of all, you've been the only thing half the guys at school have talked about for the past week. It's getting annoying, frankly."

Lucy grinned. She didn't see what that had to do with her magical power, but ...

Caleb looked steamed.

"And second, him." Alex pointed at Caleb. "He never chases girls like this. He only dates girls who chase him."

"I do not!" Caleb said indignantly.

"Yes, you do."

"I do not!"

"You do. Now, try to think with a clear head if you're capable of it, and come to the logical conclusion."

Caleb looked ticked off, but his face screwed up for a moment. Then horror dawned. "Wait ... No way."

"Yes way," Alex said.

"No way, what?" Lucy asked.

Caleb pointed at her, outraged. "*You!*" he shouted.

Now Lucy was really confused. "Me what?"

"You made me fall in love with you!"

Lucy giggled and flipped her hair. "I'm sorry, but there's just no way that we could—"

"Forget that!" Caleb exploded. "Forget all of that! That was your power! You're, like, some kind of siren!"

Lucy blinked at him. "I'm what now?"

Lucy's father poked his head into the living room again with a suspicious look. "Did I hear someone say they were in—"

"Her!" Caleb shouted, pointing at Lucy. "Her power is to make guys fall in love with her! I can't believe I fell for it!"

Horror darted across her father's face. "Iris?!" he yelled back to the kitchen in a panicked tone.

"That's not what it is," Lucy said, offended. "I'm just really cute. I've always been popular."

"So is Caleb," Alex said. "As far as I know, he's never begged for a date before."

Caleb folded his arms and muttered under his breath.

Lucy's mother came back into the living room. "What's up?"

Steven and Aaron followed, one holding a large bowl of dip and the other an enormous vegetable platter.

"They've figured out Lucy's power," her dad growled.

"Oh, have they?" A smile split across Aaron's wrinkled face. "Congratulations."

"They have not," Lucy said indignantly. "They've got it wrong. They're both just jealous that a whole lot of guys like me."

"What?" Lucy's mom asked, looking baffled.

"She's a siren!" Caleb accused. "She makes guys fall in love with her! Poor, defenseless guys, who have no clue that she's a vicious predator!"

Steven whistled.

"I am not!" Lucy cried.

Lucy's mother's mouth fell open. "Is that kind of power possible?"

"Very possible," Steven said. "There was a—someone born in late June who had something very like that a century ago."

"We're going to be mobbed by teenage boys," Lucy's dad said, with a hint of hysteria. "We'll never be able to get rid of them!"

Lucy's stomach twisted. What if they were right? What if that was all her magical power was?

No. She didn't want that power. That was a *terrible* power. Carrie and Matilda and Jezza would never forgive her if all their boyfriends fell for Lucy instead, not to mention Natasia's boyfriend that she'd been dating for over a year. That couldn't possibly be her power!

Wait ... that *couldn't* possibly be her power.

"If that's the case, why weren't you affected?" Lucy demanded, pointing at Alex. "Or half the guys at school?"

Alex shrugged, pointing at himself and Steven and Aaron. "Those of us with circumstances like ours might be immune."

"Okay, then why not every old guy I've passed on the street? Why not every male teacher in school?"

"There could be an age limitation," Aaron suggested.

"Okay, then how about this? I've only been asked out by nine guys this week."

"*Nine?*" her father asked.

"Don't worry, I told the rest they have to wait to ask me until next week," Lucy said carelessly. "I knew this weekend was booked."

Her dad didn't look comforted.

"Anyway ..." Lucy said, tossing her hair, "none of them were guys I've told to get lost in the past, and some of those jerks are really pushy. Explain that."

"Attraction and repulsion, maybe?" Aaron murmured.

Lucy gave him a blank look.

Understanding dawned in Lucy's mother eyes. "You mean she only attracts the guys she wants to? And makes the ones she doesn't want uninterested in her? That's a pretty amazing power. I would've killed for that in high school."

Lucy's father looked terribly disgruntled.

Her mom elbowed him in the ribs. "This is the point when you say I didn't need a power to attract you."

"There wouldn't be much point to me saying it now that you already have, would there?"

"Say it anyway!"

"You're not my superior officer. I don't take orders from you." But he planted a kiss on top of her head.

"Nice theory, but that doesn't explain what happened to me," Caleb said, folding his arms.

Lucy carefully avoided his eyes.

"Unless it *does!*" he added indignantly.

"You're cute," she said with great dignity. "I won't apologize for noticing that."

Alex's lips trembled, and he started snickering quietly.

Chapter 10
Not Quite the Fear

KNOWING that there was probably a magical reason why Jonas had finally noticed her made their date that afternoon seem both more and less fun. More fun, because she'd had the biggest crush on him in elementary school, and it was satisfying to know that he liked her even more now than she'd liked him back then. Less fun, because ... well ... the fact that it was happening because of magic was outright disturbing.

Still! She decided there was nothing she could do about it, since her power seemed to be one of those things that didn't turn off, so she might as well enjoy it.

Well, as much as she could enjoy a hockey game, anyway. The game was pretty violent, and Jonas kept shouting with glee over it, which she totally didn't get. But the ice skating part was cool. It seemed like it would probably be fun to play.

But boyyyy, was she dreading Monday. She'd texted Carrie eight billion times over the weekend, apologizing every time, but Carrie had ignored them all. She hadn't heard from any of her other friends over the weekend, either.

Not that she'd had any reason to expect to hear from them, because she hadn't texted or called them, but she was still dreading to find out whether Carrie had ranted to them about the whole thing on Friday. What if they all hated her now?

Lucy walked into the school building with great trepidation. Almost the first person she ran into was Jezza.

"Hey, Luce!" Jezza called, waving. There were dozens of wooden bracelets on her arms, and they clacked together as her arm raised. "Heard about what happened on Friday!"

Lucy's heart clenched.

"Hilarious!" Jezza added, grinning. She tossed her head, which shook her wild black curls. "Don't worry about all the rumors. Those girls are just jealous."

"Thanks," Lucy said, a trifle relieved.

That's one friend I still have.

After a few minutes of idle chatting with Jezza, she saw Matilda amble past them, chatting with a hot football player named Brian. He was one of the not-a-prize guys Lucy had told to get lost in the past.

"Hey, Matty!" Jezza called, waving. "Get over here!"

"Huh?" Matilda turned around and saw them.

Lucy's shoulders stiffened as Brian looked at her, but there was no apparent interest in his eyes as he glanced past her, gave Jezza a flirtatious raise of an eyebrow, and then swaggered off, leaving the three girls alone.

"Did you hear the story about last Friday?" Jezza exclaimed.

Lucy wanted to die.

"No," Matilda said blankly.

"Lucy and Carrie went on a double date," Jezza said eagerly, "and Carrie's latest boyfriend totally fell for Lucy instead! I wish I'd been there to see it! It sounds hilarious!"

"Ugh. Poor Carrie," Matilda said, wincing.

"Eh, don't worry about her," Jezza said, waving her hand. "You know what she's like. She'll get over it in, like, two minutes."

"You're right," Matilda said, nodding slowly. "Anyway, you did that to me once before."

"Wah ha ha! Sorry!" Jezza cried.

Lucy strongly disagreed. There was no way Carrie was going to get over that situation so easily. Still, Lucy wasn't going to argue with her friends when they were acting like it had just been a joke and not a reason to be angry with her.

And then Natasia walked past, holding hands with her long-term boyfriend, Sean.

Lucy tensed. Panic lanced through her mind. *Don't think he's attractive, don't think he's attractive, don't think he's attractive ...*

She had never even bothered to look at him that way, since he was Natasia's boyfriend. But now it felt like somebody had told her not to think of pink elephants. The more she tried, the harder it was not to do so.

She desperately tried to not notice how cute he was with the curl of hair over his ear, the dimple in his left cheek, those super long eyelashes—

ARGH ARGH ARGH ARGH!

At least the two were walking away. Lucy was going to have to avoid Sean forever. Did she have any classes with him? He was a junior and she was a sophomore, so it was possible they didn't. She'd never paid attention to that. She hoped not.

"Hey, Nat! Did you hear what happened to Lucy and Carrie?" Jezza called.

And to Lucy's horror, Natasia and Sean turned around and headed over to them.

Don't look at me, don't fall in love with me, don't look at me, don't fall in love with me! Lucy thought in frenzied terror.

"No," Natasia said, as Sean picked up her hand that he was holding and kissed it. Those two were usually ridiculously sappy, so this was typical for them. "What happened?"

"Lucy and Carrie went out on a double date, and Carrie's boyfriend fell for Lucy instead!" Jezza howled.

"Oh," Natasia said. "Well, maybe if she didn't start calling guys her boyfriends on the first date ..."

Sean kissed the back of her neck, and she turned around and kissed him full on the lips.

Lucy groaned, as she usually did. *We're in public!*

"Anyway, so you'd better watch out for Lucy," Jezza teased. "She might be a boyfriend-stealer."

Lucy tensed. That wasn't something to joke about!

Sean barely flicked a gaze over at Lucy. "I've only got eyes for Natasia."

"And I've only got eyes for you," Natasia purred.

The two of them started smooching again.

Lucy stared at them in astonishment. *Then Sean wasn't ... affected?*

Maybe she had the ability to turn her power off if she really wanted to. Or maybe she hadn't really been attracted to him. Or maybe her power didn't work on guys who were already in love with somebody else.

She hoped it was that last one. Then she'd never have to worry about stealing boyfriends. That would be a relief.

Lucy said bye to her friends and headed to her locker, feeling buoyant. Things were okay. Nothing had changed.

Carrie was waiting at her locker for her.

Lucy gulped and slowed to a halt. She didn't want to move forward. She wanted to turn and run away. But Carrie looked up at her, her gaze fixed and stern, and Lucy realized she had no choice if she wanted any chance to make up with her. Slowly, she walked forward, cringing inside at every step.

"So," Carrie said, as soon as she got there.

"Hi," Lucy said awkwardly.

"You texted me a bajillion times."

"I'm sor—"

"You *said* that."

"Yeah, I did."

They stood in silence for a moment.

"Caleb's a wuss," Carrie said. "It wasn't going to work out with us anyway."

Lucy stared at her, startled. "It wasn't?"

"I saw Alex and Caleb playing basketball near my house on Saturday," Carrie explained. "Alex *creamed* him. Can you believe that? Caleb is such a loser!"

Lucy's mouth fell open. *Does Alex want to date her? She doesn't seem like his type at all! Or wait ... is he planning to lose to somebody else before long?*

"Alex even invited me to watch him at practice after school today," Carrie giggled. "Isn't that great? He's so cute! I can't wait until our first date!"

"Uh, y-yeah," Lucy said weakly. *That answers that question.*

"No stealing him!" Carrie declared, pointing at her fiercely.

"Never again!" Lucy said, crossing her heart. "I swear!"

"Good." Carrie hesitated for a moment. "Well, I'll see you at lunch," she said at last, and walked off.

Lucy breathed in and out, a sigh of relief.

She'd never dare go on a double date with Carrie again. That was clearly asking for trouble. In fact, double dates at all might be off the table for the foreseeable future, which was a shame. But otherwise, things could now go back to normal.

"Hey, Lucy!" Evan cried, catching sight of her and running over. "You said that we could try to set up a date this week, right? It's Monday."

"Oh, Lucy!" Ian cried, spying her. "It's Monday!"

"Right!" Donnie cried, running over.

Okay ... not *completely* back to normal.

Maybe it's not quite such a curse to be Virgo, after all, Lucy thought with a mischievous smile.

AUTHOR NOTE:
Ever hear of "reverse harem"?

Well, as a current genre trend, it drives me crazy. It started out in Japan with shōjo manga and otome games, most of which were rated G or PG, and they were fun. Think Harutoki, Fushigi Yugi, The Queen's Knight, *or* Yona of the Dawn. *Nowadays, however, the trend has become for reverse harems to be raunchy.*

So I figured I'd stick my tongue out at that trend and write a clean reverse harem fantasy. For crying out loud.

I may be a bit defiant and opinionated about things.

NOT QUITE A BLESSING

Chapter 1
Not Quite Allured

Tapping her pencil against the side of her face, Lucy eyed the back of the guy who was sitting in front of her.

Alex really is attractive, she thought, an impish grin spreading across her face. *Shame about the personality, but he's sure cute. Those strong arms, and his hair ...*

Those arms tensed, as did the neck above them.

Lucy giggled softly. *Did I just make him fall for me? Whoops! Didn't mean to do that. Those dates he took me on last year were a total snore. He's sooooooo boring. Still, I mean ... he* is *really cute. Maybe I could give him a third date, after all ...*

"Time's up," the teacher called from the front of the room. "Hand in your tests."

Lucy sighed loudly and slammed her pencil on the desk. She hated math, and tests were the worst part of all. Not only were they actually more boring than lectures, which was ridiculous because the lectures were a snore, she knew she'd failed the whole thing again.

She probably hadn't even gotten one question right. Which meant a math tutor again, which meant no Fridays ...

Something sharp poked her in the back, and Lucy jumped, turning to see the jealous-looking girl behind her had poked her with the sharp end of her pencil. Lucy had a lot of enemies at the moment, because all the unattached cute boys at school kept falling for her.

Smirking knowingly at the jealous girl, Lucy took the stack of test papers and added her own to it. Then, noting with approval the adorable little curl right behind Alex's ear, she tapped him on the shoulder.

He turned around, his expression flat, as usual. "Stop it."

"I'm just passing you the papers."

"That's not what I meant," Alex said, reaching for them.

"Then what'd you mean?" she demanded.

"You know what." He passed the stack forward to the student ahead of him.

"No, I don't."

He sighed heavily. "Stop thinking about me, Lucy."

Her mouth fell open. "You don't get to be my thought police!"

"I do when you affect *my* thoughts," he shot back. "There's such a thing as self-control. Use it."

Lucy slouched back against the back of her chair, indignant. *It's not my fault boys fall in love with me when I'm attracted to them! Besides, there has to be something good about this dumb curse!*

The Virgo curse was sort of hereditary, and she was the current bearer of it. The way it worked was that it would keep messing with her head, trying to turn her personality into the ideal Virgo, until it finally succeeded and then she died. Talk about gag.

Alex was cursed, too. That was why he knew how her power worked, and that it even existed. Her curse was Virgo, and his was Gemini. Their curses worked the same way, only the power his gave him was different. If she remembered right, he could read his twin's mind or something.

The bell rang, and everyone gathered up their books and stood from their desks.

"Hey, how long've you been—y'know?" Lucy asked Alex.

"I don't know what you're talking about." He tucked his books neatly into the backpack beside his chair.

Lucy smacked her hand on her desk. "You know exactly what I'm talking about! It's the word I can't say!"

That was another annoying thing about the curse. It kept you from talking about it directly.

"Oh, that," Alex said, his voice perfectly level. He looked up. "My father died when I was two months old."

Lucy's breath caught in her throat. *When ... you were ...?*

Forget the fact that his father must have been the last Gemini, which was bad enough. Lucy couldn't imagine losing a parent to the curse and then inheriting it. She'd only lost her Aunt Aggie, a person she hadn't known well or cared about all that much. Alex had been cursed since he was *two months old?*

She couldn't help doing the math instantly, even though she couldn't stand math. The longest anyone had ever lived after inheriting a zodiac curse was twenty years.

"Aren't you seventeen now?" she asked.

"Yeah." His rueful smile answered the unspoken question.

Lucy stared at him in horror. That meant he had less than three years to live?! Ugh! Cute was cute, but ... man, that was way too short!

Maybe she'd feel differently if she'd been cursed for a long time herself, but she'd only just inherited her curse a few weeks ago. She hoped to live for twenty more years, at least. Heck, she wanted to set a new record and go for a hundred.

Alex looked both slightly amused and a bit sad. He'd probably seen that look a dozen times before, anytime a person who knew about the curses realized how long he had left.

Lucy swallowed. She felt like a total heel. So what if he didn't have that long left? She could be nice to him. She could go out on dates with him. He was really cute, and it wasn't like a few dates in high school was a lifetime commitment ...

"Lucy," Alex said gently but firmly. "Stop it."

"But—" Lucy protested.

"I mean it. Turn your attentions to somebody else, please."

Then he picked up his bag and left.

Lucy picked up her hated math textbook and followed him out into the hallway, her usual enthusiasm dampened. She'd felt so sorry for herself for being cursed, but man, some people had it way worse. Even if turning her down was kind of jerky ...

"Hi, gorgeous Lucy!" Pablo called, waving to her from across the hallway. "We still on for Saturday?"

Lucy grinned, distracted. She loved what a flirt he was.

"Yeah, cutie pie!" she called.

"Hey, what about me? Aren't I cuter than him?" Brad hollered from his locker.

Lucy was about to flirt back, but then she noticed a poisonous glance being aimed in her direction.

Oh, right. He has a girlfriend, she remembered.

"Not when you have a girlfriend, you aren't!" she called back.

"Oooh! Burned!" his friends laughed.

For some reason, that didn't abate the girl's venom at all.

Sheesh, Ellie, lay off, Lucy thought grumpily. *It isn't my fault that my power triggers whenever I notice a guy's attractive.*

All the same, she recited to herself over and over again, *Guys who think it's okay to cheat on their girlfriends are not cute. Guys who think it's okay to cheat on their girlfriends are not cute.*

Because, for real, that wasn't an attractive trait at all. If she ever wanted to have a steady boyfriend, which she didn't right now, she would want him to be faithful. *I mean, duh.*

So, really, truly, honestly, Brad *wasn't* cute. If he was hitting on her while he was dating someone else, he was gross. As long as she could remember that, it should help.

She got stopped by three other guys on the way to her locker, all of them guys she'd absently noticed were a bit attractive at some point today, and let them fill up the rest of her week with scheduled first dates. They all seemed thrilled that she knew their names before they introduced themselves.

Yeah, but I know everybody at school's name, Lucy thought, a bit embarrassed that they probably thought that was significant. She even knew all the teachers' first names.

She finally waded through the crowd to reach her locker, where all four of her friends were waiting. Jezza was checking her makeup in a mirror, Matilda was playing a game on her phone, Carrie had a sour look on her face, and Natasia was smooching her boyfriend Sean. Those two did not understand the concept of "not making the people around them uncomfortable."

"Oh, look, it's Lucy and her harem," Carrie said acidly.

Lucy glanced back to see five cute guys who were shyer than the ones who'd just asked her out quickly scatter. Apparently they'd been following her as she walked down the hallway.

"Good word for it," Jezza laughed. "You always make such a scene."

"Sorry," Lucy said sheepishly.

Sean and Natasia were whispering in each other's ears and ignoring the rest of them.

Sean was a weird mystery. It was a relief that he seemed to be immune to Lucy's power, since she didn't want to steal her friend Natasia's longtime boyfriend, but she didn't understand why. She definitely thought he was hot. In fact, the fact that he was so sweet to Natasia just made him more attractive, no matter how hard Lucy tried not to think of him that way.

"So what's the plan today?" Matilda asked, looking up from her phone.

"Carrie and I were talking about the mall earlier," Jezza said. "There's that earring sale you want to check out, right?"

"Yeah, but she can't go!" Carrie said quickly, glancing at Lucy.

"Huh?" Lucy stared at her. "Why not?"

"Because I like the guy who works at the hot dog place, and if he sees you, he'll fall for *you!*"

Lucy gulped. She may have accidentally attracted three of Carrie's crushes in the past two weeks.

"Okay," she said in a small voice, not wanting to start a fight. "No big deal. I have homework tonight, anyway."

Chapter 2
Not Quite Welcome

Morosely, Lucy walked out of the school building on her own.

I left the whole afternoon free to hang out with my friends, she thought, kicking a rock on the sidewalk. *And they ditched me. It's true that I have homework, but I wasn't planning to actually do it!*

Since one of the traits of a Virgo was cool-headed practicality and diligence, Lucy felt no desire whatsoever to be more responsible than usual. She'd skipped out on math homework almost every night a month ago, and she wasn't going to start changing that now, even though the thought of leaving things unfinished that she was supposed to do was starting to bug her a little.

As she walked down the sidewalk, guys she knew whistled at her and waved. She halfheartedly waved back or ignored them. Because Lucy wasn't paying attention to any strangers she passed, nobody new seemed to react to her.

A roar passed by her, and a motorbike stopped at the curb.

"Hey, Lucy!" said a guy in a helmet. He removed it, and a familiar face appeared from underneath. "Nice to meet you!"

"Alex?" Lucy said, baffled. This seemed unlike him.

"Nope! Try again."

"Oh!" Lucy snapped her fingers. "You're his twin, Xander! Your parents were super uncreative and gave you almost the same name!"

"That's me!" He reached into a bag by his side and pulled out a second helmet. "Here. Hop on."

Lucy stared at him. "You must be joking."

"Nope, not joking at all. C'mon. I'm cute. You like cute guys, right?" He grinned.

Lucy stared at him flatly. "I've heard about you from Alex. I don't trust you."

"What've you heard?" he asked easily.

"That you're trouble."

"Yeah, well, Alex doesn't understand me."

"He *knows what you think!*" Lucy exclaimed. Always being able to read his twin's mind was the Gemini's power.

"Doesn't mean he understands me." Xander tossed the helmet up in the air and caught it. "If your parents could read your mind constantly, would you think they understood you?"

Lucy shuddered at the idea. If her overprotective father could read her mind, he'd never let her out of the house. "Nooooo."

"There ya go." Xander held out the helmet and grinned.

"That doesn't mean I trust you!" Lucy retorted. "I've never met you before!"

"Exactly," Xander said, his eyes glinting. "That's the whole problem I'm trying to fix. C'mon. You like me, don't you? I can tell because I've got a real thing for you."

Lucy coughed and tossed her hair to stall for time. It hadn't occurred to her that a guy who knew about her power would understand what it said about her feelings.

"Well, maybe I do," she said coyly. There seemed no point in lying when he knew for a fact she did. The fact was, he was just as attractive as Alex, and she liked his flirtatious manner way more than Alex's quiet brooding. "But I'm not getting in a vehicle with a guy I just met. Especially without my dad's approval."

She had no interest in being grounded for the rest of her life if her dad found out about it.

"Okay, fine." Xander plopped on his helmet and drove off.

Lucy felt oddly crestfallen, watching him disappear around the corner. *Really? That's it?*

He'd seemed so interested, and he was so cute. She wouldn't have minded him trying to convince her for awhile longer, even though she wouldn't have told him yes.

She shook her head, adjusted her backpack, and told herself to forget the odd conversation as she kept on walking down the hill away from the school. She reached the bottom of the hill and waited for the crosswalk sign to light up. It was taking forever.

Loud footsteps came running behind her.

She spun around to see Xander jogging to catch up to her.

"Hey! Where's your bike?" Lucy called.

"I parked it at the school parking lot!" he called, catching up to her. He barely even panted to catch his breath, which implied he was in great shape. She liked guys in great shape. "If you won't let me drive you, I'll walk you home."

Lucy couldn't stop herself from grinning. That ... was kind of adorable. "Okay, fine. If you insist."

With triumphant glee, Xander linked his arm through hers as the crosswalk light changed. They headed across the street.

"So, where should we go?" he asked casually.

"I assume my house, since you're walking me home."

"No, no, no, don't be boring. We should stop somewhere on the way. I know a great ice skating rink."

"That would make this a date, and this isn't a date."

"Who says?" Xander asked with a gleam in his eye.

"My dad," Lucy said dryly. "He forbade me to go out with you after how Alex described you, and he has to approve every one of my first dates before I'm allowed to go out with them. It's a drag, but I'm not breaking that rule, because I want to still be allowed to go out."

Xander looked a little sulky. "Well, we'll have to convince your dad I'm a prize specimen, then."

Lucy giggled at the petulance on his face. "First you'll have to convince me. I'm still not sure I trust you."

They were nearing Brudger's Ice Cream Heaven, where a lot of students hung out after school.

"Here!" Xander said, pointing. "How 'bout here?"

Lucy considered that for a moment. It was a possible date spot, but it was also a spot where you could just hang out with a friend. She'd been here quite a few times with Natasia, Jezza, Matilda, and Carrie. "Okay."

They went inside and waited at the end of a long line. The booths inside were pretty crowded, like they usually were after school.

Xander pulled out a coin and started to flip it.

"What're you doing?" Lucy asked curiously.

"Picking a flavor. I always pick randomly." He caught the coin and looked at it. "Tails. Okay, now for the next digit."

"Next digit?" Lucy repeated.

"Yep," Xander grinned. "There are sixteen flavors. Perfect for assigning them numbers in binary and flipping a coin to pick."

That sounded suspiciously like math, which Lucy wanted to have nothing to do with. She made a face.

"C'mon," he laughed. "It's way more fun than you'd think. Surprise is the spice that makes boring things delicious."

"Ice cream isn't boring," Lucy retorted.

"Ah, but it can always be *more* interesting." Xander tossed the coin in the air again. "Life's only an adventure when you make space for randomness."

He might have a point, Lucy admitted.

"Okay, pick randomly for me, too," she said impulsively.

Xander grinned. "I knew there was a reason I liked you."

Lucy's lighthearted mood vanished. "There is a reason, and it's not as innocent as love at first sight."

"Aw, c'mon!" Xander punched her in the arm. "I don't care, so why should you? As far as I'm concerned, if it got us together, it's a good thing."

"We're not 'together'!" Lucy insisted.

"Not yet, maybe." He smirked.

Lucy did her best to hide a smile. She didn't want to encourage his cockiness, but the fact that he was so sure of himself was fun. She felt like she didn't have to worry about bruising his ego, unlike some guys, who were super fragile.

Plus, it was really, really nice to meet a guy who knew about her power and even consented to it using itself on him. Sometimes it really bothered her that she never knew if a guy's feelings were real or fake. At least with Xander, it didn't matter, because it was the same to him either way.

"Hope you like pistachio with almond slivers," Xander said as they got to the register. "'Cause that's what you're getting."

"Fine, but only if you're paying. I have no idea if that'll be good or not."

"Twist my arm," Xander grinned, taking out his wallet.

Oh, wait! Lucy realized. *If he pays, that means this is a date!*

"Never mind," she said hastily, scrambling in her jeans pocket for her wallet. "I'll pay for my own —"

"No, no, no, no. You said it. You can't take it back," he said, swatting her wallet away.

"Well, it's still not a date!" Lucy protested.

The guy behind the cash register looked very amused as he swiped Xander's card.

Chapter 3
Not Quite a Date

Great the pistachio ice cream was not, but it wasn't half bad once she coated it in whipped cream and poured chocolate chips all over it.

"That's cheating," Xander opined.

"Well, then I'm glad I'm cheating," Lucy shot back.

Xander cackled.

"Easy for you!" she added. "You got butterscotch fudge ripple with cookie dough mix-ins!"

"Wanna try some?" he asked. And then, without waiting for her permission, he grabbed a spoonful and poked it in her mouth.

"Hey!" Lucy protested with her mouth full. She paused. "Wow, that's really good. But hey! Your germs are on that spoon!"

"You mean we've *shared germs?*" Xander asked with mock horror. "Guess it won't matter if I kiss you afterwards, then."

Lucy gave him a narrow-eyed glare. "Don't try it. I don't kiss on the first date."

"I thought you said this isn't a date."

"It isn't! I don't kiss guys I'm just hanging out with, either!"

"Guess I'll have to see if I can tempt you out of that policy." Xander's eyes were gleaming.

Lucy folded her arms. She wasn't sure yet if she really liked him or found him really exasperating.

"Tell you what," Xander said, leaning forward. "Let's go on a first date tonight."

"Can't," Lucy said. "I have a date with Ivan."

Xander's eyes looked suddenly dangerous. "Who's Ivan?"

"A guy at school," Lucy retorted. "You'd know that if you weren't a dropout."

Xander sat back, looking amused. "I'm not a dropout. I just go to a different school."

"Uh huh. Right."

"No, really. I can recite you the whole thing I had to memorize for English class last week. 'To be or not to be' — "

"I don't care," Lucy cut in. "Your life is your business. We're not dating, anyway."

"Wanna see the equations I memorized for Trigonometry?" Xander slid out of the booth, snatched the pen from the register, and grabbed a napkin from the dispenser. He started to scribble on it. "Here's the first one — "

"I wouldn't know the difference between a real and fake equation if it reached out and bit me," Lucy informed him.

Xander stared at her in confusion. "Aren't you in the same math class as Alex?"

"Yeah. I'm failing out of it," Lucy said sourly.

"Sounds like you need a math tutor."

"You volunteering?" she asked with interest. One of the guys she was currently dating, George, had started out as her math tutor last year.

Xander guffawed. "Not hardly! Sounds like the most boring date idea possible."

Lucy had to agree. Besides, she didn't totally believe he wasn't a dropout. It made no sense for him to go to a different school. Unless it was a private school, she supposed, but then why would he go and not Alex?

"Why do you go to a different school?" she challenged.

"Because Alex doesn't like being around me," Xander said with a lazy smile. "He thinks I'm embarrassing."

"*Are* you embarrassing?"

"Only because it's really funny to embarrass him." Xander grinned.

Lucy put her hands on her hips. "You sound like a prize of a brother."

"Hey," Xander snapped, sitting forward. "When you've had a ... condition for seventeen years, then you can judge people. It's not just him it's hard on, you know."

That's right. Lucy swallowed. *He's known for pretty much his whole life that he was Alex's heir. He's known his whole life that his brother would die before they're adults, and then he'd be the next to go.*

"I'm sorry," she said in a low voice. "I only got mine a few weeks ago. My parents explained about what would be coming when I was six. When did you find out?"

"I don't wanna talk about it," Xander said abruptly. "Let's talk about something more fun. When *are* you free for a first date?"

"Umm ..." Lucy tried to remember. "I think I'm booked through next week, and I don't want to schedule anything further than that, because then I'd have to start keeping track, and that would be a pain."

"You're super busy, and you don't keep track?" Xander asked with a mocking smile.

"No, I don't!" Lucy snapped. "Being organized is one of the personality traits I'm trying to avoid!"

"Ah." The smile dropped from his face. "So you're trying to fight it."

"Of course I'm trying to fight it!" Lucy said indignantly. "What kind of person wouldn't?"

"You'd be surprised." Xander shrugged. "I've seen six different people die now, and not all of them made an effort to fight it. Two of them liked using their abilities so much that they succumbed within a few years."

Lucy was silent. She'd been so busy thinking that she had only twenty years left that she'd forgotten even that much time was an outlier.

"Aunt Aggie died after nine years," she said slowly. "What's the average?"

"She'd've lasted longer if she hadn't given up trying to fight it," Xander said. "It can be fast if the person doesn't try to fight it—

maybe two or three years. For someone who does fight, fourteen or fifteen is more common. It depends a lot based on how close your natural personality is to ... well, you know."

Lucy swallowed. She *did* know.

"Well, thankfully I'm almost the opposite!" she said, trying to look on the bright side. She was anything but the ideal Virgo.

"Yeah, but using what you can do makes the effect stronger," Xander said. "Those who never turn theirs off die faster. Enjoy being yourself while it lasts."

Lucy's breath caught in her throat. "That's so unfair! I *can't* turn mine off! I can't control it at all!"

"Yeah duh it's unfair. I don't make the rules."

Lucy squeezed her fists tightly. There were tears in her eyes.

"Hey. Hey." Xander slid out of his booth and sat next to her. He put his arm around her shoulders. "It stinks, I know. But I assumed you wanted the truth, not a pretty lie."

Lucy nodded, breathing shakily. Her eyes were blurry.

"Here." Xander reached out and grabbed a handful of napkins out of the dispenser on the table. "Blow your nose or something. Just don't wipe it on me. That would be gross."

Lucy giggled despite herself and took the napkins, blowing her nose loudly.

"Is there an elephant in here?" Xander looked around in mock bafflement.

"Shut up!" Lucy giggled through her tears and punched him in the shoulder.

Xander seemed to be debating saying something, and then finally spoke up.

"Look," he said reluctantly, "you can't have a boyfriend."

Lucy looked up at him, confused.

Xander grimaced, looking like he was pulling teeth. "If you're naturally impulsive and flighty, and you've never dated anyone exclusively before ... wanting a loyal relationship is probably what your ability is trying to push you into. If you give in to that ... it'll make it easier to become stable and predictable in other areas of your life. Before you know it, you'll be different, and you won't even think that's a bad thing."

Lucy stared at him, astonished. "Is that why you think I have this ... ability?" She couldn't say the words *magic* or *power*.

"Yeahhhhh ..." Xander looked deeply disgruntled. "Based on what I've seen with others, I'm pretty sure it's something along those lines. It's certainly not trying to push you to enjoy having a dozen guys in love with you at all times. Most likely, it's trying to make you feel like that's a burden so that you'll want to settle down."

Lucy kissed him on the cheek. "You're an amazing person to tell me that."

"I wish I weren't," he grumbled.

"It shows that you really love me," she said, patting his cheek. "You don't want to see me die."

"Yeah, or I'm an idiot," he muttered. He glanced over, and a slight glint grew in his eye. "So, have I earned a real kiss?"

"No!" Lucy swatted his arm. "But you can walk me the rest of the way home."

Chapter 4
Not Quite as Fun

Her highly organized mother pestered her into doing all her math homework as soon as she got home, because apparently the math teacher had called her mom about the state of Lucy's test today. Joy.

She barely had enough time left to get dressed in a new outfit and spray on perfume in preparation for her date with Ivan.

"One good thing about Lucy going out every night is that it'll lower our food budget," she heard her mother teasing her father in the kitchen.

"I'd rather just pay for her food," he grumbled.

"This is a second date, Dad, so you've already met Ivan," Lucy said in a bossy voice as she strode into the kitchen. "There's no need to embarrass me by trying to approve him again."

"Who's Ivan?" he asked suspiciously. "I don't remember that name."

"Black curly hair, beautiful eyes?"

"Don't remember that at all."

"You made a really big deal about the nose ring?"

"Oh, yes." Her father glowered. "I didn't like him."

"You never like *any* of my dates, Dad."

"Well, maybe if you didn't go on quite so many of them — !"

Lucy's mom was snickering openly.

The doorbell rang, and Lucy ran to get it. Ivan, it seemed, was more punctual than she was. He was only five minutes late.

"Hi, Ivan!" she said cheerfully. She was startled when he shoved a dozen brightly colored flowers at her. "What are these?"

"Gerbera daisies," he said proudly. "They weren't cheap."

Okay? Lucy thought. She didn't care how much money a guy spent on her.

"Hey, Mom!" she called. "Can you come put these flowers in a vase?"

Her mother came to the front door. "Oh, lovely! I haven't seen gerbera daisies since the last time your father bought them for me!" She raised her voice in what was probably intended to be a subtle hint. "It's been a REALLY LONG TIME!"

"I bought you silk ones last time! They haven't wilted yet!" her father called back.

"Have fun, Lucy." Her mom kissed her on top of the head. "And Ivan, make sure you treat her well."

He drew himself up. "I have excellent plans," he said in a pompous voice. "She'll love them."

Lucy stared at him out of the corner of her eye. *Which means what?*

It turned out to mean La Belle Caille, a French restaurant that was the most expensive one in town. Lucy only knew that because her mother had begged her father to take her there for their anniversary, and he had looked up the prices of the menu online and screamed.

They'd eventually gone, but only because her mother had promised they could get pizza for their next anniversary.

Lucy felt more than a little out of her depth as a snooty waiter herded them into chairs by a table in a dim room that was mostly lit by candlelight. All the other people in the room were adults, and all of them were dressed really fancily.

"Um ..." Lucy said awkwardly. "You know, Dave's Pizza Buffet would've been fine."

"Nonsense," Ivan said with a superior smile. "Any guy can take you there. Could any guy at school take you *here?*"

Do I want any guy at school to take me here? Lucy thought doubtfully, looking at the menu. It was entirely in French. There were illustrations for some of the meals, but not all of them, and in the dim lighting, she couldn't be one hundred percent sure that none of them were frog legs.

Or snails. Didn't French people eat snails? She didn't want to eat snails. Sweat prickled on the back of her neck just thinking about it.

She still hadn't decided what was safe enough to order by the time the waiter came. Ivan ordered what he wanted, rattling it off in what sounded like French and watching to see if Lucy was impressed.

Lucy was not impressed. It was probably his foreign language at school. She was taking Spanish, and could order just fine from the menu of a Mexican place, thank you.

"And for you, mademoiselle?" the waiter asked politely.

"Ummm ..." Lucy scrutinized the menu. She was afraid to try any of the dinner options. "Do you have salad? With, like, chicken or bacon or something and no frog legs or anything?"

"Oui, mademoiselle. We have one that has both chicken and bacon. It also has tomatoes, croutons, and cheese. Our croutons are specially made, and they are magnificent."

"They're made out of bread, right?" she asked nervously.

"Yes." The waiter seemed to be trying to keep a straight face.

"And no frog legs? Or snails?" she asked anxiously.

"No, mademoiselle."

"Perfect," Lucy said with relief.

He made a note on his notepad. "What kind of salad dressing would you like?"

"Ranch."

"Very well, mademoiselle."

The waiter left.

Ivan's face was pinched as he looked at her. "You don't have to order the cheapest thing on the menu. I can afford better."

"I'm on a diet," Lucy improvised.

The I-don't-want-to-eat-frog-legs diet, she added silently.

Ivan looked disgruntled as he shook out his cloth napkin and placed it on his lap.

Lucy eyed the breadsticks on the table and wondered if they were safe to eat. Maybe she should ask the waiter if there were snails inside them when he came back. Just in case.

As they sat in awkward silence, her mind wandered to her not-a-date with Xander earlier. If he were here, he'd probably order something random off the menu and make her do it, too. Then she'd wind up eating frog legs for sure. But maybe they'd turn out to be not so bad. Or even if they were, he'd laugh his head off about the face she made eating them.

Lucy shook her head. *Keep your mind on the date you're on.*

Into the awkward silence, Ivan started talking.

And talking. And talking.

About himself. Without pausing to take a break.

"Uh huh," Lucy interjected every so often, nodding at the right places as she ripped apart the breadsticks to check them for snails and wished she could just go home. "Yeah, sure."

Such noncommittal replies seemed to be all the encouragement he needed to keep on going, and going, and going.

Lucy's mind wandered all over the place as she gave up on listening. Mostly it kept wandering over to Xander.

It had been so nice of him to tell her what he'd figured out about her power, especially when he clearly hadn't wanted to. Knowing that the curse was trying to make her want a steady boyfriend, and therefore it was something she shouldn't want, paradoxically made her really want one. She'd always assumed she would get one eventually; she'd just never been in a hurry.

And even the risk of shortening her lifespan had to be better than a hundred more dates like this.

Ivan was still talking. And talking. And talking. She wasn't even nodding and saying "uh huh" anymore.

Sheesh, could the guy take a hint?!

It felt like the date lasted forever, but it was really only about an hour. When Ivan finally took her home and walked her to the front door, she nearly breathed a sigh of relief.

Then he leaned forward and kissed her. Hard. With tongue.

Lucy shoved him away. "Goodnight, Ivan. I'll see you at school."

"When can we have our third date?"

"Never!" she shouted. "I didn't have fun! Take a hint!"

His face fell in devastation, and Lucy rapidly escaped inside, slamming the door. She was sorry to hurt his feelings, and she would've been nicer, but come on! What had he been thinking?!

"How was the date?" her dad asked, walking quickly from the kitchen, a mug of chamomile tea splashing on his hand. He was never far from the door when she was off on a date.

"Awful," Lucy snorted. "I'm never going out with him again."

"Really?" Her dad's face brightened. "I'm sorry to hear that!"

Lucy rolled her eyes. "You could try to be a teeny bit less transparent, Dad."

"I could try. I could definitely try." He beamed and kissed her on the head. "Goodnight, Lucy. Have sweet dreams."

"Goodnight, Dad. You can give the flowers to Mom if you want to. I don't mind."

"Great idea! She loves gerbera daisies."

"Cool. Then someone can get something fun out of that date." Lucy headed up to her room, in a rather sour mood.

Her father skipped up the stairs to bed, whistling cheerfully.

Chapter 5
Not Quite the Plan

NATASIA AND SEAN had plans the next day, Matilda and Jezza were working on a group project they were doing for art class, and Carrie had a first date with her newest "boyfriend," who apparently was not the guy who worked at the mall, but one of the guys on the basketball team.

So Lucy was, again, left to walk home alone.

Not so alone, though. Because Xander was already waiting outside the school building, helmet under his arm.

"Do you know me enough to ride with me now?" he asked.

"No," Lucy said with a teasing grin. "But I don't mind walking with you again."

"Okay." He zipped the helmet into a bag at the side of his motorcycle. "What if we made a detour to Dave's Pizza Buffet this time?"

"It's not on the way to my house."

"But it *is* in walking distance from the school."

Lucy snorted with laughter. "All right. But it's still not a date, you know. We're just hanging out."

"Whatever you want to call it," he said grandly.

As they walked across the school grounds to reach the exit on the other end, a dozen jealous boys eyed them with angry eyes.

With a glint in his eye, Xander took Lucy's hand and kissed it flamboyantly.

"Xander!" Lucy exclaimed, snatching her hand away.

"I'm not allowed to show my affection?" he asked innocently.

"Not when you're clearly just trying to make them jealous!"

"I'm not trying to make them jealous." Xander smirked. "I'm trying to show them that they haven't got a chance because you belong to me."

"If you act like a dog and try to mark your turf, I'm going to slap you," Lucy said darkly.

Xander guffawed. "So much for my clever plan!"

When they arrived at Dave's Pizza Buffet, Lucy was appalled to notice that five different guys from school had followed them here and were waiting in line behind them.

"I know it isn't safe for you to date one guy exclusively, but I recommend not taking dates from guys who act like stalkers," Xander said casually, indicating the crowd behind them with his head.

"Yes, thank you, that same thought's occurred to me," Lucy said tightly.

She glanced back and stared surreptitiously at the five guys, one at a time, looking for a reason to find each one unattractive. Darian had a mole on his ear—she'd never noticed that before. Dale had a single hair growing out of his left eyebrow that was almost an inch long. Adrian's neck was way longer than usual. Stewart had grubby fingernails. Eddie, well, he was perfect, but the fact that he had followed her here was enough to make her feel like he was kind of creepy.

There, Lucy thought, turning around. *I hope that's enough.*

Her power could be a bummer sometimes, but at least it *did* stop working on the guys she stopped finding attractive. That was very helpful. It was also one of the reasons she felt no guilt about squashing Ivan's heart yesterday. He'd recover fast.

Unless, of course, his feelings were real, which was certainly possible. But she hoped not. She hoped the only guy who ever had real feelings for her would be the one she'd choose to be a permanent boyfriend.

Permanent? Lucy thought, smacking the side of her head. *You know you can't do that. It'll make you die sooner and lose who you are faster. Stop thinking about that!*

They reached the front of the line, and Xander paid for both of them before she could stop him.

"Hey!" Lucy objected, waving her wallet.

"Oops, I forgot," Xander said innocently, not looking sorry at all.

They loaded up their plates with various slices of pizza, and Lucy checked the entrance. To her relief, two of her five followers had left, and the other three looked like they were rethinking why they were here.

"So, let's see if I can find some good first date questions ..." Xander said, pulling up the browser on his phone.

"This isn't a date!" Lucy repeated.

"Here's a good one," Xander said with a grin. "What was your favorite Disney movie as a child?"

"This *still* isn't a date," Lucy informed him.

"Okay, I'll take a guess." Xander grinned and put his chin in his hand. "I bet it was ... hmmm ... *Beauty and the Beast*."

"What? No!" Lucy exclaimed. "It was *The Little Mermaid!* Belle's okay, I guess, but she is way too obsessed with books. And the talking plates creeped me out."

"Really?" Xander raised his eyebrows teasingly. "You prefer the girl who chases after a stranger like some clueless stalker?"

"For your information, Prince Eric is *cute!*" Lucy swatted him in the arm. "Any girl would fall in love with him at first sight! You can tell he's really nice, and he's got dimples, and—"

"Uh huh," Xander said, grinning.

"Anyway, she's not the best part of the movie," Lucy defended. "King Triton is."

Xander stared at her. "The overprotective dad?"

"Yes!" Lucy exclaimed, putting her hands to her chest. "Oh, my gosh, he's so sweet! He loves his daughter so much, and he'd do anything for her, and then he *does*, and oh, my gosh!"

"... Right," Xander said, looking baffled. "If you say so."

"Well, what was your favorite?" Lucy asked, picking up one of her slices of pizza. "Wait, let me guess—it was *Robin Hood*."

"Nah, too much romance," Xander said. "It was *The Sword in the Stone*."

"Really?" Lucy wrinkled her nose. She'd only seen that movie once, and hadn't thought much of it. "I wouldn't have guessed you were the knight in shining armor type."

"Are you kidding?" Xander exclaimed. "I love King Arthur! Chivalry and all that stuff—it's awesome! Half the reason I bought a motorbike in the first place is because it's as close as you can get to being a modern-day knight."

"Seriously?"

"Seriously!"

"Wow, you are weird."

"Says the girl who likes the overprotective dad character."

"He's *sweet!*" Lucy cried.

They finished off their pizza slices, bantering and laughing together, and then headed out of the pizza buffet and towards her house.

When they got there, Xander impulsively grabbed her hand and kissed it.

Lucy giggled, opened the door, and darted into the house without saying goodbye.

Unfortunately, her dad was home and standing right there.

"Who was that?!" he roared.

"Alex's brother Xander," Lucy said, deciding that telling the truth was the best option.

"The Gemini's heir?!"

"Well-remembered."

"You can't date the Gemini's heir!" he exploded. "Your mother was born in the Gemini dates! If you married him and had a kid who was Gemini, she'd be the next to inherit that curse!"

"I never said I was going to marry him!" Lucy defended. "I'm not even dating him! I'd've brought him to meet you if I was! Sheesh!"

"I just saw him kiss you!"

"On the *hand!* I'll kiss you, too!" Lucy pecked her dad on the cheek. "See?"

"It looked very different from what I was seeing," he glowered.

"That's because you're King Triton."

He looked baffled. "Who?"

"Never mind." Her lips twitched. "I love you, Dad, and I'm going upstairs. Stop worrying about me."

She ran up the stairs to her room two at a time, tossed her backpack on the floor, and glanced in the mirror to notice her hair was a mess. She grabbed the hairbrush from her dresser and started to brush through her hair, humming. Since she had *The Little Mermaid* on her mind, it reminded her of a scene where Ariel did the same thing—

Oh, no. Lucy put the hairbrush on her dresser and looked in the mirror.

She was falling in love with Xander, wasn't she?

Darn it! This was not the plan! she thought fiercely.

Chapter 6
Not Quite Relaxed

Obviously going on another not-a-date with Xander was out of the question, so Lucy threw herself into all of her other dates that week, and asked various guys at school to drive her home on the days her friends weren't available to hang out with. A lot of them jumped at the chance.

Meanwhile, she had the fun ordeal of three first dates for three nights in a row. One of them went well enough that she agreed to give him a second date sometime. The other two resulted in her politely dodging the question and looking for a reason to find the guy unattractive, hoping he wouldn't ask her again.

So she was rather looking forward to Saturday, when she had a fourth date with a guy she knew she liked quite a lot.

Unfortunately, that date wound up the most awkward of them all.

"So," Pablo said when he picked her up in his car, "you know how your dad, um, wanted to meet me on our first date?"

"Yep," Lucy said, nodding. "He insists on embarrassing me."

"Well ..." Pablo wriggled. "Guess what."

"Your father wants to meet me?" Lucy guessed.

"And my mother, and my uncles, and my aunts, and my sisters, and my grandmother." Pablo laughed awkwardly.

"That sounds like ... a lot of people," Lucy said slowly.

"I know." Pablo clunked his head against the steering wheel. "I've told them not to bother you, but all my relatives showed up an hour before I was supposed to leave to get you and said that they wouldn't let me back in the house until they met you."

"Wow." Lucy was taken aback. "They're pretty hardcore."

"You don't have to go," Pablo said quickly. "I mean ... they might drive all over town looking for us if we don't, but ... we can *try* to hide from them if you want!"

It almost seemed like he thought that was the better option.

Lucy snorted with laughter. "They're really serious about this, aren't they?"

"They make your dad look like a softie," Pablo groaned.

"Wow." By this point, Lucy was more curious than intimidated. They couldn't possibly be as bad as he was making them out to be. "Sure, I'll meet them. Why not?"

"You might find out why not," Pablo said darkly, turning the key to start the car. "My relatives would try the patience of a saint."

"Well, sainthood is something no one's ever accused me of before!" Lucy said with a laugh. Seriously, at this point, she was burning with curiosity to meet these people. Could they really be as bad as he said?

As it turned out ... yes.

Yes, they could.

"LUCY!" A plump Hispanic woman greeted her at the door as soon as Pablo rang the doorbell. She proceeded to chatter in a high-pitched, excited voice. "I'm so pleased to meet you! Pablo, she's so pretty! And you two look so good together! Imagine how cute your kids will be!"

"Uh ..." Lucy said, a little slack-jawed.

"Mom ..." Pablo said, with a hand over his eyes.

"Come in! Come in!" the woman cried, gesticulating wildly for them to come inside.

They were ushered into a room crammed with people and a clamor of voices. And crucifixes. Lots of crucifixes. More crucifixes than people. She wasn't sure which was more intimidating.

"Is that her?!"

"Hey, she's prettier than Pablo deserves!"

"Aw, my little nephew's so grown-up! He's finally bringing a girl home!"

Lucy glanced over at Pablo, overwhelmed at their excitement. He was hanging his head and looking like he wanted to die.

"H-hi," Lucy said, waving sheepishly. "I'm Lucy Martin. Nice to meet you all."

"Have a seat, have a seat!" A man who had to be either Pablo's father or one of his uncles grabbed Lucy's hand and pulled her to a chair that was within easy view of everyone else.

With a sense of impending doom, Lucy sat in it.

The flood of questions began.

"You *are* Catholic, right?" an old woman who had to be Pablo's grandmother demanded.

"Y-yesssss?" Lucy said hesitantly. She'd never gone to mass for any other reason than Christmas or Easter, but technically yes.

"How long have you and Pablo been dating?"

"This is our fourth date—"

"Are you serious about him? Are you going to marry him?" either a cousin or a younger sister giggled.

"Um, it's way too early to say—"

"Do you have a middle name? Pablo's never told us."

"It's Jennifer—"

"Do you have brothers and sisters?"

"A sister. She's in college right—"

"Have you and Pablo talked about the number of children you'd like to have yet?" a father or uncle asked briskly.

"Um?!"

"I think you should get married in June!" declared a cousin or a younger sister.

"Like I said," Lucy said, beginning to feel slightly panicked, "it's way too early to—"

"And if I'm going to be a bridesmaid, I want a pink dress, not a yellow one. Yellow makes me look fat. I'm just saying."

Lucy kept a desperately fixed smile on her face and tried to answer the questions that were lobbed at her at a dizzying speed.

After half an hour of really personal questions, culminating in an unbelievable one from an aunt about whether infertility ran in her family or whether she personally had any "period issues" that could potentially cause it, Pablo leapt up and said:

"Oh, look! We have to leave right now to make our dinner reservation in time! Come on, Lucy!"

Before anyone could react, he seized Lucy's hand, tugged her up to her feet, and fled for the door with her in tow.

Of course, half of his relatives leapt out of their seats and chased after them, but Pablo and Lucy were faster.

He must have left the doors unlocked, because he had the passenger's side open for Lucy in a flash, and then was in the driver's side before the first of the sisters-or-cousins reached the car and banged on the window.

"Sorry! Gonna be late!" Pablo called, turning his key in the ignition.

Lucy was panting for breath and giggling uncontrollably as she tried to buckle her seat belt while they screeched around the corner to escape the crowd of younger-sisters-or-cousins yelling after them. "Do we really have dinner reservations?"

"Yup," Pablo said, his eyes glued to the road as he drove thirty miles over the speed limit. "I specifically called Dave's Pizza Buffet and told them to expect us at five o'clock so that we'd have an excuse to get out of there."

Lucy was giddy. "You know they don't reserve tables, right?"

"It's amazing how much I don't care!"

They screeched around another corner, and then finally slowed to the speed limit once they were well out of sight of the house.

"So ... when you said they were worse than my dad, I thought you meant they *wouldn't* like me," Lucy commented.

"Oh, no, they like you. You're the first girl I've ever dated more than one time," Pablo said in an exasperated tone. "Naturally, they all think that means they can assume wedding bells."

Lucy started giggling uncontrollably. Now that they were away from his relatives, their extreme nosiness seemed hilarious. "Are you the only person they've done that to?"

"Ha!" said Pablo. "No! You should've seen them when my cousin Teresa got engaged!"

"I think I'd like to hear the story," Lucy said with a grin.

"Oh, it's a long and terrible tale," Pablo intoned. "It all began when she showed up at the door with a boyfriend she hadn't told anybody she was dating, which was probably a wise move on her part ..."

"Hang on," Lucy said, holding up her finger. "First, um, I just have to ask. Why all the crucifixes?"

"Huh?" Pablo glanced over at her, looking mystified. Then his face cleared. "Ohhhh! My mom collects those. Would you have preferred to have been in the living room? That's where she keeps her antique teapots."

Crucifixes versus fragile antiques that could easily break? That took less than a second of thought. "Nope, I definitely preferred the crucifixes."

"Yeah, me too. I wish she'd get a display cabinet instead of keeping those teapots on the tables. It makes the living room impossible to sit in comfortably."

Lucy suddenly started to giggle, imagining what would happen if she and Pablo did someday get married, and her father met Pablo's family in a living room full of fragile antiques strewn every which way. It'd be hard to tell what part of the situation would panic him more.

"What's so funny?" Pablo asked curiously.

"Nothing." Lucy straightened her face. "So, tell the story!"

Thankfully, Pablo wasn't nosy. "Okay. So, my cousin Teresa showed up out of the blue one day ..."

Chapter 7
Not Quite Alone

By the time Tuesday rolled around, Lucy was doing quite a good job of not thinking about Xander.

Matilda and Jezza invited her to go to the mall with them on Monday, her first date with Billy that evening was fun, her father only *slightly* humiliated her during his usual intimidation of a new guy, she was back to completely ignoring her math homework, and overall, things were going well.

Until Xander showed up in the middle of her sixth date with George.

They were waiting in line at the movie theater, negotiating about which of the not-very-interesting movies looked less snooze-worthy than others, when Xander sauntered over with a leather jacket slung over his shoulder.

"There you are!" he called. "Have you been avoiding me?"

Lucy tensed and looked at George.

He gave her a questioning look.

She nodded.

"Nah, she's fine!" George called. "Want to join us?"

Lucy stared at him in horror. *I meant yes, please get rid of him, not yes, invite him along on our date!*

But it was too late. Xander was already joining them.

"What're the options?" he asked, craning his neck to look at the ticket window.

"Nothing great," George said. "But I saw the trailer for that one with the explosions, and it looked pretty good. Lucy thinks the romance looks more interesting, though."

Xander surveyed the posters on the wall beside them. The line moved forward as someone at the front chose their tickets and went into the theater. "Let's go to the romance," he said. "Then Lucy gets what she wants."

George grinned crookedly. "Good point. I assume you've got a thing for her, too?"

"Yeah, obviously," Xander smirked.

Lucy stared at her date in exasperation. George was one of the least jealous guys in existence. It was something she'd always liked about him, but did he have to be this comfortable about sharing her right now?

She wound up sandwiched between the two guys to watch a

soppy romance movie, with a giant tub of popcorn parked on her lap that the two had agreed to split the cost of. Both of them casually reached out and took her hand that was near them, which meant she had no hands to grab popcorn to eat herself.

This, Lucy thought sourly, *is completely ridiculous*.

The forgettable movie plot ended eventually with a kiss in the rain at the sunset, and then the three of them headed out of the theater, the two boys chatting like old friends about a basketball game they'd seen on TV.

"I've seen you around at school," George said. "Aren't you on the basketball team?"

"Nah, that's Alex. We're twins. I go to a different school. I'm not on any teams, but I'm better at sports than he is. Try getting him to admit that, though." Xander grinned.

"Xander," Lucy interrupted, "I hope you realize this is my date with George."

"Yeah, true. Thanks for letting me cut in, dude," Xander said.

"No problem." George gave him a thumbs-up. "I know Lucy likes having as many guys around as possible, and I want her to have a good time."

Lucy stopped and gave him an aggrieved look. He didn't seem to notice.

They reached the spot in the parking lot with George's car, and he unlocked the driver's side door.

"Hey, you got a ride home?" he asked Xander.

"Nah, Alex dropped me off when I saw Lucy standing in line," Xander said. "I can call him to get me."

"Eh, won't be necessary." George unlocked the back. "Just tell me where your house is, and I'll take you there before I take Lucy home."

Lucy let out a loud sigh. She'd always liked how casual and low-pressure George was, but really? Now he was treating their third wheel like an old friend? Really?

Xander glanced at her and caught the look on her face. He raised his eyebrows with a mischievous smirk and said, "Sure. That'd be great."

His "house" turned out to be a run-down apartment building with his motorcycle parked right by a dumpster. Through the window, Lucy could see Alex sitting on a worn out sofa, flipping the page of a book.

"Thanks, man," Xander said, getting out of the car. "Hey, do you mind if I ask Lucy something in private before I go?"

George laughed. "If it's a date, I think she's already booked through next week."

"Nah, it's about something else. It'll only take a second. Is that okay?"

"Sure," George said, shrugging.

Lucy rolled her eyes heavenward and got out of the car, following Xander across the parking lot so that they were out of earshot. She folded her arms. "What?"

"Just want to point out that you should hang on to him," Xander said. "He's a good choice."

Lucy blinked. That wasn't what she'd expected. "What?"

"Dude seems incapable of jealousy," Xander said. "I could tell you were annoyed about that, but you shouldn't be. That's just what you need: at least two guys who don't get jealous. You could dump all the rest and still be pretty safe."

Lucy's stomach flipped over.

"Are you saying you're the other one?" she challenged.

"I wouldn't say I'm *incapable* of jealousy, but ... yeah, I can handle it." Xander grinned. "Especially since I know why you can't choose only one. And I don't mind him."

"Thank you so much for having opinions about my love life," Lucy snorted. "Maybe you could try not horning in on my dates in the future?"

"I'll do it if you'll give me a real first date."

"My dad would kill me. No!"

"Aw, c'mon." Xander grinned. "What's he got against me?"

"How about the thing your brother has that you're going to get eventually? The one that could endanger my whole family?"

A wall of fury slammed over Xander's eyes. Lucy swallowed involuntarily.

Then it was gone.

"Well," he said easily, "the only danger there is if we plan to have kids eventually. Even if one thing did lead to another and we wanted to get married—which is way off my radar right now!—I could always get a vasectomy or something. Problem solved."

Lucy stared at him. That was a possibility she hadn't considered.

"So?" Xander said. "You bring me to meet your dad, and I'll tell him that I'll do that if we want to get serious. Agreed?"

Lucy hesitated. It would certainly be interesting to see how her father would respond to that line of reasoning and if he'd be left speechless. But she had another concern right now. That flash of anger ... that had freaked her out.

"I'll think about it," she said. "Let me think about it. Okay?"

"Okay." He swept into a grand bow and grabbed her hand and kissed it. "Whatever you wish, my lady."

She giggled in surprise.

Watching him saunter to his front door, looking pleased with himself, Lucy's heart fluttered. He was sure cute. And she loved a whimsical romantic gesture.

How could she *not* fall for someone who did something like that so naturally?

But ... but maybe there was another side to him that he wasn't showing her.

Maybe he was dangerous.

Swallowing and trying not to look unsettled, Lucy headed back to the car where George was waiting.

"What'd he want to ask you?" he asked as Lucy got in.

"Oh, if I wanted to go on a double date with him and Alex," Lucy lied, shrugging. "I told him maybe, but only if Alex picks a girl who isn't as boring as he is. That guy has no personality, seriously."

George chuckled as he backed out of the parking lot.

Chapter 8
Not Quite the Truth

"Um, where exactly do you think you're going?" Lucy's dad asked as she walked past him down the stairs to grab her coat from the rack.

"Out with Carrie," Lucy said.

For some reason, she hadn't scheduled a date for tonight, which meant she had a whole evening free, which meant that she could spend it reconnecting with her oldest friend and hopefully salvaging a friendship that had become decidedly rocky since she'd gotten the curse.

"No, you're not," her father said.

"Dad," Lucy said with exasperation, zipping up her coat, "I'm done with my homework. It's five. I'll be back by curfew."

"Well, then the people who are coming here specifically to see you will be very surprised to find you not here."

Lucy paused, and groaned. She'd completely forgotten that her mother had called for a meeting of all the other cursed. She wanted their advice of what precise things she should be tracking in Lucy's behavior to watch for how the curse was affecting her.

"Do I have to?" Lucy hedged. "They're coming to talk to Mom, not me. And I hate that color-coded spreadsheet."

"Let's see," Lucy's father said, rubbing his chin thoughtfully. "Allow my daughter to skip out of a commitment she's made, or hold her to not being rude to a bunch of people who are taking time out of their lives to come help her out. Let's see. Tough decision ..."

"All right, all right," Lucy said grumpily, unzipping her coat. "But Carrie's going to jump to the worst possible conclusion if I call her to cancel now. She's going to think I got a last-minute date and just ditched her or something."

"Well, I'm sure she'll forgive you," her dad said, folding his thick, muscular arms as he stood in front of the door.

Lucy snorted loudly. Maybe that rock-hard face impressed the soldiers he trained down at the base, but she was too used to her dad to be cowed. Instead, she stomped up the stairs to her room, trying to think of some way to tell Carrie that she was not, in fact, on her way without explaining the complicated reason.

Bad news. Dad says I can't go, she texted finally.

Jerk! Carrie responded. *What's his damage?*

diately sat down at the kitchen table with the color-coded spreadsheet to talk about its columns or something.

"Hi, Aaron," Lucy said, waving at the brown-skinned old man who had come with Catherine. She'd met him at the last meeting. He was the Aries. "How are things?"

"The usual," he said with a wry smile. "Stiff. Sore. I can't recommend old age."

"Well, I won't have to worry about that," Lucy said flippantly.

Aaron's smile suddenly looked very awkward.

"No big deal. I've gotten used to it." Lucy waved her hand. "Mom made cookies. Do you like cookies?"

"I love them, but unfortunately, I have to watch what I eat." He looked a bit embarrassed.

"Okay. No biggie." Lucy tried to think of a subject that would be less awkward. It was hard to know how to talk to an old person you weren't related to. With a grandparent, you could always ask for embarrassing stories about your parents when they were kids.

Fortunately, the doorbell rang again.

"I'll get it!" Lucy yelled, running for the front door.

She opened it to see both Alex and Xander.

"Hello, Lucy," Alex said quietly, raising a hand in greeting.

"Hi, Alex," Lucy said, barely glancing at him. "And Xander! What're you doing here?"

"This meeting's about you, right?" he said with a teasing grin. "Wouldn't miss it."

"You had better not try to flirt with me in front of my dad," she warned. "He'll blow up."

"I can exercise self-control," he said, his eyes glittering.

She stepped aside to let them into the house. Alex walked over to Aaron and the two got into what seemed to be an engrossing conversation, no doubt about something abundantly boring.

Spying Xander, Lucy's father detached himself from the conversation with his wife and Catherine about spreadsheets, which he didn't seem to find nearly as interesting as they did, and made a beeline for the guy.

"You're the Gemini's heir, right?" her dad demanded.

"Only on Tuesdays," Xander said glibly.

"What's that supposed to mean?" Lucy's dad growled.

"It means I'm being sarcastic, Pops. Lighten up."

Lucy groaned quietly.

"You," Lucy's father said to his daughter, pointing fiercely at Xander, "are not dating that boy!"

"I'm *not*, Dad! Sheesh, I told you already!"

"I'm sure we'll correct that eventually, though," Xander said cheerfully, plopping his arm around her shoulders.

Her father's face turned several colors at once.

"Xander!" Lucy exclaimed. "Alex, stop them!"

Alex glanced over, taking in the scene of his brother and her father engaged in a lock-eyed staring contest. Looking faintly amused, he just shook his head and turned away.

"Maybe I should give you 'the talk' now," Lucy's dad snarled, his face mottled red.

"Maybe you should," Xander agreed.

"But I have *no* intention of letting my daughter date you!"

"So she's told me," Xander said jauntily. He let go of Lucy's shoulders and blew her a kiss. "See you in a minute, sweet lips."

Then he sauntered off with her father into the living room.

Lucy stormed over to Alex, interrupting his conversation with Aaron. "Your brother," she announced, "is the most annoying person in the world!"

Aaron's lips quirked as he looked at Alex. "Would you agree with that assessment?"

Alex shrugged slightly, looking a bit embarrassed. "I would even say it's not news."

Gah! Why was Alex always so ... so *calm* about everything? Was it that stupid Gemini curse he had? It had to be. He'd been the Gemini for seventeen years. By now, pretty much his whole personality had to be determined by the curse.

Lucy pulled her phone out of her jeans pocket and walked off to the corner of the hallway, looking up what the personality traits of Gemini were. Were they as mind-numbingly dull as Virgo's?

She stopped, and stared. She read the Google results, and then read them again.

"Adaptable. Outgoing. Indecisive. Impulsive. Loves being the center of attention. Huge flirt. Impulsive and unreliable."

But ... but ... that makes no sense! That doesn't describe Alex at all! In fact, it almost perfectly describes ...

Lucy's heart caught in her throat.

... Xander.

Chapter 9
Not Quite the Heir

Xander was still in the living room with her father, which meant he wasn't available to confront. So Lucy stormed back to the kitchen and grabbed the next best thing.

"Alex," she snarled, seizing his arm, "can I talk to you for a minute?"

The guy raised his eyebrows. "Can it wait until you're not interrupting the conversation I'm in the middle of right now?"

"No," Lucy snapped.

Alex looked over at Aaron.

"Go ahead," the old man said graciously. "We can continue our conversation later."

Lucy dragged Alex upstairs, out of earshot of everyone else. She yanked her phone out of her pocket and shoved the screen with the description of Gemini in his face.

Alex just stared at her unblinkingly.

"Look!" Lucy snarled, pointing at the screen.

"Am I supposed to know what you're trying to communicate?" he queried.

"You're a big—fat—liar!" Lucy snarled, pulling her phone away and jabbing his chest with each word. "You're not the one who's affected! *Xander* is!"

"Oh," Alex said. "You noticed."

Lucy was stunned for a moment. He'd admitted it that readily?

"How could I not notice?!" she demanded.

"You'd be surprised," Alex said calmly. "Aaron knows, and so do my mom and my aunt and uncle, but I don't think anyone else has figured it out. Of course, there aren't that many people who know about the curses in the first place."

Lucy sucked in her breath. He had said "the curses." That proved for certain that he wasn't the Gemini. He wouldn't have been able to say that if he were.

"Well, if that's all ..." Alex tried to head back downstairs.

"No, that isn't all!" Lucy sputtered, blocking his path. "Why would you lie about who has it?!"

Alex looked puzzled. "Does it make any difference?"

"YES!"

"Oh. Why?"

"Because!" Lucy exclaimed.

"Because ...?"

Apparently she was going to have to spell it out.

"Because I have feelings for Xander, you moron," she said heatedly. "And apparently he's on the verge of dying!"

"And you prefer for me to be the one on the verge of dying," Alex said dryly.

"I didn't say that!"

"Oh, my mistake, I thought you just did."

"Fine," Lucy said with annoyance. "I'd prefer it to be you because I like Xander better. Happy?"

"Not really, although I might feel better about it if you would turn off your power, which is, by the way, still affecting me."

"Don't change the subject!" Lucy glared at him.

"It's not an unreasonable request, Lucy."

"Fine," Lucy snapped. "Then you can tell me why you think it's okay to lie about something so important."

She closed her eyes and focused on how irritating she found Alex when he wasn't boring, which was completely different from Xander, who was irritating-but-exciting. Being irritated by Xander was annoying in a fun way, like being teased by a friend about something embarrassing. Being irritated by Alex was just annoying.

"Better?" Lucy asked, opening her eyes.

Alex shrugged. "I hope so, but I won't be able to tell until you remove it from Xander, too. I can read his mind, remember."

"Well, that's too bad for you," Lucy said, putting her hands on her hips. "If he wants me to take it off him, he can tell me himself. I'm not even sure I can, because he's super my type. He might even be my favorite guy I'm currently dating!"

"You're not dating him," Alex said with an edge in his voice.

"Dad's giving him 'the talk' right now," Lucy retorted. "If he can convince Dad, I soon will be."

Alex looked decidedly sour-faced.

"Hang on!" Lucy exclaimed suddenly. "You enormous liar! You *can't* know what he's thinking! He's the one who's affected, so his ability wouldn't work on *you!*"

"It's two-way, Lucy," Alex said with a tight jaw. "It works on us equally."

Oh. Lucy stared at him with wide eyes. *Ohhhh!*

That explained a few things.

It explained why Xander had known all that homework stuff he'd brought up, even though he probably was a dropout and didn't go to school.

It explained how Alex could pretend he was the cursed one, if he really did have access to the power he claimed to have.

It even explained why Alex seemed to think it didn't matter which one was cursed, even though it mattered a *lot*.

"Well, fine," Lucy said. "Now explain to me why you've lied about the rest!"

"I've never lied," Alex said coolly. "I just haven't corrected the assumptions other people have made when I figured the details were none of their business in the first place."

"None of their ...?" Lucy stared at him, aghast.

"Yes," Alex said in a chilly tone. "I know it might be an alien concept, but not everybody likes to gossip about their private life with every stranger they meet."

Boy, did she dislike him.

"Then why doesn't Xander tell anyone?" Lucy challenged. "Is he as unreasonably obsessed with privacy as you are?"

Alex set his jaw. "First of all, it's not unreasonable, and second, he *can't* tell people the details. Or have you forgotten how all of the curses work?"

Lucy stamped her foot. "Still! He could say it indirectly!"

"Why would he want to?" Alex shot back. "Do you think it's fun to have people pressuring you and wanting to know your mental state for every second out of the day?"

Lucy went silent. That was exactly what she'd been dodging from her mother ever since the curse had hit.

"So ... you're taking it for him so that he doesn't have to?" Lucy said slowly. A realization occurred to her. "Because you feel you owe him? Because he's the one who's going to die first?"

Alex said nothing. His eyes were veiled.

Lucy sighed in exasperation. The way he so often went quiet was *so* annoying.

"Okay, I get it," she said. "You don't want to talk about it."

"Thank you."

"Just one more thing, though—"

"I take back my thank you."

"What was he *like?*" Lucy forged on, determined to get the answer. "What did he used to be like as a kid?"

Alex was silent.

"It's important!" Lucy cried.

"Why?" Alex's voice was very quiet. "It's a permanent change. It's not like he's going to revert."

"Because—" Lucy's voice cracked a little. She swallowed quickly and continued, trying to keep her voice level. "Because if I fell in love with somebody, I'd want him to love *Lucy*, not somebody else inhabiting my body. I'm guessing Xander feels the same way."

Alex looked at the floor and didn't speak.

"So what was he like as a kid?" Lucy asked urgently. "It's the closest I can get to knowing who he would be now without being changed against his will. I need to know, Alex. Please!"

Slowly, Alex looked up. His eyes were filled with pain. When he spoke, it was barely audible.

"He was pretty much exactly like me."

Then he shoved past her and went down the stairs.

Chapter 10
Not Quite a Choice

Reeling from the news, it was Lucy's turn to be dead silent, standing at the stop of the stairs as Alex reached the bottom and disappeared from view.

Xander was like Alex? Xander was like Alex?!

It wasn't good news. It was, in fact, the worst possible news.

If she had gotten any other answer, she may have been able to convince herself that she could have fallen for Xander without him being cursed.

But she *knew* Alex, and she knew she didn't like him.

Well, she liked his face, because who wouldn't? But that wasn't enough to really mean anything.

Pablo, and George, and Jonas, and Donny ... all of them were great, all guys that she was happy to go out with.

But Xander was special. Xander knew about her curse, and didn't mind it. Xander had, in fact, told her it was fine to use her power on him. With every other guy, there was the uncomfortable question of whether he'd choose to date her without the power. With Xander ... it didn't matter.

But it seemed she didn't actually have feelings for Xander. She had feelings for Gemini.

And she'd hate it if somebody fell in love with Virgo, instead of Lucy.

Which means I have to stop it, Lucy thought, clenching her fists so hard that her fingernails bit into her palms. *If I'd hate someone doing that to me, I can't do it to somebody else. It's wrong.*

She had to stop liking Xander. She had to stop finding him

appealing. She had to make sure her power stopped working on him, so that he could run away to protect himself.

Because he surely wouldn't like her if she gave him a choice. He must have overheard her conversation with Alex. He knew she didn't love him; she loved Gemini. And unless he was suicidal, the last thing he ought to want was to hang out with a girl who was the perfect match for his curse. If he did, he'd fall into Gemini faster and faster, and die sooner.

Lucy closed her eyes and tried to think of things that were unappealing about Xander.

It was an uphill battle. Every time she thought of something she didn't like, such as the fact that she was pretty sure he was a dropout, one of those cocky grins or flamboyant hand-kisses sprang to her mind to drown it out.

But at last, she figured out something she was absolutely sure she didn't like, and which she could convince herself might be even worse than it seemed: those occasional flashes of anger.

I wondered if he might be dangerous, she reminded herself. She pushed aside all benefit of the doubt and tried to feed her worst possible imaginings. *He's charismatic. He could secretly be a psychopath. That's definitely not incompatible with Gemini.*

She pictured Xander as the psychopathic villain of one of those suspense movies she had seen on one of her many dates. Scarily, it wasn't that hard. Xander's personality and the one the villain had shown in public weren't that dissimilar.

He has very little control over himself. He knows he's doomed. He has nothing to live for, and nothing to lose. Isn't that the sort of person who could easily become an ax murderer?

Lucy's heart raced. She was starting to believe that it might be true. Why hadn't she seen this before? She should never have started to trust him in the first place!

"Are you kidding me?!" a voice exploded from downstairs.

Lucy's eyes flew open.

"LUCY!" her father bellowed from below. "Get down here!"

She ran down the stairs, tripping twice in her haste. She barely saved herself from a twisted ankle by seizing the handrail.

Her father was standing in the living room with a purple face and a crumpled piece of paper in his hand.

"This!" he shouted, waving it at Xander, who was lounging against the wall and smirking. "THIS!"

"What is it, Dad?" Lucy asked, carefully avoiding looking at Xander. She didn't want to undo all her hard work.

"I asked a perfectly reasonable question about his intentions," Lucy's father bellowed, "and he said, 'I'll draw my feelings for Lucy!' and then he drew *THIS!*"

He thrust the crumpled ball of paper in Xander's direction.

The guy cackled.

"What is it?" Lucy asked curiously, reaching for it.

"You're not looking at it!" her dad screamed, wrenching the ball of paper away. "It's obscene! And *you!* Get out of my house! Never come back!"

"Sorry, sweet lips," Xander said with a mocking sneer so cold that it made chills run down Lucy's back. "Guess it won't work out between us. Oh, what a shame."

He made a rude gesture, barged past them, and headed out the front door. There was a sound of keys in the ignition of a motorcycle, then the roar of it leaving.

Lucy shuddered, feeling like she'd dodged a bullet. If that had been his first reaction to losing his feelings for her ... well, that showed his true colors, all right.

Of course, he might have done something completely against his character in order to make it easier for her to stay disgusted with him because he was a nice guy ... but no, she shouldn't give him the benefit of the doubt. That kind of thinking was dangerous.

"Well, there goes my ride home," Alex commented, coming out of the kitchen and glancing out the front window. "And Catherine and your wife are still too busy talking about what to name the columns to even start the meeting. I don't suppose you could drive me back after we've finished?"

Lucy's father breathed heavily, face still red with outrage. "Only if you promise to make sure that—that—*thing* stays away from my daughter forever!"

"Yes, that's easily promised," Alex said calmly. "I don't want them dating, either."

Lucy sniffed and gave Alex a chilly look as she walked past him. He seemed inordinately pleased about that. It was a good thing she disliked him so much, since her ever being attracted to Alex again would also affect Xander.

Soon after that, Steven arrived, apologizing for being half an hour late and blaming traffic. Then the meeting of all the cursed finally started.

It was every bit as interminable as Lucy had expected. They made her take eight billion personality quizzes, and Catherine had way too many ideas about how to compile them into a useful scoring rubric.

Lucy's eyes glazed over during a discussion about whether "impulsive" or "flighty" should be combined into one trait or kept separate. It was so boring that she was beginning to long for her math homework—

Wait! No! No, she wasn't!

There was only one thing for a self-respecting not-wanting-to-turn-into-Virgo to do.

"I'm leaving to go see my friend Carrie," Lucy announced, standing. "Have fun with your charts and things."

"*Lucy!*" her mother exclaimed, looking outraged.

"Wait, no!" Steven said, pointing to one of the columns on the spreadsheet. "That's exactly the sort of behavior she should be exhibiting if she's trying to resist being changed!"

Lucy's mother stared at the color-coded spreadsheet on her laptop, then at Lucy, clearly torn about what the right answer was.

"Okay, fine," she said reluctantly. "Go have fun with Carrie."

Trying not to grin too broadly, Lucy grabbed the car keys out of her mother's purse and headed out to the car, pulling her phone out of her pocket to call Carrie.

An ironclad excuse to get out of all responsible and dull things? she thought, unlocking the car. *Sure! Twist my arm!*

It was nice to have some advantages to being cursed.

AUTHOR NOTE:

I intended for Xander to be an "evil twin," a main villain, but he vehemently refused to do it. He insisted he had to be lovable, that uncooperative brat.

Alex is the main character of The Zodiac Curse *quartet, which happens a year after* The Virgo Curse *trilogy. Xander is very much a part of that story, too. It was the series I originally designed the worldbuilding around, and then Lucy popped up and demanded I tell her story first.*

Okay, okay, demanding one ...

NOT QUITE CHANGED

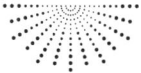

Chapter 1
Not Quite Fine

"Queen Lucy's adding to her harem again, I see," Carrie said snidely.

Lucy glanced uncomfortably over to the side. Was Tom …? Yep. Natasia's older brother was watching her from behind the grill with an admiring look on his face. She'd always vaguely thought he was cute, and apparently her power had activated on him.

"Lucy can't help it if she's hotter than the food he's cooking," Pablo teased, plopping his arm around her shoulders.

"Ouch!" Lucy mock-squealed, jumping away. "You're even hotter than I am!"

"If you want to make a date with him, I can take a turn at the grill so you can talk to him," George said seriously.

"No!" Carrie snapped. "This is Natasia's birthday party! Don't you dare make it all about you, Lucy. You already have two dates going on right now!"

Lucy laughed sheepishly. Yeahhh, she'd sort of brought two dates to Natasia's backyard birthday barbecue. But there was a reason for it!

Not that she could tell anyone that reason.

The reason was that, wellllllll, she'd made a rule that she couldn't go out with the same guy more often than once every third date. That was because she didn't dare start going out with any one guy exclusively. It was what the curse wanted her to do.

And, meanwhile, she'd had a date with Pablo only last night. But Natasia had invited Pablo to the party herself because he got along so well with all of their group, and Pablo was so fun that Lucy knew it would turn into a date if she didn't bring somebody else to be her technical date for the event, sooooooooo ... she'd invited George.

The other options would have been Jonas or Billy, guys she liked almost as much as George. But both of them got annoyed whenever she flirted with other guys while on dates with them, and she couldn't *not* flirt with Pablo when he was nearby, so yeah, she'd brought George.

"Don't go to the grill," Lucy told George with a teasing smile. "I like where you are right now."

George smiled and stroked her hand that was near him.

Pablo's arm around Lucy's shoulder tightened, and he scooted possessively closer. It seemed that while George was perfectly comfortable sharing her with Pablo, the reverse was not true.

"Now taking bets on who Lucy picks as a steady boyfriend!" Matilda stage-whispered from the other end of the table. "Ten bucks on George because he's the cutest!"

"Fifteen on Jonas because she's known him the longest," Jezza shot back.

"Twenty on Pablo because I think she likes him the best," Natasia grinned.

"Thirty on no one," Carrie smirked. "Queen Lucy is incapable of monogamy."

"You guyyyyyyys!" Lucy exclaimed.

"I'll place a bet on myself, if that's allowed!" Pablo called.

"Oooooh!" Jezza and Matilda giggled.

"I'm going to chop vegetables for the veggie platter!" Lucy informed them, shoving back her chair. "Nobody follow me!"

Laughter rolled across the group as she stormed off.

It's not that I'm incapable of monogamy! Lucy thought angrily, stomping up the stairs of the deck in order to reach the kitchen. *In fact, if I could pick Pab—one of the guys I like best, I would. But I can't! It would make the curse kill me faster!*

If she picked Billy because they had the exact same taste in movies, or Jonas because she'd had a crush on him as a kid and he still had the same wickedly sarcastic sense of humor, or George because he was the nicest guy she'd ever met, or Pablo because he was, well, duh, *Pablo*, it would mean letting the curse win. And she didn't want to give the curse any victories.

It wasn't like any of those guys were perfect, either. She'd only met Billy two weeks ago, so even though they got along great, she didn't know him that well. Jonas's jokes could be cruel and cutting. George's complete lack of jealousy got on her nerves. And Pablo …

Well, okay, Pablo *was* pretty much perfect. But his family was annoying.

Just last night, his unbelievable aunt had followed them to a restaurant to take pictures of one of their dates to put into their "future wedding scrapbook."

Granted, the way he'd yelled at her in Spanish about keeping her nose out of his business had been awesome.

And it still made her giggle to remember one of the things he'd yelled in Spanish, which she was sure he didn't realize she'd understood: *"Yes, I'd love it if she wants to marry me someday, but if that happens, it'll be on our timing and not yours, and I'll thank you to not scare her away!"*

He was so, so, *SO* great. But … that didn't mean she could afford to choose him.

Smile dropping from her face, Lucy shoved open the screen door and found Natasia's boyfriend chopping up celery.

"Hi, Sean," Lucy said, waving. "Can I help?"

"Nah, there's only one cutting board."

She looked down at the veggie platter. "Can I put the ranch dressing on there?"

He gestured at the refrigerator. "Sure."

Lucy squeezed too hard, and way too much ranch dressing splatted into the center. The excess ran over into the baby carrots. She grabbed a baby carrot and tried to shove the excess back into the middle as it kept pouring back.

She glanced sheepishly over at Sean, only to see that he was still methodically cutting tomato wedges with his back turned to her. He clearly hadn't noticed her minor misadventure with the ranch dressing, which meant he hadn't turned around to look at her once.

Chop. Chop. Chop. Chop. He kept on going without missing a beat.

Lucy frowned, puzzled. Sean was a weird mystery. He was the only guy she found attractive that she'd never caught trying to sneak glances at her. That was a good thing, since he was her friend Natasia's boyfriend, but she'd never been able to figure out why.

"How are you immune?" Lucy blurted out.

Sean looked up, clearly puzzled. "To what?"

Lucy wanted to bite her tongue. None of her friends knew about the curse, and she wanted to keep it that way.

On the other hand, she *did* want the answer to that question. As far as she knew, the only way for her power to not activate was for her to not find a guy attractive.

"Let's say there's such a thing as love potions," Lucy hedged. That was far enough away from the truth that the curse would let her say it.

"Okay?" Sean looked clearly mystified.

"Let's say it splashed on somebody, and it was an accident, and it couldn't be turned off."

"Okay ...?"

"And let's say it happened to me." Lucy took a deep breath. *"How are you immune?"*

Sean stared at her for a long moment.

"I'm not," he said, shrugging.

Lucy stared at him. *"What?"*

He looked a bit embarrassed. "I assume you're talking about the way you suddenly got really hot a few months ago, and every guy at school noticed? I dunno what it is, since you look the same as ever, but I get why the other guys are always staring at you. I just don't care. Natasia's the only girl who matters."

Lucy's mouth opened in astonishment. That possibility had never occurred to her.

So the curse isn't everything? They still have a choice?!

That was good news. No, it was great news. No, it was amazing!

"You're a great guy," she said, managing to keep her voice level instead of showing off her jubilation. "I'm glad Natasia has you."

"Me, too!" He glanced back at her with a grin.

Lucy picked up the veggie platter and walked over, moving tomato wedges from the chopping board as he prepared more.

She breathed a sigh of contentment. This meant she never had to worry that she'd steal Sean, because Sean wouldn't be stolen. He'd chosen Natasia, even with magic trying to tempt him away. That was the best thing ever.

Her hand hovered over the platter, and she swallowed a lump in her throat.

But I'll never have what they have, will I?

Because none of the guys she was currently dating had ever been given the opportunity to choose her. Not really. None of them knew that their feelings were probably magically induced.

Xander's curse had been a dealbreaker for Lucy. Lucy's curse might be a dealbreaker for any of them. So they deserved the chance to hear the truth and say "no."

Lucy took a deep, shaky breath.

That doesn't matter, she tried to convince herself. *As long as no relationship ever gets serious enough that I HAVE to tell the guy everything, it's fine to keep it a secret. It is!*

But the more she thought about it, the more it bothered her.

CHAPTER 2
NOT QUITE LONG

"—VISIT HIM," Lucy's mom was saying as she arrived back home from the birthday party a few hours later. "Oh, Lucy! I have bad news! Aaron fell and broke his hip!"

"Aaron Ahlstrom?" Lucy hazarded. That was the football player at school that Carrie was currently crushing on. She'd spent a solid fifteen minutes of the barbecue talking about him.

"Aaron Watson!" her mother said impatiently. "The Aries!"

Ohhh, him. The nice old guy. Lucy flinched a little. *I hope nobody calls me "the Virgo." I hate that Mom thinks it's okay to refer to people by their curses.*

"I'm sure it was painful," Lucy's mom nodded, misinterpreting her grimace. "We're going to go see him at the hospital. You got home just in time. You can come with us."

"Do I have to?" Lucy blurted out.

The dangerous look in her mother's eyes told Lucy that this had been the wrong thing to say.

"I mean, do I have to go with you?" Lucy amended quickly. "I want to go by myself. It'll be more personal that way."

"Oh." Her mother's expression softened. "I suppose so. You can borrow the car after we get back."

"Perfect," Lucy said, giving a cheerful thumbs-up.

It was all she could do to keep from grumbling inside as she went up the stairs to her room, though.

It wasn't that she didn't care about the old man. Breaking a hip sounded awful. But she didn't actually know him that well, and if she were the one in the hospital and maybe doped up on pain medication, she wouldn't want a bunch of almost-strangers coming to visit her. She'd want them to leave her alone.

On top of that, she'd just come home from a long afternoon of trying to seem cheerful and normal, and she wanted to hide in her room for awhile away from people.

Are Virgos introverts? she wondered, struck by the terrible thought at the top of the stairs. *This could be the curse trying to affect me.*

"Wait!" Lucy called, charging back down the stairs. "I changed my mind! I think it'd be better if we all visit him together. Less chance we'll tire him out or something."

"That's a good idea," her mother said approvingly. "Harry! Are you ready?"

"I don't see why we have to go in the first place," Lucy's dad grumbled, coming in from the living room with a well-worn copy of *The Art of War* in his hand. It was his idea of some relaxing light reading. "We barely know the man."

Lucy hid a giggle behind her hand.

"Harry," her mom said in a reproving tone, "it's important to show respect and solidarity."

"No, it's important for me to enjoy my day off."

Lucy felt significantly more cheered as they tromped to the car. It helped to know her father felt the same way she did.

She played a cellphone game during the drive there, and her father kept reading his book.

When they arrived at the hospital, they went to the right floor, checked in at the desk, were told Aaron's room number, and all headed there together.

Lucy crossed her fingers, hoping the old man would be asleep and they wouldn't have to make stiltedly awkward conversation, but no such luck. He was sitting up, wide awake, and in a friendly mood.

"Harry! Iris! Lucy!" he said, turning off the TV. "How good of you to come!"

"We heard about your hip," Lucy's mother said with concern, walking over to the bed and sitting in the chair beside it. "How are you doing?"

Aaron shrugged. "I can't say I'm exactly good, but ... I'm all right. How are you doing?"

"Oh, we're fine," Lucy's mom said, waving her hand. "Is there anything we can do for you?"

"No, I'm fine, fine. Tell me what's up with you."

"We're not important right now. You are. Are you hurting? Are they giving you everything you need?"

"Mom," Lucy cut in, "he's obviously trying to say, 'Please don't feel sorry for me, because it makes me feel like an invalid.'"

Lucy's dad coughed in a way that was clearly trying to hide a laugh.

Her mother glanced back at both of them, glaring.

Aaron's lips twitched. "Well ... she's not wrong, Iris. I'd rather be distracted from my own life right now. So please. Tell me how things are going with you."

Lucy's mother frowned, but she eventually launched into a long description of the way she had been tracking Lucy's behavior over the last few months and the worrisome places she thought she had seen hints of changes.

Aaron responded to the topic with evident interest, and they talked about it for awhile, which Lucy found intensely boring and intensely embarrassing.

She glanced over at her father with agonized eyes.

"Let's go get Aaron a snack from the vending machine," he suggested, removing his finger from his book and tucking it into his pocket. He had been sneaking glances at it every few seconds. "Aaron, is there anything you're not allowed to eat?"

"Oh, I probably shouldn't eat candy, but I'd love a Snickers."

"Good to know." Her dad gestured with his head. "C'mon, Lucy. Let's go get him something."

Lucy followed him out of the room with relief.

Once they were out of earshot, she whispered furiously, "Why is Mom so ... so ..."

"She cares about people," Lucy's father said firmly, in a tone that made it clear he wasn't going to listen to any badmouthing. "That's why she's trying so hard to track your behavior. I know you don't like it, but it could be important to keep you alive longer."

Lucy sighed heavily. She knew that. She *knew* that, but she still hated it.

"Hey," her dad said, putting his arm around her shoulders, "I'll buy you something, too. What are you in the mood for?"

Not being in a hospital, Lucy thought, but that didn't seem like the right answer. "Peanut butter M&Ms," she said.

They found a cluster of vending machines, including one with Snickers bars, but none with peanut butter M&Ms.

"No problem," her dad said. "I'm sure there are a bunch of vending machines on every floor. Let's check out all of them."

Lucy was glad for the excuse to stay out of the room as long as possible, so they went on a long treasure hunt around the hospital until they found a vending machine with Reese's Pieces, which she determined were close enough.

They headed back up to Aaron's floor and came in with the Snickers bar for him. Lucy's mother, still engaged in conversation with the old man, didn't notice them enter until Aaron interrupted her to wave and say hi.

"Here's a Snickers," Lucy's dad said, walking over and placing it on the bed beside Aaron.

"Thank you," the old man said with a smile. "That's very kind of you. Iris, may I talk with Lucy for a few minutes?"

Lucy's mother nodded, as if this was something they had discussed earlier, and took her husband's hand and guided him out of the room without comment. Their footsteps faded down the hallway.

Lucy stared at the brown-skinned old man, mystified. Why did Aaron want to talk to her? Was he going to tell her to pay more attention to her mother's stupid spreadsheet?

He didn't say anything at first. He just peeled the candy bar and took a bite, chewing it slowly as if he was savoring it.

Lucy frowned, puzzled and wondering why she was here.

At last, Aaron swallowed and set the rest aside.

"I'm not going to live much longer, Lucy," he said.

Her eyes widened. "What? Are you sure?!"

He smiled softly. "Well, the odds of a senior citizen living longer than a year after breaking a hip are fifty percent. I'm not going to beat those odds."

"You could," Lucy said hotly. "That's fifty percent. Half do!"

"But I don't want to," Aaron said quietly. "I'm content with the life I've had, and I'm not eager to spend another ten years losing myself to my condition, especially given the ability it grants me. Do you understand?"

"No!" Lucy said heatedly. "I *don't* understand!"

"Think about what I can do, Lucy."

Lucy frowned. "You can persuade people to do things, right?"

"Yes. Now think about that in conjunction with the personality

I'm inevitably going to be stuck with by the end of my life, unless I pass away of natural causes long before then."

Lucy stared at him in puzzlement.

Aaron waited patiently, his hands on his lap.

Lucy pulled out her phone and looked up *Aries personality traits*. Google found what she was looking for immediately.

"Passionate. Motivated. A confident leader. Blindly optimistic. Always convinced that they're right. Competitive. Impulsive. Selfish. Annoyed by details and nuances. Doesn't think things through."

Her mouth went dry.

Chapter 3
Not Quite Safe

Even though she didn't say anything, Aaron seemed to know what she was thinking just by the look on her face. He chuckled.

"Yes. I see you've realized."

You've got a mind-control power! Lucy wanted to yell, but couldn't say. *And you're going to turn into someone who thinks they're always right and who wants to be in charge of everybody they meet!*

Aaron picked up his candy bar, peeled back the wrapper a bit farther, and took another bite. He chewed and swallowed. "As you might guess, I don't think it would be particularly safe for the world for me to live much longer."

"But—you can't—I mean, you shouldn't—" Lucy wasn't quite sure what she was fumbling to say. She just knew that it sounded way too much like he was planning to commit suicide.

"I'm not going to end my life deliberately," he said calmly. "For one thing, every day I live is another day my granddaughter isn't affected. I'd rather she have as much time unaffected by this situation as possible."

Lucy breathed a sigh of relief.

"But I've signed a do-not-resuscitate order," Aaron told her. "And I had a mild heart attack last year. I won't take my own life, but I won't take steps to prolong it if my time comes, either. I see breaking my hip as a sign that I should prepare to die soon."

Tears rose in the corners of Lucy's eyes. "That's stupid!"

"You're young," Aaron retorted. "You don't know what it's like to be old, bored, tired of life, and ready to see if there's something else afterwards."

"Then why are you telling me this?!" Lucy exclaimed. "If I can't understand, what's the *point?*"

Aaron said nothing at first, but took another bite of his Snickers bar. It was almost gone now. He chewed and swallowed for what seemed like a really long time. Then, at last, he spoke.

"My granddaughter is only seven years old. Her name is Ellen, and her family's going to be moving here in anticipation of what happens to her after I die."

She was his heir, in other words. That was one of the words cursed people never seemed to be able to say.

"I want you to look after her," Aaron continued. "She's always wanted a big sister, and I think she'd look up to you."

Lucy's mouth opened. "Me?!"

"Yes. When I'm gone and she's part of the ... group, I want you to make sure she's included and happy. She'll be the only child among all of you, and I suspect that will make her unhappy and unlikely to listen to advice from a bunch of strangers, especially after just barely having been forced to move to a new city. Her parents haven't explained any of this to her yet. If you take her under your wing, I think that will help her."

Lucy gulped. "But I don't know how to be an older sister."

She knew how to be a *younger* sister, but ever since Lila had gone away to college, she'd mostly felt like an only child, and she enjoyed it. She and Lila got along much better when they only talked on the phone, instead of squabbling over who had stolen whose pants from whose closet yesterday.

Never mind that the pants thief was usually Lucy.

"But you do know how to be friendly and engaging," Aaron countered. "Your mother says you make friends easily, and you certainly seem to have a lot of them. I'm not saying that you have to

He's being MY DAD.

Ugh! I hate him! Carrie shot back.

Lucy winced. She didn't want to see Carrie insulting her dad, especially when he was a great guy most of the time. But there wasn't really any other way to keep Carrie from getting mad at her than to use her father as an excuse.

Sorry, Lucy said. *I've gotta work on stuff now. I hate math homework, yuck!*

Then she turned off the screen of her phone and tossed it on her bed, flopping back and putting her arm over her eyes.

Lucy sighed loudly. It really stank to be cursed. Now she was lying to her friends?

Maybe she should check her math homework again just so that she wouldn't have been lying to Carrie. She got out of bed, fetched her backpack, and pulled out the textbook and binder with her homework paper.

She found something she'd gotten wrong, and erased it and redid the problem. She saw another mistake and fixed that, too. Hey, this was actually starting to make sense for once in her life! It was almost like she was seeing things in a brand new way—

Lucy stopped abruptly, her pencil hovering over the paper. She reached out for her phone and pulled up a browser. When Google came up, she typed in, *Are Virgos good at math?*

Why yes, Google informed her, they were known for that!

Lucy snarled and slammed her phone onto her bedspread.

So now she had to be suspicious if she ever started to get better at school. Great. That was just great.

"Lucy!" her mother's voice called from downstairs. "Aaron and Catherine are here!"

Who's Catherine? Lucy wondered.

That turned out to be the Leo, she discovered after she went downstairs. She hadn't met the woman at the previous meeting because she was a high-powered executive who was usually busy at work, but she'd managed to come today.

Catherine and her mother hit it off way too well, and they imme-

treat her as if she's blood-related, but a little bit of making sure to single her out and pay attention to her and be nice to her will go a long way."

Lucy was silent. It wasn't too much to ask, and it wasn't like it would make her Virgo curse worse. Making friends easily was something she did naturally. But it was uncomfortable to have someone asking her to be friends with someone else she'd never met. What if the girl was a royal brat? What if they had nothing in common and just didn't get along?

"I guess I can try," Lucy hedged.

Then a horrible realization crawled up the back of her neck.

"You didn't just convince me, did you?!" she gasped, her whole body stiffening.

Aaron sighed heavily. "No, Lucy. If I had, you wouldn't have been able to consider the possibility. You would trust me implicitly."

Scariest. Power. Ever. Lucy shuddered.

Aaron finished off the last bite of his candy bar. He crumpled the wrapper in his hand and set it on the table beside the bed. "Thank you, Lucy. Knowing that someone will be watching over her eases my mind. If I can do anything to help you, please let me know."

"You're welcome. I'll keep that in mind," Lucy said to be polite. Honestly, she couldn't see what an old man with a broken hip and a terrifying power could do to help anybody. But he was nice, so she wouldn't hurt his feelings by saying so.

"I mean it," Aaron said, reaching out and squeezing her hand. His wrinkled skin was soft and loose, like melted chocolate. "If I can do anything, let me know."

"Okay, I will, I promise," Lucy said uncomfortably, extracting her hand.

She glanced over her shoulder. *When is Mom coming back?*

In the end, it took ten more minutes for her parents to return, leaving her and Aaron in uncomfortable silence for awhile.

Her mother said goodbye to the old man, giving him a gentle hug without squeezing him too tightly, and Lucy's father waved goodbye with a poorly disguised expression of relief.

In the car, Lucy's mom glanced back from the driver's seat before backing out, and said, "Well? Did you agree to help his granddaughter?"

Of course Mom had known what Aaron wanted to ask her. "Yeah," Lucy said. "She sounds nice. I hope she is."

"That's good." Lucy's mom smiled. "I'm sure you would have appreciated an older sister figure if you'd inherited your curse at her age."

I already have an older sister figure, and she's Lila. "I guess," Lucy shrugged.

"Personally, I don't see much point in asking Lucy to befriend a stranger she's never met," her father opined. "Not to mention one that's nine years younger. I don't think they'll have that much in common."

"Harry!" her mom said in annoyance.

Personally, Lucy was inclined to agree, but she knew better than to take sides when her parents were arguing. Whenever she did, the parent she sided with would jump to the other's side, and then she'd turn into the one they were annoyed with.

So she just smiled to herself and started a game on her phone. She glanced up a minute later to see her father tapping his finger on a paragraph thoughtfully.

That had better not be an idea about how to embarrass me in front of tonight's date, Dad! Lucy thought indignantly.

She had a first date tonight. Yet another one. She really ought to start turning those guys down. But without a steady boyfriend as an excuse, she couldn't do that without hurting their feelings.

And, well, she couldn't have a steady boyfriend, because that would be bad.

Stupid curse.

The more she thought about her conversation with Aaron, though, the more it disturbed her. Not the favor, but the fact that he wanted to die soon to protect the world from his power.

He could change minds.

She could change hearts.

He was warning people that his power existed. She wasn't.

Lucy bit her lip uncomfortably. *Do I need to start?*

Chapter 4
Not Quite Right

"Please make an exception for me," the guy in front of her pleaded.

Lucy groaned in exasperation. Tonight's first date, Andrew, would not be getting a second. But he was trying to insist on her scheduling one on the front step of her house before they parted ways anyway. What a loser.

"No," Lucy said firmly. "I don't make dates more than a week in advance, and I'm busy the rest of this week. Sorry."

"Please!" Andrew exclaimed.

Lucy pursed her lips and stared intently at his face, looking for any flaws. None stood out, which was probably why he was still attracted to her. It was hard to make herself stop liking a guy who was that good-looking.

But she'd better do it, because he was getting on her nerves. Maybe she could focus on his voice, which was now sounding distinctly whiny. Or the fact that he seemed to be clumsy.

Boys who beg for dates after spilling soda all over my lap are not attractive, Lucy told herself firmly.

"Sorry," she said, pulling her key out of her pocket to open the door.

Andrew lunged forward and tried to kiss her. Lucy yelped and jabbed her hand out to protect herself. Her key slashed the side of his face.

"Oww!" Andrew shouted, clutching his cheek. "What was that for?!"

"I don't kiss on the first date, and certainly not guys who don't bother to ask first!" Lucy yelled back. "Why would you think that's okay?!"

"But I have to! My friend bet me fifty dollars I couldn't get you to kiss me!"

Lucy stared at him incredulously. Then she spun around, jammed her key in the lock, flung the door open, stalked in, and slammed the door in his face.

"Sounds like a successful date," her father called gleefully from the living room, where he was watching a football game on TV and sipping a cup of chamomile tea.

"Such! A! Nightmare!" Lucy exclaimed, storming over to the living room. "Why do first dates so often stink?"

"Because you go on way too many of them," her father said smugly, muting the television set.

Lucy flopped into a chair, unwilling to admit she agreed. "So what's the solution?"

Her father gave her a lazy smile. "Well, there's always—"

"I'm not going to quit going out on *all* dates, Dad!"

He guffawed.

"Of course, I'm sure it didn't help that you told him if he proved to have more hands than two, you'd be happy to relieve him of the extras," Lucy added, folding her arms.

"Just protecting my little girl," he said with a grin.

Lucy flopped back against the couch, sighing. "I wish I could stop going on first dates, but I can't do that without making it look like I'm about to choose a boyfriend to commit to, y'know? And I don't want to raise P—um, anyone's hopes."

"So why don't you just choose a boyfriend to commit to?"

Lucy stared at him. This, from her overprotective dad? "What?"

"It seems to me that that's the obvious solution. If it doesn't work out, you could dump that boy and choose another."

"But I can't do that!" Lucy exclaimed.

"Why not?" He looked puzzled.

"Because! Because I think that's what the thing-I-can't-say wants me to do!"

Her father blinked. "You think the curse cares if you have a boyfriend?"

"Yes!" Lucy exclaimed. "I think the whole point of the thing-I-can-do is to make me sick of having tons of guys after me and want to settle down with just one, which is totally the kind of thing a person with my birthdate should supposedly be doing!"

Lucy's father opened his mouth, as if he were about to say something. Then he shut it again, looking puzzled.

"Okay, setting aside the fact that my sister stayed single for her whole life, and still died of the Virgo curse," he said at last, "why would you think it's a good idea to not do things you want to do just because the curse wants you to do them?"

"Because I don't want to die!"

"Yes, I approve of that goal." Her father nodded. "But you might want to consider this: if you don't want to be single for the rest of your life, then the sooner you find a relationship you want to stay in, the better a chance you have of finding someone who likes you, and not Virgo."

Lucy swallowed. That thought had never occurred to her. "But if it makes me die sooner—"

"If you'd stayed to listen to any of Steven's advice at the last meeting," her father said with a hint of exasperation, "you'd know that permanently single people tend to die more quickly of the curses than people in a relationship. His theory is that having someone who cares even more than you do about you staying alive and staying yourself is very helpful."

Lucy swallowed. Well, now that he made it seem like her getting a boyfriend was her best chance to stay alive longer, she paradoxically didn't want one. That sounded scary.

"But you'd hate that," Lucy argued. "You hate it when I go out on dates!"

"No, I hate the endless parade of strange boys showing up at our house that I don't trust with my daughter." He snorted. "At this point, seeing you settle down with one boy I know moderately well and don't mind would be a relief."

Lucy was starting to feel panicked. Did he mean she had to pick somebody? She wasn't ready to pick somebody! If she did, she'd have to break a bunch of other guys' hearts, and she didn't want to hurt anyone!

Besides, what if she got dumped and had no backup plans that she could live with waiting for her?!

"Of course, there's no rush," her dad said. "If you'd rather take a break from boys until college, for instance, that would be fine."

Until college?! "Daaaaaaaaaad!" Lucy exclaimed.

Her father sipped his probably-now-cold chamomile tea and grinned.

"I'll figure it out myself," Lucy fumed, hopping up to her feet. "Thanks for nothing, Dad."

"You're welcome for nothing, Lucy."

"I can't believe you're trying to convince me to get a boyfriend! I don't want a boyfriend! You're crazy!"

"Excellent. Nothing would make me more ecstatic than you not dating until you're old enough to get married."

"But that doesn't mean I *won't* get one!" Lucy flared.

"Then I suppose I'll tolerate that."

"Now you're just assuming I *will!* Don't try to make decisions for me! Ugh!"

Her father looked highly amused. "So you have the opposite opinion of whatever I say? Fascinating. In that case, I'd love to see you go out with hundreds of boys forever."

Lucy stamped her foot. "Stop making fun of me!"

"Then don't make it so easy."

"I don't want to dump any of the guys I like!" Lucy cried. "It'll hurt their feelings!"

"Leading 'em on will just hurt them worse."

Lucy hesitated. "So you're saying maybe I should narrow it down to only guys I might consider dating exclusively?" she asked in a small voice.

"Oh, no," her father said. "I'm saying nothing of the sort. Not when it seems to be opposite day."

Lucy snorted and turned to stomp out of the room.

"Lucy?" her father called after her.

"Yeah?" she asked saucily.

"Not the one with the nose ring, okay?"

"Dad, I dumped him two months ago!"

"Oh, good." Her father sounded pleased.

Chapter 5
Not Quite Fair

Zipping through a rack of jeans to see if she could find a pair that was both cute and fit her during this week's massive sale, Lucy was startled to hear a familiar voice off to the side.

"Aw, Mom, c'mon. Can't we just buy the first one?"

"No, you're going to try on all five."

There was a disgusted groan and the sound of footsteps stomping off.

Lucy ducked below the rack she was examining and peeked around the side, checking to see if it was the person she'd thought. Yep, that was Caleb's retreating back.

Phooey. That made her shopping trip much less relaxing.

Lucy contemplated whether she should hurry off before he noticed her, or whether she should just pretend he wasn't there and keep looking through jeans she might want to buy.

Avarice won out. It wasn't her fault that Caleb insisted on making it awkward whenever they ran into each other, and she had sixty dollars of birthday money she wanted to spend on new jeans today.

She turned her back to the men's changing rooms, hoping he wouldn't recognize her from behind when he came out, and went back to browsing.

Ooh, those jeans with the flower pockets were cute! And they were a good price, too. The size was a little too big, though. Did they have a pair in her size? She slid her way through a bunch of identical ones, looking for a pair that was the right size so she could try them on.

"Hey, look, they fit," Caleb's voice said from behind her. "Just like I said they would. Now can we buy these and go?"

"Nuh uh," said a bossy woman's voice. "You want me to pay for your clothes, I get the privilege of approving them. Now turn around so I can see how they look from the back."

Caleb groaned loudly.

Lucy stifled a giggle with her hand. Their conversation was reminding her of going back-to-school shopping with her mom when she was a kid. But seeing as Caleb was her age, hearing him whine like an elementary schooler was hilarious.

"Okay, good," the woman's voice said. "Those are a maybe. Now try on the next pair."

There was a loud exhale, clearly meant to be a less-than-subtle complaint, then the sound of footsteps treading away again.

Lucy couldn't resist. She turned around and asked the woman, "Is he always such a baby about clothes shopping?"

"A total infant," the woman said, shaking her head. She had dark brown skin, a bald head, and enormous earrings that swung as her head moved. "I wish my daughter was the one who needed new clothes. Maybe then this would be fun, rather than an ordeal."

"Or it'd be *more* of an ordeal, because she'd be begging you to buy her extra stuff every two minutes," Lucy said impishly. She and her sister tended to do that to their mom whenever they went shopping together. It drove their mom nuts.

"Good point," the woman said. "I guess my son will do. I'm Tammy. What's your name?"

"Lucy," Lucy said.

"Cool." Tammy surveyed her. "How old are you?"

"Sixteen."

"Perfect. My son's age. You can give your opinions on how the jeans look on him. I don't really have much perspective on whether he looks attractive to a teenage girl or not."

Lucy stifled a hysterical giggle behind her hand. "Um, I don't think Caleb wants my opinion."

"Why not?"

Caleb emerged from the dressing room, strode over with a bored-to-death look on his face, and then stopped abruptly. "*You!*" he shouted.

"Hi, Caleb," Lucy said sheepishly. She knew she shouldn't have started a conversation with his mom, but honestly, how was she supposed to have resisted?

"You know each other?" Tammy asked, looking confused.

"She's the one with the making-people-fall-in-love-with-her power!" Caleb shouted.

Lucy glanced around in alarm, hoping nobody she knew was nearby and listening in. Fortunately, none of her friends or other people in school were in sight.

"Oh, really?" Tammy asked with interest. "I've heard a lot about you from Steven. What's that power like? Is it fun?"

"No, it's awful!" Lucy blurted out. "I never know if anyone *actually* likes me, and the only two guys who've known about it have rejected me because I had it!"

Technically that wasn't totally true. Caleb had done that, but she'd rejected Xander, not the other way around.

Still, he definitely hadn't come back.

Which didn't hurt or anything. Really, it didn't. It was just, well, maybe part of her had hoped he'd fallen in love with her for real and would come back saying that he didn't care about the danger to himself; he just wanted her. The fact that he had done the exact opposite ...

... didn't hurt at all. Really, it didn't.

Besides, she liked Pablo way more anyway. He was just as fun as Xander, and he didn't have that nasty temper. Plus, his personality was his own.

But he also didn't know about the curse. She didn't know how he'd react to finding out what her power did. And when she imagined Pablo sneering at her in that cold, contemptuous way Xander had right before leaving, she wanted to cry.

It would be bad enough if he indignantly rejected her, like Caleb had. But contempt ... she couldn't stand it if he looked at her with contempt. She just couldn't.

And what if all her backup plans did the same thing?

Caleb was folding his arms and looking utterly unsympathetic.

"Sounds to me like the only way to find out is to tell them," Tammy said.

"Yeah, at the start, so they won't feel tricked and deceived," Caleb said acidly.

Tammy flicked him hard in the arm.

"Ow!" he complained, grabbing the spot.

"Ignore my son's denseness. Of course you can't tell them the truth from the start," Tammy said briskly. "It's a question of privacy, isn't it? You don't want to be the gossip of the entire school."

Lucy swallowed and nodded.

"So pick a set amount of time in which you'll either break up with a guy or trust him enough to tell him the truth. One or the other. That's what Steven did. He told me about being the heir to a curse on our sixth date. Kind of a shocker, let me tell you."

Lucy bit her lower lip. *But ... I mean ... obviously I trust Pablo and George and Jonas and Billy to not tell anyone by now. I just don't trust any of them to not break up with me!*

Lucy cringed. Now that she'd put it into words, that seemed disgustingly selfish.

"Do I have to pick a set amount of time?" she hedged.

"Absolutely," Tammy said. "If you don't, you'll keep making excuses to put it off long after the point where you could have done it, and that isn't quite fair. Don't you think?"

Bingo. Lucy felt a little queasy.

"But I *can't* tell them the whole truth," Lucy argued, knowing she was grasping at straws. "That's how it works. I can't explain anything directly."

"Then get somebody else to do it," Tammy shrugged.

"I'll do it!" Caleb said with a grin. He punched a fist into his hand. "Let me at 'em."

"I'd rather die," Lucy retorted.

Caleb snickered. "C'mon. I'll only embarrass you *half* as badly as you humiliated me."

"I didn't do it on purpose! And don't you have jeans to try on?"

"Good point," Tammy said, pointing to the changing room. "Let's see you in the next pair."

"They're all exactly the same," Caleb grumbled. But he left.

Lucy sighed and turned to leave.

"Hey. It's not as bad as you think," Tammy called after her. "Some people are okay with dealing with hard things."

"Easy for you to say," Lucy said angrily, wiping the edge of her eyes to get rid of wetness that was totally not forming there. "You don't have what I've got."

"Yeah, I'm just in the middle of treatment for breast cancer," Tammy said sarcastically. "You think the threat of dying maybe a decade from now is bad? Big whoop-de-freaking-doo."

Lucy swallowed. She had somehow managed to forget that there were problems that weren't supernatural that were every bit as bad as a curse.

"Thanks for your advice," she said almost inaudibly, and then hightailed it out of there.

Chapter 6
Not Quite Brave

Justifications and excuses weren't any use, so Lucy vowed that she would tell Billy the truth on their date the next night.

He was the perfect choice to tell first. He was on the list of guys she might consider a possible boyfriend, but he was at the bottom of the list. That meant if he rejected her, or if he did something horrible like betray her trust and turn her curse into a rumor at school, she'd be able to handle it.

Meanwhile, if everything went well, she'd be all the more prepared to tell the truth to Jonas. Or George. Or Pablo.

Her pulse accelerated in panic.

No, not Pablo. Not him. Not yet. She had to save him for last. He was the one she was most afraid would reject her. His family was so controlling and pushy. She was certain he'd hate the idea of her curse doing the same thing to him, only more insidiously.

But maybe ... if the other boys she liked best were all okay with it ... he'd turn out to be, too.

Lucy took a deep breath, pulled her hair back, changed her clothes, and sprayed her wrist with her favorite perfume.

There. Now she was all ready for tonight's date.

Oh, wait! Billy's allergic to perfume! She dashed to the sink in the upstairs bathroom to scrub it off.

When Billy arrived, she felt jumpy, and her voice sounded too loud whenever she answered a question. He didn't seem to notice, though, and soon they were in a movie theater, sharing a bucket of popcorn.

Well, I can't tell him now, Lucy told herself, relaxing back into her seat. *I'll have to wait till the movie's over.*

Once the movie was over, they drove back, chatting about the scenes they'd enjoyed most and the moments they'd thought were stupid. As always, they had the same opinion on everything in the movie. That was what Lucy liked about him.

Then they were back at the door, and Lucy realized that she hadn't told him anything important yet, or even tried to bring up the subject.

"Billy," Lucy began, pleating her hands nervously. "There's, um, there's something you ought to know."

"Huh?" He cocked his head to the side.

Lucy swallowed. Her heart pounded. Even the vaguest words that the curse would allow her to say stuck in her mouth.

"Never mind!" Lucy cried, and grabbed the doorknob. She flung the door open, ran a step inside, and then turned back and gave Billy a hurried kiss on the cheek. "You're a great guy, Billy. Thanks for being so fun to hang out with."

"You're welcome," Billy beamed, giving her a thumbs-up.

Lucy shut the door and leaned against it, shoulders heaving.

I'm a coward, she thought, filled with self-recrimination and despair. *If I can't tell Billy, how can I ever tell anybody?*

If only there were some way to become brave overnight. The curse was like a constant shoulder devil, and it wasn't fair. Why couldn't she have a shoulder angel, too?

Because there's nothing that works like the curse except for the curse, Lucy thought bitterly.

She headed upstairs to her bedroom and flopped on her bed, kicking her shoes off and staring angrily at the ceiling.

I'm such a coward, she thought furiously. *A total coward.*

Maybe the curse would be helpful for something. Maybe she just had to wait until it changed her. She rolled over to tug her phone out of her pocket, turned on the screen, and asked Google, *Are Virgos brave?*

The results made her jaw drop in horror.

They're known for being cowards?!?!

She sat bolt upright, teeth clenched. She slammed her phone on the bedspread.

So it might not be her who was the coward. It might be Virgo acting through her.

She was not going to let it win!

She grabbed her phone and started a text to Billy. Maybe over the phone wasn't ideal, but she had to tell him somehow. But what should she say?

She could use words like *curse* or *zodiac* or *Virgo* when typing things into Google, but she couldn't type them to show to a human. She couldn't tell him that she had a power or be specific about how it worked, either.

She could always ask her parents to write an explanation for her and send it, but that seemed way too impersonal. Making your parents do something for you that you were scared to do yourself was cowardly, anyway.

Lucy drummed her fingers on her bed, trying to figure out how to make the meaning obvious despite all her limitations.

I've got a thingy that's bad and does stuff I can't control and I know it's affected you too, she typed in.

Lucy's finger hovered over the "send" button. *That makes sense, right?* she tried to convince herself. *Right?*

She groaned and deleted it. No, it didn't. It was complete nonsense. Only somebody who knew about the curses would have any chance of decoding it.

Maybe he does *know about the curses!* Lucy thought hopefully, sitting up straight. *Maybe he's one of the unknown cursed people, and he has a curse with personality traits that wouldn't make it dangerous for him to be around me! Maybe they ALL are!*

That would be amazing. Then she wouldn't have to explain

anything, and they'd all be fine with it, and being with a guy who knew what she was going through would be the best thing ever.

But, well ...

Lucy sighed. *That's a stupid thing to hope.*

First of all, she didn't actually want any of the guys she liked to have a curse that would make them die early.

Second, if any of the lost zodiac curses had stayed in town or wandered back into it, the families who knew about the curses would have noticed them long ago. The five unknown people with a zodiac curse had to be scattered randomly across the country, maybe across the world.

Third, it wasn't a good idea for two cursed families to mix.

And fourth, how stupid was she? Helllllllo! She didn't want a boyfriend who was going to lose his personality to a curse! That was why she'd made herself stop liking Xander in the first place!

Well, no ... she'd mostly done it for his own sake. But there was also the teensy tiny selfish fact that she didn't want to date a guy whose original personality was the same as Alex's, because come on, *Alex?* Did he even *have* a personality? The guy was as boring as dirt!

Lucy grinned wryly. Of course, if she said any of that to Pablo, he would tease her by quoting something from the Bible about the importance of being nice to people and not judging them or whatever, because it turned out he was way more religious than he looked at first glance, but since it was better for everybody if she kept disliking Alex and Xander and wasn't charitable to them at all, she would keep on being rude to them in her head, thanks very much.

She looked down at her phone, which still had nothing useful typed in, and groaned. *I'm procrastinating, aren't I?*

See, this was exactly why the curse was such a pain in the neck. She couldn't just explain without having to thinking about it, and she couldn't think about it without letting her mind wander, and she couldn't afford to let her mind wander because that would give the curse more time to turn her into a coward.

She wanted to get it over with, and she wanted to be brave, but she couldn't seem to figure out how to make those happen.

I need a shoulder angel! Lucy thought with frustration. *I need some-*

thing that will turn me into the kind of person I want to be, not what the curse wants me to become!

But it was impossible. There was nothing that worked the same way as the curse. Nothing except ...

Lucy gasped and leapt off her bed. She ran downstairs.

"Mom! Dad! Can I borrow the car? I want to visit Aaron at the hospital!"

Nothing except the current power of the Aries curse.

Chapter 7
Not Quite Wrong

AARON WAS asleep when Lucy entered his room, and the lights were out. She should have realized he would be; it was almost eight thirty pm, and old people always seemed to go to bed early.

She stood there awkwardly, fidgeting, wondering if she should wake him up. Visiting hours ended at nine pm, so she'd thought she'd be okay, and she really, really wanted to talk to him about this right now, but if he was asleep ...

She moved forward, wanting to check if he was really asleep or if he was just getting ready to fall asleep, because if he wasn't quite asleep yet it would be okay to wake him up, and tripped over one of her undone shoelaces. She stumbled and fell forward, her elbow whacking the bedside table with a hard thump.

"OWWW!" Lucy yelled, grabbing her elbow.

Aaron's eyes slowly opened. "Hello?" he asked groggily.

"Um. Hi," Lucy said sheepishly. This wasn't quite how she'd wanted to start the conversation, but it would do. "It's me, Lucy. Um, are you awake enough to talk? I, um, I wanted to ask you something."

"Mmm. Sure." Aaron sat up slowly and creakily, turning on the lamp at the table beside his bed. The lamp was crooked from Lucy jostling the table when she'd whacked her elbow on it. "What is it, Lucy?"

"Um. Um. Um." Lucy's mind raced. How could she put this in a way that wouldn't make him say no?

She wished she had his power to convince people. Well, no, she didn't. Wait, yes, she did, because then she could use it on herself and all of her problems would be solved.

"Remember you asked if you could do anything to help me, and to just let you know?" Lucy blurted out.

"Yes," Aaron murmured, rubbing his eyes and trying to stifle a yawn. "Did you think of something?"

"Yes!" Lucy said rapidly. "I want a shoulder angel."

Aaron stared at her with mystification written across the lines of his face.

"So, you know the bad thing we both have?" Lucy asked.

"The word we can't say. Yes."

"And you know how it works?"

"I daresay I do," Aaron said dryly.

"Well, *your talent* works the same way. Right? I mean, when you use it on someone, it's basically exactly the same thing."

Aaron stiffened. He didn't answer, and seemed wary.

"But that's a good thing!" Lucy added excitedly. "Because it can be used in a good way!"

"No, it cannot," Aaron said, his voice a hoarse whisper.

"Yes, it *can!*" Lucy said. "Because it works the same way as the other thing, it could be a *cure!*"

Aaron was silent for a long, long moment.

"I think," he said, very slowly and quietly, "that you're wrong about that. The other thing is much too devious for a brute force approach to work as a cure."

"Oh." Lucy wilted slightly. But she rallied. "Well, then it'll work as a treatment for the symptoms! I mean, when I have a cold, y'know what's making me miserable? The symptoms! So cough medicine's enough to make a difference!"

"Yes ... pain medicine's helpful, too." Aaron frowned. "But pain medicine can be dangerous."

"So are knives," Lucy said. "But you can't cut up food without them."

"I don't want to mess with your head."

"I don't want you to mess with my head, either. I want to fix my own head, and I want to use the thing you can do as a tool."

"Two wrongs don't make a right."

"They do when the two wrongs are opposites and the right thing is somewhere in between."

Aaron stared at her, pondering.

"What exactly are you asking me to do?" he asked finally.

Hurray! Lucy dug into her pocket for two pieces of paper she had hastily scribbled on while she was waiting for the elevator downstairs.

"This is the bad list," Lucy said, handing the first paper to him. At the top, the paper said BAD in all caps, underlined several times. "These are the personality traits I want you to convince me to avoid. They're stuff the bad thing in my head is trying to make me become that I don't want."

"I see." Aaron squinted at the paper. "It's a good thing my handwriting is worse than yours, or I'd have trouble making this out. Let's see. 'Organized. Obsessed with spreadsheets. Good at math.'" He blinked and reread it. "'Good at math'? Really?"

"Yup. I hate math, and I reject its having a place in my life entirely."

"You might regret that later in life."

"No, because hating math'll help me *have* a 'later in life.'"

Aaron gave her a bemused look. "That's ... one perspective, I suppose. Do you have a good list?"

"Yes," Lucy said, pulling the other list out of her pocket. It tore slightly, so she flattened it with care before handing it over. "These are the traits I want you to convince me to develop over time. Not immediately, but, y'know, gradually. Some of them are traits the bad thing wants me to have, but I want them anyway. The rest are ones the bad thing wants me to lose or not gain in the first place, so I want them even more."

"This is a long list," Aaron said, his eyebrows raising.

"Yeah, there are lots of things."

"'Affectionate. Loving. Loyal,'" Aaron read. "'Honest. Brave.

Impossible to intimidate. Clingy.'" He paused. "'Clingy'? This is on the good list?"

"Yeah, clingy's part of who my dad is, and he wouldn't be himself without it."

Aaron stopped. "Are these all describing your dad?"

"Yup."

"I thought you were modeling yourself after an abstract concept."

"I've never met any abstract concepts."

"I see ..." Aaron read through the rest silently. At last, he set the two papers in front of him. "Well, theoretically, I don't see any reason why this wouldn't work."

"Yesssss!" Lucy cried, pumping her fist.

"But that's a *theory*," Aaron stressed. "That doesn't mean there won't be any unpredictable negative consequences that can't be fixed. I've never tried anything like this before. It could be a huge risk."

"Risks are okay," Lucy said. "Much better than a guaranteed bad thing."

Aaron tapped his fingers on the papers, seeming hesitant to get started. "Do your parents know about this?"

"No, because it's none of their business."

"What if something goes wrong?"

"Then it's my fault, not yours. If I turn into a braindead zombie or something, you can tell them if you want to, but I'd rather you didn't because it's none of their business and they shouldn't blame you. Anyway, I don't think anything bad is going to happen, so. Y'know." Lucy took a deep breath. "Can we get started? I think visiting hours are going to end soon."

Aaron glanced at the watch on his wrist. "What time do they end?"

"Nine o'clock."

"That's five minutes from now."

"Then let's get started now! Pleeeeeeeease?"

Aaron hesitated. "Are you really sure you've thought this through?"

"I've thought it through enough, and I don't want to go home tonight without a shoulder angel, because you might die tonight, and then where would I be?!"

Aaron put a hand to his face and laughed wryly. "I notice 'tact' was on neither of those lists, so I hope you develop it eventually ... but you do have a point. Okay, Lucy. Okay."

Lucy cheered silently.

Chapter 8
Not Quite Time

"No!" Lucy said in frustration, slamming her phone down on the bed.

She was back from seeing Aaron, and she couldn't tell if his persuasion had helped at all, but that was probably a good thing. It was supposed to be subtle and long-term, not instant and obvious, after all. The thing was, she didn't feel especially braver than before, which meant she was right back where she had been an hour ago.

I have to do it now, Lucy thought with grim determination. *I have to do it now, so that I don't chicken out.*

But she wasn't any smarter than she'd been an hour ago, either, and she was finding that no explanation would come that made sense and didn't sound vague and meaningless.

Lucy flopped back on her bed and groaned.

Okay, fine. I'll have to do it in person. I can play charades. Or use crossword puzzle-like hints. If I do it with all four at once, one of them's bound to guess correctly, and then I can say "yes" and move on until they get the whole thing.

That seemed so, so, so stupid, though.

Of course, maybe she just thought it was a stupid idea because she was looking for excuses to procrastinate it further.

Rashly, Lucy grabbed her phone and typed in, *Come to my house at four pm tomorrow! I'm going to tell you my big secret. Here's a hint: five-letter word, rhyming with "purse." Come with your best guess what it is!*

Then she added a dozen winky faces and pushed the button to send it to all four of the guys at once.

Lucy dropped her phone and breathed a sigh of relief.

There. It was done. She hadn't told them all yet, but the time was coming, and it was soon. And she couldn't possibly chicken out, because there was no good way to explain away that hint without telling the truth.

She had eighteen hours left to figure out how to do that.

LUCY SPENT all morning ignoring her classes and scribbling down possible explanations in her notebook, none of which made any sense when she reread them. It was frustrating. She was starting to think it really wasn't possible to explain things on her own.

Yes, there was charades, but did she really *have* to play charades? What if none of them guessed the right words? It wasn't exactly a normal thing she was trying to explain.

Maybe she should ask her mom or dad to give the explanation for her. But no ... no ... no ... nooooooooooo ...

Finally, listening to the bell ring to end math class as she scribbled out her fifth terrible attempt, she looked up and saw the guy in front of her stand up. A brainwave came to her.

"You can do it!" Lucy exclaimed.

Alex gave her a blank look. "Ex ... cuse me?"

"You can explain things," Lucy gabbled all in one breath. "Because you're not what I am, but you know what it's like, and you also know what it's like to be under my, you know, what I can do. Can you tell some people how the thing works?!"

Alex's face held no expression.

"Please?!" Lucy pleaded.

"Why?" Alex asked flatly.

"It—it's for four guys I like," Lucy said in a rush. "'Cause I don't want to keep using it on them without their permission, but I can't ask their permission if they don't know, and I can't tell them myself, and nobody else would do it right. Mom would try to make me sound completely blameless, Caleb would badmouth me, and my dad —well, actually, I dunno what my dad would do, but there's no way he's unbiased on the subject of me dating. He's super overprotective. Oh, please!"

Alex stared at her for a long moment. He didn't blink.

"Please, please, please, please?!" Lucy swallowed, her heart pounding, as she pleated her fingers in front of her.

"It's true that I bear you no ill will," Alex said in a slow and measured voice. "And I wish you well in your endeavor. But I have no wish to be recognized as part of it."

"Then write it down!" Lucy cried. "Make it anonymous! I can pull out a piece of paper with an explanation and show it to them, right? The thingamajiggy won't stop me, right?"

"No," Alex said slowly. "As long as the words are mine and not yours, it won't stop you from showing it to other people."

Lucy made a face. "Well, it's not like it'd let me write down anything useful anyway."

"You'd be surprised," Alex said. "You can use any of the words that are normally forbidden as long as they aren't meant for communication with another human being. A journal can be kept freely, for instance."

Lucy stared at him, startled. "Are you sure about that?"

"Yes. My father kept one."

Wow. Lucy's mouth opened. *Guess that would explain why I can type whatever I want into Google. And guess I couldn't ever show someone my search history to help them figure it out. The curse is weird.*

Alex seemed to be pondering.

"All right," he said finally. "As long as you will keep me fully anonymous, I'll write an explanation that you may show to them. I'll put it in your locker in half an hour."

"Oh, you can just write it in my notebook right now," Lucy said, proffering it.

"No," Alex said firmly. "It needs to be typed so that my handwriting cannot be recognized."

Lucy couldn't stop an impatient groan emerging from the back of her throat. Him and his obsession with privacy.

But Alex was as good as his word. When she reached her locker half an hour later, after strolling through a gauntlet of flirting guys emerging from their last classes of the day and making excuses to her friends about why she couldn't hang out this afternoon, she opened her locker door and saw a piece of paper waft out and fall to the ground.

She picked it up and saw exactly the explanation she needed:

To whomever it may concern:

Lucy has a magical power to make boys fall in love with her. It affects both physical attraction and emotions, but seems to work primarily on physical attraction. It is not something she fully has control over, as it is only possible for her to turn it off by not being attracted to the individual.

If she is showing this to you, she probably suspects you've been affected by her power, and she wants you to be aware of it in case that changes your opinion on whether you wish to continue having feelings for her.

Be aware that this is not a power she chose to have. It is an accompaniment to a curse that cannot be broken, will shorten her lifespan, and will change her personality over time. It is a grim curse, and not one she chose.

She cannot explain any of this directly herself, as an inability to speak directly about the curse is another part of the curse.

Please do not share this information with anyone else. Lucy is sharing this with you because she trusts you to be silent and not spread this private information to others. Your absolute discretion is appreciated.

Lucy's lips twitched up into a wry smile. She would've known this was from Alex even if she hadn't asked him to write it. Only he would put such a strong emphasis on the need for privacy, despite the fact that that was something she could say for herself just fine.

Still, she appreciated it. He was a nice guy. Annoyingly quiet, but nice.

She folded the paper into messy halves and quarters, and then shoved it into her jeans pocket, wrinkling the edges as she shoved it in to fit.

Now she was ready.

Now it was time.

Chapter 9
Not Quite Real

When Lucy got home, she found her mom outside weeding the garden, pulled the note out of her pocket, showed it to her, and said that four of her guys were coming over so Lucy could show this to them and maybe pick one of them as a real boyfriend, so could Mom pleeeeeeeeeeease take Dad out of the house for awhile?

Fortunately, Lucy's mother understood immediately why it mattered, and it wasn't long before she was dragging her husband out of the house with the announcement that they hadn't been on a real date in almost a week, and she was tired of her teenage daughter dating more often than they were.

"There's a solution to that," Lucy's dad grumbled as his wife shoved him out the front door. "Lucy could go on a few less—"

The door shut behind them.

Lucy buried her face in a pillow from the sofa and giggled.

The first of the guys arrived only ten minutes later.

"Verse?" Pablo asked as he came in the door.

"Nope!" Lucy said. "But good guessing!"

"Do I get a second hint now?"

"Not till everyone's here!"

George was the next to arrive.

"Have you guessed the secret word?" Lucy asked teasingly.

"Huh?" George looked befuddled for a moment. "Oh. Right. What was the clue again?"

"Five-letter word, rhyming with 'purse.'"

"Reverse?" he hazarded.

"That's not five letters!"

"Sorry, I'm not very good at crossword puzzles."

Billy was next, and Jonas arrived soon afterwards. Billy guessed "nurse," and Jonas guessed "worse."

It's a good thing I didn't decide to go with clues and charades, Lucy thought, exasperated.

"Okay," she said with a bright smile, pulling the well-crumpled paper out of her pocket. Her heart was pounding, and her hands shook slightly. "Well, here's my secret! I—I can't read it to you, so, um … I'll put it on the table, and you can all read it together!"

She darted to the coffee table, unfolded the paper, and laid it out so they could see it. Pablo and Jonas got up from their seats to move closer, while George and Billy leaned forward to read.

George finished it first. "Is this a joke?" he asked.

Lucy's mouth went dry. She tried to summon a teasing smile, and failed. Instead, she just shook her head.

Jonas finished next. "That's, uh … wow."

Lucy nodded, fidgeting nervously.

Billy finished slowly, mouthing the words. He merely looked up in puzzlement, as if he still didn't understand.

Pablo was last. His face was ashen when he finished.

Lucy's heart accelerated into panic mode.

"So … this is *true?*" George said, pointing at the paper.

"Yes," Lucy whispered. "It is. It's—well, it says there why I want you to know."

She found herself grateful that Alex had slightly overexplained. Even though the curse wouldn't have blocked her from saying her reason for telling them, the words stuck in her throat anyway.

"Well," George said with an awkward laugh. "Well. I guess that doesn't really matter. I mean, the curse sounds bad, but the power—it doesn't really matter if my feelings are real or fake."

Lucy breathed out. "Really?"

"Sure." George shrugged.

"Yours are probably real, anyway," Lucy blurted out. "You've liked me for over a year, and this started three months ago."

"Oh, really?" George looked pleased. "Cool."

"Huhhhhh …" Jonas muttered, rereading the note.

Lucy swallowed. "Um. Yes?"

"Three months ago, huh?"

"Yeah," she said in a small voice.

"Okay. I'm out." He stood up. "That's when I started thinking you were hot. I dunno why he's okay with it, but I'm not. Turn it off or whatever you do, okay?"

Lucy felt sick to her stomach. "It—it might take awhile. I have to stop liking you."

"Okay. Then do it." Jonas walked over to her and patted her on the shoulder. "Sorry, Luce. You're nice. You're fun to hang out with. But I'm not good with this. I'm gonna go, and you talk with them. It's probably best if we avoid each other from now on."

Lucy nodded, a huge lump in her throat.

After Jonas left, Billy, George, and Pablo all stayed silent. George was watching the other two. Pablo had his face in his hands, and his shoulders were tense. Billy just kept looking baffled.

"B-Billy?" Lucy prodded nervously. "What do you think?"

"Ummmm ..." Billy looked down at the paper and then back up again. "I don't think I get it."

"It's what it says!" Lucy said, trying not to get angry.

"Yeah, but magic doesn't exist."

"Yes, it *does!*" Lucy shouted. "Are you an idiot?!"

Billy stood up, looking huffy. "I don't wanna date someone who thinks I'm an idiot."

Lucy's throat tightened. "I'm sorry. I didn't mean—"

"I mean, what kind of sick joke are you playing?"

Lucy stopped. She stared at him.

"You're right," she said finally. "I do think you're an idiot."

"Well, bye then," Billy said with irritation, stalking to the front door and walking out. He slammed it behind him.

That just left Pablo.

Who was being very, very silent and seemed very upset.

Lucy's fists clenched and unclenched as swirls of panic spiraled through her.

You've still got George, she tried to tell herself. *No matter what, he's okay.*

But it *wasn't* okay if she wound up with George! She wanted *Pablo* to choose her! She'd been trying to convince herself she'd be okay with any of them, but she wouldn't, and it had to be him, and what if he said no?!

At last, after what seemed like an eternity but was probably only about twenty minutes of silence, Pablo looked up.

"Can I talk with you in private?" he asked in a low voice.

Lucy's heart raced. She looked over at George.

"Sure," he said gently.

She took Pablo to the laundry room, which doubled as the downstairs bathroom, and shut the door.

Even then, he was silent. He looked like he was about to cry.

"You don't want me, do you?" Lucy said in a broken voice. "That's why I was afraid to tell you. I thought you'd say no."

"To what?" Pablo mumbled.

Lucy fidgeted and looked at her hands. "To being my boyfriend because I love you and I couldn't ask you unless you knew the truth and now that you know it, you don't want me!"

Her voice got rather loud at the end.

Pablo stared at her in astonishment. "You ... you were going to ask me ...?"

"Yeah, because you're *awesome!*" Lucy exclaimed. "You're everything I've ever wanted in a boyfriend!"

"You're everything I've ever wanted, too," he whispered.

Lucy's eyes widened with hope. "Really?"

"Yeah, but ... I don't think you want me." He looked away, his eyes fixed on the washer and dryer. "Because I'm gay."

Lucy's mouth sagged open. "... What? That's impossible."

"I sure wish it were."

"But you've never shown any sign of it!"

"Yeah! Because I don't want to be! I prayed for years that I'd find a girl I could fall in love with, and then I finally did, and now I find out it's *fake!*" His voice broke at the end.

Lucy swallowed. "So you don't want to be in love with me?" she asked in a small voice.

"What?" Pablo gave her an incredulous look. "Of course I do! I'd rather not live a celibate life, I just thought it was the only way to be faithful to God if I never found a girl I wanted to m—never mind—and then I did, and now it turns out it's *fake!*"

He looked like he was about to cry.

Lucy took a deep breath. She was still recovering from the shock. But ... really, one thing was obvious. "Who says it's fake?"

Pablo didn't look at her. "The timeframe—"

"No! I didn't ask if it was caused by the thingamajiggy I have, because clearly it was. I asked if it's *fake!* If you want to be in love with me, and you *are* in love with me, and I want to be in love with you, and I *am* in love with you, then that means it's real. Q.E.D.!"

Pablo stared at her for a moment. Then his shoulders started to shake. She was worried for a second, and then she realized he was laughing. "I don't think you know what 'Q.E.D.' means."

"It means 'I totally proved it,' right?"

Pablo was laughing openly now. "Well, yes, but ..."

"There we go!" she said triumphantly.

"What I'm saying is, I'm not sure your logic is sound!"

"Psshhhh!" She waved her hand. "I don't care about logic. I care about choice. Do you choose me?"

He was silent for a moment. Then he took a deep breath.

He walked over and took her hand.

"Yes," he said. "Yes, I do."

Chapter 10
Not Quite Done

GEORGE WAS WAITING for them in the living room when they left the laundry room together, hand-in-hand. She'd almost forgotten he was still there.

"Um," Lucy said awkwardly. "Um ... hi, George. So ... Pablo and I talked, and we're kind of sort of thinking that I'm going to be exclusive with him from now on ..."

George sighed. "Yes, I kind of thought that was the direction this was going."

Lucy swallowed. "Sorry."

George shrugged, stood, and shook Pablo's hand. "Well, I'm happy for you. Wish it'd been me, but that's how it goes."

Lucy felt like a heel. George was a way nicer person than she would be. "Can we still be friends?" she asked hopefully.

"I hope so." George took her hand and shook it. "Your secret's safe with me, of course. I'm going to stop being a third wheel now. I'll see you both at school."

He left, shutting the front door softly behind him.

Lucy put a hand to her forehead and groaned.

"Any regrets?" Pablo said with a teasing smile, but his voice sounded a little worried.

"Nope!" Lucy said, kissing him on the lips.

She pulled back and hesitated for a second, then decided she should probably tell him.

"To be honest, Pablo ... George was my second choice, but only because I really like him and respect him. I don't think I've had feelings for him for a long time. Which in a way might be a good thing because it means his feelings are probably entirely natural these days, but it's also a really bad thing, because, well, I'd rather have a guy I'm attracted to."

Pablo was silent for a moment. "What about the reverse?"

Lucy frowned. "What do you mean?"

"Well," Pablo said, "if your curse ever breaks and your power disappears ..."

"Not gonna happen. It's impossible."

"It's better not to assume. So, think about it: if your curse ever breaks and your power disappears, that'll put me right back where I was before we met."

Lucy went silent.

"So—are you okay with me still wanting to be with you even if I'm not attracted to you anymore?"

Lucy swallowed. "That ... sounds much less fun," she said in a small voice.

"I completely agree." He touched the side of her face. "But if our relationship is based on the assumption that your power will be there to make things easier forever, it's much too fragile."

Lucy hesitated. "Well, what would *you* do?"

"I've already chosen," he said. "You asked me if I chose you, and I said yes. I meant that with or without your power."

Lucy scrunched up her face. "Well, if we, say, got married—which I'm so not ready to do right now!—and it went away and you weren't in love with me anymore, where would that leave us?"

He shrugged. "You'd be my best friend and the only person I'd want to spend the rest of my life with."

"That doesn't sound nearly as romantic!" she complained.

He laughed. "No, it doesn't, does it? But a lot of marriage relationships *do* go that way, you know. It's very common, and that doesn't mean it's right to end them. I don't believe in divorce. If we ever get married, I'm staying no matter what, unless you ask me to leave." He grew serious. "So, if we ever got married, would you take it as seriously as I would? Because if you wouldn't ... that's a deal-breaker for me."

Lucy licked her lips. "You're not, like ... asking me to marry you right now, are you?"

"Oh, no!" Pablo burst out laughing. "For one thing, I'm not giving my family that kind of satisfaction!"

"Good, because ... I'm so not ready for that! As for your question, um ... give me a minute to think about it."

Lucy sat down on the couch and thought for several minutes. It was a hard question. But she decided he was right: if he was willing to devote his life to her, she had to be willing to do the same. They didn't have to make the decision of whether they were going to right now, but they did have to make the decision of whether they would see it through if they did.

Pablo sat down next to her, his face questioning.

"Okay," Lucy said at last. "If we ever reach the point that we want to get married, and you lose your feelings for me afterwards, I won't complain about it, and I'll stay."

Pablo touched her face and smiled. "*That's* what makes it real."

Lucy got up, grinned, and flopped on his lap.

"Oof!" Pablo said. "You're a little heavy."

"That's okay," Lucy said coyly, playing with his hair.

"Says the girl who doesn't have a hundred pounds of weight on her lap."

"One twenty, and thanks for the compliment."

"I'm serious! You're heavy!"

"Just *try* to get me off."

"Oh, in *that* case ...!" He stood up, dumped her on the couch, and then sat on top of her.

Lucy shrieked with laughter. "You're way heavier! Get off!"

"Nope, I'm going to sit here for as long as you sat on me."

So naturally she had to tickle him.

About ten minutes later, they settled the battle by having her lie on the couch with her head on his lap while she flipped through the channels on TV, looking for anything good on.

"Hey, Pablo?" Lucy asked, looking up at his face from his lap. "I've got a weird question for you. Are there any advantages to you in being gay?"

He paused. "Excuse me?"

"I'm just wondering. Because it's not like it's going to go away. You're gonna be attracted to guys for the rest of your life, whether or not you have feelings for me. But I've just learned there's an advantage to my thingy—"

"Your curse?"

"Yeah."

"What's the advantage?"

"You, duh!"

"I said I'd stick around even without it."

"Yeah, but would you have ever considered me in the first place without it?"

Pablo pondered. "Probably not," he admitted.

"See? There's an advantage to me. So I'm wondering if there's an advantage to you in the thing *you* have that you don't want."

Pablo ran his fingers through Lucy's hair for awhile. "You know," he said at last, in a surprised voice, "I think there may be."

"Really?" she asked.

He nodded. "Before I figured out I was gay, I didn't really take my religion that seriously. I was kind of like you. I didn't really see a reason to bother with it. But once I figured out I was gay, the question of whether I believed in my religion became of crucial importance. So I did a lot of studying, a lot of praying, and a lot of thinking about it, and I determined I did. I think that made me a much better person."

"Huh." Lucy cocked her head to the side. "So is this a subtle hint that I should start, like, attending mass more often?"

He laughed. "I'm not gonna make you, but it would certainly be nice if you did."

"Okay, fine. But only if you're going with me, because then it can be like a date. A really, really, really boring date, because I assume you won't be kissing me in a church."

"I could kiss you right now," Pablo said with a grin.

"Ooh! Good idea!" Lucy got up and bounced onto his lap.

"Lucyyyyyy! You're heavy!"

"Kiss me anyway."

So he did.

"WHAT IS THIS?" a voice roared from behind them.

She spun around and saw her dad standing in the doorway, crimson-faced. Behind him was her mom, looking amused.

Lucy coughed and scooted away from her boyfriend. "Oh, hi, Dad. We've been watching TV."

"Only watching TV?!" he growled.

"All right, and kissing, too." Lucy gave him a wicked smile. "Pablo's a great kisser, and he's going to be really fun to have as a boyfriend. Want me to describe what I like about his kissing?"

Her dad's eyes looked like they were about to bulge out of his head.

"Harry," Lucy's mom said, obviously trying not to smile.

"Don't 'Harry' me!" he roared, glaring at Lucy. "You can't invite a boy over here without supervision! You know the rules! And that goes double for a boyfriend! And as for him *being* your boyfriend, you need my permission for that!"

"No, I don't."

"Yes, you do!"

"No, I don't."

"Yes, you do!"

"Sir, 'the victorious strategist only seeks battle after the victory has already been won,'" Pablo said with an impish grin. "Sun Tzu."

Lucy's father was speechless for a moment. Then he sighed and said, "Oh, all right, he'll do."

AUTHOR NOTE:

Pablo is based on a real person. One I didn't intend to write about, but that person really needed their story told, so I took a deep breath and did it.

Pablo and Lucy are minor characters in The Zodiac Curse *quartet, and also two of the main characters in my* A Courtship of Wishes *trilogy. I didn't plan for them to be, but they wriggled their way into the plot and made me rewrite the whole thing.*

I don't know if you've noticed, but my characters rarely listen to me. They usually have better ideas than I do about their conflicts and the choices they want to make.

ABOUT THE AUTHOR

Emily Martha Sorensen writes fantasy and science fiction books with realistic paths to a happy ending. She considers all her books clean, with zero swearing and not much violence, but the romance between married couples can be PG-13.

She likes clever characters with unique personalities who charge straight through her plot and spend it spinning wildly off the rails. (Those brats.)

She likes magic systems with strict rules and intriguing limitations.

She likes romance after the happily ever after. That's where the relationship begins!

She likes plot twists that will make your jaw drop.

She likes hope and fun and humor.

She likes darkness that exists only to help characters grow towards greater light.

She likes —

Wait, where did those uncooperative protagonists put the plot *this* time? They just ran off with it, cackling maniacally!

Well, she hopes they'll leave you grinning.

You can find her books at http://www.emilymarthasorensen.com.

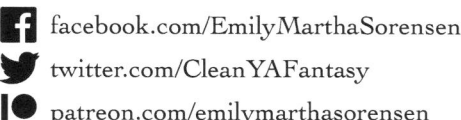

facebook.com/EmilyMarthaSorensen
twitter.com/CleanYAFantasy
patreon.com/emilymarthasorensen

ABOUT THE COVER ARTIST

MEREDITH DILLMAN is an artist and illustrator originally from Minnesota. She now lives in Wisconsin. She is known for her colorful watercolors which blend Art Nouveau, fantasy and Asian influences.

She enjoys painting fairies, woodland creatures and other fantasy and medieval themes and has been drawing such since childhood. She is inspired by Pre-Raphaelite artists, Japanese comics, and turn-of-the-century book illustration.

She graduated from Minnesota State University Moorhead with a BFA degree in Illustration in 2002. Her work has since been published in instructional books and licensed for a variety of products and collectables. Meredith is the author and illustrator of the books *Watercolor Made Easy: Fairies and Fantasy* and *Fantasy Fashion Art Studio*.

Her enchanting paintings are made with attention to detail, starting with refined pencil and ink drawings followed by many transparent layers of watercolor. You can see more of her works on her website: meredithdillman.com.

 facebook.com/meredithdillmanart
 instagram.com/meredithdillmanart
 patreon.com/meredithdillman

ADDITIONAL COPYRIGHT INFORMATION

All works on this page are copyright Emily Martha Sorensen unless otherwise noted, and are included by permission of the author. Works are listed alphabetically by title.

"Advanced Precognition" copyright © 2013. Originally appeared in *Worlds of Wonder* collection.

"The Apple of Discord" copyright © 2013. Originally appeared in *Worlds of Wonder* collection.

"The Dragon and the Santa" copyright © 2013. Originally appeared in *Worlds of Wonder* collection.

"Dragon's Dawn" copyright © 2019. Originally appeared in *Tales of Tie-ins* collection.

"Dragon's Egg" copyright © 2016. Originally appeared as a standalone work.

"Dragon's Hope" copyright © 2016. Originally appeared as a standalone work.

"Dragon's Yowl" copyright © 2019. Originally appeared in *Tales of Tie-ins* collection.

"Entrance Interview" copyright © 2019. Originally appeared in *Tales of Tie-ins* collection.

"His Unicorn" copyright © 2021.

"Introduction" (essay) copyright © 2021.

"Knock Three Times" copyright © 2018. Originally appeared in *Magic and Mischief* collection.

"Legacy of the Corridor" (essay) copyright © 2021 Joe Monson.

"The Mark on Her Right Hand" copyright © 2021.

"Not Quite a Blessing" copyright © 2020. Originally appeared as a standalone work.

"Not Quite Changed" copyright © 2020. Originally appeared as a standalone work.

"Not Quite a Curse" copyright © 2020. Originally appeared as a standalone work.

"Ogre in Boots" copyright © 2019. Originally appeared in *Tales of Tie-ins* collection.

"**On a Long Camping Trip**" copyright © 2013. Originally appeared in *Spellbound* (Fall 2013), edited by Raechel Henderson.

"**On Dragons and Curses**" (essay) copyright © 2021 Joe Monson.

"**On the Way Through the Woods**" copyright © 2013. Originally appeared in *Worlds of Wonder* collection.

"**One Midsummer's Night**" copyright © 2013. Originally appeared in *Spellbound* (Summer 2013), edited by Raechel Henderson.

"**The Rise of Starlight**" copyright © 2018. Originally appeared in *Wings and Wonder*, edited by A. J. Flowers.

"**The Spinning Talent**" copyright © 2013. Originally appeared in *Worlds of Wonder* collection.

"**Third Princess**" copyright © 2018. Originally appeared in *Tales of Ever After*, edited by H. L. Burke.

"**To Prevent Similar Views**" copyright © 2021.

D.J. Butler
A collection
of his short works

T**he *Florilegium of Madness***
978-1-64278-008-6 (tp)
978-1-64278-001-7 (ebook)

**Available everywhere
books are sold!**

hemelein.com
It's worth your time.[TM]

Something for everyone to enjoy!

LTUE Benefit Anthologies

Trace the Stars | A Dragon and Her Girl | Twilight Tales | Parliament of Wizards

Legacy of the Corridor

The Florilegium of Madness | Dragon Soup for the Soul | Down the Arches of the Years

Legacy of the Corridor

Killing London

HEMELEIN PUBLICATIONS
It's worth your time.™

Find out more at hemelein.com

A UNIVERSE OF STORIES AWAITS YOU!

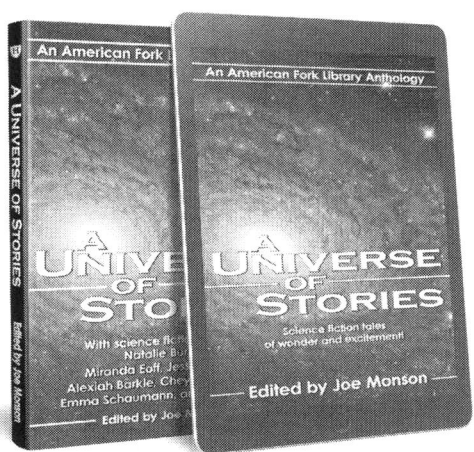

Unique and interesting visions from up-and-coming science fiction writers!

A Universe of Stories

Trade paperback — $10.99
978-1-64278-007-9

Ebook — $4.99
978-1-64278-001-7

Pick up your copy today!

HEMELEIN PUBLICATIONS

It's worth your time.™

hemelein.com

Made in the USA
Columbia, SC
02 December 2021